Darkenbloom

Darkenbloom

EVA MENASSE

Translated by
Charlotte Collins

SCRIBE

Melbourne | London | Minneapolis

Scribe Publications
18–20 Edward St, Brunswick, Victoria 3056, Australia
2 John St, Clerkenwell, London, WC1N 2ES, United Kingdom
3754 Pleasant Ave, Suite 100, Minneapolis, Minnesota 55409, USA

First published in German as *Dunkelblum* by
Verlag Kiepenheuer & Witsch in 2021
Published in English by Scribe 2024

Typeset in Garamond Premier Pro by the publishers

Printed and bound in the UK by CPI Group (UK) Ltd,
Croydon CR0 4YY

Scribe is committed to the sustainable use of natural resources and
the use of paper products made responsibly from those resources.

978 1 922585 48 6 (Australian edition)
978 1 914484 40 7 (UK edition)
978 1 964992 04 4 (US edition)
978 1 761386 03 9 (ebook)

Catalogue records for this book are available from the
National Library of Australia and the British Library.

≡ Federal Ministry
Republic of Austria
Arts, Culture,
Civil Service and Sport

scribepublications.com.au
scribepublications.co.uk
scribepublications.com

for Laszlo

Dramatis Personae

Lowetz (35), returns to Darkenbloom in the summer of 1989 because he has inherited his parents' house

Kalmar, Fritz (45), carpenter, lives next door to the Lowetz family; suffered a head injury as a small child at the end of the war that impaired his speech

Kalmar, Agnes (69), Fritz's mother and Eszter's friend; recurring episodes of mental illness since the end of the war

Malnitz, Flocke (23), primary school teacher, daughter of Toni and Leonore Malnitz; interested in coming to terms with the past, and in the town chronicle; was friends with Eszter Lowetz and inherited her Vauxhall Corsa

Malnitz, Leonore (56), known as the 'Queen of Darkenbloom' because of her beauty; wife of Toni, mother of four daughters, including Flocke; born in Kirschenstein, came to Darkenbloom only after the war

Malnitz, Toni (56), her husband, winemaker who won awards after switching to organic methods early on; father of Flocke

Rehberg (49), local travel agent and enthusiastic town historian, nephew of the late Elly Rehberg

Gellért, Dr Alexander (69), tourist; takes a room in the Hotel Tüffer in the summer of 1989 and starts conducting investigations, sometimes with the help of Flocke Malnitz

Grün, Antal (67), grocer, shop at Tempelgasse 4; he and his mother Gisella were the only Darkenbloom Jews who returned after the war; initially rented part of Agnes Kalmar's house before they were able to get their own house back

Reschen, Resi (71), almost-omniscient boss of the Hotel Tüffer on the town square

Graun, Veronika (71), known as Vroni; notorious alcoholic, widow of the murdered Josef Graun, mother of Young Graun, former childhood friend of Resi Reschen

Young Graun (43), her son; wine grower who wanted to be a musician

Graun, Karin, his wife; loyalty shifts between her husband and mother-in-law

Sterkowitz (77), local doctor; took over the practice from his Jewish predecessor, Dr Bernstein, in 1938; still practising because of an error by the health insurance company

Ferbenz, Dr Alois (79), former Deputy Gauleiter of Styria; returned to Darkenbloom in 1965; owner of Boutique Rosalie; respected citizen and town benefactor

Koreny, Herbert (55), electrician, reluctantly acting as mayor during Mayor Balf's illness

Historical Timeline

September 1918: Collapse of the Austro-Hungarian Empire; Austria and Hungary become two separate republics

December 1921: The border is officially drawn between Austria and Hungary; Hungary cedes Burgenland to Austria

February 1934: Austrian Civil War

March 1938: Nazi Germany annexes Austria, known as the *Anschluss*

September 1939: The Second World War begins in Europe

March/April 1945: American troops enter Austria; the Red Army of the Soviet Union crosses the eastern border; occupation under the Allies begins

May 1945: End of the Second World War in Europe

May 1955: Occupation under the Allies ends; Austria becomes an independent country

November 1956: The Hungarian Revolution is crushed by the Soviets; Hungarians flee across the border to Austria

1988: 50th anniversary of the *Anschluss*; Austria finally confronts its Nazi past on an official and national level

May 1989: Dismantling of the border fence between Austria and Hungary begins

August 1989: The Pan-European Picnic. Hundreds of East Germans holidaying in Hungary cross the border into Austria and travel on to West Germany

September 1989: Opening of the border between Austria and
    Hungary
November 1989: Fall of the Berlin Wall
October 1990: German reunification

PART I

The Austrians are a people who confidently look forward to the past.

PROVERB

I.

IN DARKENBLOOM, THE WALLS have ears, the flowers in the gardens have eyes; they turn their heads this way and that so nothing escapes them, and the grass has whiskers that register every step. People here *sense* things. Curtains flutter as if fanned by quiet breathing, in and out, essential for life. Whenever God looks down into these houses from above, as if they had no roofs, when he peeps into the doll's houses of the model town he constructed with the Devil to be a warning to us all, in almost every house he sees people standing at the windows, behind their curtains, peering out. Sometimes — often — there are two, even three, in the same house, in different rooms, hidden from one another, standing at the window. One wishes on God's behalf that he could only see into houses, not into hearts.

In Darkenbloom, the locals know all about each other, and the few tiny details that they don't know, that they can neither fabricate nor simply omit — these are not unimportant, these loom largest of all. That which is not common knowledge holds power, like a curse. The others, the incomers and those who have married in, don't know much. They know that the castle burned down, that the counts' descendants now live in various far-off countries, but usually return to celebrate weddings and christenings, when the whole town joins in the festivities: the children gather flowers from the cottage gardens and wreathe garlands, the old women dig out their hundred-year-old traditional costumes, and everyone stands the length of Herrengasse and waves. The foreign brides notice, with tight little smiles, that, despite the republican takeover all those years ago, one can still rely on one's subjects here, on high days and holidays, at least.

It's been a long time, though, since any counts were buried here. Their crypt can be visited, but it is no longer receiving occupants. It wasn't until twenty years after the war that the comital family could even be lured back to Darkenbloom, on the advice that the crypt was no longer watertight. Immediately after the war, by contrast, someone — no one knows who — had, with astonishing diplomatic finesse, kept them away. The news that was conveyed to them about the state of the burnt-out ruin was greatly exaggerated. *Demolished — alas, the castle must be completely demolished*: this was the assessment presented to them, with much wailing and gnashing of teeth. And the recently widowed countess-in-exile believed her former stewards and tenants and secretaries and maids, or whoever was behind the story, or whoever passed on things they knew from hearsay, or things they had been forced to say themselves. Perhaps the Countess wanted to believe them. She was too lazy, or too cowardly, to come and see for herself, too low on funds to pay for a surveyor's report. And so the castle was pulled down, and a huge piece of prime real estate became available in a previously inaccessible central location. Someone must have profited back then, because someone always does. Since then, the centre of Darkenbloom has been architecturally and atmospherically divided: the centuries-old rustic half, with its winding streets and whitewashed houses with their blue or green shutters, and the other half, hideously functional, all steel and silicone, practical, easily wiped clean, just as people would have liked to be themselves, back then, in the period of reconstruction.

And so, twenty years later, the Countess's affable eldest son returned for a flying visit, a man who could be described as many things, but never sentimental. *The ancestors are seeping!* he trumpeted. The crypt was opened, and what needed to be sealed was sealed. Afterwards, the priest blessed everything, emphatically and for all eternity, and the crypt was closed again. It is said that there were still women of Darkenbloom who kissed *His Serene Highness*'s hand after the ceremony, curtseying as they did so. Ferbenz, meanwhile, put up posters announcing happy hour in Café Posauner at the exact same time as the ceremony. This attempt to divide the community did not, however, meet with success. When the Count and the priest required their presence, most people knew what was expected of them, even if the majority shared Ferbenz's view. The Count took precedence. After all, he was so seldom there. And so Ferbenz sat in Café Posauner with his hardcore, loyal followers, and they drank till their noses glowed, and although it looked like a defeat, all of them knew that they would always remember who was there and, more to the point, who was not. And the bullnecked among them — which was most of them — were already ruddy-naped with anticipation, because, with the Count's departure, the balance of power would soon be restored in Darkenbloom.

Ever since the counts had sealed their crypt, and with it their exodus, time had essentially stood still. Seasons and hemlines changed; television programmes became more varied and more numerous. The people of Darkenbloom grew older, as people do, but because they drank copiously, their ageing went almost unnoticed for a good long while — glinting eyes, rosy cheeks — until at last their old friend John Barleycorn struck, swiftly and without mercy. He was a professional killer. His chosen victim would start coughing, just a little, when he got up in the morning; then, over breakfast, he would bring up the first of many gobbets of blood, which followed one another in ever quicker succession until, within a quarter of an hour at most, it was all over, leaving behind — for those who were left behind — an impressively disgusting mess that almost never served as a deterrent. Fritz, the village idiot, would be informed, and would measure up the fine oak planks in his workshop that very day, happy as a sandboy whenever he received a commission, whistling a ragtime tune while he prepared the so-called *wooden pyjamas.*

The drinkers to whom this had not yet happened believed, for that very reason, that it was unlikely to do so. For decades, Ferbenz had sat with Berneck, the Heuraffl brothers, Stitched-Up Schurl, and Young Graun in either Café Posauner or the Hotel Tüffer — once so elegant, now blighted by peasant ceramics and braided straw — explaining the world and its history to his drinking companions and scheming against the mayor of the day, or the bank manager, or the chairman of the tourist board, until one of the aforementioned walked through the door and bought a couple of rounds, securing Ferbenz's unconditional support. Ferbenz himself actually drank very little, but was skilled at pretending otherwise. He knew how to emerge from any situation in life unscathed.

Just two streets over from the Tüffer, at Tempelgasse 4, Antal Grün packed and unpacked boxes in his grocery with ant-like industriousness. He was a teetotaller, and experience had taught him that many things were possible, although he never talked about them. In his blue overall, with three meagre strands of grey hair combed diagonally across his round head from the right temple to the opposite ear, he unpacked fresh goods, packed up the ones past their sell-by dates, dragged crates and boxes back and forth, made open sandwiches for a dozen schoolchildren whose parents could afford to pay for such luxuries and wanted to, as a way of showing off, obligingly read out to elderly ladies the small print on the cummerbund around the balls of wool (20 per cent Dralon, 80 per cent polyacrylic, no, my dear lady, there doesn't seem to be any cotton in that at all), and took particular pleasure in threading a new roll of paper into his till. Each time, he was astonished that it had worked. Each time, he anxiously imagined the mechanism malfunctioning, the paper curling up, that instead of being drawn in it would be spat out, rejected. The prospect filled him with clammy unease. If he started obsessing about it, he had to go and wash his hands for a long time to distract himself. And only when there really was nothing else to do, when the roll of paper was fat and new, every shelf filled, the stone floor swept, only then would he turn thoughtfully to the newfangled metal stands for newspapers and postcards that he had recently allowed a dubious salesman with a foreign accent to talk him into buying, and which now, rather strangely, even displayed hand-tinted historical photographs of Darkenbloom Castle.

The general practitioner Dr Sterkowitz, on the other hand, did drink, but in moderation, and only because it was the done thing around here. Elsewhere he would have chewed tobacco or eaten sugar balls; he set greater store by harmonious coexistence than was usual in Darkenbloom. Sterkowitz was almost always in his car, currently a flashy orange Japanese model, making house calls. He insisted that house calls allowed him greater flexibility, because if he needed to spend a bit longer with those who were bedridden he could just leave out the ones who weren't that sick anyway, or who were, on the whole, hypochondriacs. The surgeries he was required to hold three mornings a week, despite his home visit service, were correspondingly chaotic — newly vaccinated children bawling, feverish old people collapsing, and more than once he had thwarted double pneumonia at the last minute with a cocktail of broad-spectrum antibiotics — because, even after all these decades, not everyone knew that Dr Sterkowitz came to your house on principle, not just in an emergency, or else they preferred to come themselves rather than see that flashy car pull up outside their half-finished bungalows and run-down farms. Sterkowitz refused to be dissuaded from his service concept.

The truth was that he just liked being out and about. Perhaps he was so keen on driving because he had a particular aversion to being in closed rooms; who knows. Wherever he went, he would throw open the windows. You need to breathe, he would scold, sick people need fresh air, you'll suffocate before you freeze. Yet it seems that in our town everyone would rather stew in their own fug!

Dr Sterkowitz was now several years past statutory retirement age, but so far this hadn't been a problem. He felt fit, his test results were fine, and he had only acquired the brand-new orange Honda a few years ago. That would have been a pity. Where else was he supposed to drive it, if not to his patients? Gradually, though, he was starting to wait: for his so-called twilight years, and the replacement the public health insurance company had promised. These days, he sometimes thought about his predecessor, too, and how he must have waited for him.

Time, frozen. Because people, unlike animals, always need to be doing something; even if only renovating their dwellings, they create for themselves the apparently necessary impression that they are moving with the times. The people of Darkenbloom naturally believed this, too. In reality, though, they had at last been left in peace, disconnected and marginalised as they were. The fateful local beast that brought death and ruin whenever it began to stir, obliterating for decades not just people but moral principles as well, had lain in an enchanted sleep for so long that people had slowly begun to forget it. It seemed to have been finished off for good. Now it really was adorned with little nails — metal ones, not cloves, as Brahms's pretty lullaby would have it. That murderous lindworm lay immobile in a bed of concrete and barbed wire, and the drama of the world played out elsewhere. The last time the deadly serpent had made its presence felt, it had been what was essentially a long sigh, a deep, sorrowful exhalation, as if in an oppressive dream. That was how it seemed, any-way, looking back; but that time, the last to date, a female resident of Darkenbloom had suffered a dramatic breakdown. In early November 1956, after hearing the news on the radio, Agnes Kalmar snatched up a blanket and a few items of food and ran barefoot with her bundle, screaming and crying, right through the town and out into the forest in the direction of Kalsching. Many people saw her run past; nobody drew the right conclusions. Some assumed that something else had happened to her son, Fritz. As a small child, he had been shot in the head during the final phase of the battle for Darkenbloom, and ever since had been considered the village idiot. But the fourteen-year-old Fritz was already apprenticed to the carpenter by then, and it wasn't until the next day that he mentioned his mother was missing. It was another two days before Agnes was found. She was dragged out of the forest, hypothermic, dishevelled, witch-like, her lips and teeth blue from bilberries; she screamed and struggled, and was taken to hospital a long way away, where she stayed until things had quietened down. Fritz learned to look after himself back then, after a fashion, and all those who knew him were relieved. And it was then, with his mother gone, and in spite of the turmoil in the town, that his friendly, helpful nature was first revealed. After he finished work, he would show up at the old primary school, which had been converted into a makeshift dormitory for the refugees, and every evening he assisted Dr Sterkowitz and Antal Grün by running errands, carrying things, or doing minor repairs. Without discussing it — in fact, without ever making a conscious decision — the doctor and the grocer took on the organisation of the whole operation. They worked till they were ready to drop. Fritz was almost always there with them. Late at night he would bring them a pot of soup that someone had pressed upon him, would fetch cigarettes and pour cups of bitter thermos coffee for the people lying on the mattresses. This went on for weeks. Yet in January, when the carpenter first showed his apprentice how to construct a coffin, Fritz didn't seem to make the connection to the young woman who had frozen to death and whose body he himself had helped recover by stretcher the previous night.

That, then, was the last time the serpentine monster had raised its head, sighing in its sleep, this creature of many names, *határ, meja, hranica*, all of which are too innocuous, because none evoke the fire and the poison, the explosive mixture of past crimes, premonitions, fears for the future, hysteria. Only one thing is certain: nothing good has ever come from it, from the border.

2.

THIRTY-TWO YEARS AND A few months after Fritz helped carry the dead woman out of the snowdrift, a man was on the bus to Darkenbloom. It was a hot day in early August 1989. This man wanted to arrive as a stranger; he wished to see things from an unbiased perspective. But Darkenbloom knows how to clout people on the back of the head so they immediately topple straight into the old gutters, face down in the muddy puddles of their own prejudices. And so a malicious twist of fate slipped the man the regional edition of a daily newspaper, and he leafed through it, bored, an activity that demanded more of his fingers than his brain. Outside, fields stretched as far as the horizon in regular, colourful, transverse stripes, green-gold-green-gold-green-blue, everything straight as a die apart from the avenues of poplars at the edges of the picture — children's book aesthetics. There would be more topographical variation once they passed Kirschenstein. Only at the very end of the journey would the landscape begin to rise, or at least heave itself to its knees, for just outside Darkenbloom, in time immemorial, the Earth's crust had bulged slightly, forming what Darkenbloomers proudly called a *mountain*. The colours of the fields alternated in regular rhythm; the strip of sky remained immaculately blue, without so much as a scrap of white cloud. The traveller grew sleepy.

A Nazi salute on holiday is a 'travel defect' that justifies a reduction in price; the removal of a towel, however, is not.

What? Excuse me? Sorry — beg your pardon? A jolt, as though at the very last moment he had escaped tumbling into a ravine, when in fact it was just his heavy head falling forward and being snatched back by the final vestiges of consciousness.

The bus bumped over the seams in the ready-mixed concrete slabs that were once so popular in road construction and which it had unfortunately not yet been possible to replace completely, just like the asbestos fibres that still infested everything, just like the old Nazis. In any case, the combination of the intervals between these concrete speed bumps and the bus's leisurely pace generated a hypnotic earworm in the passenger's head: *Nazi salute is a travel defect, Nazi salute is a travel defect, dum-di-dum-di-diddley-dum* ... This was what happened if you didn't keep your mind constantly under control.

What the hell was a *Nazi salute on holiday*? The newspaper had slipped from his lap when he'd dozed off. All around him, people had already started unwrapping the marbled white greaseproof paper from their bananas and Extrawurst rolls. At least no hard-boiled egg had yet been peeled to spread its Mephistophelian smell.

He picked up the newspaper and leafed through. He couldn't possibly have imagined the Nazi salute; it had to be in there somewhere. Now it was hiding from him, presumably to make him doubt his own mind. He had long known, though, that doubting the mind was an unnecessary expenditure of energy — doubting it, and firmly believing it, too. Don't think too hard when dealing with the mind, that was his motto. Ignoring things was a natural response.

So where was the Nazi salute, then? Not in the politics section, which consisted of barely one and a half double pages. Not in the local news — fire brigade festival in Kalsching, barn burns down in neighbouring Ehrenfeld ... a curious connection that the newspaper neither made nor commented on. Presumably the volunteer fire brigade had partied a little too wildly — *everyone needs to let off steam sometimes* — and the young people *who courageously put their lives on the line day after day* (according to the photo caption, which also made a mockery of the overweight lads with the impressive drinker's noses) had sacrificed the barn that night to their *festive fun*, as the article called it; bravo for the alliteration and bugger the barn, let it burn, who needs it, certainly not us. Not in the sports section, almost more extensive than politics, interspersed with adverts and classifieds: Dragica offers *inspirational massage*, as if she doesn't know she's inspiring the body, not the mind; Ilonka offers a *gentle* escort service. The Unterrainer farm is selling direct from the farm shop again, starting on Sunday, and there's a children's jumble sale in Sternsingergasse. Also: Heuraffl, Graun and Malnitz have started selling the new wine, same as every year. But here, under the heading *World News: Nazi salute on holiday deemed a 'travel defect'*; subhead: *Removing a towel from a sun lounger is not.*

A holidaymaker had been dissatisfied with his holiday: he had bravely served out his time, partaking of the sun and the buffet, presumably under inner protest, already composing his complaint. Inner protest like inner emigration: always difficult to prove after the fact. But he did want some of his hard-earned cash back; well, no one gives us anything for free, do they, and what better trump card to play than political sensitivity? The judges did not accept the man's complaint that the towel he had spread out at the crack of dawn had been cleared away, his successful reservation of a front-row sun lounger by dint of self-righteous early rising unacknowledged. One might say that the sun lounger left the judges cold. In fact, the holidaymaker's declaration that he only got his towel back after a thirty-minute argument had prompted the judges to respond with a sentence that made the man reading the newspaper burst into hearty laughter, a sort of bright, summery, bus-journey jubilation: *Insofar as the complainant regards it as a 'defect' that the removal of the towel resulted in a thirty-minute argument, it must be taken into account that an argument requires the participation of at least two individuals.*

The heads of the banana eaters and sandwich-paper rustlers turned towards the man and jerked away again. Not a single glance actually grazed him. The jerking heads were a criticism. None of these old lizards wanted to know why he was laughing. They certainly didn't want to laugh with him. They didn't have time for laughter. Not with him. The jerk of the head was intended to convey that his laughter had been noticed and disapproved of. Which, with the lizards, was almost one and the same: no sooner did they notice something than they disapproved of it. But they could have taken this attitude rather earlier, he thought: fifty years ago, say ...

So he hadn't had any luck with that complaint, our holidaymaker. The Nazi salute, though! He'd got them with that. The club entertainers had performed a cabaret in which they had demonstrated the typical greetings of different nations. When it came to Germany, the entertainers had affected a rigid goose-step, flung up their arms, and roared *Heil!* A German-speaking paying guest would not feel esteemed and welcome on seeing this, the court agreed, and awarded the plaintiff damages in an amount that would at least enable him to order two or three good lunches in a reputable restaurant in the region. For two, naturally — himself, and his wife, who had sustained similar damage. These damages, then, did not constitute an appreciable reduction in price, but an acknowledgement of the plaintiff's hurt feelings.

If only the visitor had not read any further! If only the little report had ended there! He would have swayed on to his destination, amused and mollified, a little sweaty from the fake leather seats; the world is full of idiots; Na-zi sa-lute is a tra-vel de-fect, Na-zi sa-lute is a tra-vel de-fect; he might have dozed off again; he would have shown some sympathy to the banana eaters, given the sandwich-paper rustlers a smile. The young day would have pretended that it was innocuous and peaceful, but that, let's be honest, is what days never are, not one, so we shouldn't allow ourselves to be deceived. The final sentences of the report stood out in contrast to the dry news-agency-speak; they had clearly been added by the editor. These final sentences not only unexpectedly lifted the anonymity of the holidaymaker, they also provided people from the region with a torrent of subtext, like a mudslide. *In an exclusive interview with our newspaper, Dr Alois F. expressed his satisfaction with the judgment pronounced. It had never been a question of the size of the compensation, he said, but of putting a stop to the Egyptian entertainers' tasteless jokes, for the benefit of future guests. Furthermore, Dr F. said he would forgo expensive foreign holidays in future: his homeland, he said, was quite beautiful enough.*

The traveller crumpled a corner of the newspaper in his fist and glanced around in fury. He had been reminded of where he was. Where he was heading. As if in confirmation, the other passengers chewed, stared into space, and rustled. Suddenly his bones ached. He wasn't on a pleasure trip; he was sitting in a dull, sweaty, stuffy bus, travelling in a direction he had avoided for decades. The bus would soon be stopping in Kirschenstein, then in Tellian, Ehrenfeld, and finally Zwick, which was already part of Darkenbloom. The holidaymaker was no amateur complainant, some pensioner from Landshut or Amstetten whose long-standing diabetes made him permanently irritable — though it would also have been interesting to know what it was about the Nazi salute that bothered such a man! — nor was he a peacenik, a thoroughly-come-to-terms-with-the-past family man of the '68 generation, who would have given an anguished nod and murmured, *Serves us right.* No: it was the notorious Dr F. of Darkenbloom. It was he, no doubt about it; there was no need for them coyly to abbreviate him. Presumably he was proud of his symbolic victory. And of course it was not the Nazi salute per se that bothered him, but the fact that it had been executed by *Egyptian entertainers*, which in Alois F.'s world was a synonym for, at best, *homosexual scoundrels*. The editor of the local paper was sure to know this; everyone here knew it, all the way to the nearby national border. Dr F. was renowned. An uninformed reader from the capital or another province, on the other hand, would notice nothing at all. The uninformed would be touched to hear that F. had — you could bet on it — donated the damages, almost four hundred schillings, to a recently widowed young mother or a disabled man whose 'wheels' were in need of expensive repair. For Dr Alois was also renowned, well beyond Darkenbloom, for his charity.

The main square, the terminus, was deserted. The sun stood directly above the plague column. For the past two hundred years, a half-naked sandstone beggar had held out her beaker accusingly to new arrivals. Even without the harsh sunlight you believed she really was dying of thirst. The two saints at her side, Roch and Sebastian, whose sensitive noses had been eroded by wind and rain so they looked like affronted sphinxes, had given her nothing to drink for more than two hundred years.

Long after the bus had turned round and headed off back to the more lively, normal world, or to a mysterious depot where it mustered the strength to make its escape, the visitor was still standing there in the sun, a compact leather bag at his feet. The other passengers had quickly and soundlessly disappeared, like mice into their holes. He took his time, looking around, confirming to himself that he really was here again. The tower, the sole remnant of the castle's former glory, stared back at him through sullenly narrowed window slits. *Asia begins just over there*, the people of Darkenbloom liked to say, shuddering melodramatically in the direction of the border, *we're the final foothills*. The loss of the castle had resulted in a photograph of it, framed, occupying a prominent position in almost every house. And they still sold picture postcards of it. He knew this because he had recently received one — colourised! They missed it now. Back then, when they pulled it down, they wouldn't have known how to spell the word tourism: *guest rooms* were what people offered, as a sort of favour. The phrase *historic town centre* didn't exist then, either. Things weren't historic in those days, just old.

Shortly after the war, a little wall in the old, whitewashed style had been built onto the left and right sides of the tower, as if it were a grotesquely inflated decorative element in the wall of a park or cemetery. And thus it had stood ever since, a giant whose minuscule, clipped wings were insufficient to keep the new, utilitarian buildings on either side at bay.

Hotel Tüffer stood directly opposite. It no longer belonged to the founding family; the Reschens had taken it over years ago, but at least they had had the good sense to allow their trophy to retain not only its name but also the elegant pink 1920s lettering. All in all, they had not made many changes. In this instance, there had been a conservationally fortuitous conjunction between their vague intuition that the original owners' taste accorded better with the expectations of well-travelled guests, and obsessive provincial parsimony. The visitor pushed open the door and inhaled cautiously. For a few nostalgic seconds the smell of the rooms — patchouli, eau de cologne, floor polish, and candles — transported him back in time: he was young again, barely eighteen, ladies of all ages were smiling at him. It was the scent of before-the-madness, of better days nearing their end, elegant, suspended. This harmonious building with its dark wooden panelling, brass lamps, and green glass lampshades was no longer in keeping with the times, certainly not with high society. Proof, if proof were needed, stood awkwardly at the Art Nouveau reception desk in the form of Zenzi, the hotel maid, wearing a cheap dirndl and gawping at new arrivals.

'I'd like a room,' he said, 'for a few days, maybe more.'

She handed him two keys. The chunky fob that, in hotels all over the world, is intended as a reminder, if only by dint of its weight, that this item of hotel property should never be removed from the premises but always handed in at reception, took the appropriate form of a huge, ornate mortice key. They probably used to open the castle gate with a monster like this.

'Is it a nice room?' he asked.

She hesitated, set the first key aside and gave him a different one. 'That's the nicest I can give you, that is.'

'I'll be sure to verify,' said the traveller, almost moved by her doubling of the relative pronoun. Then he winked at her, because he felt sorry for her, and because she might prove useful to him later on. It seemed she hadn't picked up from his accent that he was from the region.

3.

AS IT LATER TRANSPIRED, the mysterious visitor arrived in Darkenbloom at about the same time as Lowetz, whose first name no one could remember, as he himself didn't seem to use it. Lowetz planned to spend the summer figuring out what to do with his parental home. His mother had died a few weeks earlier. She had not been ill, nor was she especially old, yet, as expressed in the unintentional witticism produced, with some effort, by her inconsolable neighbour Fritz — the injury he had received as an infant made him difficult to understand, but the Lowetz family were attuned to his guttural stammer — she still *woke up dead one morning*.

Lowetz had not been born in Darkenbloom; his father had, though. His mother was from Over There, but over the decades she had skilfully succeeded in making people forget it. She was linguistically talented and, above all, an excellent mimic. Life was hard on the border — she sang the aria along with all the Darkenbloom women of her generation, an immaculate soprano lament. In rare moments of disharmony between mother and son (or, earlier, between husband and wife) an expression would cross her face as if a tiny hand had carefully pulled back a curtain and she was looking deep within.

Lowetz had got out as soon as he could. He had intended never to return. He had learned to talk like people in the capital; he never said *t'gether* any more, for example, because there they said *together. Let's get together.* And then *Let's sit together.* Avoiding *t'gether* altogether was almost camouflage enough. But he was tired of their ignorant, rapturous squawking, all the clean-shaven metropolitan movers and shakers and their narrow-hipped girls who saw Darkenbloom and its environs as provincial perfection, because within easy reach, while also fully expecting and decreeing that it remain provincial, for the highly unlikely eventuality that they might one day require a refuge. Quiet, empty vistas, and untrammelled nature! As if there were such a thing. Quiet, empty vistas in people's heads, and an untrammelled conscience — that's more like it. We can agree on that. We can come together on that. T'gether, even.

Darkenbloomers, on the other hand, have aspired since time immemorial to be the principal town, at least by their own standards, as in, to have a higher status than the surrounding rural villages. And they succeeded — thanks not to their own efforts, but to a decision made in the Middle Ages by the family of the now-emigrant counts. A crossroads of trade routes, the panoramic view from the plateau that had been promoted to *small mountain* — who knows what caused them to lay the foundation stone? A count started to build the first part of a castle, which grew at a leisurely pace and nurtured the town through its castellar umbilical cord. It could just as easily have happened in Zwick or Kalsching, but this concept was utterly alien to the people of Darkenbloom; they would have laughed so hard you would have seen right down to their rosy tonsils. An awareness of their limited grasp of the possible could, in fact, have told Lowetz all that was most important about them.

So the people of Darkenbloom continued to live, unabashed, in a state of fortuitous privilege. The fate of their castle and the counts had given them not a moment's pause; they acted as if it were wholly unconnected to them — what could they do about it?

There was always so much to do, we couldn't pay attention to that.

After the war, they just carried on, as everyone did — the majority, anyway. As everyone did who wasn't excluded from carrying on; because they were dead, for example.

One day, the Darkenbloomers began to yearn for their first asphalted road, and got one. Soon they craved a supermarket; then a second, as competition; finally, a chemist's. And since they had acquired a home-improvement store, its electric sliding doors stood open for every conceivable crime against good taste, as late as five pm on Saturdays. Three times in the past hundred years they had demolished the train station and rebuilt it, worse. Its present incarnation had glass bricks, aluminium windows, and the colour of crepuscular vomit. However, no sooner had it been completed than it was taken out of service. It was under-utilised; no one took the train any more, not since every hut- and cottage-dweller could afford a car. *Could* afford was inaccurate, though; afforded, without the modal verb. For this, savings were made elsewhere; where exactly was something people had to work out for themselves. In Darkenbloom, the poor and the better-off had one thing in common: everyone had flash cars. Only Lowetz's mother drove an old, spinach-green Corsa, almost until the end, which could be seen as a polite act of resistance. Shortly before her death, she passed it on to a young girl she liked, who, she told her son on the phone, sometimes came and gave her a hand.

The Lowetz house was at the bottom of a cul-de-sac in the old part of town. They could have shot films here depicting life in the olden days, and the set would have needed little decoration. They could have sent extras dressed as Jewish merchants scurrying down the narrow streets with their baskets full of lace trimmings, fabrics, ribbons, buttons, and an imposing, definitely moustachioed actor in the role of Iron Edi, with his rucksack full of whetstones.

Edi was from the Lovari travelling folk; he journeyed around the country in spring and autumn, sharpening knives and scissors. He did it so well that many back then were convinced he had magical powers. One day, the current Heuraffls' father, who was jealous and quick to anger, forbade his wife to give Edi her knives and scissors. He would sharpen them himself, he declared. But he couldn't seem to manage it, though he asked the advice of everyone in the region — even Over There — who had anything to do with metal and blades. He simply couldn't get his knives as sharp as Edi could, and they blunted much faster, too. This just fuelled his anger at Edi, but Edi, as usual, didn't come back for half a year. Frau Heuraffl, who in those days was a fresh-faced, sturdy blonde, had to borrow knives from the neighbours to slaughter the animals. The little town awaited the arrival of the knife grinder with anticipation. Curtains twitched. People could *sense* something. Nobody warned Edi when at last he arrived. They waited behind their windows, which were ever so slightly ajar. Without preamble, Edi was dragged into the Heuraffls' farmyard and beaten up. When he finally let him go, old Heuraffl bellowed his question into Edi's bloody face: why did the knives stay sharp for exactly half a year, just until Edi returned? Why couldn't a magician like him either make the knives stay sharp for longer, or perhaps even not as long, then he could come more often and make even more money, you filthy bastard, you charge enough, after all! Edi, who had a broken nose, had lost two teeth, and was struggling to get to his feet without looking at his tormentor, murmured in his peculiar accent that they simply didn't last that long.

They won't last any longer, it wouldn't work.

He kept murmuring this, even as he dragged himself off to visit his remaining customers. Many claimed to have heard this explanation: *It won't last any longer, it doesn't work.* And of course the superstitious among them remembered this sentence a few weeks later, when old Heuraffl, who was only about forty at the time, fell off a ladder in the upper vineyard and died. Dr Bernstein was sent for, Sterkowitz's predecessor. With some people, the heart just won't last any longer, explained the doctor, who seemed not to know about the business with the knife grinder. Nothing to be done, and no way of predicting it either, unfortunately.

But gypsies can see the future, the superstitious people murmured, they read palms. Gypsies know what'll last and what won't. They said it not to Dr Bernstein, but to each other. The 'other' Heuraffls, as they were back then, old Heuraffl's brothers, the wild uncles of the current Heuraffls, may perhaps have considered taking revenge on Iron Edi, but if they did, the idea was forgotten in the tumult that followed the arrival of the Führer. The whole lot of them suddenly had other things to do; a great deal, in fact, to do and organise and change: they were intent, for example, on raising the white flags as fast as possible, and afraid that Kirschenstein would get there first. And so it is not at all certain that Edi ever came to Darkenbloom again. Or who actually sharpened the knives and scissors after that.

In any case, this is what it was like in the pretty, homely part of Darkenbloom: uneven cobblestones, which Lowetz's mother, before she had fully mastered the language, used to call *chessboard stones*. Winding streets, scarcely wider than a horse and cart. Long, low, little houses, hunched like fearful schoolchildren, with whitewashed façades. The window frames painted in bright colours, with matching shutters, mostly blue or green, but there was also an upmarket version: a kind of mustard yellow bordered with a shade of red that was difficult to define. Not really claret, it inclined towards ruby red, but veered off just before it got there; it did not, however, become Tuscan red, and was of course nothing like the red of the fire brigade. It was simply Darkenbloom red, particularly striking in combination with the yellow, and found on the better, slightly larger, old houses. Everywhere there were flowers: geraniums, forget-me-nots, vines climbing the walls, and pots full of herbs sitting on the ground in the entrances to buildings. The old part of Darkenbloom was a world unto itself, disorientating, labyrinthine, secluded, and cool in summer. It could feel uncanny, like a surreally beautiful maze that could swallow you up, but also like a refuge where no one who wasn't from here could find you. The two possibilities lay side by side, like cards dealt out by chance.

When Lowetz turned the corner and raised his eyes, his parental home stood before him like an apparition, and he looked at it as if seeing it for the first time. Fritz next door had kept the garden and window boxes regularly watered. Apart from that, everything was growing however it pleased, and it almost looked enchanted. The apple tree had lowered its heavily laden branches over the cracked wooden fence as if politely asking for help. Inside the house it was a little dusty — light, decorative dust that had descended out of the air since his mother's death, like a chronometer. It was only now, because she was no longer there, that Lowetz noticed her unusual taste; both his parents', in fact. They had never followed any fashion — they let themselves be guided by their own preferences. They possessed only a few old but much-loved pieces of furniture, some of which had been given to them when neighbours were refurbishing. A black-and-white photo of Lowetz as a child, aged about eight, was stuck to the fridge, and beside it was the postcard of the castle that had recently reappeared in the shops. For a few years now there had at least been a dishwasher, a small one. His mother wouldn't believe that the small one was more expensive than a big one. She had insisted on getting the small one, for a small kitchen, a small house. A small life?

The greenery outside the windows created a sense of being under-water, at the bottom of a not very deep sea. Lowetz was surprised to find that he felt at home. Darkenbloom lay all around him, there was no denying that — on the way here he had seen Stitched-Up Schurl

with his horribly scarred face, straining to push open the door of the
Tüffer, and he pictured the rest of the company inside, with their red
noses and vicious jokes. But this house was an island. He sat down
and let his arms dangle. There had been something different about
his parents, but he couldn't put his finger on what. They had always
joined in with everything: church on Sunday, the carnival parade, the
annual shooting club fete. Lowetz's father had not been a member of
the *fellowship association*, nor did he go to the morning drinks where
these *fellows* predominated. But by no means everyone went, only the
loud and the cowardly. Which really wasn't always the same thing.
Had it been hard or easy for his father? Not to be part of it all? It
was the first time Lowetz had wondered this. He thought of the old
families whose names cropped up in the cemetery more often than
others, and the Malnitzes came to mind. Everyone was angry with
Toni Malnitz and his father, Old Malnitz — he didn't know why.
It had always been that way. His own father, on the other hand, had
been more neutral, or so Lowetz thought. But what did he know? He
had got out as soon as he could. 'If we'd at least had a chance to learn
languages in this godforsaken town,' he had sometimes complained, 'I
could have got further away than just the capital!'

'You can do whatever you like,' his mother had said. 'Don't put off
anything you really want until later.' It had never occurred to him to
learn his mother's language.

Now it seemed to him that it had taken all his strength just to
avoid the town. He hadn't been capable of more. He had simply run
away; he hadn't anchored himself anywhere else. And that was why
he was back; Darkenbloom only had to tug on the chain. He sat in
the almost empty living room on a bentwood chair that had belonged
to his maternal grandparents, whom he had never known. It had
provoked a row with the other, Darkenbloom grandparents, which
even he had heard about when he was little. First he brings back a girl
from Over There, then she doesn't want our chairs!

A stray bumblebee lurched across the room, sounding like Mother's old hand-held mixer. The sun stretched a few fingers of light through the undergrowth, in at the windows and over the rough wooden floor. This is where the treasure is hidden, it seemed to say, right here. Lowetz realised that he couldn't sell the house straight away. He loved it as much as he hated the town around it. He had to hold on to it; he had to reconcile with the house, at least. There was no one else left.

4.

THE ELDERLY GENTLEMAN WHO had been staying at the Hotel Tüffer for the past few days was friendly and inquisitive, in a manner that people here were not accustomed to and did not really appreciate. He strolled attentively through the town, the very embodiment of a tourist. Darkenbloom had not been blessed with these to date, the regional politicians' promises notwithstanding. The cyclists and hikers who trickled in for a few hours at the weekend when the weather was fine generated hardly any extra income for the taverns and hostelries, and it was not the rarely occupied rooms that kept the Tüffer from going bankrupt, but its bar, which was open seven days a week, the cut-price lunch menu, and old Frau Reschen's self-exploitation. The little town had nothing to offer people interested in art history, apart from the plague column and an altarpiece, half burned in the war and inadequately restored, that depicted several devils behind and beside the apostles, small, feathered ones, and a large one with a horse's hoof. The castle tower was so dilapidated it could not be accessed, and if you wanted to visit the counts' family crypt you had to make a booking.

Plans for a museum of local history had been under discussion for some time, but they could not be implemented because the town council had split into two uncompromising camps. One, led by Rehberg, the travel agent, envisaged a sort of comital theme park where the Darkenbloom dynasty's family trees, coats of arms, tapestries, wigs, suits of armour, and the famous gold Passion of Christ (hammered, two metres by three) would be exhibited, though no one had asked the counts whether they would actually put all this at their disposal. The others insisted it should be an expression of rural culture, a craftsmen's and wine growers' museum that must, at the very least, be furnished with a historic winepress.

Since the start of summer, some long-haired students had been working in the old Jewish cemetery, mowing and weeding, burning brambles and righting fallen gravestones, but of course there was nothing worth exhibiting there, either. People had almost forgotten about this cemetery's existence; it had been invisible behind its high wall. It was strangely affecting to see the gates now standing open, except on Saturdays. No one understood what it was all about. You didn't voluntarily stroll around a cemetery if you didn't have a grave to tend, and if anyone had wanted to, the Catholic and Evangelical ones were nice enough. The savings bank had even donated benches for them years ago, eight for the Catholics, three for the Evangelicals.

But these young people had produced a document from the capital, so they were welcome to cut back the elder bushes if they had nothing better to do. That was the view of the reluctant, overburdened mayor, Koreny. He had never put himself forward for election. He had only ended up as deputy mayor because he was a good-natured fellow and a loyal supporter of the dynamic Heinz Balf. However, Balf, an estate agent and hobby marathon runner, had recently been chauffeured to the capital by Dr Sterkowitz himself, with swellings in his armpits. They were saying he wouldn't come back for a long time, if at all. And so, to his utter horror, chubby, ginger-haired Koreny had become mayor.

And it was Koreny who had given permission for this undertaking, and the more that suspicious citizens made enquiries, the more emphatically he reiterated his position. It had come from on high, after all. But people here opposed everything, because they understood nothing about politics. The long-haired youngsters had a legal document from the city, and it stated that the Jewish community had charged them with the restoration of the cemetery. They're paying for it, as well, and there's an end to it. No, it's not costing us anything. Yes, of course it's true that the fiftieth anniversary year is finally over. But our chancellor also said that we shouldn't remember Austria's annexation only on the memorial day itself; that remembrance should be something that endures. The cardinal said so, too. Or was it even the president?

There had been a little incident at the end of the town council's last meeting before the summer break — tiny, insignificant really. A young woman had made a stupid remark that exposed the frazzled state of the mayor's nerves. Flocke, Malnitz's youngest daughter with his wife Leonore, had come to pick up her father, and had apparently been listening for a while in the half-open doorway. Rehberg from the travel agency had just got to the end of his speech about the local history museum. Rehberg had wanted to be a priest, but he had become a travel agent. Since then, although he wasn't conscious of it, he expected the world to show consideration for his disappointed ambitions, and tried to project himself as a beacon of culture, good manners, and strategic overview. He rarely succeeded. Most people, with the exception of Ferbenz, were his oratorical inferiors, but that didn't bother them. They didn't even listen to him; they overruled him or shouted him down. Rehberg, who had a voice like a worn-out fan belt, had again invoked the crowds of visitors who flocked to exhibitions elsewhere, like 'The Kuenring Family Treasures', 'The Babenberg Women', and 'The Habsburg Castles', because noble families and the aristocracy were, quite simply, the attractions of the future. People were nostalgic for the good old days. Rehberg felt he was especially knowledgeable in this particular field of tourism. The wine growers and tradesmen, who for some obscure reason usually voted socialist in this part of the world, had expressed their displeasure with interjections like *Shaveling!* and other, even less friendly remarks, but they had at least let him finish speaking. Mayor Koreny was about to end the meeting and adjourn this item of the agenda, or the other way round, and was just wiping his handkerchief over his wet forehead once more to calm himself and gain time. And then the cheeky little Malnitz girl squawked from the doorway something about a border museum, something special that no one else has but us. Us, in collaboration with people from Over There, everything in both languages — there were links, we'd just have to dig them up, that alone would be a unique selling point. With this awkward term she appeared to be imitating Rehberg, who had probably just used it himself. Those were just the sort of words he came out with, as if he were some sort of intellectual.

'That's enough,' shouted Koreny, and his freckled fist slammed down on the table before him as if of its own volition. For a moment, everyone looked up, even Dr Ferbenz, who, on account of his age, was only a humble minute-taker these days: at their service, saying nothing, remaining on the sidelines, but of course he was always there, and never missed a word that was spoken, or indeed any that went unsaid. 'Meeting's over,' Koreny roared, and found venting his feelings surprisingly refreshing. 'I'm tired, and it's hot; the date of the next session will be announced in due course.'

The inquisitive elderly gentleman from the Tüffer even found out about this. He strolled through the town, chatting at garden fences and farmyard gates. He visited the local taverns and tasted their wine. He stood admiring Rehberg's Travel until the owner came outside. In keeping with the time of year, the window display featured a pile of sand, a potted palm tree, and a leather camel. The gentleman was so interested and attentive that Rehberg, gaining confidence, confided that a tour operator had given him a splendid inflatable steamer with which to advertise their cruises. But he wasn't sure whether or not to put it in the shop window. He knew his clientele. You couldn't sell cruises here, even with the best will in the world. His most reliable business consisted of arranging trips to the Adriatic: bus to Kirschenstein, train to Graz, where you transferred to the bathers' bus, which stopped in all the Adriatic seaside resorts and dropped tourists at the door of even the smallest hotel, as long as they had reserved in advance. Rehberg's clever idea was to provide an extra service: he paid a student in Graz to meet the travellers on the train platform, with a list of names and a yellow-and-red Darkenbloom flag, and accompany them to the departure point for the bathers' bus. It was only two streets away, but people immediately felt unsure of themselves as soon as they left their familiar environment. He was proud of ideas like these. His clients came from all over the region, even further than Kirschenstein. Rather than head off alone into one of the noisy, bewildering cities, they preferred to come to him. This was why Rehberg was still optimistic. The travel sector was growing everywhere; it would grow in Darkenbloom, too. He had already sold Dr Alois a beach holiday in Egypt, although he had been unhappy with a few little details — he was a fastidious gentleman. Generally speaking, Rehberg was hopeful. But the beautiful steamer? With its lovingly printed portholes and the little figures waving on the top deck? Wasn't it — grandiose?

The stranger listened to all this and gave Rehberg a piece of advice that immediately convinced him. His personal view, said the visitor, was that shop windows should display the unattainable, so that customers have something to dream about. You enter a shop because — and although — there's far more in there than you can afford.

You want a little bit of Paradise, not Paradise itself. Even the scrap merchant from the market, he said, has a truffle salami on Saturdays, albeit a tiny one, to go with his mountain of freshly sliced Extrawurst. In short: people had to believe Rehberg was capable of planning and organising the most luxurious of cruises on the most splendid of ships, then they would feel confident enough to book a little trip with him. 'People want to stretch out, not hunker down,' said the friendly man who was staying at the Hotel Tüffer, 'we're all the same in that respect.' And Rehberg was so grateful that he invited the stranger into his shop, and, before blowing up the steamer, poured him a glass of schnapps and allowed himself to be persuaded to divulge his humble opinions on the very old, very nasty stories about Darkenbloom — it seemed to him that this man was the right person to hear them. Towards the end of this memorable meeting, they could be seen clambering about behind the plate-glass window, using a dustpan to relocate the pile of sand, shifting the palm tree, and placing the huge, picture-perfect, truly heartwarming white steamer with all the laughing faces on a long, wavy strip of blue wrapping paper, such that one might think the Danube ran all the way to the Pyramids. Or was it supposed to be the Nile? Surely the Nile was not as blue. For the rest of the summer the leather camel stood in the front-right corner of the window and marvelled.

After a few days of walking and looking around, the guest at the Tüffer had found someone to drive him. He was seen sitting in the passenger seat of Flocke's battered, spinach-green car with the windows down, in good spirits, turning his head this way and that. How had he come across Flocke? No one knows. It's possible Rehberg mentioned her outburst at the local council meeting, but it was probably much simpler than that. Rehberg wasn't to blame for everything that went wrong in Darkenbloom, even if, for years, Berneck, Stitched-Up

Schurl and the Heuraffl twins had delighted in telling him exactly that.

'So, Rehberg, what've you done now?' they would ask, linking arms with him on both sides, if he had the misfortune to cross their path of an evening after their extended session in the pub. He never answered, did not defend himself. He tried to turn his head away, but couldn't, as they were all around him. He tried to wrench free of their grasp, not forcefully, but feebly, whining. He wriggled like a child. 'Let go,' he wailed in his unfortunate voice, 'let me go, I haven't done anything.' They pushed him around a bit, just for fun, fists on his forearms, jeering: Rehberg's innocent, Rehberg hasn't done anything, and what he did do he didn't mean to do, didn't even know he'd done it, hahaha!

Once, years ago, when they were still young and wild, they had given him a couple of kicks up the backside, just as an experiment. He had fallen so awkwardly that he couldn't get up, had done something to his knee or ankle, not broken but torn. Lowetz's mother had found him there, on the corner of Tempelgasse and Sternsingergasse, motionless but still conscious. He hadn't dared call out, for fear the lads would return; instead, he told Frau Lowetz he must have passed out for a moment. To Dr Sterkowitz, too, he insisted that he had stumbled in the dark, over an animal, perhaps, Doctor, we've got raccoons now! Sterkowitz suspected the truth. 'I have to report this to the police,' he said, testing the water, but Rehberg puffed out his chest, looked him dead in the eye and asked, 'Can't we even stumble any more? Do we get reported for breaking a leg? What's the world coming to?'

Sterkowitz observed the high-frequency tremor in Rehberg's hands and legs, prescribed a mild sedative, bandaged the leg, and didn't mention the police again. He said something to Ferbenz later, though, and Ferbenz said something to his lads, who just got a bit carried away sometimes, wasn't that so, and after that they only ever pushed Rehberg around, gave him the odd bruise, tugged at his jacket and sometimes his ears. *Nothing serious, just having a laugh, eh?* That was all that was needed.

Rehberg really wasn't to blame for everything, only his shop-window decoration. So one can think of many possible occasions on which the gentleman from the Tüffer and Flocke might have got talking; perhaps, quite simply, when he visited her parents' tavern. Flocke had come home for the summer holidays. And she, too, liked to roam about, regularly visiting Fritz and the grocer Antal Grün. She helped him do the stock-taking; for some reason it made him so nervous that he couldn't cope on his own. She brought cider and sliced-sausage rolls to the students at the overgrown cemetery. Flocke Malnitz had a mind of her own, but having a mind of your own did rather run in the family. Apparently Darkenbloomers did at least differentiate between these own minds, because they described the girl as a *hippy*. It would never have occurred to anyone to say the same of her father.

And now they saw her driving the stranger around in her car. They drove up the so-called local mountain, which was known as the Hazug, an Over-There name; it didn't have a German one. So most Darkenbloomers just said *the mountain*. At the top, Flocke and the visitor gazed down at the countryside, of both countries. A beautiful view, all spread out below them, undulating, dappled, vivid, and inviting. You could make out the border installations; seen from on high, they looked as if they had been cobbled together out of wire and toothpicks. Here, as there, miniature tractors drove diligently across the fields, the little, spiky church spires pointed straight up towards God, and the vineyards looked like decorations, frilly velvet ribbons between smooth squares. The towns and villages as if sprinkled in between, frayed at the edges. From above, the architectural eyesores of the post-war period were barely visible, just the occasional flash of bright orange or sky blue in the gaps. But you could clearly tell from up here that the centre of Darkenbloom was extremely dense. As if packed more tightly, tied up, pressed together, as at the lowest point in a crate, where everything bears down two or three times as hard from above. In Darkenbloom, it bore up from below. But density can be nice, too, warm and full of energy. *People simply didn't need as much space in the old days.*

The guest from the Tüffer suggested they drive to Ehrenfeld; he had had friends there, a long, long time ago. The smaller town of Ehrenfeld had seemed to him altogether more harmonious, more peaceful.

'Hmm, I don't know about that,' said Flocke doubtfully.

The guest said he had read in the paper that a barn there had burned down recently. Had she heard about it?

'Heard?' Flocke replied. She laughed, stuck out her lower lip and blew her fringe up off her forehead, a tic of hers. 'That was our barn; my mother inherited it. And the fire brigade were busy getting hammered in Kalsching that very evening. Isn't that a coincidence!'

5.

THE OWNER OF THE burnt-out barn, Leonore Malnitz, was the queen of Darkenbloom. Describing her as a *provincial beauty* would have been an understatement. In her youth she had often been told she should enter beauty pageants, but Leonore had merely snorted at this. By the time the pageants started up again in the late fifties, she was married and had had her first two children. And a few years later, when it had become customary for Darkenbloom men to sit in the bar of the Tüffer baying at the screen as girls in bikinis walked across holding their numbers, she had provoked a fistfight.

'Disgusting and sexist,' she had declared loudly as she strode through the television room with a delivery note, because back then the Reschens still served Malnitz wine. 'Don't any of you meat marketeers ever think of your own daughters?'

The men roared, some tried to smack her bottom, and she turned and gave the nearest man a theatrical slap. Unfortunately, this nearest man leapt to his feet, grabbed her arm, and pulled her right up close to his red face. Leonore leaned back as far as she could, more in disgust than fear.

'Berneck, stop it,' screamed the landlady, Resi Reschen, but it was too late. To Berneck's surprise, Young Graun, no more than twenty at the time, flung an arm around his neck from behind and squeezed, using his elbow as a lever. Leonore stumbled and wrenched herself free. Frau Reschen dragged her behind the bar, and from there into the kitchen and out through the tradesman's entrance. Outside, Leonore checked she still had both her earrings, thanked Frau Reschen, and advised her to chuck those *animals* out, the whole lot of them. This did not go down well with Frau Reschen, who had always wanted to tell those self-important Malnitzes what she thought of them — if only she had been able to find the right words.

The older Leonore got, the less she seemed to fit in in Darkenbloom. She was well aware of this. It was one thing to be an attractive, quick-witted girl for a few carefree years, but continuing to look good, remain slim and athletic, and dress with taste was not the genetic plan in this part of the world. Other than her, there were no ladies for miles around, only old or very old women. Leonore did not become broad and fleshy, despite her four children; her small breasts, which had bothered her in her youth when a different ideal prevailed, also retained their shape. And she cherished the culture that she, the daughter of a Kirschenstein teacher, had brought with her from home, music and literature in particular. *Just because you make good wine, it doesn't mean you have to be an ignoramus* was one of the precepts with which she raised her daughters.

She and Toni soon knew people both in the capital and further afield. On one occasion, Leonore even caught the eye of the Count. When the renovation of the counts' family crypt was completed, twenty years after the war, she did wear a dirndl to the ceremony, though she certainly did not kiss his hand — that would have been going too far. But when everyone gathered in the town square after the service, the two embarked on a long conversation that was covertly observed by many of those present.

Leonore did not have the same effect on people in the capital, she knew that. Her accent was too strong. People found it off-putting, which would not have been the case for a man. Equally, she sensed that the metropolis called for different codes, different qualities, in order to succeed and stay on top. These were things that couldn't just be acquired. In the city, to which she would escape, sometimes often, sometimes less so, a residual uncertainty clung to her, as indelible as the provincial twist to her speech. It frustrated her, as did the uneventfulness of Darkenbloom. What she really needed was female friends who were her equals. It wasn't surprising, then, that she had the idea of luring to Darkenbloom the kind of people she missed so badly: artists, intellectuals and creatives, daredevils, and eccentrics.

Leonore's marriage to Malnitz, though it had endured for decades, was highly problematic. Both were high-handed and stubborn; it was why they had fallen for each other so hard in the first place. They were both big talkers, they both had dreams, and, in his family at least, Toni was the first fish determined to crawl on land, maybe even to fly. This was probably why he resolutely married up, half a step at least, into the Kirschenstein bourgeoisie. Leonore's parental home had a Bösendorfer grand piano, and it came with her to Darkenbloom.

They would have made a perfect couple — energetic, curious, inventive — if only there had been a few more people like them around. But because there were none, they also needed each other as opponents, the other being the only person worth arguing with. With the first three children born in quick succession, and Leonore's conservative parents-in-law being part of the business, things soon got very heated. With big dreams come big disappointments. Leonore would volubly curse the miserable little border town she had let Toni drag her to, full of Nazis, liars, and drunkards. Toni would get up and walk out, slamming the door, and occasionally smashing a few plates or vases on his way. Darkenbloom listened in, rubbing its hands with glee. But perhaps that was the glue that held them together: they refused to give the old soaks the satisfaction. And then there were their clever, confident daughters, the prospering business. Toni was one of the first to become interested in organic farming: less pest control, older varieties, smaller but better harvests. He focused on the high-price market segment. He stopped exporting inferior blends, which at the time seemed inconceivably stupid. Everyone profited from the sweetened wine they sold to Germany, and had stopped bothering with anything else. Toni was the only one to go down a different path. He represented the business himself, travelling all over the country, visiting the newly emerging high-end caterers; he started to experiment with sparkling wine and fine spirits. He fell out with his parents over it, so badly that — maximum escalation — they moved to Zwick to live with their younger son, a wine grower of the old school.

As soon as her parents-in-law had gone, Leonore cleared out their beautiful old house and had it renovated. She installed a sauna and decorated the bathrooms with exotic tiles; she furnished the rooms with wrought-iron French bedsteads and antiques. She bought works by young artists and hung them on the walls. A soft brown puppet dangled from the ceiling in the entrance hall like a hanged baby. What really got Darkenbloom talking was that some rooms supposedly had freestanding bathtubs, in full view of the beds. The plumber's apprentice had told his uncle, Stitched-Up Schurl, who cheerfully passed it on.

Resi Reschen from the Hotel Tüffer had laughed at first when she heard the room rates that crazy Malnitz woman had the barefaced cheek to ask. But when one of the Malnitz daughters asked a Reschen grandson at school whether he actually knew how many letters made the difference between *quality* and *quantity*, the Reschen grandson said two, the Malnitz daughter declared the correct answer was three, and the two children had a fight — when, moreover, Resi learned that people were actually paying Leonore's fantastical prices, she stopped serving Malnitz wine.

Meanwhile, Leonore made friends with a permanently inebriated author from the capital, who reserved rooms with her in the summer for himself and various friends. Other members of the cultural in-crowd followed suit. It wasn't long before Malnitz's organic farm was considered an insider tip: *in the heavenly, unspoilt border region, replete with wine and history*, as one magazine described it. Sometimes, on hot summer weekends, even the Tüffer was booked out with the author's hangers-on — Leonore, tipsy on Toni's vintage sparkling wine, started referring to it as *Tick HQ*. Guests she could no longer accommodate had to call ahead themselves, though; there was a limit to the service she was willing to provide.

Then the country was rocked by the wine scandal, and the younger Malnitz brother went bankrupt. Toni, on the other hand, could have sold that year's vintage several times over. With a bank loan and what was left of his savings, the elder Malnitz bought the filling station for his son; so now, over in Zwick, they smelled of petrol rather than grape juice, and radiated inflammable hatred. Toni brought them a case of wine every week, and left it on the driveway without a word.

In her early thirties, after the beauty pageant fistfight in the Tüffer, and before the Count kissed her hand in front of the whole town, Leonore permitted herself an indiscretion. Her parents-in-law were still living with them then, they were restructuring the business, and money was tight; sometimes she couldn't keep track of whom she had just quarrelled with and with whom she had reconciled. Their eldest daughter, who looked like a grumpy little Toni with plaits, had informed her over lunch that she hated her because she was always telling Papa off, while the youngest, sick and crying, kept clinging to her and smearing snot all over her blouse. Only the middle daughter was agreeable; she played outside all day and didn't bother anyone. Leonore took the youngest to her mother-in-law, squeezed out a *please*, a *thank you*, and a smile, and got in the car. She drove to her parents' in Kirschenstein, but fled again after coffee, because the only thing her tired, sick father wanted to talk to her about was his will.

Young Graun was standing on the main road southwards out of town, with his thumb out. Ever since he had leapt to her defence in the fight at the hotel, she seemed to bump into him everywhere. He was at least ten years younger than her, scarcely more than a child, and he always looked at her as if he depended on her for his survival. She pulled over and picked him up. She was making a detour to Ehrenfeld to look at a plot of land that belonged to her father. It was on a slope on the outskirts of town; the countryside fell away spectacularly behind it. Her father had said there was a very good chance it would be redesignated for construction.

'What do you think, could someone build a hotel here?' she asked the trembling Young Graun, as they picked their way through the long grass together.

He shrugged. 'Who wants to stay in a hotel that's practically on the border?' he asked.

'It's got a nice view,' she said, 'all the way Over There.'

Leonore rattled at the door of the old barn. 'So where do you want to go?' she asked him, rather ambiguously.

'To the conservatoire,' he said.

She turned. 'What do you play?'

'Violin,' he said.

'Nice,' she said. 'So you're not going to be a wine grower?'

He shook his head vehemently.

Inside, by the barn door, which Young Graun eventually managed to get open for her, a big rake was leaned against the wall in the dim light, and because he gestured for her to go first, she trod on its rusty prongs. She cried out and fell, landing softly on old straw. A thin streak of bright red blood trickled down her shin. Before she knew it, he knelt in front of her and kissed it away. He was a good-looking lad in those days, before Ferbenz got his claws into him, with tousled hair that was rather too long. At the end of this surprising afternoon, she couldn't help telling him that you should only give ladies precedence when entering familiar rooms, not unfamiliar ones. 'Men always step first into the unknown,' she teased him, laughing, 'but how could you be expected to know that, you twerp?' When she became pregnant for the fourth time, she abruptly ended what she secretly thought of afterwards as the *little romantic barn interlude*.

Shortly before the inquisitive guest arrived at the Hotel Tüffer, and shortly after the august foreign ministers met nearby to cut through the border fence with big, but not very sharp, parrot-nose pliers — from what people said, it had already almost rusted away — Leonore decided to buy a second pug. She suspected herself of getting the first as a child substitute, though she and Toni were not short of labour-intensive grandchildren. Her eldest daughter, Andrea, already resented her acquisition of the first pug, but she had always been the most intractable of children. 'Anyone might think you bought this creature so you'd have an excuse not to look after your grandchildren,' she had said, in that tight-lipped, corner-of-the-mouth way that at least meant you could pretend you hadn't heard her.

'Pugs are very child-friendly,' Leonore had retorted stoutly. 'Once the children are bigger, they'll have tremendous fun with him.'

In fact, Leonore thought it less conspicuous if she walked around talking to the pug instead of just to herself. Her loneliness had not diminished with the years, although the wine business and the country hotel were flourishing and she was constantly surrounded by people who wanted something from her. And perhaps that was why she felt so sorry for the solitary pug that panted around after her every step and almost choked with delight when she knelt on the floor and pretended to tussle with it over a tennis ball.

The drive to western Styria was a long one. She resolved not to buy a second dog if there wasn't one she really liked. Koloman snuffled on the back seat. She had named him after the martyr; she found it amusing. Leonore wondered whether returning to his birthplace would make Koloman feel sad, or whether this, too, was a burden that only affected humans. Her parental home in Kirschenstein had stood empty for years, but she still hoped one of her daughters would want to do something with it.

To her surprise, the current litter was black, not beige with black masks, like Koloman. The breeder praised Koloman's lean physique. Leonore was exhausted, and it all felt a bit much. There she sat, with a cup of bitter coffee and the puppies tumbling about her like little black devils. She would have liked to bring Flocke with her, but the girl was off out somewhere again. Koloman pressed himself against her foot and feigned disinterest. The black puppies clambered on top of each other as if trying to build a pyramid, like Chinese acrobats. They kept slipping and trying again; it looked like a stunt that kept going wrong.

'The thing is, I didn't really want a black one,' she told the breeder, who suddenly knelt down and rummaged in the pile of pugs.

'I'll come back with my daughter when you've got the other ones again,' she continued, and stood up, but the breeder wasn't listening.

'Good heavens,' she said, when he had prised the black furballs apart. Underneath the others, flat and still, eyes closed, lay the smallest puppy of them all. The breeder carefully lifted it up.

'Is he dead?' asked Leonore.

'No, no,' said the breeder. The dog opened its eyes and started to run in mid-air, like a cartoon character. The breeder set it down on the ground. It staggered a few steps, made a puddle, and fell right into it.

'Can I take him now, or is he still too small?' asked Leonore.

'I can't give it to you any cheaper, you know,' the breeder resisted. 'Breeding is breeding.'

'No, no, that's not what I ...' said Leonore. 'But ... is he sickly? Is he going to die?'

'It's a bitch,' said the breeder, 'and if you take her away from the competition here, she'll be fine. She's no beauty, though.'

'You mean she won't win any Miss Pug beauty pageants?' asked Leonore, amused.

'Definitely not,' said the breeder. 'Look at her — scrawny little thing.'

'Do you know any female martyrs?' asked Leonore.

The breeder considered. 'Hildegard von Bingen?' he suggested.

Leonore laughed. 'Oh well,' she said, 'never mind.'

6.

'YOU DON'T HAVE TO do everything Dr Alois says,' Young Graun's wife hissed as he got up from the breakfast table.

What do you know about it, he thought, but he said nothing as usual, just pressed his lips together and pulled the door shut behind him. On the long drive — he generally did the deliveries himself — he had plenty of time to wonder whether all men were put under this much pressure by their wives. Or whether he had got a particularly raw deal. They always found something to grumble about, wanted to do everything differently to you, and nagged if you opposed them. He suspected it wasn't really about the issue, but the principle; so, ultimately, about power. There was no freedom of speech with women. He exempted his mother from this — though only partially — because there must be other reasons, probably personal, for the fact that she a) was an old soak, and b) had always had something against Dr Alois. Reasons he didn't know, that didn't interest him in the slightest, but that went back a long way, to the war years, you could bet on it. Young Graun knew all too well what was whispered about Dr Alois in town. But it could hardly be to do with that, the political side of things. Because Young Graun's mother, and his father, too — him especially — they'd been just the same, back then ...

He twiddled the radio dial and stumbled across a talk show. Then he had to let go of the dial, because out of the corner of his eye he saw ... a black wave, high as a house. A huge, wide lorry was coming straight at him, well over the central line. He threw himself onto the horn with both hands and all the strength in his body. The lorry swerved back into its lane, tall trailer wobbling. '*Arsehole!*' shouted Young Graun as they passed each other. Behind the other windscreen, for a fraction of a second: wide eyes in a pale face, a good half-metre above him. Probably another Yugo who'd won his driving licence in the lottery, dear God in heaven ...

It took him a few deep breaths to calm down. Electricity poles flashed past outside, as upright and intact as bottles in the filling line. But he had come within a hair's breadth of being smashed to pieces: spikes, splinters, blood, the end.

'It's women who choose their partners,' said an impertinently self-satisfied female voice, 'it's women who decide for or against a man. In more than 80 per cent of cases in our survey — and naturally we asked people from every income bracket — women also make the decisions on decorating the home, not just individual items of furniture but the whole style, whether to go for classical, modern, or rustic. But of course the most significant decisions are those that affect the partnership. More and more often these days, it's the woman who leaves. The number of divorce petitions filed by women has been rising steadily for years. Women are less afraid of being alone: nowadays, of course, that's also to do with changes in pay and working conditions, but it's true that, compared to men — and I'm talking now about older women, as well — even after several decades of marriage, they're much less afraid of ...'

Young Graun switched it off. He had noticed lately that the radio sometimes responded almost directly to what he was thinking. It only happened in the delivery van, never in his private car. Perhaps because no one but him ever drove the van, so the radio had set up a direct line to him in there.

He glanced at the clock. He had been on the road for a good half-hour; the day had only just begun. But he could guarantee that Karin would already have dropped in on his mother and told her everything. You could usually talk to his mother in the mornings — sometimes she might even still be on top form, a financial wizard. The few times in recent years when he had really been at his wits' end, when the people at the bank and the tax consultants had made his head spin with their tables and progression curves, she had come to his rescue. You had to pick a good morning. That was what made the difference. A Tuesday or a Wednesday morning. On Mondays, her system was still so overloaded from the weekend that it could barely cope with anything else. By Tuesday, the level would have sunk a little, though nothing upsetting must happen, no run-ins with him or Karin, or the children, or the teenagers who shouted insults at her on the street. Keep her around other people, because at least when others were about she did pull herself together a little. Be friendly. Don't provoke one of her furious stormings-out. If Tuesday went well, you could carefully distract her in the evening with the prime-time wildlife documentary, and a first taste of the new vintage, just to postpone the fetching of the schnapps. But there could be no looks, no gestures, certainly no comments when she eventually hauled herself to her feet, shuffled off to her room and returned with one of the unlabelled bottles. If she offered you a drink, then it was fine, things had gone well. Wednesday would be a good morning, the right morning. It was an egg dance that required the cooperation of the whole family. But if it succeeded, she was still astounding: narrowing her eyes at the financial officials' many confusing papers, snapping her fingers for calculator, notepad, pencil. When it was especially complicated she called for strong coffee with a shot of alcohol. But every time she made her final decision with the confidence of a judge, or an auctioneer bringing down the hammer. For example: Yes, it's right to refinance, but certainly not at that rate. These are the terms you ask for ... And she would hand him a note with the percentages and durations as she was already turning away.

'But if ...' he had said doubtfully, the first time. She had turned back and looked at him with her customary contempt. As a child, he had always sensed her disappointment: that it was just him there, and not his father any more. *What? Just you, you little clown? Making such a racket?* It made him furious, every time, as if his edges were on fire, but he also couldn't stop himself shrivelling into a small, grubby heap, a little pile of dirt, even though the dirt was smouldering.

'If what?' she asked, and started laughing, a rusty laugh, as if at any moment she might start coughing up tar and phlegm. 'If they don't give it to you? Then they'll be the ones to lose out, won't they? The other bank'll give it to you, anyway. But we won't go there.'

'No, we won't go there.'

It was no comfort to Young Graun that his mother didn't know the difference between major and minor, and as for *dominant seventh chord*, if she had recognised this at all, she would have thought it was in the language of Over There. Sometimes, alone in the car, he would say *Dominantseptakkord* as if it were Over-Thereish. You just had to shift the As and Os in the opposite directions: darken the As and open up the Os, but not completely, just a little. It was important to stretch the E in *sept* like an elongated *eh* and pronounce the word as if you were swaying along to a schmaltzy tune in a beer tent, lilting, taking your time. He liked to think about the relationship between the speech rhythms of specific languages and a country's characteristic music. Whether — and for which instrument — you could write études that would sound like English, French, Spanish. He couldn't speak any other languages, apart from the little Italian that consti-tuted the language of music, but for precisely this reason he believed he could feel and hear their tones. Especially Over-Thereish. It was memorable — he would recognise it anywhere. A vowel-soaked swaying that could shift at any moment into a rattle of machine guns. A combination of woodwind and brass with lots of tritones. What people referred to as *gypsy music* was different, though, more cheerful.

He had once greatly amused Dr Alois with this idea: that they must once have had a different music Over There, one that sounded more like their language. 'You're right,' Dr Alois had shouted, laughing, 'you see, that's what happens if you don't preserve your own cultural heritage! Negroes and gypsies come in and take over!' Young Graun had tried to explain to him how gypsies had a special kind of musicality, the few he had met, at least; without even being able to read music, they ... But you couldn't talk to the Doctor about this — he was stuck fast in all his old crap.

'A people needs other primary talents in order to be worthy of the name,' Dr Alois had declared, his chin trembling as it always did when he lost himself in the old heroic exploits. Young Graun had given up; you couldn't change people, after all. Not Dr Alois, and not Karin, either: not her profound antipathy towards the Doctor. Perhaps antipathy wasn't the right word. But fear was probably putting it too strongly.

He shouldn't have told her about the plot of land. What did it matter to her why the Doctor wanted it! It didn't matter to Young Graun. Dr Alois just wanted it, and urgently, it seemed. It was clear to everyone, though, that Malnitz wouldn't sell to the Doctor. They weren't even on speaking terms. Apparently, the Doctor said, it belonged to her, to Frau Malnitz. The lovely Leonore. Young Graun could have confirmed this. And how. On the other hand, he couldn't tell the Doctor why he was uncomfortable about asking Frau Malnitz if she would sell it to him. The Doctor seemed to assume he was on good terms with Frau Malnitz. Well yes, he said hello to her, they encountered one another on a regular basis, you couldn't avoid it in the neighbourhood. But he hadn't actually talked to her for more than twenty years. And this old, secret history was probably the reason why he had told Karin about the land. His own uneasiness with the matter had made him spill the beans. As if he had been begging her to object.

'You don't have to do everything Dr Alois says!'

No, he didn't have to. But he ought to. And he wanted to! He felt obliged to him, even though he really didn't always agree with his views. Just because he sat with him at the regulars' table — did you have to agree with someone's views on every little detail? Young Graun wasn't interested in politics, anyway. Liars, the lot of them. Let the old boy yatter on, with his trembling chin — Young Graun would never forget what he had done for him. Without Dr Alois, he would have ended up in court that time, maybe even in prison; he wouldn't have married Karin, or taken over the farm; there wouldn't be any children, those dear, noisy little snotrags ...

And now Dr Alois just wanted this plot of land, for God's sake, and needed him to be a straw man. Straw man? He grinned. Yes, there was still straw there, in the barn ...

Come on, why not? Why shouldn't he help? What was the problem? Naturally, it was a bit complicated. As everyone in town knew, he not only had no money, he was in debt. But there were possibilities. The Doctor had already thought of something: a loan, securities, a company that he would be part of, that would handle it ... The only thing was, he would have to deceive Leonore. She would be very angry when her plot eventually ended up with Dr Alois ... On the other hand — let her be angry. After all, it was because of her that, back then, he almost ... And he wouldn't now ... Perhaps he would enjoy it, he thought, picturing the scene: he encounters Leonore, with the ridiculous lapdog she's had for a while now; she makes a fuss — which he couldn't really imagine, because she had always been gentle and ironic, frosty only at the end, so for the purpose of imagining the scene he substituted Karin. He stands there, waits till she's finished scolding him, and then he says to her face, he says to her face ... He doesn't know what he says to her. He can't think of anything suitable.

He would probably just take the car keys and go, the same as always. He murmured *Dominantseptakkord* again instead, as if he were someone from Over There. Finally he reached the motorway slip road, and found a classical music station on the radio.

By late afternoon, everything had been delivered and Young Graun's back was aching. The table wine, the two-litre bottles, the grape juice. Five crates here, a pallet there. Small trade that didn't interest him in the slightest. He didn't employ a cellar master, like the Malnitzes; he didn't invite sommeliers (none would have come to him, anyway); he didn't age in barrels. All that was too extravagant for him; besides, he had never had money to invest. And so he supplied small, provincial inns and cafés, even stalls at swimming pools and sports fields. They got by, somehow. Maybe Karin would nag less if business were better. He was driving through Kalsching when he remembered the argument at breakfast. Ehrenfeld was next. Maybe he should stop and take another look at the plot of land. Maybe he'd figure out what Dr Alois wanted it for. Surely he wasn't going to build anything new, at his age?

The fence around it was in good condition, had probably been repaired, but the land itself was overgrown. Young Graun glanced around and climbed over the fence. A trodden-down track ran through the weeds and undergrowth towards the barn. It looked as if someone — several people — had been here recently. Probably teenagers. Let's hope they were careful if they were smoking in the barn. Frau Malnitz really ought to get someone to mow this, it would only take a couple of hours.

The barn looked just as it had back then, the last time they'd met here. The door wasn't locked, and his body suddenly remembered how his heart had pounded whenever he stepped inside. Everything in his life had only got worse since then. Had she trodden that track? Did she still use the barn to meet men? You twerp, he berated himself.

She has very different options these days. These days, she can go to Venice with her lovers. Why did he think of Venice? Probably because the timetable for the bathers' bus had been in the window of the travel agency for weeks, along with that stupid camel and the heap of sand. And because Karin was so keen to go to the Adriatic one day. Maybe they would be able to afford it next year, or the year after.

The roof of the barn was sound, but the sun shone in thin strips through cracks in the walls. It all looked quite unremarkable: no rubbish, no fag ends, no beer bottles, which implied it wasn't a teenagers' hangout. Even they had other options these days.

But this barn could belong to him; not properly, but on paper, for a few weeks at least. He wasn't interested in the plot of land, just the lovely old barn. He suddenly had the urge to lie down on the ground, stretch out his arms and whistle. Lying there, he saw that the roof was full of birds' nests. Directly above him, in the middle of the room, dust was dancing in a pillar of light.

'What are you doing here?' someone asked sharply. She appeared in the doorway, so that to him she was just a black silhouette. She stood there as if she had a baby on her arm. This confused him for a moment, catapulting him back to the time of his greatest despair. She had still said hello to him, back then, soon afterwards, when she was pushing a pram again. But her eyes no longer saw him; it was as if her pupils were stuck on.

'Leo, it's me,' he said, once he had cleared his throat. He scrambled to his feet.

'You,' she said, the hostility gone from her voice.

Silence. They both hesitated.

'What are you doing here?' she asked again.

'I saw it needed mowing,' he said. 'I wanted to take a closer look.'

'Mowing,' she repeated, as if this were hard to understand. But she stepped a little closer.

'What have you got there?' he asked.

She laughed. 'Allow me to introduce Hilde! A scrawny little thing, just like you, back then.'

In her arms she was holding an ugly little dog, the kind that, in his house, they would have drowned on the spot. His mother had taught him this from a young age: *For God's sake, don't be sentimental.* Flies, mosquitoes, unsightly cats, mangy puppies, a fat, well-fed hen or pig — they were killed, in various ways and for various reasons, because they were useful, or because they were no use at all.

Young Graun meant to say: I could mow it for you, but instead he said, 'I could kill it for you.'

'What?' she asked. 'Are you insane?'

'Sorry,' he said, '— sorry, that wasn't what I meant to say, what I meant was ...'

She backed out of the barn into the sunlight. 'Come out here,' she ordered. 'I want to look at you!'

He stood in front of her like a poor sinner who didn't dare raise his eyes. 'I'm sorry,' he said, 'I really didn't ...' He gestured with his chin towards the bundle of dog in her arms. 'It's just, that thing, it looks as if ...'

She looked at him and shook her head. 'You're all such simpletons,' she said.

'But Leo,' he began again, 'the meadow, why don't you let me mow it, I could do that for you, and you can sell it for a good price ...'

'Sell it for a good price?' she repeated. 'They refuse to give us planning permission, so it's not worth anything. You can guarantee Ferbenz is behind their withholding it all these years. It'd be a nice bit of land, wouldn't it?'

'For a hotel?' he asked, boldly. He didn't dare look her in the eye; instead, he looked at her neck, where the delicate scar was visible. Twenty-five years ago it had been fresh, and red; he had never touched it. He could only do what she permitted. She showed him the way. He wasn't allowed to choose his own.

She always used to wear a scarf, but she'd stopped doing that a long time ago. You could hardly see the scar now. Back then, though, in the barn, the scarf had often slipped, or come off altogether, and he had seen the scar. And that was the only reason the black velvet choker caught his eye, at the posh shop in town where he was delivering wine for a company anniversary; the mannequin in the window was wearing it exactly where Leo had her scar. He had noticed that there were gems, little stones, stitched onto the velvet band; that was what was pretty about it. But the fact that it was expensive, precious — he hadn't realised this when, at an opportune moment, he slipped it into his pocket. That it had sapphires and pearls on it and God knows what else. Or that the moment was far less opportune than he had thought. He was just a twerp; no, he was more than that, he was a full-blown idiot.

When he looked up, he noticed that she was inspecting him from top to toe. His hair had been falling out for a while now. He supposed she could see that. There wasn't much left on the back of his head. There wasn't much left anywhere, compared with before ... Even so, she shouldn't look at him so disdainfully. He felt hot, and his edges began to burn. The scar was like a mark indicating where you should strangle her. A line to aim for, like the black circles on the torsos of the cardboard cut-outs at the shooting club. Just a lot less noticeable. If you want to strangle her, this is where to do it, the pert little scar seemed to say.

The crippled dog whined. Leo gazed at it tenderly and rocked it like a baby. 'Didn't know Grauns were sentimental,' she said. 'Now get off my land!'

7.

JUST A FEW DAYS later, the Ehrenfeld barn went up in flames, and Berneck, whose heavy, red-necked form was the embodiment of the insurance company's regional office, waited, without interest, for the assessors' report. Then, one morning, Lowetz and the guest from the Hotel Tüffer encountered one another at the grocer's.

As previously mentioned, there had been supermarkets in Darkenbloom for years. They were not yet the brightly lit, air-conditioned, UFO-style hangars of later on, but even then — smaller, greyer, more cramped — they sat amid perfectly levelled fields of asphalt where people could park their snazzy cars for all to admire. This was where the first generations of Darkenbloomers to move into physically undemanding white-collar jobs treated themselves to modest consumerist delights.

But if anyone was short of a few onions or drawing pins, or suddenly found themselves in need of a mousetrap, washing line, crossword puzzle, stamps, or a bar of soap, they bought these small items from the grocer, Antal Grün. For a while, after the war, the shop had been in another house just a few metres away. But for almost twenty-five years now it had been back in its original spot, Tempelgasse 4, and with it Antal Grün, and for a long time his mother, Gisella, too. Before that, her parents, Josef and Mathilde Wohlmut. Before that, Josef's parents. And so on and so forth, probably all the way back to the late seventeenth century, when Emperor Leopold, egged on by his wife, threw the Jews out of Vienna. Margarita Teresa of Spain, very Catholic, was mourning the loss of her first-born, and her pain was so searing that only a tangible scapegoat promised relief, a reason for this senselessness: someone who could first be blamed, then got rid of. A response that restored the authority of action, after the helpless kneeling and screaming at the little child's bedside. If the Jews were gone, the children that came afterwards would stay alive. The way they went about it in those days was relatively civilised. The Jews were given an eight-month grace period. Eight months; that's adequate, that's really not short. Hitler lasted only ten times as long. Vienna's fifty richest families received an invitation from the Elector in almost inconceivably faraway Berlin. The others found shelter much closer to home: in the south-east, under the wings of princes and counts who set greater store by the weight of their treasure chests than by their priests' and spouses' superstition. Here, in the south-east, the Jews were then protected and left alone for more than two hundred and fifty years; their lives were so comfortable and secure that they were especially surprised when this period came to an end. Especially naive and defenceless.

A family business; an institution. Not *Grün's* — no, that would have been overly familiar — but *the grocer's*. Impossible to imagine the town without it. It had joined the A&O Cooperative long ago, but apart from the logo stuck in the shop window and the standardised plastic bags, little had changed. The contract probably meant that Grün had access to a bigger, more modern range of goods. And perhaps the A&O banner also helped non-locals to recognise the little den, packed to the rafters, for what it was.

When Lowetz opened the door, Grün looked up at him from the half-light at the back of the shop as if Lowetz were the Saviour himself. He scurried out from behind his counter — thinking about it later, Lowetz had the impression that he had been backed right up against the shelves, retreating from the stranger speaking to him — came over, and shook his hand at length. Lowetz didn't have time to be startled; Grün was already ambushing him with a torrent of words about the house, the garden, his poor, dear, wonderful mama whom they all missed so much. Lowetz felt as if he were having to ward off a hail of soft, sweet projectiles. But he was fond of Grün; he used to visit his store as a child to pick up shopping for his mother, often putting it on account, and Grün would slip him lollipops. Then, as a teenager, he would help him with the inventory, because sometimes the grocer got confused and had to stop counting. In moments like these he couldn't write, could hardly breathe, and would crumple up the form; Lowetz remembered one occasion when his mother had carefully eased the clipboard with the lists out of Grün's hands. He always recovered quickly from these attacks; he just needed to sit down and drink a glass of water, and someone else to take over the counting and the writing things down. Now, though, good old Grün seemed to have gone a bit weird. He was chattering at Lowetz as if someone were paying him to do it. The man in the background gradually edged closer, as if he were part of the conversation. He was smiling, seemed friendly and engaging, and was clearly waiting for a pause in order to say something.

The stranger took another step forward. Now he was standing right beside them; they had become a group of three. Antal Grün broke off, almost in mid-sentence, gestured towards the stranger, and mumbled something about a historian from the region — or in the region? — but he really couldn't be of any help, unfortunately, please believe him, he hadn't even been here at the time in question.

The man, whose eyes were dark and serious, though the rest of his face did not stop smiling, shook Lowetz's hand and introduced himself. As so often in moments like this, Lowetz didn't quite catch his name but was too slow, too shy, or just insufficiently interested to ask him to repeat it.

'What is it you're looking for?' Lowetz asked.

'The graves,' the man replied, with his winning smile.

'The graves,' repeated Lowetz, not understanding, not even shocked; he must instinctively have thought of mummies or Celts or the early Stone Age, because weren't people always finding small stone axes, flints, metal coins and broken pottery, quite near here, as well? But Antal Grün shook his head, back and forth, his eyes closed in disapproval, or despair, or pain; shook his head, back and forth, forth and back.

No, Lowetz had never heard of them, although he had grown up here. 'I mean, come on,' said Lowetz, with a little snort, 'I was born in fifty-four. Obviously I know a lot of stuff went on here during the war. Same as everywhere along the border, right?'

'Yes, unfortunately,' the stranger confirmed, 'the same as everywhere. But in Tellian and Kirschenstein, and over in Mandl and Löwingen, we found them long ago.'

They all stood and stared at the floor. Grün wiped his palms on the front of his overall, as if to brush himself down. Lowetz felt he ought to ask a question, but he couldn't think what. 'Not a nice job,' he said, after some consideration.

'It is, actually,' the stranger replied. 'Once they're found, they can be given a proper burial and can rest in peace.'

'Dead's dead, though, isn't it,' said Lowetz.

Grün said, 'Come now, lad.'

'Sorry,' said Lowetz.

After a long pause, the historian said, 'Listen, Tolli, I'll come back another day. When you've got more time. Right now, I'd just like to buy a few postcards ...'

He turned to the new rotating display stand. The lower sections were full of newspapers, magazines, and wrapping paper; higher up were little wire baskets for envelopes, greetings cards, postcards. He spun it around a few times, as if admiring its well-oiled rotation, before finally stopping it at the postcards of the castle. He took one out, held it up, and asked, 'Who does these, by the way? Who gets these cards printed? They didn't use to have them, did they?'

Grün wiped his palms on the front of his overall. 'They came with the others,' he said, 'the new ones of the plague column and the aerial view. The aerial view is very popular, too; you should definitely take an aerial view.'

Lowetz picked up one of the postcards of the plague column. The monument had been photographed in portrait format against a blue sky, and the focus seemed excessively sharp; every detail was clearly visible, including the fact that the noses of both saints had crumbled away.

'When I was a child, I asked my mother if that was old Frau Graun,' said Lowetz, pointing to the ghastly beggar holding out her cup. At this, both Grün and the stranger burst out laughing, quite amicably.

Lowetz studied the card. He hadn't looked at the plague column properly in years. The figure's face was contorted, her hand clutched the cup, and the rags she wore were almost slipping off her breasts. Fortunately, both breasts and rags were made of sandstone. It seemed to Lowetz that it wasn't appropriate to portray a person like this, even if there had been no real model for the figure, or only one who had been dead and forgotten these past two hundred years. Because something about the beggar woman seemed so real that you felt her living prototype might walk through the door at any moment, weeping and wailing. Was it simply the expressiveness of the scene, the aspect of frozen despair?

Old Frau Graun, though, isn't made of stone, thought Lowetz, which is why she has to drink to such miserable excess.

It seemed the visitor was a mind reader. 'I wonder if it was just her husband's death,' he said, 'or whether there's another reason?'

'I don't know what that might be,' said Lowetz, shrugging. 'I'd have thought it was enough for a young woman to suddenly be left on her own with a child and a farm to look after.'

'From that point of view,' the other man continued, 'she did a fantastic job: raised the child, scraped a living for herself and the farm until the son was able to take over. And then she threw in the towel ... Is that how it was?'

'You could say that,' said Lowetz, 'except she always drank. But you're right, of course. She managed, though you do wonder how.'

Lowetz put the card back in its little basket. The stranger took the whole batch of castle postcards and placed them beside the till. Antal Grün counted off the cards and put them in a little paper bag. 'Stamps with those?' he asked.

'Just four for now,' said the man. 'But, Tolli, one more question: tell me, when did you get the shop back?'

'After Horka left,' Antal Grün said, reluctantly. 'He just disappeared one day, and his wife sold it to me there and then. She seemed to know he wasn't coming back.'

'And the wife?' asked the visitor.

'Went to live with her family in Styria,' said Antal Grün. 'There's none of them here any more.'

'When was that?' asked Lowetz, who barely understood what this was about, though the name Horka stirred a memory of something he had forgotten.

'Sixty-five,' said Grün, 'the year the Count sealed the crypt. You were a young lad then, you helped me with the move. Don't you remember?'

'No idea,' said Lowetz, shaking his head.

After the stranger left, a small wave of customers swept in and out of the shop. Frau Koreny needed cooking string, pork belly, and dog food; some young strangers, presumably from the cemetery, bought sliced-sausage rolls and drinks; finally, Zenzi from the Hotel Tüffer picked up a big box of pre-ordered goods that she took away on the chassis of an old pram. When things had quietened down again, Lowetz and Grün sat on the stone steps outside the entrance, smoking cigarettes.

'You didn't like that guy earlier,' commented Lowetz.

Antal Grün played dumb. 'Who?'

'You know — the one who bought all the postcards of the castle,' said Lowetz.

'No, no, not at all,' Antal Grün protested, 'I just really can't be of any help to him, I wasn't even ... I simply know nothing about it.'

'Then he'll just have to ask someone else,' said Lowetz.

'Quite,' said Antal Grün, 'but I suppose he's already tried that.'

'Horka, though,' said Lowetz, a few minutes later, 'I'd forgotten about him until today. They used to threaten us with him back then, when we were young.'

'I can imagine,' said Antal Grün.

'Horka was the bogeyman of Darkenbloom,' said Lowetz, and laughed. 'And you bought this house off that horrible creep? I don't remember your old place at all.'

'Ah, come now,' said Antal Grün. 'I was right next door to you, where Fritz has his carpentry workshop these days. You were always running back and forth when you were little, until one day Eszter told you you should only go through the garden.'

'So the doorbell doesn't ring all day,' said Lowetz, the sentence floating up from the same depths where he had just come across the threatening but as yet still faceless Horka.

'So the doorbell doesn't ring all day,' Antal Grün confirmed.

'But you don't have a bell at all any more,' said Lowetz.

'It stopped working. I'm mostly at the front of the shop, anyway. And if not, people just call me.'

'I'll take a look at it,' said Lowetz, getting to his feet.

'Leave it,' Antal Grün demurred. 'I don't need it.' But Lowetz had already gone into the shop. He brought out the ladder, propped it in front of the door, and peered inside the bell. He held up his lighter for a closer look. 'There's just something stuck in there,' he called down. 'Quick, pass me a knife or a screwdriver.'

Carefully, Lowetz eased from the doorbell a small, greyish-white lump, which at first he thought was a big piece of dried chewing gum. But the lump had a hard centre, and afterwards, sitting on the steps and smoking another cigarette, he scratched at it with his thumbnail. Inside was a little porous pebble, a tiny, asymmetrical, slightly tapered cone with a small, round head, almost like a Ludo playing piece.

He wanted to show it to Grün, but he was busy replacing the roll of paper in the till, though Lowetz noticed that the old one wasn't even empty. To punish him, he closed the door and immediately yanked it open again. There was a piercing jangle, and Grün flinched.

'You did it yourself,' Lowetz teased, holding the little stone out towards him. 'There's no way this got up there on its own. Be honest, Uncle Grün: you wanted to silence the bell, didn't you?'

'No, no, I didn't,' he answered, focusing intently on threading the freshly cut roll of paper into the machine. 'I told you, one day it just stopped working.'

Lowetz rolled the little stone around in his palm. 'It almost looks like a piece of bone,' he said. 'Why would someone have glued this in your doorbell?'

Antal Grün pressed a button, the till whirred, and the roll of paper began to turn, but the front piece didn't go through the slit; it backed up, crinkled, balled up, pressing itself desperately, fearfully into the machine before spewing out of the top in a paper fountain.

'Nononono,' Antal moaned, 'now look what you've done ...'

'Me?' asked Lowetz. 'What have I got to do with it?'

But Antal Grün was so bewildered, staring helplessly at his

rattling till as it gobbled the roll of paper, that Lowetz had to press the button and switch off the machine. He grabbed a pair of scissors, pulled out the length of crumpled paper and cut it off. He cut off two more corners at a steep angle to the outer edges, so that the end of the roll of paper looked like an arrow or a sharp tongue. People said they did this with the loo roll on Malnitz's organic farm, but Lowetz couldn't remember who had told him that — they even fold the toilet paper up there, but then their guests probably shit primroses and lilies of the valley! He pressed the button again, the apparatus whirred into life, he fed the paper arrow into the slit, and the arrow slipped in and through, as imperturbable as a trained lion leaping through a burning tyre. Lowetz pressed down the cover of the till and cut off the superfluous tip, grinning. Antal Grün stroked his chest and belly with outstretched fingers. 'See, Uncle Grün,' said Lowetz, 'sometimes it's just a question of technique.'

8.

THE QUESTION OF WHETHER there is really such a thing as evil, in a pure, self-sustaining form, is antiquated, quasi-religious, and serves no useful purpose. Everything can be explained: by childhood, poverty, and, in particular, by the violence a person has suffered, which really does, as the Bible says, keep on begetting itself. In any event, we must accept that, in some rare cases, inauspicious circumstances and distinctly bad inclinations coincide to create a person who is like a loaded gun. Where later, however closely you look, it is impossible to identify any point when their life could have taken a different direction — no moment's pause, no fork in the road — that would have led, if not to virtue, then at least to less harmful domains.

Just such a one was Horka, given name Georg, known locally as 'Schorsch', born at the end of the first decade of the century in a hut on the outskirts of Zwick. Beaten by the drunkard who undoubtedly begat him; beaten, kicked, strangled, and worse by his brothers, who scrabbled on top of one other in their smallholder's cottage, vying for oxygen, attention, food. Inconceivable sanitary conditions. Inconceivable social, psychological, sexual conditions. No daughters, or else the daughters mercifully all died young, because this settlement had more than its share of dead children, as well. Horka was the youngest. After he was born, his mother gave up, though her giving up dragged on for a few more years. Somehow, though, the youngest Horka got by, and this was what he was better at than so many others: getting by, against all odds.

Even the Horka children saw the inside of a school for a few years. There was a strong tradition of schooling under the monarchy, from Maria Theresia onwards, and the Republic was mindful of it, too. They might be raping each other or beating each other half to death at home, but children went to school. They at least learned the basics of reading and writing. Lessons, incidentally, were in Over-Thereish, because for Horka's first decade they still belonged to Over There.

On the big holy days, food was distributed to the poor — a hungry child like Horka had grasped this by the age of six. Also that on the morning of 24 December you could get warm clothes from the factory owner, Thea Rosmarin, at her garden gate, and sometimes even boots. If you were especially deserving of support. Which Horka knew how to demonstrate almost every year, as soon as he had grasped the requirements.

The youngest Horka child was far from stupid. In fact, he was the smartest of the brothers — apart from one, the eldest, but there is no way of comparing the two. This brother left not just the cottage, not just the region, but the country and continent as soon as he could, and he also changed his name. While unlikely, it is conceivable that one of the latter-day descendants of this emigré brother — a chubby-cheeked girl from Litchfield, Ohio, or a white-blond boy from Irving, Arizona — has studied history there, on the other side of the world, has read about the case of Darkenbloom, and, for one privileged moment, trembled with moral disgust.

Horka's intelligence was of a particular kind. Like a sturdy, tailor-made coat, it held his other qualities together: his physical strength and agility, the desire to torment and humiliate, and the violent temper that could send him into murderous frenzies. However,

Horka was also, surprisingly, capable of deferred action. This was the function of his intelligence, which assumed command if he was liable to compromise his own advancement. He had controlled this ability since adolescence. He controlled himself. Yet his intelligence went no further than this: the requirement to deploy the Horka fighting machine judiciously. Specifically, if his intelligence had been that little, but decisive, bit greater, it might, for example, have suggested to him that there was something more to life than simply battling through it in the most literal and physical sense.

On his first day at school, Horka was seated next to Alois Ferbenz. He was instantly provoked by the other boy's clean shirt and meticulous side parting. At the first opportunity, during break, which the children spent on a patch of rough grass beside the school, he leapt on him from behind. He clung to the boy's neck, and was already baring his little brown teeth with the intention of biting off an earlobe, at the very least, when he was ripped away, as if by magical forces, and flung to the ground. It was like at home, where his big brothers, out of boredom, would sometimes throw him to and fro between them like a ball, a ball you didn't necessarily have to catch. Horka lay on the ground; several boys sat on him, and one began to strangle him, but almost incidentally, with his eyes still fixed on their leader. Alois Ferbenz straightened his shirt, looking smug. As Horka's face turned from dark red to purple, Ferbenz gave the order and gestured to them to let him go. For the rest of the school day, Ferbenz's loyal followers stood around him, glancing suspiciously at Horka. Horka kept his distance, plotting his revenge. If he could persuade some of his brothers, it was sure to succeed. He would kill Ferbenz. Not right now, but one day. He would wait.

But after school, Ferbenz, again with little more than a wave of his hand, indicated that from now on it was Horka who was allowed to carry his bag home for him. Another vassal reluctantly surrendered the polished leather satchel. Ferbenz was the shoemaker's son, and as he was from Darkenbloom itself, not the settlement where the riffraff lived, he arrived at the school with his own power base. This was his singular talent. It would stay that way all his life: he always had people around him who would willingly subordinate themselves. Right from the start, Ferbenz was a little prince, and Horka his loyal footsoldier. Horka adapted himself because it pleased him to belong. Ferbenz was clever enough to favour him, ever so slightly. That way Horka could convince himself that it was his own choice to put his menacing strength at another's disposal — only one person, the best.

And Ferbenz protected him for decades. He knew Horka's inclinations, and knew that in giving him certain dirty jobs you were practically doing him a favour. Ferbenz made sure that he himself was very far away on such occasions. Just for safety's sake, because of what people might think, because of the inevitable gossip. He knew, though, that Horka would never betray him. The urge to betray was an impulse for which Horka was, in a way, too unsophisticated. Beatings, torture, murder, lies, deception — all this he was happy to turn his hand to, any time. But no betrayal, and no scheming. Horka knew who was boss. As far as his emotions were concerned, he was not crooked, but entirely straightforward. The crookedness he left to Ferbenz, who, thanks to Horka, never had to get his hands dirty. So each hand washed the other — the crooked and the bloody hand washed each other with artless, Teutonic innocence.

Because, initially, the times were very obliging to people like Horka and Ferbenz, they were lifted up, as if by the water in this image by Stefan Zweig: *Whenever time suddenly rushes forwards, rushes into things, the characters who know how to throw themselves into the wave without a moment's hesitation are the ones who gain the advantage.*

Too young for the First World War, they were ripe and ready for everything that followed. The rivalry with the white flags, for example: that was the first occasion on which Horka showed his talent for organisation. And that, too — organising — requires at least a modicum of intelligence. In those decisive days, he was everywhere at once, pitching in all over the place, and it was probably only thanks to his tireless efforts that Darkenbloom was able to raise the white flags a few hours before Kirschenstein, and days before Tellian, before Löwingen, before almost everyone.

Not long after this glorious day, but before the start of the war, Horka killed a man for the first time. Contrary to what was claimed so firmly afterwards, the victim was not a gypsy (no one would have batted an eyelid at that), but an itinerant labourer called Miklos Jobbagy. He travelled from village to village on his bicycle, offering his services for mucking out stables, haymaking, harvesting, or when a fence or a barn needed building. Unfortunately, he couldn't hear very well, and may not have been the brightest of men, either; both were probably his undoing.

Horka wanted to get his new house painted. Anyone who suddenly acquires a house without paying for it wants to make changes straight away, to make it his own. We've heard the stories: the previous owner's saucepans still warm on the stove. But who knows — perhaps Horka's new house really hadn't been painted for ages. At any rate, he stopped Miklos on the street and informed him that he had work for him. This wasn't outside the new house in Darkenbloom, Tempelgasse 4, where Miklos might have understood better what was wanted of him, but on the outskirts of Zwick, where Horka had apparently been doing something near his parents' house, if that was how one could refer to the lopsided cottage. In any case, doddery old Miklos Jobbagy misheard the name, or else he still thought of Horka as someone from the settlement: half wrong, half right.

'What's yer name again — Horváth?' he asked, putting his hand behind his enormous ear, from which a thick tuft of hair sprouted like grey wire. 'Me, whitewash a gypsy's house? I dunno about that.'

Horka punched him, full force, on the temple. How dare he call him Horváth! Death was sudden. Horka left everything just as it was. He spat, turned his back, and went on his way. He still needed a painter and decorator, after all; if they were so difficult to find these days, he'd better start looking right away.

After a while, the police showed up, with Dr Bernstein, by which time the bicycle had already made off of its own accord. The dead labourer was lying all alone in the dirt. Because Dr Bernstein maintained his professional ethics, despite the difficult environment, and because he still had such authority that no one interfered with his reports, he did mention on the death certificate the cranial fracture he had identified with his fingers. It wasn't that nobody cared, not yet; they did carry out an investigation. There was even an interrogation. However, there was also a call from someone close to Ferbenz, who was already a long way away by then, at the pinnacle of his career. Ferbenz, now a doctor of law, a jurist, of all things, and, more importantly, a Deputy Gauleiter, got someone to call the Darkenbloom police station and have Horka brought to the telephone; only then did he speak to him himself. Horka listened for a while, said only, 'Understood,' and hung up. The final report stated that Horka had acted in self-defence against an aggressive gypsy who had apparently illegally evaded resettlement.

The mortal remains of Miklos Jobbagy, whose relatives, if there were any, could not be located, were buried in the Catholic cemetery — not in the knacker's yard with the heathens, the unbaptised, and suicides. In retrospect, it almost looks as if someone had a bad conscience. Who that someone might have been, nobody knows. And perhaps, after all, it was just an error, a consequence of the turbulent times, in which it occasionally even happened that something, some tiny detail, actually worked out for the better.

9.

HORKA'S SINISTER REPUTATION, WHICH he wore in later years like an aura and protective shield, was largely due to his part in defending Darkenbloom in the last days of the war. In the preceding months, he had commanded a forced labour camp. For seven years, Darkenbloom had been *Jew-free*, but then, when everything really was falling apart, they sent wagonloads of half-starved, ragged creatures over from Budapest. Along with the *foreign workers*, for whom conditions were slightly better, and anything in the region that could still stand, walk, and hold a shovel — this was mostly local women and older children — they were assigned to build the so-called South-East Wall. The Wall was one of the last grand ideas to emerge from the Führerbunker in Berlin. In order to repel the Red Army, the plan was to construct a defence system unlike any the world had ever seen. The Great Wall of China, the Roman *limes*, closely followed by the South-East Wall — something like that. Their own armies were still on the other side of it, but were they to be beaten back — and they would be, anyone who could read a map and was following the Wehrmacht reports knew this — they would find, upon their retreat, a splendid line of defence, with spherical bunkers and gun emplacements, into which they could slip like a hand into a glove pre-warmed, laid out and ready. From here they would continue to defend the Thousand-Year Reich. The Führer had already thought of everything. That was why thirty thousand, forty thousand people were digging and shovelling from the White Carpathians to the Drava; it was to be a monumental construction, insurmountable, invincible. That, at least, was what the propaganda, always particularly shrill when least corresponding to the facts, was shrieking. Yes, new records were set by the number of crimes committed along this line, the number of senseless, brutal deaths died in its name. But the sheer effectiveness of the structure ...? This is what it looked like just outside Darkenbloom: a first Soviet tank drove carefully into the ditch, a second drove on top of it, thick beams were laid atop the two tanks, and behold: a makeshift bridge for the Soviets. Elsewhere, apparently, the Wall was more effective, but that was no use to the people of Darkenbloom.

So there they were, the Soviets, and the *Volkssturm* man who greeted them with a rocket-propelled grenade from behind the war memorial was as pleased as Punch when he saw that he had finished off their first T-34. Perhaps he was already picturing himself with a medal on his chest, or perhaps the adrenaline was pumping too hard for such sweet dreams — *if you weren't there, you can't imagine ...* In any case, the joy and pride lasted two minutes at most, until the second Russian tank wiped him out, along with the war memorial and part of the house on the corner of Karnergasse.

Horka and Old Graun spent the forty-eight hours after the Soviets captured Darkenbloom — the first time they captured it — in the attic of the Stipsits house. This attic had a distinctive feature: on the narrow side was a false wall that separated a strip just over a metre wide from the rest of the room. This wall, covered in cracked and yellowing plaster, looked just like the others. In front of it, stretching almost halfway across, was a massive old wooden wardrobe, not an attractive piece with carved wood and decorative rustic paintings, just a heavy, worm-eaten, three-door cabinet. This, though, was the entrance. The left-hand section had five shelves, starting halfway up, with the back of the wardrobe, painted blue, clearly visible behind them. Underneath them, though, it was missing. Anyone who climbed in and ducked under the lowest shelf practically fell into the hidden room. The arrangement was a very old one, and no one outside the Stipsits house knew about it. A Stipsits ancestor had either hoarded treasure in this hiding place or indulged in other covert activities; who knows what they might have been.

Old Graun had discovered it as a schoolboy, when it was empty of all but dust and mouse droppings. For a while, there had been a substitute teacher at the Darkenbloom school called Jenő Goldman. Goldman was young, liked children, and had modern ideas, one of which was occasionally to take the children out of the school and let them draw in the open air. He did this once or twice, after which it was made clear to him that he should not do it again. There were still people in Darkenbloom back then who didn't see why their children should have to go to school instead of helping on the farm, especially if they were just being taken on walks around town. In one of those two, at most three, outdoor classes, Jenő Goldman told the class to sit on or near the steps of the plague column, choose a section of the main square, and draw it. Lots of children chose the castle, with its imposing tower, but the schoolboy Graun, who could draw particularly well, picked the end of Reitschulgasse, the street facing him, the row diagonally opposite the Hotel Tüffer. The first building was the school, the second the Stipsits house, the third an office building with thick walls that belonged to the Rosmarin industrialist family. The Rosmarin villa itself, Reitschulgasse 8, with the wrought-iron railing around the garden and two stone pillars flanking its wrought-iron gate, couldn't be seen properly from the plague column, which was why Graun decided just to indicate the iron railing at the edge of his drawing. But he put a lot of effort into the windows, doors, and roof tiles of the other three houses, rubbing out, cross-hatching, smudging the cross-hatching with a moistened index finger, to depict as many different surfaces as possible. Jenő Goldman praised him. 'You've got a very good eye', he said, but Graun just grimaced slightly. He knew people thought this teacher was a fool, so he wasn't going to be friendly with him. Although he liked the drawing lessons. He didn't say this, either. You did as you were told and kept your head down; that was how it was back then. And that was how it was later, as well. But in that hour at the foot of the plague column the observant schoolboy Graun recorded the proportions of the houses he was drawing very precisely. And when, just a few days later, he happened to be delivering something to the Stipsits house, and Frau Stipsits asked him to carry a heavy basket up to the attic for her, he noticed almost immediately that the room was missing a skylight that was visible from outside.

He couldn't get this puzzle out of his head. The evening of the summer solstice, when all Darkenbloom was out and about, seemed like a good opportunity to investigate further. Discreetly, he crept away from the solstice fires, climbed the stairs to the Stipsits's attic, and looked around. He opened the dormer window on the far left, just a crack, afraid that someone might notice him from outside. A sideways glance was enough to ascertain that the office building started right alongside. So it had to be the other narrow end. There were all sorts of things piled up against it, including the enormous wardrobe. Graun opened the left-hand door. He was no taller than one metre fifty at the time, meaning he only needed to bend down slightly to see under the lowest shelf. In any case, he smelled, or sensed, that he had found what he was looking for. In he climbed, and discovered the secret cubbyhole behind it. He took a swift look around — just mouse droppings and dust — and was about to slip quickly away to go and think how he might put this new knowledge to use. But there, standing outside the wardrobe, grinning, was Horka, who had been tailing him again. And so both of them knew it was there — and more than twenty-five years later, in that life-or-death moment, both of them remembered.

To begin with, it felt like a trap, the two men holed up in the little room, with the invaders gathering outside the windows. No matter when they came out, the assumption that they were not innocent civilians would be as logical as the only possible consequence: they would be shot dead on the spot. Both had lost visual and audio contact with the other defenders, and had suddenly heard the enemy tanks instead. In that moment, they were as shocked as everyone else, as they had firmly believed in the protective effectiveness of the Wall; they had reckoned with the possible arrival of soldiers, but not this line of tanks that were making the earth quake. At the very last minute, they had each, independent of the other, managed to get into the Stipsits house. Someone — Graun? — had at least thrown some provisions through the opening beforehand, and they had enough ammunition, as well as a Panzerfaust 30 anti-tank grenade launcher apiece. So now here they were. The space was big enough for them to sit facing each other with their legs outstretched, or both under the window, slightly staggered, with their knees bent. They spent forty-eight hours like this, talking, not talking, smoking, listening. The hidden chamber became the ideal strategic post. In the early morning of Good Friday, they heard cannon fire again. 'They're coming to liberate us,' hissed Horka, who had been scratching the plaster off the wall on the street side with his knife all this time, in the hope of loosening a tile and pulling it inside. They didn't dare look out of the window during the day, and at night there hadn't been much to see, just the occasional torch and the glow of poorly shielded cigarettes, at which they would dearly have loved to shoot.

Darkenbloom was a ghost town, although not all the inhabitants had fled. A few had stayed, because they feared for their house and property, or because they had calculated that they had an even smaller chance of surviving indefinitely in the forest in winter. The old, the sick, women, and children hid in wardrobes and coal cellars, in cattle sheds and haylofts, waiting for an end that none of them could really envisage. Would Austria become communist? Time and events are fluid as you swim through them, but people seldom remember this years or decades later, when they say things like *the end of the war*. They think of it then as a clear marker in the flow, something fixed and easily recognisable, solid, like a breakwater.

Darkenbloom is the best example of this. It seemed that everything was already over; the Russians had overrun the South-East Wall more or less in their sleep, and now they and their tanks were standing in the main square and in the surrounding roads and side streets. They had set up their main observation post at the top of the castle tower, as anyone would have done. For forty-eight hours, the scales hung in the balance. There were no white flags; not this time, not in Darkenbloom. Darkenbloom did not surrender, as many other places did; it was deserted, and hostile. The Russians had no contact with any of the locals; it was as if the ground had swallowed them up. Anything that moved was shot at. The names of the victims are inscribed in the town chronicle: Theresia Wallnöfer, Aloysia Malnitz, Hubert Gstettner, Eduard Balaskó, and a child, eight-year-old Edwine Grubar. None of them had been prepared to surrender, to come out with their empty, unarmed hands above their head. There were those who had even been shot dead doing that, surrendering: by the Russians, or by their own people, from behind, in the back. Not here, but elsewhere. All this was well known. At the time, on balance of probability, there wasn't much to choose between dying and surviving, not even for the civilian population. So they preferred to stay in their hiding places and wait. If they were caught, it was because they were scuttling about, from the privy back to the hayrick, or from house to potato cellar. The Russians realised that things were not over yet, and called for reinforcements.

Instead, the Germans returned, in unexpected strength and numbers. The scales had flung up their right arm again; they had an idiosyncratic sense of humour. By this time, Horka had finally loosened a roof tile, and carefully pulled it inside. The noise of battle grew louder. Anti-aircraft guns rattled, firing into the town instead of at planes. The Russian tanks began to withdraw; from the attic, they couldn't see where to. And this was the big moment for Horka and Graun, who unexpectedly found themselves positioned behind the enemy. Horka flung open the window and finished off the last two tanks as they were driving away, with the two grenade launchers, one after another, quick as a flash, before the second tank could even turn round. And that was no mean feat from their position, no mean feat at all. Afterwards, they left their hiding place, running under cover of the walls and alleyways they knew so well, taking shortcuts through gateways, farms, and vegetable patches. They pursued the Russians out of town, street fighting from house to house, yelling and cheering when they finally joined up with the astonishingly large units of the Waffen SS Panzer Division Wiking. This was made up of fanatical Germans, Austrians, Dutch, Flemings, and Balts, yet the two Darkenbloomers must have appeared to them like invincible fighting machines, emerging and attacking the enemy from behind the way they did. That, at any rate, was how the story was subsequently told, because their pursuit of the retreating Russians was often raked up again, especially by Ferbenz on the memorial days, which they commemorated in Café Posauner: the thirteenth of February, the twentieth of April, the first of May, and the ninth of November. And they would slap Young Graun on the back in his father's stead, the Heuraffls, Berneck, Stitched-Up Schurl, and the rest.

'Hell of a pair, Graun and Horka,' said Ferbenz, again, and the older he got, the more his chin trembled. 'German heroes,' said Ferbenz, his red eyelids growing moist. 'They don't make them like that any more. But we'll be back. Maybe not in my lifetime, but just you wait; you'll see, all of you ... we'll be back.'

The Heuraffls, Berneck, and Stitched-Up Schurl all nodded. They knew what he was going to say next.

'Because he will endure for centuries,' said Ferbenz, and his old man's voice rose in pitch until it was almost as high as Rehberg's — 'no, a thousand years, a figure who will be studied by all the best minds one day, including Jews.'

Young Graun sat there, unmoved. He wasn't embarrassed; it wasn't important to him, he was indifferent. It was like the weather, his wife's nagging, and his mother's drunken stupors: it came and went, and you sat there at the end of the working day and drank your schnapps. He didn't reflect on how the heroic expulsion of the Russians was only half the story, only one part that, in view of the outcome, was the least significant, as it had led to a whole week of reconquest, the deaths of twenty Darkenbloomers, mostly women, little Fritz Kalmar dragged out from under his dead grandmother with a piece of shrapnel in his head, more than a hundred dead soldiers and *Volkssturm* militiamen, and an unknown number of dead Red Army soldiers; on top of that, the reduction of two dozen houses to rubble, not to mention the castle, fired on and set alight by its own people because the Russians, perched up in the tower, had to be brought down. And then the castle had burned as the fighting continued; it had burned for days, a torch visible for miles around, because unfortunately they could not extinguish the fire in the midst of the battle.

Graun and Horka, Horka and Graun, two heroes who gave it their all. In this story they were transformed into best friends, simply because that was the picture the wartime anecdote painted, more or less automatically. But the stories don't fit together: stupidity and heroism; surrender or bloody resistance; friendship, enmity, or just the exploitation of a fortuitous advantage in a desperate situation, after holing up in the secret chamber? Young Graun would have been the last to reflect on this. His lack of reflection could almost be considered an achievement. Because it was an accepted fact in Darkenbloom, at least among the older residents, that it was Horka who, almost exactly one year later, shot his fellow combatant Graun in the forest and burned him, along with his dog, until there was almost nothing left. It was an accepted fact, but no one talked about it.

IO.

FLOCKE WAS HOME FOR the summer holidays. For two years now, she had been teaching at a primary school a hundred and fifty kilometres away, and every time her mother asked her if she wouldn't rather apply for a job nearby, she said it did her good to get some distance from Darkenbloom for part of the year. 'It would do you good, as well, incidentally,' she added, and laughed.

Malnitz, her father, loved her best of all the four children, although in many ways she was incomprehensible to him. Flocke had a mind of her own, and it differed fundamentally from both his own pig-headedness and that of his beautiful, headstrong wife, Leonore.

Because he loved her so, things between father and daughter often went awry. He interfered too much in her affairs and, like other old-fashioned fathers, he masked his worry with authoritarian behaviour. Lately he had been wondering, with increasing urgency, whether she was really *all right*, though he would not have wanted to define *all right* more precisely, not even to his best friend, if he'd had one. *All right*, in this instance, meant *straight*. It was not possible to talk to Leonore about this.

'So, has she finally got a boyfriend?' he tried once, casually, Leonore having just put down the phone after a long call with Flocke.

'What do you mean, finally?' Leonore responded, turning her eyes on him like cold spotlights.

'Well, it's about time, isn't it,' he said, in his defence, and immediately realised that this was a mistake.

'Not everyone is as stupid as me these days,' retorted Leonore, and that, of course, had made him angry.

'I'm not talking about getting married and having kids right away,' he roared, 'but surely I can ask whether she has a boyfriend, whether she's ever had a boyfriend, and whether, as her father, I might be permitted to know?!'

He had left the house, slamming the door, because although he was able to ask the right questions when angry, the dramaturgy of his anger meant he couldn't wait around for the answers.

Since Flocke had got home, she had mostly been hanging about the Jewish cemetery. It had been their joint discovery that there was something going on down there. They had breakfasted together as usual, just the two of them; Leonore was constantly preoccupied with the new pug, whose flattened little head harboured a single, stubborn conviction, namely: that, as a dog, it was incumbent upon her to do her business exclusively indoors. She refused to be persuaded otherwise. She went wherever she happened to be standing, or walking: number one and number two. Rugs had already been removed because of this — only temporarily, Leonore protested. She chewed to pieces, or tried to, anything that wasn't snatched from her jaws: shoes, scissors, logs. Koloman, the established pug, trotted after her, sniffing at the destruction, as if he couldn't believe what this new dog had the nerve to do. So far, Leonore had not cared about the objects, only about the two teeth Hilde had already lost.

'If it carries on like this, it'll be toothless before it's a year old,' said Malnitz, but his wife was at her wits' end and was not to be provoked.

One might be forgiven for wondering why she had more patience with this infuriating creature than with all the rest of the world.

'Mum can make a fresh start with the dog,' Flocke informed him, spreading jam on her bread roll. Even as a child she had pronounced her opinions as if they were accepted truths. 'The dog doesn't say stuff like that to her, because it can't. You probably don't realise, but you're always criticising her.'

'How?' he asked, uncomprehending.

'Telling her she's more patient with the dog than she is with you, for example.'

'I didn't say ...' Malnitz began, but Flocke's expression made him change direction mid-sentence. 'Why are you women always so touchy!'

So they had already almost had a row over breakfast. Afterwards, he just asked quietly if she wanted to come with him to the new vineyard. To his surprise, she said yes, and smiled as if nothing had happened — not the rest of breakfast eaten in silence, nor the pointed offer to her distressed mother to take both dogs for a long walk later on, *until Hilde simply has to go outside.*

But they had scarcely been in the car five minutes when she cried, 'Stop, Dad, stop — look, look over there!'

The gates of the Jewish cemetery were gaping open, an almost alarming sight. They were much bigger than one would have thought; before, they had seemed to merge indistinguishably with the wall. But now — now they yawned widely, after decades of sleep, revealing an enormous gap through which the head of a mythical green creature appeared to burst forth, trailing shaggy hair around its nose and mouth. As if the greenery had forced the gate open from the inside, head first. People had forgotten that anything was there. That the wall actually enclosed something. For as long as they could remember, the cemetery had just been an uncanny obstacle, a block you had to walk or drive around. A piece of stolen scenery. Now it stood open, and that made it seem imperious, as if it was about to expand, like a new universe, unfolding for potential accessibility. And of course Malnitz's youngest daughter, whom he found it so hard to see as an adult, was determined to go in. 'Dad, Dad, stop right now, I have to take a look.'

Inside: not construction workers, but a group of baby-faced incompetents in jeans and trainers. Malnitz wanted to laugh out loud as they sat there sweating, perched on beer crates and contriving to look despairing, haughty, and resolute all at once. There were girls among them, too, their trousers already knee-deep in burrs. One had scratches on her face: she must have become closely acquainted with the brambles that bound the thickets together like barbed wire. They did at least have handsaws, garden shears of different sizes, shovels, rakes, an axe, and a dented wheelbarrow. But their only electrical implement was a small hedge-trimmer, which could have been used to trim a box bush into a ball, a spiral, or an upturned flowerpot. Its relationship to this jungle was like that of a spoon to a mine. He could see from his daughter's eyes that he had better not say anything along these lines, so as not to come across as a typical provincial macho, interfering, inhospitable, resentful, the way Berneck or the Heuraffls would have been. So he confined himself to a humorous, 'What're you up to here, then, eh?'

The young strangers didn't answer; they just shrugged their shoulders.

'You speak German, though, don't you?' he asked, suddenly uncertain.

'Almost perfectly,' said a man in a red T-shirt, possibly the leader, with a disdainful look.

'Need anything?' asked Malnitz, in a conciliatory tone. 'I'm guessing a motor-axe wouldn't go amiss?'

He saw the frown disappear from Flocke's forehead. The young people stared at them.

'A chainsaw,' Flocke translated. 'Do you want to borrow our chainsaw?'

And so Malnitz went back to the car and fetched a chainsaw,

lubricating oil, the work gloves with the Kevlar lining, the petrol can, a crate of mineral water, a long-handled pruning saw, a couple of ropes, and whatever else he found that might be useful, then left Flocke with her peers and drove to the new vineyard by himself. But a few days later, when he brought the obligatory case of wine to Zwick and left it on the drive for his family, his sister-in-law, to whom he hadn't spoken in years, briefly opened a window and hissed something at him. He didn't understand what she said. He drove off — and it was only then, in the car, that he realised what the word must have been. He slammed his foot on the brake and did a U-turn in the middle of the road; Young Graun, heading towards him in his van, kept his hand on the horn, trailing the sound behind him like a banner of outrage until he disappeared from view. Malnitz bumped over the kerb, stopped, left the engine running, and loaded the case of wine back into the boot of the car. Behind the windows, now firmly shut, the curtains moved almost invisibly, as if fanned by quiet breathing. *Jew-lover.* There was no need for them to drink wine made by such a person any more, so he took it away again.

In all her twenty-three years, Flocke had never seen a Jewish cemetery. She didn't know what she had expected, but she must have assumed that the Jews' resting places looked similar to theirs, or she wouldn't have been so amazed. The otherness of the place was enhanced by the infinitely slow destructive power of the vegetation — far slower even than lava, but just as relentless. Already it had done its work. Roots eat their way up from below, levering everything aside, no matter how heavy. With their gouging fingers they make the gravestones weep; their invisible tears crack them apart, and the branches and leaves that reach down from above only pretend to bring comfort. All they are doing is concealing the battlefield — they are collaborators. But everything here was different, not only what was smashed and broken: the colours, and the shapes. The gravestones, low and white, or tall, thin, black ones, stood like startled children, frozen in mid-air, as if caught playing Grandmother's Footsteps. They were waiting for the verdict. Who wobbled? You're out ... Most of them were narrower than in the normal cemeteries, and closer together. Lots — the little white ones — were shaped like church windows, with a pointed arch on top. Many had already fallen over and lay helplessly on their back, or front. Further down, along the outer wall, were little palaces of remembrance, kitschy mausoleums with columns and flights of steps, domes and steles; there were pyramids and sarcophagi. But these, too, unmistakably the graves of the rich, were cocooned in metre-high nettles, hazel bushes, field maple, elderflower. In between was the plant they called sticky willy, with its clinging leaves. And brambles, everywhere.

Sleeping Beauty did not in fact sleep behind rose bushes for a hundred years, but behind brambles. Flocke had learned this when she was little, from Frau Lowetz, who lived next door to Fritz. Back then, Flocke had thought she was a witch, because of her hair. Later, though, they became friends, if that's the right word for two people so far apart in age.

A rose bush is nothing, Frau Lowetz had said, compared to a fence of brambles, which are tough as nails. Only brambles could really protect Sleeping Beauty, because no one can get through them. Protect, or lock away? thought Flocke, who suddenly felt that there was violence in the way this place, already half swallowed up by nature, was being ripped open and exposed.

'Why are you actually doing this?' she asked the others.

'Do you want to leave it like this?' asked a girl with a shock of curly black hair. Flocke had noticed her earlier, as she came in through the gate with her father; the girl had picked up her video camera and pointed it at them.

'The new ones'll need to go somewhere, as well,' added the boy in the red T-shirt.

'What do you mean?' asked Flocke.

'The reburials,' he said, in a tone that meant any further questions would imply intolerable provincial stupidity.

The next day, Flocke dropped in on Fritz and asked him if he wanted to come with her to see what was going on in the third cemetery. The *third*, she said, without giving it too much thought. And it was true: there were three cemeteries altogether, one on each road out of town, although this third one had vanished from people's consciousness. Soon everyone was saying it. It was a way of avoiding the other word that no one liked to pronounce, neither Antal Grün nor the once-young louts, now old, who still tormented Rehberg from time to time, poor, cowardly Rehberg with his falsetto voice. The *third cemetery*: a nice, blank name for a *good place*.

Fritz was the right person to ask; he always liked to help. He was much handier with the chainsaw than Flocke. He knew how to apply it, even in the more inaccessible corners, knew which thickets you could get rid of and how to do it, and he felled several young acacias so judiciously that he was able to take the wood away for his own use. His guttural stammer wasn't a problem — the young people from the city acted as if they didn't notice it. *There are plenty more like him in the city* — the comment floated up from somewhere at the back of Flocke's mind, a nasty old Darkenbloom sort of comment.

The standoffish girl with the video camera was particularly nice to Fritz; she filmed his hands, oiling the chain, tightening it, and, during a cigarette break, whittling a little manikin out of a root. It looked grumpy, indignant, its rooty hair standing on end. Fritz gave it to the camera girl, mumbling, 'Looks like you.'

With Fritz's help, in just a few hours they managed to lay bare the first of the big tombs that stood along the length of the wall. It had stone steps, a pseudo-antique peristyle in front, and a door reinforced with metal strips, which no one tried to open. The Tüffer family tomb: Malwine and Leopold, Hermann and Felix, who must have been their children, and one Salomon Kalischer, whose relationship to the Tüffers was presumably no longer known to any living being. Next to the names was written, in metal letters that had stood the test of time:

Seek to bury your life
in others' hearts together,
even in death, you then
live on in them forever.

And when they had got that far, had taken the first of a thousand steps, cleared the weeds from a first, tiny area, made it accessible and viewable, and been scratched and stung by all sorts of thorns, nettles, and startled insects, the first of the Darkenbloomers came by; they stuck their noses in at the great gate hanging off its hinges, shook their heads, and laughed awkwardly. A mother from the new housing estate barked at her children to come back; she was afraid the gravestones might fall on them. Some people were unfriendly and just wanted to know who had actually given permission for this; others gazed around, wide-eyed, and offered up all sorts of tips on how to tackle the jungle. Zenzi, the buxom waitress from the hotel, brought a tray of plum cake that her boss had sent. Because Flocke was there, she opened up: they'd been talking at the regulars' table, she said, and the boss had intervened, been surprisingly fierce, said they should all shut up, the lot of 'em, it's nice that the young people are doing something, a bit of weeding, after all these years, not like you lot, all you've ever done is drink and fight! Frau Reschen had gone quite red in the face during her outburst, and the Posauner landlady, chain-smoking Gitta, who'd run out of cigarettes again, which she usually got from the Tüffer — she'd backed her up and said, yes, right, so just stop it, all of you. She was from Styria, though, so she didn't actually have a clue. She didn't even know where the castle used to be.

'Oh, are the women taking over now?' Berneck had said. 'Look what we've come to!'

It was only after this explanation that Zenzi took a closer look at *the temple*, as she called it. She read the poem, moving her lips silently, sighed that it was beautiful and true, and only noticed the names right at the end. 'Tüffer — has that got something to do with us?' she asked, her mouth hanging open for a moment at the end of the sentence.

'Best ask the boss,' said Flocke cheerily.

And it was in these days that Mayor Koreny, who suffered so badly in the heat, was constantly having to tell anyone who wanted to know — and there were quite a few — no, it isn't costing us anything, it's all been taken care of. It doesn't matter who by, it's not our money. No, and it's nothing to do with the anniversary year, either; yes, of course that's over, we all know that. It's not tax money either, certainly not!

He had to raise his voice once or twice, although he wasn't 100 per cent sure whether or not it was in fact tax money. Weren't all public funds ...?

But he made the claim, anyway, because all the gossip and questions annoyed him. Why on earth should they care! 'What do you care?' he said, in the bar of the Tüffer or at the Posauner. 'Someone's paying, and it isn't you. Why do you all keep fretting about someone else's money?'

People here didn't usually talk back to a mayor for very long. But to him, the insecure substitute, they did. One day, a daring but irrefutable argument materialised in Koreny's mind. It must have been the heat that caused it to materialise, right at the back; all he could see at first was a promising outline. He took another swig of beer, then seized it with determination. Wiping his handkerchief across his sweaty brow, he placed his bill and payment on the counter, leaned forward, raised his eyebrows as high as he could, lowered his voice in a conspiratorial murmur, and tapped the top button of his opposite number's shirt lightly with his forefinger. 'And what if — *if*, I said! — the money came from abroad? There, see — hadn't thought of that, had you?'

And with that he got up and left. Tax money! Perhaps you could grow into the role of mayor, he thought, as he walked to his car; perhaps even he, plump, ginger-haired Herbert Koreny, who had only ended up in this uncomfortable situation because he would have done anything for his good friend Balf. But Balf, unfortunately, was not at all well.

II.

HE WENT TO VISIT Balf regularly. If Mayor Koreny had to spend the night in the capital, he stayed in the Pension Baldrian, which Rehberg had recommended. In its musty rooms, surrounded by velvety green fabric wallpaper patterned with golden vines, most of the other guests he encountered were also from the far south-east. The sounds of the breakfast room, where two bread rolls, two pats of butter, and two little plastic tubs of jam (red and yellow) were laid out for each person, were familiar, other conversations like muffled barking.

The guesthouse stood in the shadow of a giant flak tower. Several of these high-rise bunkers were still standing in the capital, because the thick Nazi concrete was almost indestructible, a building material comparable to Ferbenz's soul. Blowing up the bunkers would have meant reducing whole neighbourhoods to rubble. Strangely, the houses around this bunker were particularly magnificent, the Gründerzeit showing off with its multi-paned transom windows, semi-circular oriels, stucco, decorative friezes, tendrils and flowers, heads of angels and Titans. Houses just like these, whole streets of them, must have been demolished to make way for the colossi, which looked like elephants that had blundered into a toy-sized landscape. The name was all they had in common with the spherical bunkers on the outskirts of

Darkenbloom, where Koreny had played as a boy before the entrances were filled in. Back then, they used to find munitions everywhere, had dug up hand grenades, even, on one occasion, a steel helmet. There had been a fight over that, which the Malnitz brothers had won. In bed that evening, remembering Toni and Mick sauntering off triumphantly with the helmet under their arm, young Koreny had wept with disappointment.

They were all well past that now: being young, playing and digging, scrapping in freshly mown grass. Especially Balf. He was in the big city, in the biggest hospital; the mere thought of the building made Koreny break out in a sweat. It could have housed the whole of Darkenbloom. Its two towers bore a strong resemblance to the flak tower next to Pension Baldrian. If the bunkers were classic grey elephants, the hospital towers were brown giants: bison, or aurochs. Inside, there were three zones, blue, green, and red, almost the way a body's insides are differentiated on medical wall charts: arteries, veins, organs. Koreny still hadn't grasped the relationship between the towers and the coloured zones; he had, however, reached the hypothesis that the interior of one tower was red, the other green, but blue was a colour you might encounter anywhere if you weren't paying attention. His friend Balf lay almost at the top of the red tower. From there, you looked down over the city laid out as if on a plate, the sky stretched delicately over it like a transparent cloche. The view was exciting, not meditative green like the view at home from the lookout tower at the top of the Hazug: the way the houses merged into streets, the streets into individual, wildly uneven districts; the way the cars scurried about like ants and clumped up in traffic jams. Koreny would have liked to spend longer gazing at this animated complexity, but he was here to visit the invalid.

At first, Balf had acted as if he were being forced to lie here for no apparent reason. At first, he had paced about the little room, firing instructions at Koreny, and slapping his palm on the windowpane for emphasis. Later, he could no longer get out of bed, was hooked up to all sorts of tubes, lost his hair, his eyelashes, his eyebrows. But even then he was still himself; he stared at Koreny from the bed, a born commander and leader, ever since his schooldays. He never doubted himself. His favourite word was *strategy*. The strategy must be ... From a strategic point of view ... Or, worse: Bertl, you're thinking completely unstrategically! Koreny wished he would scold him like that again. Without Balf's regular guidance, his own strategy was bound to have collapsed already into the hopelessly unstrategic. He hoped, though, that it wasn't all his fault. Some of Balf's assumptions had proved incorrect: for example, that the farmers would abandon their resistance to the water authority if he, the mayor, just had a private word with each of them individually. He had tried. He had driven from farm to farm. He had let them drag him across meadows and fields, to springs and soggy hollows which they saw as evidence that there was plenty of water down there, all they needed to do was link up the individual sources sensibly and feed them into the Darkenbloom network. In particular, he had let their leader, the farmer Faludi, torment him with national and international statistics on the use of water meters. Wherever these meters had been installed, he said, water usage had dropped dramatically. Water meters, and some new pipes to access our own water sources, and we can remain independent! A self-sufficient commune! Darkenbloom water for Darkenbloom! Anyone who didn't dodge Farmer Faludi in time would be ambushed with this. He had held an information evening in Café Posauner. With a slide projector, and a Green from Lower Austria, supposedly an expert. A Green! Apparently, a surprising number of people had gone along. Just to hear what he had to say, their wives assured Koreny's wife, when they bumped into each other out shopping — well, we want to know all the pros and cons, don't we? Since Farmer Faludi had started his campaign, most of the farmers had turned against the original plan. Because something like the water authority is essentially a social-democratic idea, Balf had explained to Koreny, when he was still able to speak. The farmers, on the other hand, are the stooges of a different political strategy, namely that of the Raiffeisen Agricultural Bank! We must pursue a counter-strategy! And so on.

Laying additional pipes and constructing an elevated tank or suitable storage reservoir would cost money — as would the charges payable to the water authority. A lot of money all at once, or a little money forever, that was the choice that lay before them: a cold shower, or a constant trickle. You could believe those who claimed that, in the long run, the water authority would be much more expensive because they would be at its mercy. Or not. Balf had not believed them. Their claims were strategic, he said. But Koreny had different reasons for stubbornly, desperately backing Balf's decision. It wasn't because preliminary contracts had already been signed, as his opponents on the town council speculated, or because these preliminary contracts were so restrictive and unfavourably worded that it was better not to even think about whether they would ever be able to get out of them again. That was the malicious whisper put about recently by Ferbenz, who still got people's attention if he so much as opened his mouth. And someone was probably already claiming that Balf and Koreny had been bribed by the water authority. This was the most popular accusation, one that could be made against politicians at any time: as soon as citizens were unhappy about something, they started to spread rumours that this or that person must have been bribed.

No; Koreny basically didn't care where the extra water came from, in the hot summers when it was in short supply. Anything that was good for Darkenbloom was good for him, too. However, to his anxious, overburdened ears, the water authority sounded like a gift from Heaven: you joined, and the water flowed. He didn't even want to think about the other option; no, he would tell himself, reining in his thoughts whenever they reached this point, we finalised the contracts long ago, and there's a year and a half until the next election! Committees, test drilling, construction plans, tenders, redesignations, recalcitrant neighbours who want a say in where the new pipes cross their land, and so on. Huge holes, excavated sections, everything topsy-turvy, the whole area a building site, for months, at least. He would have needed to govern with a firm hand, not just administrate. That may have been precisely Balf's motivation: too much trouble, too much work, too many imponderables. Back then, almost a year ago, Balf had imperiously pushed through the town council's decision to join the water authority. He had blindsided his councillors by putting the item on the agenda at the last minute. A strategic master stroke; no one had grumbled, they had already had an unusually dry spring the previous year. After the vote, Mayor Balf invited everyone to join him in the Tüffer bar and bought a few rounds to toast the *historic decision*. Not long afterwards, Dr Sterkowitz, an experienced diagnostician, had found the lumps in his armpits. Balf was even chauffeured to the faraway hospital in the doctor's orange Honda. His case was clearly so serious that only the best clinic was good enough. But if Koreny didn't succeed in upholding and defending Balf's decision, he might as well just go and lie down with him.

Balf was not awake this time, either. The room was in darkness. When Koreny pulled aside the curtain, the sun burst in. You couldn't see much of the city; it was too bright. Exhaust fumes swirled down below, greyish brown, mingling with red brake lights. Higher up, the haze became more golden, sun-coloured, until it merged with the white-blue sky. Koreny stood at the window and stared out, squinting.

'So, Heinz,' he began, 'nothing much is new. I've had to impose water-saving measures again. Severely restrict the watering of private gardens — they just won't be able to have a nice lawn. Same for agriculture, like last year. Some of them are still worked up about the young people at the cemetery, but not as many as before. The other day, I said it was being paid for from abroad; I think that was a good strategy for once, Heinz. They'll all be telling each other that now, so at least I'm shot of one thing. Anyway, it'd be nice if you'd wake up again soon. Because there's something going on, I don't know what exactly. It's just a feeling. But people are talking; they stand around all huddled together on the street. They say Young Graun was up in the Rotenstein meadow with Malnitz the other day. Hard to believe, really, those two chatting away all of a sudden, they've always been at each other's throats, but I don't think anyone's made it up, because it's so unlikely. They were inspecting something up there, apparently. "Are you sure it wasn't Faludi?" I asked, of course, but no, they said it was Graun, no doubt about it. And on top of that — I don't know, it's probably not important, but Malnitz's daughter, the youngest, you know, the mouthy one, she's always asking around these days about some stories from years ago; she wants to open a museum, or a private exhibition, anyway, on that land of her mother's over in Ehrenfeld. Except the barn there has just burned down ... She told our Frau Balaskó that she was looking for Darkenbloom war criminals. Imagine that — war criminals, in our town! The girl's barely twenty. Young people used to be interested in other things, in dancing and flirting ...'

At this, Koreny faltered. Perhaps it wasn't such a good idea to talk about being young — here — about dancing and all the rest of it. Why had he even mentioned the girl? Because he had got annoyed with her the other day for being such a know-it-all. He closed the curtains again, pulled up an armchair beside the bed, and forced himself to look his friend in the face. Unlike before, one eye was now ever so slightly open.

'The old people are a bit worried,' he continued, 'because of all the refugees. The numbers are building up on the other side of the border. They're showing it every day on TV. It makes no difference how often we tell our people that they don't want to come to us, they just want to get out and then travel on to Germany. Genscher is already sending buses. But the old people are scared. The Russians are coming back, they say, there'll be shooting again soon, just you wait and see.'

'Aaaah,' said Balf, with an effort, and the other eye opened a crack as well.

'Heinz,' cried Koreny, 'are you awake?'

'Water,' said Balf.

Koreny looked around. He found a feeding cup, opened it, sniffed it. Cold tea, probably. He held it in front of Balf's face, as if for confirmation. 'Do you want to drink something, Heinz?' he asked.

'Water,' said Balf.

'I'm afraid there's only tea,' said Koreny.

Balf made a movement that might have indicated a shake of the head.

'Should I call the nurse?' asked Koreny.

Balf made the movement again.

Koreny didn't know what to do. He brought the feeding cup to Balf's lips and tipped it carefully for what he hoped would be a pleasant little sip.

'All right?' he asked.

'Water,' said Balf.

'I don't know,' said Koreny uncomfortably, and wondered if he should just get up and leave.

'Heinz, I'll get the nurse,' he said eventually. 'I don't want to do anything I shouldn't.'

When Koreny opened the door, Sterkowitz was standing outside. 'Hello, Herbert,' he said, 'I thought I'd find you here.'

'He's awake,' said Koreny nervously, 'and he wants to drink some water, but I don't know if he's allowed.'

Sterkowitz went over to the bed. 'No, Herbert, he's not awake, and I'd have been very surprised if he were.'

'He just asked me for water, twice,' Koreny objected.

There was a pause. Sterkowitz looked at the backs of Balf's hands, where the tube from the IV drip went in, and straightened the blanket. 'I came to tell you that we have to drive back in a minute. They've dug someone up in the Rotenstein meadow.'

'What?' asked Koreny, putting his hand to his throat. It was so hot, and it was so terribly close in here, in this dark room that was much too high up, much higher than people ought to build, surrounded by reinforced concrete, seventeenth floor, but perhaps it was only up here that you could actually breathe, because from up here you could see very clearly all the filth that swirled around down there. 'What in heaven's name have they dug up — a Jew?'

'Human remains,' said Sterkowitz. 'Which could be anything, of course: Wehrmacht, Russians, Ancient Romans. Nothing recent, from what I can gather. Come on, the mayor needs to be on the spot.'

'Me?' responded Koreny, aghast. 'Me?' He followed the doctor to the door as if in a trance. Just as he was about to close it, Heinz Balf called loudly from inside, 'Water! Hold out!'

'Did you hear?' said Koreny. 'He just spoke again!'

Sterkowitz said, 'He coughed, the poor man.'

12.

SINCE BEING BACK IN Darkenbloom, Lowetz had watched time passing. He *lived for the day*, and this suddenly seemed beautiful and adventurous to him, like *living on the edge*. Each day was brilliantly sunny; each day could have been the previous day, or the next. The garden buzzed and hummed in its underwater green, and the little faces of the flowers followed the sun intently. Lowetz didn't want to do anything, didn't want to think. He could imagine what his ex-girlfriend would have said about him moving into his mother's bed; towards the end she had been, above all, cuttingly ironic. But Mother's bedroom faced east, and he liked to be woken by the first morning light. Soon after Father's death, his bed had been brought into the big room and pushed up against the wall. Ever since, covered with a lambskin and brightly coloured cushions, it had passed itself off as a kind of sofa. It no longer seemed to know what once it was, or that it had been separated from its companion. To Lowetz, idle and mentally porous as he currently was, the redesignation of his father's bed seemed to typify his mother's character: she didn't go on silently railing at Fate, as other widows did, by crawling into a half-empty double bed every evening. She took the bed — and with it, somehow, Lowetz fancied, his father, too — and assigned it a new place: at the centre of her life, exuding not grief but tranquillity. So he felt that, in relocating his sleeping quarters, he was not lying in the marital bed but continuing Eszter's tradition of constantly reassessing things. One aspect of this was that he would occasionally try to talk to her. Quietly, in a whisper, although no one could hear him. It felt less embarrassing if he whispered. He didn't try to persuade himself that he regretted anything. He knew that, if she were still alive, he wouldn't be here, and he wouldn't feel the need to talk to her. That was just how it was. Things change, although this particular change had been completely unforeseen. She had only been sixty-four, yet she had gone, leaving just her body behind, as she would have said. And so now the house was his, and it was new to him in a way that it could only be without her.

'But where have you hidden your books?' he whispered one morning, standing in the main room in T-shirt and underpants, clutching his first coffee of the day. He had gone over to the window, as he did every morning, not curious, just seeking to reassure himself that nothing had changed, if you please. Summer, sunshine, flowers in full bloom; often, during the week, the screech of machinery from next door, from the joinery. That was all part of the pleasure: that Fritz — on an ordinary working day, at least — was at work, whereas he, Lowetz, was in here playing summer holidays. But today was Sunday. Turning back, glancing around the room, he suddenly noticed that the books were missing. His mother had been a reader; she loved Hesse and Werfel and Stefan Zweig, and when he really couldn't think of a present, he would give her nonfiction popular-science books, with a historical focus. Over the years she had built up a little collection of works on regional history: the First World War, the Second World War, even something ethnological about the Roma and Sinti. There used to be a medium-high bookcase next to the daybed that was always overflowing; printed matter seemed to wander over there at night and freeze in the morning in fresh configurations, as if caught in the act. It was only now that he realised it was missing: the wooden floorboards were paler just there. Instead of the bookcase, a drawing hung on the wall in a thin silver frame, just a few wobbly lines in black ink, the head of a melancholy-looking girl.

He didn't know who it was, and it seemed to him that he should. Was it his mother as a young woman? Someone in the family? He wasn't sufficiently interested to ascertain whether it was old or new.

An asthmatic horn honked outside the window, as familiar as the smell when you entered the house. He looked out. The sturdy boughs of the apple tree creaked against a background of spinach green. His mother was back. For the blink of an eye, he lost his mental equilibrium; it was as if he were waking from a strange daydream in which his mother had gone away and he had taken possession of her house and bed. Then he knew once more that it was the other way round: that the improbable was reality. For the first time, he was glad to be in Darkenbloom; he didn't want to be anywhere else. However, he was also aware that he was not wearing trousers, and would not have time to put some on, local etiquette being what it was. Honking signifies: Here I am. An open door signifies: Come on in, any time. So he just stood where he was and tried to assume a slightly ironic attitude.

'Hi, Lowetz,' said the slender, heavily fringed creature who appeared in the kitchen a moment later. 'I'm Flocke. I hope I'm not disturbing you.'

'Might I perhaps put on some clothes?' he replied.

'You might,' she said, and laughed. 'I'll make myself a coffee in the meantime.'

When he returned, she was standing on a chair pushed up against the sideboard, fiddling around behind its carved, decorative trim, her elbows above her head and her tongue peeking out of the corner of her mouth. Eventually she produced a red tin with French writing on it that looked as if it had once contained biscuits. The visitor clambered down again, pulled the chair back to the table, sat down, and took two teaspoons of sugar from the tin to put in her coffee.

'Why....?' asked Lowetz, pointing up at the sideboard.

'She had a terrible craving for sweet things,' said the girl. 'That was why she hid the sugar up there — so it would be an effort every time.'

'She never took sugar before,' said Lowetz, after a pause. 'She didn't eat much in the way of sweet things, either, as far as I know.'

'It was because of the tablets,' she said, looking at him curiously.

'What tablets?' Lowetz asked.

She shrugged.

'If you know your way around so well,' he said, 'maybe you know where she put her books?'

'She gave the books to me, but I wanted to ask if you've got the papers?'

Lowetz answered that he had of course received the will, birth certificate, passport, and so on and was keeping them in a safe place — not here, though; in his apartment in the city. Flocke shook her head. She told him about interviews Eszter had given to Rehberg, for the town chronicle. Eszter had wanted to look through them all again and proofread them, so she had taken the transcripts home with her. Then there were the other things she had dug up herself ...

'What things?' asked Lowetz, who was starting to wonder if they were talking about the same person. But this girl had the Corsa and knew where the sugar was hidden.

'Newspaper cuttings, mostly,' said Flocke. 'We went to the library in Kirschenstein, and she photocopied the newspapers from back then. Other things, too — court documents, and ...'

'From back when?' asked Lowetz, feeling like the idiot he presumably was in this pretty young woman's eyes.

'You know — then,' she said, still giving him that wide-eyed, open look, as if this were all, while very friendly, nonetheless an examination. 'Forty-six. When Old Graun was shot in the forest, and the two witnesses a few weeks later. But there were some from twenty years later, as well, when Horka disappeared, the one they say did it all. That was in the papers, too, back then.'

'But none of it's valuable, is it?' said Lowetz. 'Anyone could make more copies any time.'

'Why valuable?' asked Flocke.

'I thought you were saying they'd disappeared?'

'No,' the girl corrected him, 'I just wanted to know if you had them.'

They even went up to the attic, but they didn't find anything: no files, envelopes, or photocopies. Apart from a few cookbooks, the rooms seemed to be devoid of paper, which Lowetz found enviable, given the state of his own apartment and desk at work. But there had at least been photos before, a couple of albums, and old letters from Father, too ... He put off thinking about it until later.

The girl stayed, even after they had stopped looking. She didn't say anything about the bedroom, although it was obvious that he was sleeping there now. She stood at the kitchen window and looked out the back, at the brick shed the Lowetz and Kalmar families had always shared. All it contained these days was firewood and a few old gardening tools. The shed had bashfully allowed itself to be overrun with climbing plants; the plaster underneath was falling off, and the bricks were starting to dislocate, like an old man's vertebrae. Lowetz's parents used to distil schnapps in there, and when the weather was warm they would sometimes sit in front of it in the evening, and Agnes and Fritz might join them.

'Why doesn't Fritz have a father?' asked Lowetz.

'Died in the war ... I was going to go and see him next.'

'He'll be round in a minute anyway, when he sees the car.'

They made coffee again, together. She put two teaspoons of sugar in every cup, as deliberately as if it were a ritual. The biscuit tin, filled to the brim, was allowed to remain on the table. Later, Lowetz made fried eggs; she had some bread in the car, and went to fetch it.

So there they were, together, in a house they both knew. They were both on holiday, and they hit it off immediately. They had their background in common, as well as having established a certain distance from it. They weren't narrow-minded provincials, but neither were they contemptuous types who would be ashamed of it. At least, Lowetz succeeded in giving that impression, which he would not have pulled off anything like as well a few weeks earlier and two hundred kilometres further north.

As is usually the case with young people in fairly small communities, Flocke knew some embarrassing details about him. A few youthful escapades and school leavers' practical jokes, which already sounded to him like apocryphal tales: a disco ball stolen from the legendary Südsee Club in Kalsching; a pair of the hated young PE teacher's trainers nailed to the blackboard one morning, much to the aged Latin teacher's distress, when he eventually noticed. A raised hunting hide that collapsed during a birthday drinking binge. Only this last — the hide, an injured ankle (not his), hospital, plaster, police investigation — rang a bell with Lowetz; he must have been present, but he remembered it more like a story he had heard told over and over again. Sometimes it seemed to him that he had never been young at all, or that he suffered from a rare form of memory loss that applied only to everything that had supposedly taken place in Darkenbloom.

From Flocke he learned that she had been a premature baby, so tiny and translucent that her sister had said she looked like a snowflake, a *Schneeflocke*. It was a while before it occurred to him that he had been in the same class as one of her sisters. He had no idea which. Andrea, Christl, Barbara? He couldn't remember a first name, only that she was a Malnitz.

'Easy,' said Flocke. 'Was she a swot with plaits, or a tomboy, or a girl who cried all the time?'

'Swot with plaits,' he said, 'class spokesperson every year.'

'That's Andrea,' cried Flocke. 'Are you really that old?'

'Well, I look a lot younger,' he said, and grinned. To himself, he thought: I really am that old. Do ten years constitute a generation? He didn't ask the question out loud; it wasn't important. And yes, of course they could go swimming sometime. Yes, he could come for roast suckling pig at the organic farm and bring Fritz with him. He even agreed to let her show him the third cemetery, although this took him into more uneasy territory. For the past three years, ever since that obdurate liar Waldheim had entered the Hofburg Palace as president, this had been the point on which he regularly came into conflict with his peers. He didn't believe protests changed anything; he believed that history would take its course. They would all die soon, anyway, the liars and the order-followers; all the noisy protests meant they were still being glorified. For years now, people had been selling off old insignia, identification cards, medals, at the flea market near his apartment. And that, he felt, was as it should be; throw them away, flog them off, ignore them. Don't put them on a pedestal, not even the pedestal of evil. He found it hard to explain, and consequently his ex-girlfriend, that metropolitan daughter of the bourgeoisie, had accused him more than once of being indolent. But he found the uproar that broke out long afterwards, never at the time in question, only when it was already far too late, oddly discomfiting. To his ex-girlfriend, he had said it was about as much use as someone with measles frantically trying to wash away the spots. It couldn't be done with soap and a brush, not even with a pumice stone. The measles patient would just get weaker and weaker, with the infection at its height. She hadn't understood the comparison, and when he tried to explain it better, his words and thoughts became muddled. In the end, he had declared melodramatically, 'I'm protesting against my own spots,' and Simone had tapped her forehead.

Here and now, though, he decided, he would simply see it as a regional speciality, like funnel cake and hot sweet polenta. They had to do something, after all. There was nothing to be done here. They could restore the plague column, for example, and the altar triptych with the feathered devils — that was historical work, too. Instead, they had opened up the third cemetery and removed tons of biomass, and yes, he believed this bright young woman when she said there were things to be discovered in there.

But saying that the town chronicle would have to be completely rewritten — that sounded a bit over the top to him.

'I thought Rehberg had only just started writing it?'

'I mean everything people have been saying all these years,' said Flocke. 'At most, only half of it's true. There are some who don't even want the town chronicle — you know what they're like, history written by the victors, all the stuff they go on about in the bar.'

'History's always written by the victors,' said Lowetz amiably. 'It's been like that ever since the Ancient Romans.'

'Well, Rehberg seems to have started with the Ancient Romans,' said Flocke, laughing, 'that's why he'll never finish. But the mayor's approved a grant of five thousand schillings now, for expenses, research, copies, reproductions of photos. So it's official. And later we'll scrounge the money for the print run from all over town, from the shops and supermarkets and the insurance company and all the tourist places. They'll get adverts in the back in exchange, that's how it's done these days!'

Flocke stood up and plucked the photo of the boy Lowetz from the fridge. 'This would make a nice exhibit, too, actually,' she said, gazing at it. 'Black and white, lederhosen ... Would you let us use it?'

'Dunno,' said Lowetz defensively, 'is there something special about it?' But of course he would. If she wanted this photo, or anything else, he would gladly give it to her. His mother had given her the car and her books — he could understand why. Perhaps he would find his mother's files for her, too. The stuff had to be somewhere; perhaps

Fritz had taken it over to his place. He would help, and in return he cautiously imagined Flocke in a bikini, this slim, tanned person with the heavy fringe. Simone, his ex-girlfriend, had been much more womanly, not her figure so much as her general demeanour. She had a firm walk, and when she wore shoes with heels she hammered them emphatically into the ground, as if testing it to see if it would hold. Now Simone was single again, just in time; she was studying for her PhD and, with her parents' help, had made an initial downpayment to buy her own apartment.

He watched Flocke trying to stick the photo back up again. The magnets were flat and round like button batteries, and they seemed to be pretty strong. She tried working the nail of her forefinger underneath. The tip of her tongue peeked out of the side of her mouth. Outside in the sunshine a car horn sounded, not asthmatic but peremptory. A big dark car drove up onto the pavement behind the Corsa. 'My father,' murmured Flocke, without turning her head. She had finally loosened the magnet, and was about to stick the child-hood photo up again when the postcard alongside it, of the castle, fell to the floor. She bent down.

'Hello, Lowetz,' said Malnitz, shaking his hand firmly. 'I saw my daughter's car.'

Flocke straightened up again. 'Look at this,' she said, and handed Lowetz the postcard. Across the back, in capitals, was written: *Stop lying.*

'That's not her writing, is it?' asked Lowetz.

Flocke stared at him in dismay.

Her father took a few paces about the room, as if looking around, but without really seeing anything. Then he stopped and bounced his knees a little, like a boxer before a fight. Finally, he clapped twice and said: 'They've dug someone up in the Rotenstein meadow, Flocke. I thought you'd be interested.'

13.

ONE THURSDAY, SHORTLY BEFORE six in the evening, Rehberg took a felt-tip pen and wrote across a sheet of paper: *We look forward to seeing you again on Monday!* Next to it he drew a steamer with a thick, laughing cloud above its chimney, and stuck it inside the shop window. He locked the door to the shop, went upstairs to his living quarters, changed his shirt, put on a waistcoat and jacket, picked up his already-packed suitcase, and set off on his trip. He drove to Kirschenstein, took the local train to the capital, ate a too-fatty sausage in the station restaurant, washed it down with Gösser beer, then settled in in his sleeping compartment. His outer garments he hung on a coathanger that he had brought for the purpose. He lay on the bed in his underwear, and although it swayed from side to side, he slept well. By nine in the morning he was already in Zurich; the sky appeared to have been wiped clean, and from the glimpse he caught of it from the station, the city looked dinky: doll's houses with crown-glass windows. When he alighted in Lugano at midday, he admired the palm trees, which here were even cultivated in tubs.

This, he said to himself, is certainly very different.

The people he asked for directions were friendly and understood a bit of German. He had a little something to eat in a café. At four o'clock on the dot he called on the Countess. He had bought three peach-coloured tea roses for her, and wondered anxiously if that was too few. There was nothing to be done about it now, though, and even these three little flowers had cost about four and a half times as much as they would at home. A rough calculation; he didn't want to work out the exact figure.

The door was opened by a woman in a pleated skirt and woollen cardigan. He had been expecting a butler in tails, but it seemed times really had changed. He was made to wait for a while in the entrance hall of the villa, then the woman led him into a gigantic conservatory. The lake glittered behind a vast expanse of glass. The Countess was sitting with her tea in front of her, and nodded when he bowed. She looked exactly as he had imagined her: a small, desiccated lady with beautifully coiffed silver hair, the network of veins on the backs of her hands as purple as her silk blouse. He proffered the flowers; the woman in the cardigan reached across him from behind, took them, and walked out. The Countess gestured towards the empty seat.

He sat down. Neither of them spoke. Rehberg waited. The Countess said nothing. Rehberg cleared his throat. 'Most gracious lady,' he began at last — whereupon the distant door opened again and the servant returned with his tea roses in a delicate crystal vase. He was glad he had not bought more — they looked perfectly wonderful in it. The woman placed the vase precisely between them; he could no longer see the Countess properly. It seemed to him that, in doing so, the servant flashed a malicious, lopsided smile, revealing a crooked canine. But he must have been mistaken. When he looked at her she seemed exactly as before, her mouth sternly closed. She poured him some tea and disappeared again. Rehberg shifted his chair a few centimetres to the side, as unobtrusively as possible. The Countess gazed out over the water. Boats motored past. There were sounds of splashing and laughter.

'Most esteemed and gracious lady,' he began again, and as

she said nothing, didn't nod or turn to look at him, he carefully recited his speech. As he spoke, he tried at least to take pleasure in his own well-chosen words, and to sound as deep and sonorous as possible. It had occasionally been pointed out to him that he had an unusually high voice for a man, and he wanted to compensate for this shortcoming. His voice filled the room. He spoke of the long, fruitful relationship between the Countess's family and the town of Darkenbloom, of how one could not be imagined without the other. This centuries-old relationship ought finally, finally to be depicted and exhibited, in all its facets, in an appropriate setting. He extolled the tolerance the counts had always shown towards minorities: the patent for the Jews in the seventeenth century, the plot of land in Zwick for the gypsy settlement in the nineteenth. 'Your family brought education and culture, open-mindedness and prosperity to our rural area, dear, esteemed, gracious lady,' he said, practically choking with emotion. Suddenly he wondered: was all that really true, of this particular lady? One had heard otherwise. He couldn't consider that now. He couldn't allow himself, and especially not his voice, to admit any doubt concerning the entirely justified praise of the counts of Darkenbloom.

The Countess remained motionless.

'Your relationship to our region, your influence down the centuries,' said Rehberg. 'That, to this day, is our distinguishing characteristic, our USP. Perhaps it is presumptuous of me to claim' — once again he regretted that he had repeatedly been discouraged, in the nastiest possible way, from standing for public office in Darkenbloom, because, when it came to rhetoric, he could not recall any mayor who had been able to hold a candle to him — 'presumptuous, dear lady, to claim that we in Darkenbloom are more saddened by the loss of your splendid castle than even you yourself and your family.'

He observed that the Countess was looking at him, with a fixed, watery gaze. He lowered his eyes. 'I know you were born and grew up there,' he said, more quietly. 'I had no intention of reopening old wounds. It is an immense loss, but, believe me, that loss is felt by us as well.'

This felt like the right moment to take the postcard of the castle out of his jacket pocket. He placed it in front of her, beside the vase of flowers. In order to do so, he had to push the teapot slightly aside with his little finger. 'Such a dreadful shame,' he said. 'That incomparable, magnificent edifice. Two hundred rooms! Renaissance!'

The Countess stared at the postcard. Out on the lake, the water sports enthusiasts whooped excitedly. Then Rehberg heard a dry, quiet hiss, like a snake in a pile of autumn leaves. Where was it coming from — under the table? He glanced around warily. But it was the Countess who was hissing, tonelessly, like a fingernail on sandpaper.

'It was Neulag, that fucking son of a bitch,' she hissed. 'He gave the order. Some of my stallions burned to death. Not the best ones, but still. If you know how frightened horses are of fire ... I couldn't evacuate them all at once, some were still there, and when he gave the order to set fire to the castle, it had absolutely nothing to do with the fighting or the Russians, it was just because he wanted to break my heart. Should be strung up by the balls, the filthy bastard.'

Rehberg felt compelled to go along with the unforeseen turn the conversation had taken. He hoped he would succeed in returning to the subject later on if he allowed himself to indulge his curiosity.

Now he was whispering, too. 'Neulag? It was always said that Ferbenz ...?'

'Stuff and nonsense,' hissed the Countess. 'The cowardly Dr Alois snuck off to the west at the first opportunity. It was Neulag who was in command those last few weeks. Of everything.'

'Of everything?' whispered Rehberg. 'Including ...?'

'Of course,' hissed the Countess, 'especially that! But what he enjoyed most was setting fire to my horses, at the end. Filthy, filthy son of a bitch.'

Cardigan Woman was suddenly standing next to Rehberg, as if she had sprung up out of the black-and-white terrazzo floor. 'It was a pleasure for Countess Darkenbloom to make your acquaintance,' she declared, and her tall figure seemed to absorb most of the light, even the bright glare reflected off the lake.

Breaking out in a sweat, Rehberg raised his hand to stave her off. 'Might I have just a few more minutes, dear, esteemed Countess — we're planning a museum that, without your invaluable assistance ...'

'Apply to the foundation,' hissed the Countess, 'contact name Herr Gotthelf, Zurich office.'

He gazed at her beseechingly, but she was looking out of the window again. This, it seemed, was her final word. He had the impression that the purple of her blouse and veins now also lay as shadows beneath her eyes. The postcard of the castle, though, had vanished from the table. Her blouse had no pockets, and whatever she was wearing on her bottom half, skirt or trousers, was concealed by the little table. It occurred to Rehberg, too late, that he should have written all the things he wanted to discuss with her on the back of the card.

'Countess Darkenbloom is pleased to have made your acquaintance,' Cardigan Woman repeated, tugging at the back of Rehberg's chair.

He stood. 'So I may write to Herr Gotthelf, then, about our museum?' he asked, in the Countess's direction, and his voice sounded unbecomingly shrill and whiny. But answer came there none.

He walked back through town towards the station, where he had deposited his small bag. There was still time before his return train. His thoughts raced back and forth. Had he merely incurred expenses and made a fool of himself, or had he, with his modest yet courageous visit, decisively advanced the interests of Darkenbloom? If only by knowing the magic words (*foundation, Herr Gotthelf*) and being able, justifiably, to claim that the Countess herself had pledged her support? You could say that she had promised it! That would only be a tiny exaggeration — not enough to constitute a lie, anyway.

In front of the station was a small park with a friendly fountain in the middle, strelitzias, palms, a few benches. He removed his jacket, placed it on a bench, and sat down.

Of course he had hoped for more. At the very least he would have liked to return with her consent to exhibit some of the artistic treasures in the counts' possession. The priceless Passion of Christ — if only briefly, just for a few weeks after the opening. Or the famous early-seventeenth-century automaton, a small gold coach that, when wound up with three keys, could travel the length of a festive table to the accompaniment of jingling bells, circled by eagles and dogs while the fat, red-cheeked, enamel god resplendent on top raised his cup in a toast in all directions. A few of the better-known portraits, at least: Árpád the Great, the castle's founder, stylised as a knight on horseback; or the Countess as a child, with brown, curly hair and hunting dogs, in front of the fireplace. It occurred to him that, although the Countess's appearance had corresponded exactly to what he had expected, he had actually thought of her as younger. Lately, there had been reports in the society pages about aristocrats who partied a lot and had crazy hairdos, who were photographed with cigarettes and sunglasses, who made pop music, or threw bags of paint that exploded onto canvas. He had imagined the Countess to be a little along these lines. That the palm trees and fashionable lake might have transformed her into something similar. Someone who would say, with a dismissive wave of her hand: Oh, the Passion, of course you can exhibit it, I really haven't any use for it. A countess with a slice of lemon decorating the rim of her glass.

'Ciao,' said someone beside him, quietly. A young man had sat down on the bench and was smiling at him. He was very pale, but he had dark hair, deep blue eyes, and eyelashes girls would kill for.

His mouth, on the other hand, was slightly crooked: an accident, or a badly repaired cleft lip? There had been a boy like this at the seminary; Rehberg found the slight deformation touching. This boy — like the other he recalled — looked as if his mouth were about to start crying while his eyes were laughing. Rehberg tried to think of an opening gambit. But in which language? Perhaps a *ciao* would suffice.

He almost flinched when he felt the hand on his thigh. From a distance, no one would have noticed; the young man had slid it deftly under Rehberg's jacket, which lay between them. Already he was slowly withdrawing it and standing up. '*Vieni?*' he asked amiably, and walked off in the direction of the station building.

Rehberg sat there, thunderstruck. Had this been the true purpose of his trip? Would he be making a terrible mistake; would he be ridiculed, beaten, as he had been once before? Worse: robbed? Or was it perfectly normal here, so far from home? He didn't have all his cash with him — the rest was in his bag in the locker. Those eyes — their remarkable colour, and the eyelashes ... And that poor, wounded mouth.

Rehberg slowly rose to his feet and surrendered to recklessness. Whatever happened, there were no Heuraffls, no Berneck lurking here to lure him into a trap and abuse him, break his nose, and take his trousers and underpants, leaving him to figure out how he was going to get home in the middle of the afternoon. Even if there were people like that here, they would be different people, with different names. The Heuraffls and Bernecks here could only insult him, not his whole family as well, especially his Aunt Elly, whom he had loved, and whose grave he tended, along with the others. The risk was manageable. Besides, he had a bit more intuition now than he'd had back then, perhaps even a better understanding of people.

Half an hour later, he and Carlo were toasting each other with bright red cocktails in the café where he had eaten that afternoon before visiting the Countess. The glasses were decorated with slices of lemon. Conversation was a little difficult on account of the language barrier, but Carlo had an uncomplicated way of laughing it off and gesticulating instead. Rehberg, who was trying, more or less in vain, to communicate in Latin, sometimes drew what he meant on a napkin. By the time they had finished their digestif, he had decided to rebook his return journey. And so they went back to the station, giggling, and changed his ticket to the following day, and then he booked a room in a guesthouse on a quiet street where no one paid any attention to whether a guest was really alone when he came in late at night. Changing the ticket had cost money; the room, the cocktails, and the dinner, which they didn't eat until late that evening, around ten o'clock, cost even more; but Rehberg finally had both the desire and a reason to spend the little money he had. All in all, it was just over twenty-four hours. He relished every single one. He could sleep later, in the swaying train. And he did indeed sleep there, like a log, one that has been warmed by the sun. And after his first proper day's holiday in a very long time, his dreams will certainly not have been of the desiccated, hissing Countess. Getting out of his car outside Rehberg's Travel on Sunday afternoon, as if in a trance, the first thing he saw was the steamer in the window. How innocent he had been when he drew it! How cheerfully his own friendly, laughing cloud bade him welcome! But barely ten minutes later, once he was back in his apartment and had opened the windows to let in some air, Flocke Malnitz drove up, kept honking the horn until he stuck his head out, and shouted to him from down below that they'd dug someone up, over in the Rotenstein meadow. And there, sitting next to Flocke, was Eszter's son.

14.

IT WAS SUNDAY; CHURCH and morning drinks had finished, and up in the Rotenstein meadow a crowd was gathering as if for a folk festival. Everyone who heard the news drove up, though once there, many acted as if they just happened to be passing, or as if this were an established meeting spot where it was quite usual for people to park all over the place right along the edge of the forest. Yet they didn't venture far from their cars — some of the women didn't even get out, sitting surly-faced in their accustomed seats on the passenger side, as if in protest. The men leaned on the car boots and bonnets, smoking; some had brought beer, cola, even suntan lotion. When Flocke and Lowetz arrived, only two police cars were there. Everyone knew Gerald and Leonhard, who had donned their professional scowls so no one would ask them any questions. They and two of their colleagues were hammering iron rods into the ground, the tops of which were bent into a loop. Through this they would thread the red-and-white barrier tape; one had the roll already in his hand. None of the spectators came any closer. They stayed off to one side, in their newly created car park. Lowetz mingled with the onlookers. You probably couldn't see anything, people speculated, unless you were right up close, actually standing in the hole, because whatever it was would have taken on the colour of earth long ago. Lowetz saw dark ochre, like loam, mixed with the thick black of the topsoil, and for a moment he imagined zebra-patterned bones. Bones? *Human remains*, people had said, or heard — that was all anyone knew. 'But someone must have seen that that's definitely what they are,' said one of the men, 'so they can't be that old, because if it's just bones, you can't tell straight away ...' The speaker tailed off. People round here often didn't finish their sentences, a good strategy for subjects like this: you indicated what you thought, but you hadn't actually said anything. This tailing off was followed by laughter and a few dirty jokes when some bright spark provided the information that, in humans, sex could usually be quickly determined by the shape of the pelvis.

'You're all such pillocks,' said a surly woman, from behind a half-open car window.

What they were actually doing was waiting for news, unsure whether they should expect something troublesome or sensational. Who had been digging around up here, anyway, and why? And who did it belong to? Someone maintained that this was where a Graun field abutted a Malnitz field, but only the owners knew exactly where. Another doubted that Graun's field still belonged to him: he'd sold everything that wasn't a vineyard.

'Who to, though?' asked the first man.

'Not Malnitz, that's for sure,' the other answered, laughing.

'Dr Alois, probably,' said a third, 'who else?'

Higher up was the start of a wood belonging to the Heuraffls. Everything below the road was municipal property. Only one thing seemed certain: it was Young Graun who had called the police. His van was parked closest to the site of the find, well away from the others; the back doors were open and he was sitting on the loading bed, legs dangling, smoking. Flocke caught sight of him as she got out of the Corsa, and observed him for a moment. There was a resemblance between the two of them that was difficult to define. It wasn't the face itself, but the expression: an intent frown, an internalised concentration that could have been misinterpreted as standoffishness and bad temper.

Farmer Faludi came stomping up the mountain. He was getting more and more ecological, if that's the word. His beard, which had been growing unchecked for some time, now bathed his breastbone, and he had taken to hiking with a long, carved walking stick that was taller than he was. Children probably saw him as an all-year-round Father Christmas, and although he didn't talk much, except about his pet topic of water boreholes, it was unequivocally clear from his bearing what it was he wished to represent: the good shepherd, taking care of people, animals, and resources, sincere, implacable care. As soon as he reached the others, he thrust the stick into the ground as if in affirmation.

'Let's just hope it's not an Ancient Roman,' he said, the words issuing from somewhere deep within his beard. Since appointing himself spokesperson for opponents of the water authority in the row over Darkenbloom's water supply, he was increasingly acknowledged as a leader — a very different kind of leader to the one Ferbenz used to be. One might ask oneself — and certain town councillors, Toni Malnitz, for example, did — what Alois Ferbenz, old and shaky as he was these days, thought about the water business. When he would make his opinion known. And who would win the war that would very likely follow: the old, brown-shirted power, or the new, green one.

A woman started to describe the seven plagues that would fall upon them from Heaven if the find turned out to be something archaeological. Her voice was not loud, but a droning, accusatory monotone that assumed an almost physical shape. The bureaucratic obstacles on which everything, the entire future of Darkenbloom, would soon founder seemed practically to rise up out of the ground between the listeners, sticky, dark-grey matter constituting everything of which *the state* was guilty. She, the speaker, had relatives in Löwingen, and what had gone on there ever since they'd found a few rusty coins and blades in a field simply beggared belief, she droned: roads rerouted, construction halted, practically expropriation. The bystanders nodded. They all knew a bit about the strict regulations of the monument preservation authorities — it really was astonishing. 'And where's our hobby historian?' someone asked. 'Rehberg? Has Rehberg actually been told?'

'He'll be here in a minute,' murmured Lowetz. 'He's only just got back from seeing the Countess.'

At that, someone grabbed his shoulder and shook him. 'What d'you mean, from the Countess? And who are you, anyway?'

'Take your hands off me,' said Lowetz. 'What do you think you're doing?'

'Leave him, Joschi,' said one of the men, 'that's Eszter's son.'

'That doesn't make it any better,' grumbled Joschi, but he let go, and in the same, now almost elegant, flowing movement he took a packet of cigarettes from his breast pocket and offered them to Lowetz. That was how it had always been here, Lowetz remembered: cigarettes were deployed like miniature white flags. You mouthed off at someone, jostled him, or kicked him into the gutter, but as soon as you realised you might have got the wrong man, he was hauled to his feet by the front of his shirt and a cigarette was conjured up and proffered. It did not signify propitiation or apology. It signified: don't go making a fuss.

Lowetz ignored the stranger's cigarettes and lit one of his own instead. To the other man, the one who had referred to him as Eszter's son, he said, 'I see manners haven't improved since I was last here.'

'Darkenbloom's never been big on manners,' said the other.

'Well then, let's give it a go,' said Lowetz. He mimicked the troublemaker, Joschi, who had retreated to the edge of the group: 'Who are you, anyway?'

'Feri Farkas, from the garage,' the man replied. 'D'you really not recognise me?'

'Sorry,' said Lowetz, in surprise. Now it was his turn to proffer a cigarette. 'Been a while.'

Feri took it, and said, 'You can say that again.'

'But what was Rehberg doing with the Countess?' interrupted the woman with the droning voice. She attempted a smile at Lowetz, but it looked to him like a malevolent grimace. He glanced around for Flocke, but couldn't see her.

'For your museum,' he said vaguely. 'You know more about it than I do. To borrow something or other.'

'Aha,' someone said, 'to borrow something, from the Countess.'

'For the museum,' the droning woman repeated.

'Bring out the best pieces,' said another woman's voice.

'Not keep 'em hidden away all the time,' said another man.

'Finally show everyone what we've got,' said a third.

'We've so much to be proud of,' the new woman's voice continued.

'We just have to remind ourselves,' said the second man.

'A treasure that just needs bringing out into the light,' said the droning woman.

And Joschi, exhaling smoke aggressively: 'A glorious past.' He observed Lowetz through narrowed eyes, as if testing him.

Lowetz looked around again for Flocke. The car was there, but where had she gone?

'Sorry, what?' he said to Feri Farkas, who he suspected had been in his First Communion class. He remembered a rosy-cheeked boy, practically bursting out of his little suit. So they did *outgrow the fat,* as the mothers used to say indulgently. When Lowetz was young, fat children were a status symbol; people would pinch their cheeks and thighs approvingly, delighting in their firm plumpness, testing it admiringly between thumb and forefinger. Beanpoles like him counted for nothing, nor did spindleshanks, scraggy-bones, and pasty-faces, because no one wanted to be reminded of hunger and war. The adult Feri had indeed outgrown the fat; he wasn't thin, but he wasn't as pear-shaped as many of the others here. And he was the only one Lowetz didn't find unpleasant. The only one he didn't immediately want to fight. Was this urge to fight neurotic? Or a healthy self-defence mechanism? What was wrong with these people? Why were they so antagonistic? Towards Rehberg and his museum, towards the archaeologists, towards anything, presumably, that disturbed their little worlds. Lowetz felt the rising anger that would often overcome him in Darkenbloom, a deep-seated aversion that his mother had claimed she simply didn't understand, not in the slightest. Which had infuriated him even more. Because he didn't believe her. She knew what he meant. She could have expressed it better than him, if she had tried, if she hadn't always denied it. That, at least, had been what he suspected, and what he reproached her for: the fact that she understood exactly what he couldn't properly explain to himself.

But weren't the reasons blindingly obvious? This rude greeting, for example, the way he was obviously being taken for a fool. Perhaps he should ask the mysterious visitor, the castle postcard fan, what he thought of the atmosphere here: as a stranger, a disinterested party.

'What are you talking about?' he asked again. 'What do you mean? What's wrong with you all?'

They stared at him, motionless as reptiles.

'Well well,' said Joschi, finally. 'Bit tense, are we?'

'They're just imitating Rehberg,' said Feri Farkas soothingly. 'He gets on some people's nerves with his activism.'

'Especially his *you-ess-pee*,' said Joschi. He poked his forefinger into his cheek a few times, his mouth hanging slightly open. They all burst into shrill laughter, crocodiles clattering with amusement. Joschi glanced around like a victor, threw his cigarette butt on the ground, and carefully trod it out.

An official-looking convoy arrived. It comprised a white minibus, several dark cars with number plates from the capital, and in the middle, as if framed by the others, Dr Sterkowitz's Honda — except that it was being driven by Mayor Koreny, who was alone. An old Fiat covered in anti-nuclear sun stickers lolloped along at the back — this was the reporter from the local paper, who habitually wore his single-lens reflex camera around his neck, especially when driving. The convoy drove up to the site of the find and stopped, right there on the embankment of the road, nose to tail. The Darkenbloomers craned their necks. They watched a dozen people emerge from the various vehicles, some in uniform, some not. There were also men in suits. They saw someone help their stumbling mayor down to the lower ground of the field, and the few steps into the pit. Boards had now been laid to stand on. They saw a man in uniform speak to the reporter, leaning in close, his hand on the reporter's camera strap. Eventually the reporter got back into his rust bucket and reversed it back towards the gawping crowd. The Darkenbloomers saw that the convoy had brought its own photographer, also in uniform, who knelt and took a few photos, with a flash, even though the sun was beating down like nobody's business.

'Forensic scientists, CID, public prosecutor,' the reporter reeled off when he reached them, 'forensics team, crime scene investigators, police photographers — it's nuts. On a Sunday.'

'How many are there?' asked Joschi.

'I don't know, maybe fifteen?' said the reporter.

'God Almighty,' exclaimed the droning woman. 'Fifteen?'

'Fuck me,' said Joschi.

The reporter looked puzzled. 'Well, if you count the four gendarmes,' he said, 'it's ...'

'He meant corpses,' said Feri Farkas. Joschi had turned scarlet.

'Oh, right,' said the reporter, and laughed. 'They've only found one so far, but that might change.'

'Please, Mr Reporter,' said a gaunt-looking woman, 'do they know yet whether it's a man or a woman?'

'Don't think so,' the reporter answered. 'Why do you want to know?'

'There's someone still missing, from back then,' said Feri Farkas. 'You know: the Stipsits daughter ...'

'My elder sister,' the woman explained.

The reporter whipped out his notebook. 'Right,' he said, 'the Stipsits daughter, of course, that would be something ...' And with that he took the other Stipsits daughter aside, for an exclusive interview, as it were.

'Dragged out of her house by the Russians and never came back,' someone whispered in Lowetz's ear, and he recognised Flocke by the smell of soap.

'Where've you been all this time?' he hissed. 'I feel like a voyeur standing here.'

'Talking to Graun,' she whispered back, 'and we're all voyeurs.'

'Can we go?' he pleaded. 'There's really nothing to see here.'

'You never know,' she said. 'Let's wait a few more minutes.'

'I'm going to sit in the car,' said Lowetz. 'I'm finding all this pretty weird — the crowd of onlookers, like that German hostage drama.'

'Don't exaggerate,' she said, 'there aren't any bank robbers firing guns around here! What if it's an ancient Celt? With precious burial gifts, swords, amulets?'

'You don't seriously believe that,' he said. 'They'll have dug up all the ancient Celts when they built the Wall.'

'But they didn't take them to the museum back then,' she giggled. 'They'll just have tossed them aside. So all those lovely Celts with their amber treasures, they must all still be here.'

15.

THERE WAS REALLY NO cause for alarm, the duty public prosecutor had assured them; this could be one of any number of things, but definitely not a recent murder. An old matter, uncovered by chance. If Herr Graun had dug just three steps further on, it would never have come to light. So it's fortunate, really, isn't it, if you look at it like that — none of us wants to moulder away undiscovered somewhere in the countryside. But don't you worry!

Yes, yes, Mayor Koreny had murmured, not a problem. And yes, thanks, he was fine, absolutely, he just always suffered in the heat, this year perhaps a little more than usual. The public prosecutor claimed to understand Koreny well, very well indeed. Yet there was not even the tiniest bead of sweat on his brow — at most, the skin under his nose was glistening slightly. Koreny observed that this region, between nose and lip, was considerably larger in the public prosecutor than in other people. The only conceivable explanation was that a caricaturist had drawn the public prosecutor like this, his face stretched apart in the middle like a lump of Plasticine, mouth and chin almost structurally separated from the rest. There was no name for this facial non-feature — at least, Koreny couldn't think of one. An indented bridge, the spot where others wear their moustache. Perhaps the public prosecutor, whom Koreny was seeing for the first time, used to sport a moustache and had only just shaved it off. Perhaps this face carried an optical echo of the recent past, because the skin there was still imperceptibly paler. Who knew. All he knew was that he couldn't help staring at it, spellbound, while the public prosecutor explained everything to him in order of what would happen next: cordon off, recover, search the periphery, forensics, *suspicious death*, possible historical investigations. Koreny stared at the spot that was, at most, glistening slightly, displaying not a trace of the sticky moisture that had blanketed every part of him, even the most intimate. And there the man stood, claiming to understand him.

Koreny nodded weakly. He didn't want to be asked again if he was okay, or if ... Or if! He was hot, and he really had had other plans for his Sunday.

But yes, he had understood everything, even if he wasn't sure he would be able to repeat it all when he spoke to the people. And speak he must: they were all standing around, they had driven or walked up, they were understandably concerned, a dead body up here, in the middle of the meadow; now they'd parked up all along the edge of the forest — surely they had other things to do — but fair enough, of course they had time on a Sunday afternoon. Even Farmer Faludi was here; he'd got a nerve. If Koreny had understood correctly, he was the one they had to thank for this discovery. Young Graun had apparently been promised something if he checked to see whether an underground stream ran through here, as the experts Faludi had commissioned had calculated. Who was actually paying for this? Were these experts working for free? Think strategically, Balf would say: who benefits if the contract with the water authority is cancelled? Right now, it was beside the point. But he must keep an eye on it, for later.

Yes, he had understood, and now he would explain to his people. Prevail upon them to leave the site. Not to obstruct the investigation any further. The results, as soon as they came back, would, at the right time ... Understood. Of course. No more questions, no. Thank you, Public Prosecutor, and thank you, too, for making time for this on a Sunday.

'No need for thanks,' the lanky man said drily, and the indented bridge puckered in a way that may have been mocking, or possibly just friendly. 'It's all work.'

'And no play,' Koreny murmured. He let Gerald haul him back up onto the road and squeezed past the orange car he had driven up in. First he would stand there and inform people about what was going on. And afterwards they would figure out how to extract the Honda from this convoy of cars.

Lowetz sat in his mother's car, smoking. He tried to view it all from a disinterested, outsider's perspective — nothing else going on in Darkenbloom, after all; it's only natural for half the town to start hopping up and down when they find a few bones — but he didn't really succeed. He had been taken aback at first when Flocke had unhesitatingly joined in, as if she had insisted they peep under the neighbours' blankets together. But it wasn't like that; it was something else, though he didn't quite understand what. Standing there in the group, harassed by Joschi and the droning woman, by the others' nonsense ... You had to ... push back against it somehow. What he found hardest was trying to imagine his mother getting involved. Chatting with this girl over coffee, hiding the sugar on top of the sideboard with her, doing historical research with the travel agent? This was not the mother he remembered.

The mother he remembered stood on the fringes, like him. She didn't associate with these farmers. Some of them looked like the Alm-Uncle! His mother wasn't part of this community; she was the wife of a quiet man, she came from Over There, they'd had different furniture and different views. She had a big heart, which was unusual here: it encompassed Fritz and Uncle Grün, and also her friend Agnes, Fritz's mother, who every few years would start screaming and end up in hospital for a while. The Lowetz family just happened to live here — that was how he used to see it; they might just as well have lived in Löwingen or Mandl, or in the capital. Mightn't they? No, the capital's not my cup of tea, he heard his mother say. And then he realised that perhaps only Darkenbloom was close enough — a hand outstretched, geographically speaking, to Over There, the place from which she came and about which he knew almost nothing. Kirschenstein or Löwingen were already in the heartland; in those places, there was no longer any doubt to which country they belonged. But Darkenbloom? Previously, before the First World War and in the preceding centuries, it had all been the same territory, but strictly speaking it had belonged to Over There. No one ever talked about this. Apart from Flocke. She liked to ask probing questions. Just as she had immediately asked him about his girlfriend, his apartment, his levels of professional and general satisfaction. Flocke was planning an exhibition about the border; she had told him about it that morning. She was dreaming of old family photos and family trees going back a hundred years, pictures of old town centres and traditional costumes, lists of venues where bands had played that showed just how intertwined things used to be. The Cecilia Men's Choir, the Pinzker Group, the Stern Jewish Ensemble, all long forgotten. And this was why she was supporting Rehberg: if he could persuade the counts to part with their treasures, there would be a place for her biographical project as well. And the farmers could even exhibit their historical winepresses!

'This is where we're from; we can't do anything about it, except do things better.' This was what she had said that morning as they ate fried eggs on toast together.

'You're one of those activist types, then,' he had responded. 'Yeah, I guess that's fashionable right now.'

She had just laughed — laughed at him, but in a friendly way, with a dismissive wave of the hand and no follow-up retort.

The red-haired mayor, who reminded Lowetz of a marmot, not least because of the funny, pleading way he held up his hands, appeared outside the window, giving some sort of explanation. This Lowetz did want to hear. So he got out of the car and went back to stand with the crowd.

'... appears right now to be an isolated find, but the site will of course be investigated across a larger area,' Koreny was saying. 'The dead man ...'

'Woman,' a shrill voice shouted.

Koreny started his sentence again without showing any reaction: 'The dead man or woman will be recovered and taken to the forensics department in Kirschenstein. They will attempt to identify them, although, as it currently seems likely that the body is several decades old ...'

'It's Neulag, that's who it is,' said Joschi loudly. Koreny faltered. Joschi stared provocatively at the mayor, cigarette dangling from the corner of his mouth.

'According to the public prosecutor,' Koreny said, 'no statement can yet be made concerning the identity of the human remains found today, here in the Rotenstein meadow, and thus within the municipal district of Darkenbloom. We will have to wait to hear what results ...'

'You'll see,' Joschi called out, 'you've gone and dug up Neulag. Remember I told you so!' He turned and walked to his car, slammed the door, laboriously manoeuvred the vehicle through all the bystanders, and drove off.

'There's nothing more to say right now,' said Mayor Koreny. 'The best thing would be for you all to go home — this is going to go on for days.'

———

Later, Lowetz remembered that it took several seconds for those present to locate the source of the commotion that followed. Heads swivelled helplessly, trying to work out where the screaming was coming from. Infants put a lot of effort into learning how to do it, but even later on, especially outdoors, people don't find it at all easy to localise a sound. And so they turn this way and that, searching, like a beetle that has reached the end of a blade of grass. The spectacle, and the time it takes them, are almost comical; fascinating to consider that most animals can't afford to be this incompetent. In this instance, it was a character familiar to Darkenbloomers, rather disagreeably so, who was thrashing a dishevelled stranger down the mountain towards the valley.

Heuraffl wasn't calling for the police as he thrashed the stranger down the hill, just loudly threatening to do so. Mostly he was ranting, in a coarse and primitive way: about the times they were living in, politicians, and how you had to do everything yourself because no one was going to help you, it was all up to you, things that, by rights, the government, and the police, *all those fucking bigwigs who don't know where their loyalties lie any more ... get on with it, you piece of shit, keep moving!* Yet he seemed completely unaware of how the man he had effectively apprehended was reacting. And so Lowetz and the others watched a man stumble down the slope, trying repeatedly to raise his hands but having to lower them again so as not to lose his balance, or in order to catch himself when he fell to the ground because he was being pushed and kicked from behind. A bearded stranger, who kept trying to turn and gesture to his tormentor, to protest that he would go with him of his own accord and not attempt to flee. But Heuraffl went on pushing and kicking like a man possessed, and when his victim stumbled, he stood over him and grabbed his shirt, dragged him back onto his feet and pushed him on. Perhaps, contrary to what one might think from his heedless thrashing, Heuraffl was in fact acutely aware of his audience, and had dialled things up a notch, because a person who shoved and yelled this much was also letting people know what a spectacular catch he had made. Or perhaps he was trying to suggest that he was particularly afraid of this other man, to justify his behaviour?

The other Heuraffl twin broke away from the crowd of onlookers and charged towards his brother. At the same time, the mayor started shouting at the two gendarmes: Leonhard, Gerald, go on, go on, what are you waiting for? Until then, they had merely straightened up and taken a few steps away from the now-secured site, like sleepwalkers, uncertain what to do. However, as soon as one Heuraffl reached the other, there was no longer any ambiguity about the situation. Two Heuraffls were beating up a third man, mindlessly, senselessly, and, above all, for no apparent reason. And so the gendarmes reluctantly intervened, taking charge of the stranger and holding him by the upper arms, left and right, which they might have been better off doing with the first Heuraffl. But they knew him, didn't they? And they didn't know the stranger.

Heuraffl had caught the man unawares in the Heuraffl hunting cabin. The man had clearly been living there for several days; he had helped himself to the supplies of biscuits, jam, schnapps, and water, although he seemed to be a good sort, and the schnapps did not appear to have been his main priority.

'Do you understand German?' asked Koreny.

'Aye,' said the man, smiling anxiously.

The Darkenbloomers exchanged glances. They realised, though, that he was indeed speaking some sort of German, albeit with a very peculiar accent, as if the vowels were getting lost at the back of his mouth, between throat and nose. He hauled them up somehow, the sounds, up out of the throat, but they didn't emerge properly, though it didn't feel as if he were swallowing them.

The surprising thing was that he vehemently refused to be taken to the capital, where, as Koreny assured him, buses and trains were leaving for West Germany: no problem, tomorrow or the next day you can easily be in Nuremberg or Giessen. Instead, he begged in his strange dialect to be allowed to stay, because he had lost his wife and daughter as they were fleeing across the border. They must still be in the forest, he said, perhaps they had turned back and would come as soon as they got another chance. But they would definitely try to cross where they had lost each other, just as they would expect him to stay close by. 'That's what you do when you lose each other,' he said unhappily. 'I can work,' he said, holding out his hands for Koreny to inspect, 'I'll pay it all back later, please just let me stay.'

'Load o' bollocks,' growled the Heuraffl who had found him.

The bearded stranger looked around imploringly.

'There'll be more like him soon, you mark my words,' said another man, eyeing the forest suspiciously. The stranger protested that he would get out as soon as he had news of his family. He pleaded with the Heuraffl — imagine, wife and daughter, Silke only sixteen — but his captor just shook his head belligerently.

Lowetz had been standing further back, craning his neck and trying to hear everything. Out of nowhere, Flocke's father appeared; he stepped forward and put his hand on the stranger's shoulder, pushing aside one of the gendarmes, who was happy to let go. 'So,' said Toni Malnitz, 'as it's clear no serious crime has been committed ...'

'What about my cabin?' asked Heuraffl. 'And my supplies?'

Malnitz grinned and slowly reached towards his back pocket, where men generally kept their wallets.

'Seriously?' said Flocke loudly, suddenly appearing beside her father.

A staring match ensued between the two Malnitzes and the Heuraffls.

'Go fuck yerselves, the lot o' you,' said the first Heuraffl at last, and turned away.

A gap opened up in front of Lowetz; those who had sided with the Heuraffls, or had satisfied their need for Sunday entertainment, were beating a retreat. And so he stepped forward, towards Flocke, her father, and the awkward refugee. The marmot-like mayor was red-faced and sweating. 'What is it now?' he asked Lowetz, holding his pleading hands in front of his stomach and apparently struggling to keep his composure.

'I just wanted to say, I've got an empty room,' said Lowetz.

16.

BACK HOME, LOWETZ WASN'T immediately sure what to do. The
bearded refugee, whose name was Reinhold, had been taken by
Flocke's father to make a phone call. When Flocke had dropped
Lowetz off in front of his house, she had said, 'See you later.'

First of all, he checked his old room, and found it tidy. He put
fresh sheets on the bed, and closed the door as firmly as if the guest
were already in there and tired. Then he remembered an old rug he
had noticed in the attic that morning, fetched it, and spread it out
in front of the shed, in the courtyard, which was what his parents
had called this little area enclosed by walls overgrown with greenery.
You could turn this into a garden, he thought; and also: that this
sort of terminology was a measure of the distance between the big
city and Darkenbloom. Darkenbloomers, those who lived in the old
town centre, at least, had no use for ornamental gardens. To them,
everything was a courtyard, a vegetable patch, or a vineyard. These
last lay outside the town. Flower gardens were for pretentious poshos.

Lowetz brought out cushions from the paternal daybed, a tray
with glasses, and an ashtray. The stiffer stalks of rampant grass were
slow to surrender. At first he hovered a foot above the ground,
undulating, as if on a flying carpet coming in to land. He rolled from

side to side a few times, like a dog or cow. And then he was lying in the green terrarium, in a madly stippled, softly blinking mosaic of light and shade. No one but Fritz and Flocke would find him. He shouldn't have emerged from his lair, certainly not to go up to the Rotenstein meadow. Grubbing in the dirt, poking around in graves! It wasn't good for you. *You don't want to get involved in anything, not after all we've lived through, on the border.* Who had said that? Another saying from the old days. But something had happened up there — a vague memory kept drifting through his mind, something he couldn't put his finger on. Rotenstein meadow. End of the war, probably. Had his father told him about it? On the other hand, stuff had happened everywhere around here, at the end of the war and before and after it and a hundred years ago, as well. And stuff will happen here in a hundred years' time, too, thought Lowetz, rolling luxuriously onto his side, his face in a hot patch of sun, when they tell each other how, one sunny August Sunday, they dug up Europe's first *Australopithecus*, overturning all previous scientific assumptions, or some hitherto unknown subspecies of *Homo sapiens. Homo darkenbloomiensis*, perhaps, as established by subsequent studies — a remarkable creature: social, musically gifted, able to walk on its hands and wag its curly blond tail, living in peaceful, vegetarian, matriarchal hordes. Completely unknown until then, and undoubtedly unique in the history of humanity. Became extinct at the first breath of an Ice Age, or the first onslaught of common club-swinging thugs, because it didn't have the right characteristics. Since then, *robustus* has been the dominant species here; only, occasionally, very seldom, by improbable genetic fluke, a delicate, captivating *darkenbloomiensis* mendelizes through, a distant descendant of the singing beauties of yore who danced upon their hands. Flocke? Outwardly, yes, with her elfin appearance — though probably too psychologically forceful. Reinhold could be one, the way he had brushed away a tear as he got into Toni Malnitz's hulking BMW. Although most people would probably brush away a tear after getting the Heuraffl treatment. And as he was from faraway Saxony, Reinhold had to be ruled out on the basis of geography. The Heuraffl twins, on the other hand: indubitably *Robustus robustus*, with a hefty dash of Neanderthal. Lowetz laughed and opened his eyes. Flocke was kneeling in front of him, with the expression of someone who is concentrating very hard on sneaking up, to ... do what?

'You gave me a fright,' Lowetz lied.

'You're making fun of me,' said Flocke.

'A bit,' Lowetz lied.

Flocke laid a book on his chest. 'Look — it's your mother's.'

'So it is,' said Lowetz, holding it up in front of his face. 'I remember this.'

Traditional Tales of Darkenbloom, the cover taped together in several places. He knew the handwritten inscription on the front page without opening it: *Eszter Lowetz, sötét virág, 1944.*

'She used to read this to me when I was little,' said Lowetz.

'Me too,' said Flocke.

'What do you mean, you too?' asked Lowetz.

'Do you really not remember me?' asked Flocke. 'How often I was here, with your mother, because mine never had the time? That's not very nice.'

A skinny girl sitting with his mother in the kitchen and lowering her eyes on the rare occasions he showed his face at home. If anyone else had asked him, he would have supposed it was several different girls over the years; it was possible that all the nice little girls of Darkenbloom would sit in his mother's kitchen at some point and help with the cooking and baking. Most of them, anyway. And in exchange, she would read to them.

'Dog gloves,' she said, reflectively. 'Dog-leather gloves. Once a year, that was the agreement.'

'Even if the knacker man sometimes didn't have enough leather,' he continued, 'he still had to provide the gloves.'

'Didn't have enough *fine* leather,' she corrected him.

'"The Count and the Knacker Man" — that was my favourite story,' he said. 'In the end the knacker man executed the count, instead of the passing traveller who'd been condemned to death.'

'It doesn't actually say so,' she contradicted him. 'I think the count was snatched away by the Devil.'

'Because he didn't send the condemned man his supper,' said Lowetz, nodding. 'Although I never understood why the knacker man didn't just take him the meal himself.'

'Because those are the rules,' Flocke explained. 'The count lays down the law; he has the power of life and death, but, like every judge, he must be benevolent and detached. By granting the condemned their last meal, by treating everyone the same, he shows that it's not about personal vengeance, he's just performing a role. Probably standing in for God. That's why every condemned person must receive a last meal.'

'I thought he just forgot,' said Lowetz.

'He forgot because he was vain,' she said. 'That's precisely the point. His own status, his furs and the beautiful furnishings in the castle, arranging the best possible marriage for his daughter, perhaps the dog-leather gloves as well — all that was more important to him than the law.'

She looked at her fingers and said, 'I've never owned a pair of leather gloves.'

'Because of that story?' asked Lowetz. She didn't answer.

'She must have read it to me very often,' he said. 'It stuck in my mind, anyway.'

'I think she used this to learn German,' said Flocke, who was kneeling beside him and leafing through the book.

'She could already speak it a bit,' murmured Lowetz. 'Back then, everyone spoke both.' He wondered whether he could tug Flocke's wrist to get her to lie down beside him in the sun. Whether perhaps the rug smelled a tiny bit, of age and neglect, associations he definitely didn't want. And whether in fact she smoked.

Meanwhile, she seemed to have become wholly absorbed in her reading. Lowetz sensed that she was suddenly out of reach. You could hear it in someone's breathing when they were completely distracted. Lowetz closed his eyes again and considered. When it happened, it was as if a hood had been slipped over their head, or rather: they were dragged away, away from you. What could it be? She was sure to tell him in a minute. He was already familiar with her urgent undertone.

'Did she write translations next to the words?' he asked finally. 'Or have you found something else?'

She closed the book and looked at him. 'Do you remember the story about the barren field?'

'I think so,' he said. 'With the youngest daughter, and the field full of Christmas roses at the end? That blossomed on Christmas Day?'

'Tell me,' she demanded.

'Oh, come on,' he protested. 'Something edifying, like in the Bible, with a miserly farmer and his field where nothing grows, and only when the youngest daughter gives a poor pedlar a piece of bread behind her parents' backs ... Hey, is it possible that the knacker man story was by far the most sophisticated? Morally, I mean? Maybe that's why we remember it so clearly?'

'Why did nothing grow in the field?' Flocke insisted, and reached, to his relief, for the packet of cigarettes. 'Think — do you remember?'

'Give me one, too,' he said.

'He had a lot of fields,' she prompted him, adopting the fairy-tale narrative voice, 'he had a great many fields, the big farmer, but in one of them nothing good would grow, even though he tried everything. The first year he planted barley, the second he planted hemp, the third potatoes, but nothing would grow, and the people said ...'

'And the people said, a hunchbacked dog is buried there,' Lowetz finished.

Flocke looked at him and nodded slowly.

He sat up and stroked her arm in what he hoped was a friendly way.

'So you never read it yourself, either,' she said.

'No idea,' he said. 'Probably not. Why?'

'Because it says here ...' She picked up the book again, opened it first, he noticed, at the contents page, leafed through, then held it out to him. 'Read it yourself.'

Lowetz looked at the sentence she was pointing at. He read aloud: '"And the people said a hunchbacked Jew was buried there."'

'I see,' he said. He closed the book and lay back again.

She finally lay down beside him.

'So my mother read to us from a Nazi book,' he said, finally.

'You probably can't really say that, either,' said Flocke.

'Why not?' asked Lowetz.

Flocke rolled onto her side and propped herself up on her elbow. She mimicked the style of the book, with an ironic tone: 'And the people said, every text must be understood in the context of its time ... The book is probably much older than that, from the turn of the century. And when Eszter read it aloud, she adapted it.'

They smoked, and said nothing.

'When you're a child, you don't wonder about anything,' she said, after a while. 'Not even what a hunchbacked dog might actually be.'

'Probably one you're better off making into gloves,' said Lowetz.

'You really are heartless,' she said. But she laughed.

Soon after that, she left. Something had occurred to her; she mentioned a strange-sounding name, and again her face had that knot of concentration at the bridge of her nose, just above her eyebrows. Lowetz assumed she meant the tourist, Darkenbloom's only long-term visitor, who had recently bought up the whole stack of castle postcards at Uncle Grün's so not a single one was left. But he only wanted to send four for now ... Hadn't he been looking for graves of some sort? Perhaps there was a connection with the Rotenstein meadow? Was it possible that Young Graun had found what that man was looking for? One thing led to another.

The sun was shining, and it was quiet in Fritz's workshop. On Sunday afternoons Fritz would sometimes sing loudly, mostly Beatles songs, clearly identifiable by the melody. You could not have identified them by the lyrics; only the As and Os were in more or less the right place. He would have liked to have listened with Flocke to Fritz's melodic roaring. Perhaps they would have hummed along. He liked Flocke. He really liked her, and it pleased him that every time she said goodbye she said *See you later*. Twice so far, in one day. That seemed to him to mean something; it sounded conspiratorial, suggestive, because they were hardly likely to see each other again today. Tomorrow, though, for sure.

He now shared with his mother, in addition to half his genetic code, these feelings for Flocke. Perhaps his mother had had a trace of *darkenbloomiensis* in her? It was very painful to think about her. So painful that he tried just to steal sideways glances at her in his mind, at specific, clearly delimited parts of her. Strong, prominently veined hands. The long grey plait, and how until a few years ago she had worn her hair loose. It had looked a bit witch-like. Had he told her that? Was that why she had stopped?

He never wanted to wonder about anything — it was one of his principles in life. Wondering about something meant you hadn't looked closely enough, you hadn't got the itemised bill. Wondering was one step below surprise, and surprises should be given a very wide berth. Except in childhood, they are almost never good. He had seen the separation from Simone coming: he didn't wonder about it when it was articulated, even though it hurt. And so it was probably normal that he was missing his mother as never before, while also having lost all sense of who she had been. He had shown an ostentatious lack of interest. He didn't know the first thing about her life in the past fifteen years — what she thought, what she was interested in, what she was like with others. So it was no wonder that he was wondering. There were so many things that he had inexcusably overlooked. If he was wondering now, it was his own fault.

Unsure what to do, he took the book of folk tales into the house and considered where to put it. The bookcase was no longer there; he stood in the living room and looked around. For a moment he thought of putting the pretty old book in the newly created guest room, but then the hunchbacked Jew and the field of Christmas roses reappeared in his mind's eye. Reinhold from Saxony had already made sufficient acquaintance with Darkenbloom's particular charm — he ought to be spared this. Lowetz put the book on the kitchen table. It felt like a contaminated object now. You couldn't even give it away, certainly not to someone with children. Then it occurred to him that he could take it to Rehberg at the travel agency. The hobby historian. There's a thought! He almost regretted that he couldn't tell Flocke at once. Already he pictured the old book lying on felt beneath a heavy glass cover, in the kind of display case no Darkenbloom museum would ever be able to afford, unless the Countess were to bequeath them part of her fortune. An amusing idea, though. The old book could only be put to educational use now, as a cautionary example, notwithstanding all the clever knacker men and counts dragged off to Hell. The book essentially resembled the tales it claimed to tell, because it concealed, and only very superficially, something terrible. *And the people said a hunchbacked Jew was buried there.*

17.

OLD FRAU RESCHEN CLOSED the bar at half past ten, after the last drinkers had staggered out. The few hotel guests were in their rooms, which was as it should be — none of their keys were hanging on the board, at any rate. Zenzi had been sent home at seven. Sundays were usually quiet, but the drama had driven more people than usual into the bar. Frau Reschen herself had not been up to the Rotenstein meadow; she had no need of that. She didn't have to go anywhere to find things out, because everything that happened in Darkenbloom found its way back to her. She kept it all quietly shut away; most things were still stored in her memory, even things from very long ago.

But just because treasure disappears into a mountain, there is no guarantee that it will ever re-emerge. The town's stories sedimented in old Frau Reschen as if in an inaccessible mine. What she absorbed remained inside, where it grew shiny and easy to handle, and from time to time she would contemplate it at her leisure. If someone asked too many questions, as sometimes happened, she would say, with her servile, crooked expression: *I don't get to leave the hotel, not ever, day or night.*

Frau Reschen's entire life had consisted of work. It would never have occurred to her that it could be otherwise. Perhaps that was why she remembered anything unusual — certain facial expressions and conversations — so clearly: because the rest was a sea of monotony, of sweeping, scrubbing, bending, wiping. So many brothers and sisters at home; she herself born and growing up somewhere in the middle; the big ones looked after the little ones, and as soon as a child was able, it had to join the others in the fields. Apprenticed at fourteen — the great coup of her life. At home, they hadn't even known she had applied. A Hotel Tüffer apprentice — for a girl like her, it was more a question of luck than judgement. She had been convinced that pretty Veronika would get the post. She had only heard about the interview because of her. The young gentleman had issued the invitation; he was very taken with Vroni, who didn't want to go alone, and brought Resi with her. And so two red-faced girls stood in reception. The gentleman seemed surprised, and eventually old Frau Tüffer was summoned. Young Herr Tüffer being so taken with her was no good to Vroni then, but her affected manners in those days may not have helped her, either. She had been teaching Resi on the way there: *By all means, gracious madam; at your service, kind sir.*

But old Frau Tüffer had picked Resi, without hesitation, and said to her son: 'That's a good girl, Wilhelm, you hear me, a good girl!' Wilhelm Tüffer twisted his mouth right over to one side of his face, whereupon the opposite nostril closed vertically, like a camel's, and replied: 'Whatever you say, Mamá.'

Vroni was sent home, and from then on young Herr Tüffer acted as if he had never known her, and only had eyes for Resi. She received her apron dress and her initial instructions from Frau Tüffer. Six years later — by which time she was already filling in on reception and sometimes even doing the weekly planning for the kitchen — she had to help Frau Tüffer with all the packing. And suddenly she was handed the big bunch of keys, with all the keys on it, to everything. Old Frau Tüffer had never let it out of her hands. 'Take good care of it, Resi,' she said. 'I'm relying on you.'

Soon the Tüffers were gone, young and old, with their clothes and hats and coats and boots, and God knows what would have happened if Resi hadn't got in with Josef Graun and his friends early on. But those young, ambitious lads, Graun, Neulag, Stipsits, and Ferbenz, sat in the bar every evening and laughed with her and called her *Boss*. Resi kept on the honest employees, and brought in two of her younger sisters. She had always been good at sums, which was lucky, and so somehow everything carried on, though the hotel was soon a very different place. Other guests started coming, a lot of them, in fact, those first few summers, though they weren't necessarily more pleasant than the ones she had come to know as an apprentice. But there were so many of them that she was even able to put a bit of money aside before it all abruptly ended.

She stood at her bedroom window, from which she could see a bit of the castle tower with its two ridiculous extensions, the low walls to left and right. They should never have built those little wings, or else they should have torn them straight back down again. If they had built directly onto the tower, incorporated it into some sort of new frontage, it wouldn't have been so conspicuous. It wouldn't just stand there like a monument. After the war, though, everyone who could afford it wanted a detached house, because they considered it a luxury to be able to keep their distance from their neighbours. They had never had that before; in the preceding years they had all lived huddled close together, closer than was comfortable for some. And old Frau Reschen clearly remembered how Horka — who, after being a big Nazi, was suddenly the Russian officers' trusted representative — had sold large parts of the site on the Countess's behalf, at a high price, to those who still had money for large, detached commercial buildings. That was where they realised their economic-miracle dreams: Wallnöfer with his car dealership, Balf with his estate agency, Berneck with the insurance company, and Stipsits with that enormous pharmacy, which he'd had to downsize later on, making room for a hairdresser from Slovenia.

The castle had been gone such a long time now, but since these postcards had started appearing everywhere, it was vividly present in her mind. She hadn't seen it burn; she had been in the forest, with her brothers and sisters. But the blackened ruins, which remained standing until the Countess gave permission from afar for them to be demolished, were a shocking counterpart to the state in which she had seen it just days earlier: the building like a radiant bride, its arms, its gates wide open, illuminated, decorated, music and dancing. They had been toiling away down in the kitchen, all the women Resi had been able to drum up when the Countess gave the order, but they too, right down to the last dish-washer, were suffused with the splendour of the evening, from which they might have guessed that it would be the last for a very long time. They hadn't known. They hadn't thought about it; they had just hoped for a miracle, for the miracle weapons to work. They had trusted in God; that, at least, wasn't wrong. Already they could hear the rumble of the cannons at the front. Who knows, perhaps that was even what had prompted Neulag to throw another party.

Old Frau Reschen lay down on the bed, in her long linen nightdress. People around here had worn nightdresses like this for generations; they used to be made of fustian. She wouldn't have known what else to wear in bed, although she had pictures in her head of these nightdresses that never should have been there. The nightdresses of Agnes Kalmar and the Stipsits girls, one of whom didn't come back. Dragged out into the street like pale ghosts; dirt, mud, vodka, blood. Nightdresses lying abandoned in the forest.

She already had Reschen by then; ten years older than her, and minus an arm. That was why he wasn't shot or arrested. 'You've got it,' he told the Soviet officers, once they knew each other better, 'I left my arm with you!' And they all drank to that.

Reschen had pounced on her, as the Russians did the others later on. He was half crazed at first — because of the front, and the pain in his missing arm — but once he had what he needed, things got better. It was a piece of luck, really; for her, it was just the one, just him. And Reschen was always able to get hold of whatever they needed. He hadn't waited for the Russians to come and take away the hotel; he had gone and offered it to them. There were those who said he had gone over to the enemy ten days earlier, when the Russians took Darkenbloom the first time. That he had laid out everything to them clearly then: the cripple who had been a mid-ranking SS officer and now wanted to be a hotel manager, as if in compensation for the arm. Resi, however — who became his wife, and, apart from those first brutal hours and days, eventually came round to it — secretly thought it didn't make a whole lot of difference whether you came to an arrangement with the Russians straight away, or not until ten days later, when the Germans had long since lost.

Asleep, she fell, as she often had lately, deep into a ramified network of caves. The fall lasted so long that she had time to overcome her fear and tell herself that she wouldn't feel the impact. Consequently, after a few moments that may also have been minutes, the fall became almost pleasant, a headlong freefall that couldn't be stopped and would end in painless, instantaneous death. But as before, she just landed and found herself in that first, dark, labyrinthine cave. She didn't know where the exit was. She groped her way forward, opening heavy doors with swan-neck handles, like the ones they'd had in the castle. At some point she turned because she heard something behind her, and a hideous face, far bigger than a human's, grinned back at her. It was Horka, his face as big as a balloon. She screamed, and woke up.

She lay in bed, listening. She thought she had heard herself scream. Outside, all was quiet. The cave in her dream looked a little like the stables underneath the castle, where the forced labourers had been housed, back then. It seemed to her that she had had this dream many times. But the ending was wrong, because it had not in fact been Horka but her former fiancé, Josef Graun, who had been standing, quite unexpectedly, behind a door, laughing like the Devil himself.

Six months earlier, in the last autumn of the war, when the construction of the Wall was at its peak, Josef had suddenly disappeared. There were no more weekend visits; he stopped coming back from Styria, where he was stationed, to see her. He showed up only once, at the back door, in the middle of the night; she could still hear the knocking. He refused to come in, just stood there on the doorstep telling her about problems, about Ferbenz, about Neulag, and about having to report something to the police.

'Remember, Resi,' he said, 'if they nab me, it wasn't me — it was the others! I don't cheat people, and I don't line my own pockets. If we lose the war, it's the fault of people like that. Heil Hitler.'

She hadn't understood much; she stood at the back door in her nightdress, and when they parted he shook her hand, as if they were two men sealing a contract. She was afraid she would never see him again. Those were terrible times. Of course she would have waited. She was really fond of Josef Graun. But a few weeks later, as she was about to bolt the front door, someone leapt out of the shadows, flung themselves against the door, grabbed her, yanked her hair, and threw her on the ground. This was Reschen. He knelt on top of her, with both legs, and locked the door from the inside, even though he only had one arm. Afterwards, he didn't run away; he went and lay down in her bed, and simply stayed.

She didn't see Josef again until the end of March, at that party at the castle. After midnight, the serving girls told her there was something going on upstairs. A group of people were leaving the ballroom. They heard them come down the big staircase making a lot of noise. Resi peeked out from behind the kitchen door, indulging a curiosity she would not have permitted in her girls. At precisely that moment, a door directly opposite flew open; behind it was a table full of guns, lined up as if in a shop window, and him, Graun, standing there; he raised his head, saw her, and started to laugh like the Devil. It was only much later that she realised why she had started to shake and had retreated back into the kitchen. She must have thought they were going to shoot Graun here, in the room directly opposite the main kitchen. That that was why they were coming downstairs; that he had accepted his fate, and had laid out the guns in a row for them. Given the situation at the time, it was not an unreasonable assumption. And when that wasn't what happened, relief initially blocked out everything else.

The knocking continued, not just in her memory. Someone was calling softly: 'Resi, Frau Reschen, are you still awake?' She gave a start, and got out of bed. She opened the window. Someone was standing down below.

'What is it?' she asked, suspiciously.

'It's Toni,' said Malnitz. 'I need to speak to your guest, urgently.'

'At this time?' asked Resi. 'It's after midnight!'

'It's important, Resi, open the door!'

'I'm sure it can wait till morning,' said Resi, and was about to close the window when she heard a voice from the balcony above her.

'It's all right, Frau Reschen,' said the guest from Room 7. 'Would you be so kind as to unlock the front door for me?'

What choice did she have?

And then the three of them were standing downstairs together in the dark, just because Toni Malnitz's daughter had taken off somewhere.

'She was going to see you this evening,' he said, agitated, to the man from Room 7. 'What did she want?'

'To talk about the find in the Rotenstein meadow,' said the guest. 'She asked me if I had any information about it.'

'Was that it?' asked Toni Malnitz, sounding strained. 'Just the old stories? And she didn't say where she was going?'

'No, I'm sorry,' said the guest.

'What's all the fuss about?' asked old Frau Reschen grumpily. 'What's going to happen to a young girl nowadays? She's just gone off to see friends.'

'She's never done that,' said Toni Malnitz. 'It's not like her at all. Someone set fire to our barn just a few days ago ... She doesn't just have friends in this town, Resi, you know that.'

'Because she's digging around in old stories, like a few others I could mention,' said Frau Reschen.

Toni Malnitz, who was tossing his car key in his hand, snorted, turned abruptly on his heel, and left. 'Thank you, sir, very much indeed,' he said, over his shoulder. 'I'll just keep looking for now.'

Resi Reschen, in her long nightdress, looked at her guest, who had been staying in her nicest room for fourteen days, though all he had arrived with was a small leather bag; one might well start to wonder what exactly he did all day. Because he had something to do with it as well, she realised suddenly, with some sort of investigation. We often pay the least attention to what is right under our nose. He went around town cross-questioning people, he had visited the third cemetery several times, and had hiked to the top of the Hazug with the Malnitz girl.

'Frau Reschen, I would like to show you something,' he said. 'If you would please follow me to my room.'

'At your service, sir,' she murmured.

His bed was still made, and on it was a large, open cardboard box. A few days ago he had received a parcel that was very light, at least in relation to its size. Numerous smaller containers now lay scattered on the floor, also pale brown, as if the big box had reproduced. The guest handed her one. She took it reluctantly, thinking: The things we have to put up with from our guests. To her surprise, the little carton was made of wood, very thin and delicate and light, with a lid, carefully constructed to fit, that you could just lift off. She eased it up with her fingernail. It was empty; there was nothing inside. She peered into the pale emptiness, which smelled faintly of wood, a whiff of sawdust, perhaps. And was suddenly filled with horror.

'When we find them, they'll be laid to rest in these,' said the guest, and his sententious tone made her want to smack him.

Frau Reschen handed back the little carton, which was about twice the size of a shoebox. 'I'm afraid I've no idea what this is about,' she said, with her crooked, servile expression.

But then — later she was almost convinced she had dreamed this, too, in her unsettling, recurring cave dream — the guest abruptly dropped the formal form of address, and spoke to her as if he knew her well.

'Come now, Resi,' he said. 'I don't believe you don't know exactly what this is about. And do you really not recognise me?'

'I don't get to leave the hotel, not ever, day or night,' answered old Frau Reschen, and turned away.

PART II

Here, too, people are used to dying; more so,
at any rate, than they are to thinking.

HANS LEBERT

I.

THAT NIGHT, SHORTLY AFTER half past one, there was a thunderstorm, the like of which had not been seen in those parts for a very long time. Many Darkenbloomers were shaken from their slumbers, people who, over the following days, repeatedly assured each other that they usually slept soundly, the sleep of the righteous. That night, though, they were woken by the thunder banging all its instruments at once, cymbals, drums, timpani, maracas, raging above the town as if trying to smash heaven and earth to pieces. Even the hardest of hearing were driven from their beds by flashes of lightning that followed so fast on one another's heels that the blackness between them flickered discreetly rather than the other way round. Everywhere people stood at their windows, looking out; they couldn't see each other, but perhaps some guessed that they were not in fact alone, they just happened to be apart. It was the first time in a long while that so many Darkenbloomers were simultaneously inactive and attentive, the opposite of their usual behaviour. *There was always so much to do, we couldn't pay attention to that ...* If God or the Devil had lifted the roofs of the houses, they could have stroked a lot of heads. But they didn't need to; they already knew.

There wasn't even anything to see outside, only a natural spectacle.

Unstoppable discharges of physical energy. Nature was pulling out all the stops to try to get itself noticed; that night was a prime example. People had built themselves solid dwellings, yet there were moments when they couldn't help doubting their painstaking little creations. Perhaps the storm wants to clarify something, thought the guest in Room 7, who had a good view of it through the balcony doors. He wondered why he had got up. Why it hadn't been enough for him to lie in bed listening to the thunder. But this storm was unusual; it was so loud, as if it demanded to be admired as it danced its hellish dance.

And so there were several pairs of eyes watching over every street and every courtyard, not to mention the market square, where six streets converged before braking deferentially and flowing into one another in front of the plague column and the castle tower. If someone — although this was quite inconceivable — had run through Darkenbloom at this hour, no matter how furtive he was, zigzagging along and hugging the walls, he would still have been seen. By many people.

In the midst of this inferno the white tower stood like a knight, overexposed by lightning, the last defender left standing. Only this great structure was acceptably in proportion to the forces raging around it. The stubby wings at its base made it look as if it were pleading for this to stop. It did not stand tall and proud; rather, it seemed to be kneeling, terribly alone in the halo of lightning. And if anyone had looked closely they would have seen the castle shimmering around it, materialising through the ugly post-war buildings like a phantom in the electrically charged air.

In their cheap bed-and-breakfast, the students from the city were thinking of the cemetery jungle, and how all the overgrown vegetation they had painstakingly cleared away and piled up to one side would be blown back over the graves. And that the brambles they had already hacked down would get even more tangled and dig in their claws, like barbed wire. Martha, the girl with the halo of tight black curls who was documenting the work with her video camera, held the little root manikin Fritz had carved for her, and turned it over in her hands. It looked like her, and like the atmosphere in this town. The root manikin was her ally, and it was not afraid.

Dimwitted Zenzi, with her penchant for horror stories, was not standing at the window, but lay quaking in her bed. She thought of the huge Tüffer family mausoleum, and imagined a bolt of lightning smashing through the stone roof and all that lay beneath. Lying there, staring at bedclothes illuminated by flashes of lightning, she inevitably pictured clichéd, white-clad forms rising slowly into the air. And where would they head for, once they had escaped their marble prison? For the place they used to call home. Zenzi had not asked the manageress about the tomb, had not asked why the name of the hotel featured so prominently in the third cemetery; her instinct had advised her not to, and her instinct, at least, was pretty good.

Berneck stood at the window in sweaty pyjamas and cursed the work he would be saddled with after this night. Storm damage, lightning damage, flooded cellars, failed harvests if it hailed as well; evaluations, phone calls, form-filling. A paper war on multiple fronts from now until Christmas. And just a few days ago that old barn in Ehrenfeld had burned down without the aid of lightning. If it had gone up in flames tonight, no one would have been surprised. But what seemed to be coming together here was a typical cluster of improbabilities, something everyone in insurance was familiar with and about which they all kept silent. Their profession was founded on probabilities. Everything was mathematics, but mathematicians in particular often had a penchant for religion or the esoteric, and with good reason. It was well known that if one plane crashed, another would fall from the sky shortly afterwards. It was always like that. The same was true of earthquakes and other natural disasters. One happened, then, shortly afterwards, a second. Unlike with acts of violence, you couldn't argue that there was a copycat effect. I don't believe it, people would say in dismay, and the insurers would reassure them that it was just coincidence, *because about the same number of good things happen as bad, overall*, they would say, with an artificial laugh. This was what they learned during their training. But they knew better. There were clusters, and then there were long periods of calm. But if you noticed that nothing had happened for a long time, and began to steel yourself for an event, it was highly likely that nothing would continue to happen. It tricked you; it led you up the garden path. Who? Who was *it*? Berneck would have liked to know this, too, but he believed in neither God nor Fate. *That's just the way it is*, he would have growled, if he had ever talked to anyone about it. And now there was this barn. A piece of land belonging to Frau Leonore's family, location as attractive as the woman herself, elevated, panoramic view, but much too close, of course, as in: right on the border. *You'll be the first to be shot up there when it all kicks off again* — those were the sort of comments you heard in this region. So she had never done anything with the land, even though she was such a shrewd businesswoman. She'd just left it standing, that ancient barn; apparently it had been so dry that it was pale grey, like an old elephant. Unlike the owner — she was taking her sweet time over the ageing and drying up. Berneck smacked his lips. 'Come back to bed,' called the old woman behind him. He pretended not to hear. He should have recognised the fire in the barn as a sign, because there'd been nothing significant for a long time before that. But that wasn't how it worked. Omens were usually innocuous; it was only with hindsight that they revealed themselves. What sort of a claim was it, anyway? A disused barn, a patch of uncultivated land overgrown with weeds. But those crazy Malnitzes had reported it as arson — on a thirty-year-old wooden shack! Unbelievable. Well, what do you expect of people who put a bathtub in the middle of the room. True, it was an unfortunate coincidence that the volunteer fire brigade had been having a party that night just three kilometres away. Anyway, he didn't have to worry about it, because the insurers didn't get involved as long as the police were still investigating. But that bloody barn had been the omen of tonight's storm, which was going to create an endless amount of work for him.

After several hours of keeping herself mindlessly busy, Leonore Malnitz took it into her head to lug Toni's leather armchair out of the living room, up one floor and down two long corridors to her bedroom. Prior to this, she had preserved several crates of fruit, then cleaned every square centimetre of the kitchen, including the oven, the icebox, and the cutlery drawer. Preserving jars were standing upside down all around, cooling off, but now there really was nothing else for her to do. She ought to go to bed, but there was no one to tell her to do so. She had cut short the last few phone calls from her elder daughters, saying she had to keep an eye on the saucepans of jam. It hadn't even been difficult for her to be the calm and sensible one (*let's just wait and see for now*), because she had never shown fear in front of the children. She considered this her maternal duty. And she still kept it up, even though the children now had children of their own. She hoped they did the same.

Toni was out in the car; the preserving jars were his. She didn't know where he was or when he would be back — probably not until it got light, knowing him. After that, others would be able to find her; in the darkness, though, he imagined only he could do it. He called Leonore every now and then, and they kept repeating the same four-word conversation:

'Anything new?'

'No.'

'Okay.'

And hang up. The line had to be kept free, just in case.

It wasn't a problem getting the armchair out of the living room and as far as the stairs. She knew that, up to a point, women could compensate for their lack of strength with a bit of careful thought. So she slid a small runner under its thick little feet and dragged its dead weight up to the half landing. There was only one way she could get it up there on her own: by tying a rope around it and pulling it up step by step. She knew what that meant: for a while she would be lashed to this piece of furniture, in a precarious position. She wouldn't be able to run to the phone if it rang, and if her strength failed her, she would have to either wait helplessly or let the thing thunder back downstairs, with ruinous consequences for walls and floor. But that was precisely the point: for her to do something that was actually too hard, that would take some time and require all her concentration.

She found several lashing straps in Toni's garage and brought them all into the house. She decided to tie them around the armchair in two big loops, and cross them over so she could slip into the ends as into the straps of a rucksack. This would make it easier to tip the armchair up onto the next step, as she would have to do; she congratulated herself on the idea. If she didn't manage it straight away, she could undo one of the belts and tie the load to the banister for a little while, which was a reassuring way out.

It wasn't nearly as bad as she had expected. She was sweaty and dishevelled by the end, but proud of herself, too. In less than a quarter of an hour she had got the leather monster upstairs. She dragged it along the corridor and into her bedroom without even glancing at the bed, because what you don't see isn't really there. She pulled the armchair right up to the window, where the first bolts of lightning were zigzagging across the sky. In that moment, she was terrified — two of her loved ones were out there — but a moment later she had accepted it as if she had been anticipating it for a long time, as if this evening could only ever have been expected to bring the worst. With a blanket on her knees, she sat in the heavy, soft leather seat that had once belonged to her father. Thunderclaps dropped on Darkenbloom like bombs, and Leonore tucked her legs underneath her. It began to pour with rain; within seconds the gutters were overflowing. She had a clear view of a corner of the roof where water was sloshing over the edge in waves and plunging down into the night. She stared at the water gushing out as if a full vase had been placed under a running tap. She wondered whether this was the water from the top, whether it was just being washed straight out again, or whether the influx pushed water from the bottom to the top, so that every molecule of water had been everywhere, top and bottom. Whether anyone knew, or could measure it. Whether perhaps she ought to know herself, or be able to deduce it — after all, the science teaching at the academic secondary school in Kirschenstein had been fairly good. But she didn't know. She just watched, and in the meantime her feet went to sleep. The water poured over the edges of the gutters; it simply refused to stay on its designated path. Occasionally the storm slapped it against the windowpane like a wet towel, but Leonore no longer flinched. The black water could have been lava or mud or oil; it was unstoppable, she couldn't look away. What have we done, she thought, on a monotonous loop, the letters rolling slowly past her mind's eye one by one, garish and flickering, as if on a conveyor belt: what on earth have we done? All that was needed now was for the ground to open up as if on the Day of Judgement.

2.

DR STERKOWITZ WAS ALSO standing at the window, like so many others. However, unlike most of them, he barely registered the menacing aspects of this storm, neither the noise nor the lightning bolts that stabbed down like knives. What preoccupied him were the black masses of water slamming against the houses and trees like hard sails, clattering non-stop instead of just sinking down and being swept away like ... wet clothes or bundles of rags, downstream into the darkness, off and away.

He had got home late. His wife took the covers off the plates, and beneath them his cold supper was waiting: bread, sausage, Liptauer spicy cheese spread, gherkins, the usual. She was already in her nightdress, but she sat with him and asked about his day. To distract her, he talked for longer than necessary about Balf, poor chap, and how hard Koreny seemed to be taking it all.

'He believes Balf's still talking to him when he's not even conscious,' he said, with his mouth full. 'He tried to convince me, in all seriousness, that he's been giving him instructions.'

His wife shook her head solicitously.

'And in the car on the way back, all Koreny talked about was the water authority,' Sterkowitz continued. 'He's panicking that they're going to overturn the decision.'

'Can they actually do that?' asked his wife.

'They can probably do anything,' he replied, 'if the whole town council opposes it.'

'Well, maybe it's as well,' said Sterkowitz's wife. 'There's plenty as say we've got enough water, why should we have to pay extra?'

'I don't know, either,' said Sterkowitz, 'but that's why we have politicians; they're supposed to know these things.'

And then he went on talking, at the easy pace he only spoke at with his wife. He told her that Fritz Kalmar had been waiting for them at the edge of town, had waved frantically to stop the car — 'He called,' Sterkowitz's wife interrupted, 'I told him you was on the way back from Vienna' — and pleaded with him to come and see Antal Grün, even though it was Sunday. And so as soon as they got to the grocer's Sterkowitz had handed over his car to the mayor, who had to get up to the Rotenstein meadow as quickly as possible.

'There was a lot of to-ing and fro-ing,' he told his wife. 'I needed to fetch my bag from the surgery, on foot, and Antal was so weak and Fritz in such a state that I thought I'd better stay a bit longer.'

'You're too good for this world,' his wife said. Soon afterwards she got up and went to bed.

Sterkowitz cleared away his dinner plates, sat back down at the table, and thought for a while. He even turned off the light, to prove to his wife, if she came down again, that he had just been on his way up. But he stayed, gazing out of the window. Thunder rumbled in the distance; the wind was picking up. The trees started swaying back and forth, as if they could already hear faraway music, someone beating time.

Antal Grün had shown up in Darkenbloom a few years after the end of the war, a dynamic, suntanned, very engaging young man. He and his mother had moved in one day with the Kalmars, widowed Agnes and her disabled child. Within a week he had converted one of the two rooms facing the street into a makeshift shop. The room was also where he and his mother slept, behind an inconspicuous curtain. For the first few years they simply conducted their business out of the window; Antal built a wooden platform with steps, which he would carry outside first thing in the morning, at opening time, and push up against the service window. The shed in the inner courtyard served as a storeroom, and right from the start he somehow managed to stock all of the most important groceries. Grün's shop made it much easier for people in the centre of town to get what they needed; Sterkowitz's wife immediately started going there, too. But before Sterkowitz himself — who, in the years after the war, worked almost around the clock — had made the new grocer's acquaintance, the latter appeared in his office one evening and asked to speak to him. Sterkowitz remembered the conversation very well. They had sat together in the surgery, smoking. Antal Grün's eyes always seemed to be smiling, because he was a little short-sighted. He had come to ask the local doctor to intercede on Fritz's behalf. Sterkowitz observed how well this shopkeeper was able to express himself, unlike the tentative circumlocution of the ordinary locals. Fritz was of normal intelligence, said Antal, but he couldn't speak very well because of his early childhood injury, so at school he pretended to be mute. Everyone there thought he was an idiot; he sat at the back, and had to draw row after row of flowers and leaves, nothing else for the past year and a half. He, Antal, had discovered that Fritz already more or less knew his letters. Would the doctor please give his expert opinion? It would be such a pity otherwise.

And so one afternoon, Sterkowitz, well aware that in Darkenbloom the doctor was an authority on a par with the mayor, the priest, and the chief of police, examined little Fritz Kalmar. Antal was right: he didn't say a word, but he could obviously read and write. Sterkowitz put a page of the school primer in front of him; Fritz read it attentively and answered questions on it, writing the answers down if they required him to do more than nod or shake his head. Afterwards, Sterkowitz palpated the boy's larynx, looked down his throat, and found nothing out of the ordinary. He told him to say something. Fritz shook his head. Agnes, the boy's mother, started to plead with her son, and Antal pleaded, too. Sterkowitz declared that he could probably help him, but in order to do so he needed to know what exactly was wrong. Little Fritz stared at the floor.

'Come now, young man,' Sterkowitz insisted. Fritz's mother kneaded the boy's shoulder, and Antal Grün promised to let him man the till after school the following day. So at last he opened his mouth, took a deep breath, and out came a hideous gurgling sound, as if a muddy river were being sucked through a suddenly unblocked drain. Fritz closed his mouth again, tears flowed, his mother buried her face in her hands. Even Antal Grün was upset. The doctor felt ashamed, but didn't show it.

'Never mind, let's forget that,' he told the boy, and decided to enquire about specialists in the capital when he got the chance. The very next day, though, he dropped by the school and spoke to the teacher, and Fritz no longer had to draw garlands of flowers but was allowed to write and do sums like the others.

On this particular afternoon, Sterkowitz had found himself thinking about the dynamic, undaunted young Antal of old when Fritz led him into an unventilated room where the grocer was laid out like a dying swan. He knew, of course, that illness and infirmity could put decades on a person, but he wasn't prepared to accept this in Antal, who was ten years younger than him. Antal, he thought that evening, sitting alone in the dark, had secretly been a role model for him, with his energy and his dogged determination to build things up again. Antal who, just a few years after the war, had championed an injured child, and built the grey-faced, obdurate women of Darkenbloom a sort of wooden platform, with steps up and down, where he served them with exemplary politeness: *Always at your service, madam.*

So as he approached his bed, he teased him: 'Come now, Antal, why the long face, it can't be that bad!' And even before examining him he went over to the window and threw it open. 'Never forget, you'll suffocate before you freeze!'

Antal didn't respond. He really did look godawful. Fritz was leaning against the doorframe, wracked with worry. Amid much good-natured murmuring and harrumphing, a habit he had got into right at the start of his career, Sterkowitz treated the cut on the head first, on which Fritz had provisionally put a plaster. He measured Antal's pulse and blood pressure, listened to him with his stethoscope, checked his blood sugar. Antal had closed his eyes. Sterkowitz sat on his bed and gave a long, rambling speech about the body and the constitution in general, how the good old machine sometimes played up over the years and you just had to look after it a bit and keep it in good condition.

'However,' he blustered — from the way Fritz was blocking the door, he was starting to suspect that he didn't want to let him out again — 'however, with a man like you, who hardly smokes and never drinks, there's barely even a trace of rust! Come on, it'll pass — don't hang your head like this!'

'My head is propped bolt upright on the mountain of pillows you've stuffed behind it,' whispered Antal.

'There we go,' cried Sterkowitz, 'our good old Antal's back again; I definitely heard a little of him there!'

He stood. Fritz planted himself in the doorway so he wouldn't be able to pass. Sterkowitz walked towards him, undeterred but with raised eyebrows, and Fritz gurgled something at him, more unintelligible than he had been for ages.

'Come now, lad,' Sterkowitz chided him, 'you can do better than that. Start again, nice and calm.' Fritz gurgled.

'He's inviting you to eat with us,' Antal whispered. 'He's cooked for me.'

Sterkowitz laughed, and said, 'Well, of course, I'd like that, but first I'll nip over to the surgery and get some drops to improve your circulation.'

And so he had stayed for dinner. Fritz had rustled up a decent goulash, although by the time Sterkowitz returned with the medication it was only lukewarm. He and Fritz ate at a little table pushed up against the bed; Antal had his plate on a tray on top of the blanket, almost like in hospital. Afterwards, when Fritz took out the dirty plates, Sterkowitz remained seated for a moment. Antal's eyes had been closed for several minutes. Sterkowitz was just wondering when he might sneak out when Antal began to speak. And the whole time he was speaking he smiled, as if it were an absolute pleasure to talk with your eyes closed. Seemingly out of the blue, he said that the Tüffers would have liked to take his mother with them when they left; she used to sew for old Frau Tüffer. The old lady, who ran the family business, had been reluctant to forgo the high-quality buttons that Antal's mother covered individually with fabric, or her bodices, which were tricky to make, on account of Frau Tüffer's unusual measurements. A broad back, and a very small bust, said Antal, which therefore required optical enhancement, but below this a narrow waist that was absolutely not to be emphasised. Only a master craftswoman like his mother had succeeded in making the boss look not like a small, stocky wrestler or swimmer who had disguised himself as a woman, but like a well-proportioned, possibly even dainty lady. A good dressmaker is a good liar, said Antal, smiling, eyes closed.

But they wanted to take only his mother with them; they had just one berth free on their ship's passage. And that was only because the Tüffer son's pallid wife had suddenly bethought herself of her Aryan lineage and filed for divorce. For Antal's mother, though, the offer was out of the question. The Tüffers, in turn, had not been prepared to exchange the mother for the son, and Antal's mother had never forgiven them for this, on principle. Antal had only just turned sixteen at the time.

They're two completely different things, she'd said later, when Antal argued that, in any case, it would have been terrible and wrong to separate them. A person should be allowed to have a say in how they would like to be rescued.

They never found out what happened to the Tüffers, whether they made it to New York or South America. Antal's mother did not forgive them. After the Tüffers left, there was no one who knew anything any more; nobody could help, they were all in the same hopeless situation. Antal's mother refused to go to the capital without a safe contact there, and so they just stayed — constantly searching for ways to escape, telegraphing everywhere, but they stayed, past the deadline. Until the truck came. 'There were fifty-one of us,' said Antal, smiling, eyes closed, 'including an eighty-year-old rabbi, and several children.' And he told Dr Sterkowitz about his night on the breakwater.

Sterkowitz sat in the darkened room, gazing out into the storm. The branches were dancing czardas now. Antal had described it all in detail. Four dozen people were loaded onto a truck and driven forty-five minutes north, where they were made to climb onto a weir in the middle of the Danube. Women, children, and old people. Onto one of those groynes constructed almost at right angles to the riverbank, intended to regulate the speed of the current and prevent erosion of the bank. They were shooed up onto it like a gaggle of geese onto a long springboard, except that these geese couldn't fly away. Threatening shots were fired into the air, again and again. Only a few people were needed to chase many more up onto the narrow ridge. The main thing was for the chasers to position themselves correctly, forming a corridor between riverbank, water, and jetty. Then people essentially had no alternative but to walk slowly forward onto the water, one after another, even when those at the front shouted back into the darkness that the dam had come to an end. That they couldn't go any further. People were backed up on a rocky dam that backed up the wide river. Did the first ones who stepped onto it in the blackness of the night hope it might take them all the way across, huge blocks of stone tossed into the river like a makeshift bridge? That once they reached the far bank they would be in freedom, albeit in wet clothes; that they could simply set foot in that other country and run away? But no: the breakwater only projected as far as the middle of the river, where it was in full spate. Where the water was already washing over this artificial barrier. So fifty-one people crouched down and clung on. Falling asleep would have been fatal. The wrong person beside you, floundering and dragging you down with them, would have been fatal. Small children cried, and their mothers slapped them just to make them hush. Others wailed that perhaps rivers had tides as well, that towards morning a wave was sure to come and sweep them all away.

Many hours later, when the sun rose, they saw a few houses on the far, Slovakian, bank. There were people standing there, waving. And these good Samaritans saved them: they fetched them in their boats, one little group at a time, and took them back to that other country. The fact that they couldn't stay there, in case they set a precedent, that for this reason they were deported back to the Reich just two days later, that the chaotic situation continued, and ended, for some of them, in death — this was not at all the point of what Antal wanted to say to Sterkowitz. What he wanted to tell him was that early that afternoon, before he collapsed, he had had exactly the same feeling in his body as he had back then, with people backed up in front of him and others pushing from behind, dogs barking, gunshots, when anyone who tried to break away to left or right would simply have met an even quicker end in the cold, black water that was already licking enticingly towards them, the only place that offered infinite freedom. Rocks, cries, shots, night. Pushing and shoving from behind, nowhere to go in front. And because he immediately recognised this feeling of panic and constriction, because his body had returned him to that long-ago breakwater, he thought that this time it must mean certain death.

A very long silence followed, in which Sterkowitz didn't dare move and scarcely dared to breathe. Finally, Antal opened his eyes and looked at him.

'I just don't understand why they did it,' he said.

Of course, he continued, soon after that it all got increasingly murderous. But it wasn't that murderous in the beginning. Seven years later, yes, clearly, things were very different around here: no one was transported anywhere by truck any more, someone like him was just handed a shovel wherever he was standing, a shovel to use for himself. Sterkowitz must have heard about it. But this earlier story — which had ended well, thanks to the Slovakian fishermen who had come to their aid — it seemed, to Antal, too lurid. As if someone had played some perverse kind of joke. Fifty-one people are chased onto a groyne in the river. As soon as the sun comes up, they can be seen from all around. After a while, they either collapse from tiredness and exhaustion, fall in, and are swept away, like wet clothes or bundles of rags, downstream into the darkness, off and away. Or they're saved by someone from the other side. But what was the point of it all? 'Just be glad you weren't here yet, at the time,' said Antal.

'Yes,' said Sterkowitz, and sighed. 'I was still studying, at the time.'

3.

THE STORY OF HOW Horka, Neulag and Co. made Dr Bernstein disappear, although he was still there, became their party piece. Or the reverse: how he was made to stay, although he had been expelled. However, for quite some time now, as far as Darkenbloomers are concerned, the story of Darkenbloom doesn't begin until much later: the day the Russians came. Put it like this: discussion of the *historical heritage* of this region, *where great spiritual, national, and cultural differences have repeatedly collided,* as Rehberg boldly wrote in his manuscript, refers to Neolithic finds, to Celts and Romans, to the important trade route that began at the Baltic Sea and passed through Darkenbloom on the way to the Adriatic. To the stone lion's head, washed out of the ground on the Malnitz farm after a storm, later identified as a Roman artwork and installed on the fountain beside the plague column. There, long ago, lies a rich, proud Darkenbloom history. But then — whoops — history stumbled somehow, and was forced to make a great leap in order to stay upright.

Which is why, after the Ancient Romans, it picks up more or less directly with the Russians and the wretched, humiliating post-war period, when strenuous efforts had to be made to re-establish the distinction between Germans and Austrians — historically, excuse me, they were never the same! Older people were as willing to talk about the suffering, the hardship, and the crimes committed against girls and women as they were silent about the period that immediately preceded it.

They told of how these primitive Russian soldiers were constantly demanding *uhra, uhra,* watches; some, it was said, would roll up their sleeves with a rachitic grin to show off four or five of the coveted prizes. The people of Darkenbloom did not speak of what they themselves had been proclaiming just a short while before; that is all too human. Most people would do the same: reach for every scrap of victimhood to hold up in front of them like a white flag. White flags for capitulation, *please spare me.* White flags for innocence.

However, it is important to know the following: it is a custom in Austria to raise a white flag over the school building when every pupil who sat the school-leaving exam there has passed. And this comes closer to the particular meaning white flags acquired back then, at the time of the *Anschluss,* in Darkenbloom and Kirschenstein and Tellian and Löwingen and Mandl, in the whole region, in this charming but very remote part of the countryside. If all the pupils pass, it means no one has screwed up. The school is immaculate, unsullied by failures, layabouts, or any good-for-nothing lowlife. And perhaps it was this parallel that appealed to Horka, a terrible student who had only managed to crawl to the end of eight years' compulsory education with the help of Ferbenz's far-reaching system of sucking up to and threatening the teachers. From the age of fourteen, Horka gave his occupation as *unskilled labourer,* occasionally showing up on a construction site or at the grape harvest. Not that often, though. People knew he carried out orders, ran errands, and that now and then part of his working day consisted of a brawl. He would provoke it, then would give his target a particularly hard punch on the nose in the mêlée. When Horka, the professional but under-utilised dogsbody, heard about the white flags, and that Kirschenstein was supposedly on the verge of hoisting theirs, he personally took up the challenge. It was entirely to his taste. He was the one who realised that not only was the thing inspiring in itself, so too was its competitive nature. Now he could show them all what he was capable of. That he too could write lists and organise things. And in doing so he gained access to a source of information about certain properties that were about to become available. Never before had he found a task so much fun — until, that is, he came up against the problem of medical care. For which he, along with Neulag, nonetheless soon found a creative solution: oh, how they laughed.

But those two, Neulag and Horka, had vanished years ago; Old Graun was long dead, ancient Stipsits recently so. So no one remembered the story any more. Ferbenz had so many other things which seemed to him worth preserving, and to which he clung with his waning mental faculties — his personal encounter with the Führer in particular — that he might only have recalled the Bernstein conjuring trick if someone had asked him about it. That's how memory works: everything seems to be gone, echoing emptiness, a deep, dark expanse, but if you feel your way around, you find gossamer-thin threads that do have something attached to them if you give them a tug.

Most of the story is irretrievably lost. Such as why, of the three doctors, they chose Dr Bernstein. Probably because he was the eldest, the most experienced, and the best-liked; perhaps also because it was assumed that, as a responsible sort of person, he wouldn't make any trouble. Which begs the question of what sort of trouble that might have been: refusing to go along with it?

It's possible the other two were never even considered. One, Lazarus, specialised in the head, teeth, tongue, neck, and ears, and was most reluctant to deal with other diseased body parts; the other, Spiegel, was professionally impeccable, but an unpopular, nasty fellow, taciturn, uptight, and unpleasant.

The list that went up outside the town hall was one almost anyone in a town like Darkenbloom could have compiled off the top of their head. The only curious thing about it was its systematics. The primary order was alphabetical by address: Feldgasse, Hauptplatz, Herrengasse, Karnergasse, Mühlgasse, Neugasse, Reitschulgasse, Schulgasse, Tempelgasse. Oddly, though, within this sequence it was arranged alphabetically by name, which meant that the house numbers jumped back and forth. On Hauptplatz, for example, it went from Arnstein, Malwine (Hauptplatz 13) via the five Tüffers (Hauptplatz 4) to Wohlmut, Karoline (Hauptplatz 7), an aunt of Antal Grün. He was listed ahead of his mother Gisella, under Tempelgasse 4. His father, Salomon Grün, had departed for the next, eternal world just in time, which Gisella and her then sixteen-year-old son came to regard as *a stroke of luck*, in the sense of Tante Jolesch's famous saying: *God preserve us from any strokes of luck.* The book about Tante Jolesch wasn't around back then, but those aphorisms were formed over centuries, like diamonds: under intense pressure.

There were eighty-seven names altogether, and Dr Bernstein's was already missing from the list. Anyone who goes to the trouble of getting hold of it can verify this. Because the list still exists, of course, if you know where to look. Under Herrengasse 3 there is only Bernstein's wife, Emma, as if Paul Bernstein had already left. Or had died just in time, like Salomon Grün.

The list was pinned up next to the entrance to the town hall, and anyone who cared to could have seen the affected Darkenbloomers appending their signature, stepping forward, furtive or upright, pen in hand: *By order of the Gestapo you are hereby informed that you must leave the municipality of Darkenbloom by 30 May 1938 at the latest. Sign below to confirm that you have noted these instructions.*

At least they were still being polite.

In his new capacity as the Nazis' local group leader, incorporating the office of mayor, Neulag, accompanied by Horka, paid a visit to Dr

Bernstein to explain what was expected of him. Bernstein wouldn't have said much; his biggest concern was probably that his wife should be able to leave as soon as possible. The two crooks assured him of this — *but of course, Herr Doctor* — they had both been treated by him since they were children, for their cuts, fevers, broken bones. And after that Bernstein packed up his things, and some of his people probably helped to carry them: Goldmans, Grüns, Arnsteins, or Wohlmuts. Late in the evening — when in an agricultural community people are least likely to be out and about — Dr Bernstein, with his instruments and medicines, was transferred to the Hotel Tüffer, in through the back entrance and up to Room 22 on the second floor, well out of the way at the end of the corridor, a room that was only ever allocated when there was a big influx of summer visitors, and usually, even then, only to servants of the guests — nannies, wet nurses, or ladies' maids.

The indefatigable young Resi, who had recently taken over the running of the hotel and was red-faced with the effort, had no objection. On the contrary: she was keen to get on the right side of the new authority. And so, just a few days later, white flags were raised over Darkenbloom, beating its rival, the more bourgeois Kirschenstein, by a few hours; there they fluttered, the evidence of a quite new, very specific form of innocence and purity: *Darkenbloom is free of Jews! The town that for centuries was infamous for its more than one hundred resident Jews is now completely Jew-free! Most have already been deprived of citizenship, because they left the territory of the Reich. As a sign of the deliverance from the Jewish plague, our Ortsgruppenleiter and mayor raised a white flag over the former Jewish temple in front of a cheering crowd.*

That is what was written in the paper. And if someone had no house and no registered address, they were no longer there, were they? It would be a while before the new doctor arrived, as there was a certain lack of doctors everywhere at present. But Neulag was very well connected. He had been forceful in requesting a replacement, and had been promised a good, young doctor, newly qualified, modern methods. *Our own people are finally getting a chance.* That was what he said to whoever might care to listen. However, anyone suffering from an acute minor ailment could easily find out where they needed to go. The information was passed on by word of mouth; there was no written evidence. The Kirschensteiners can't touch us, bellowed Horka, and laughed so heartily you could see right down to his tonsils.

Dr Paul Bernstein sat in the Tüffer, in the room at the very back, number 22, and saw patients. He listened with his stethoscope and peered into throats, gave digitalis injections, and tapped his little hammer below the kneecaps of howling children. Resi brought up his food, curtseying from force of habit. Bernstein waited, and longed for his replacement to arrive. He didn't know whether his wife was already out of the country. As far as many Darkenbloomers were concerned, it could all just have stayed that way; they were used to and trusted him, and it even felt rather elegant, going to visit the doctor at the hotel.

After a while, when the white flag competition could no longer be challenged, when it had almost been forgotten, just the first of many valiant steps into the glorious thousand-year future, they were no longer quite as scrupulous about the need to stay undercover. Dr Bernstein was allowed to leave his room in an emergency; because, for example, an itinerant labourer called Miklos Jobbagy was lying dead beside his bicycle in Zwick. Wait, that's not quite correct: by the time the police and the doctor arrived, the bicycle had somehow removed itself of its own accord.

Although it may have seemed an eternity to Dr Bernstein, he only spent just over ten weeks in the Hotel Tüffer. One evening, at the height of summer, Horka appeared and informed him in honeyed tones that he was being transferred back to Herrengasse. Herr Doctor was to pack his things; helpers would come in a few hours to carry everything over there. Bernstein asked no questions, only if Resi could assist him. Horka nodded and left; this time he even closed the door behind him.

It was late by the time the last box was carried into the practice. The Aryan helpers vanished without a word. Resi, whose thoroughness and aptitude would have made her a good doctor's assistant, had come, as well. She now explained that everything had to be unpacked and put back in its old place.

'You look very tired, though, Fräulein Resi,' said Bernstein. 'Can't it wait till morning?'

'Those are the orders,' mumbled Resi, who was already carefully opening the first box containing the bottles and pipettes.

The replacement didn't come until after noon the next day. And he came alone: Bernstein, watching from the window, saw Horka point to his front door, turn, and walk away. The replacement was young, very young, and didn't really seem quite sure how to approach the new situation. He greeted Bernstein with a snappy *Heil Hitler*; yes yes, said Bernstein, just come on in, and the young man broke into vociferous praise of the house and the consulting rooms.

He's pleased, thought Bernstein. That's good for the people, if he's pleased.

'Let's go through everything,' he said, putting the card-index files on the table. 'Do you have any obstetrics experience?'

The young man looked abashed, and replied that he had hoped to find experienced midwives here, especially as they were in the countryside.

Bernstein nodded. 'Dentistry?' he asked.

The young man mumbled something Bernstein didn't catch, but the gist was obvious.

'Now listen carefully, Doc-tor Ster-ko-witz,' said Bernstein, looking at him sternly. 'I'm writing down two names and addresses for you: the dental technician, and the midwife. The first thing you do is go to them, introduce yourself, and tell them the truth. You understand what I mean?'

The young man nodded, shamefaced.

'You'll be fine with everything else,' said Bernstein, relenting, 'as long as you always wash your hands thoroughly.'

And afterwards, after he had shown him around the lovely old doctor's house from attic to cellar and handed over all the keys, Dr Bernstein simply walked out of town, *travelling light*, as they called it later on. On foot, yes, of course: because first of all he had to get far enough away, to where no one would know who he was and so might give him a lift.

4.

A REGION WHERE GREAT *spiritual, national, and cultural differences have repeatedly collided.* When Rehberg marked the full stop at the end of this sentence, as carefully as if he were dabbing it onto thin glass, he put down his fountain pen and gazed out of the window. Although so many things had collided around here — which Rehberg felt actually required a bit of a run-up — distances were in fact short. The only thing that was remote was so-called civilisation, in the form of larger towns and cities, because you first had to fight your way over ranges of hills and through meandering valleys, heading either south-westwards or due north. Darkenbloom was situated as if it had slipped right to the bottom and into the corner of a sack. It hadn't always been like that. An old map hung on the wall above Rehberg's desk; he had inherited it, like so many other things, from his Aunt Elly. He had drawn in the contours of the sack with a fine pencil, because on this map Darkenbloom was still out in the open, the next big town only a dozen kilometres to the east. It wouldn't take more than half an hour by car, although no one knew what state the roads were in these days.

For a few years after the war they had still existed, the roads and footpaths, the local network for cross-border traffic. As a schoolboy,

183

Rehberg had regularly cycled over the hill, through the vineyards, and even as far as that nearby town, Stossimhimmel, where his aunt had an acquaintance to whom he would take small and medium-sized parcels, sometimes even a whole basket, but who only gave him sealed envelopes in exchange.

Since he had started researching the history of Darkenbloom, Rehberg doubted not only almost all assertions made by his fellow citizens, but his own memories as well. It was a strange phenomenon, one he couldn't do anything about. Something told him that everything had to be called into question, especially the things that were repeated most often and declared to be definitively true. This scruple meant that the scope of his research had increased out of all proportion, but all he could do was accept this for now and hope it would result in more professional findings.

He had started to doubt everything after realising that his memory had deceived him in the most extraordinary fashion. It had not just been any old memory, but one of his most vivid, as if it had been etched into metal. Yet when he examined it more closely, none of it was true.

Back then he had owned a bicycle, the fabulous luxury of his childhood. He used it to run lots of little errands. The bike had come from his Aunt Elly, who told him she had got it years ago from a family called Rosmarin. It was only in the course of doing his research that he realised it was not that these Rosmarins, like typical rich people, simply didn't need it any more: they hadn't been able to take it with them. A distressing thought, but there was no other explanation. Why else would anyone have given away such a treasure? Back then, as a child, knowing nothing of this, he relished the responsibility he had been given. He transported things to the other town for his aunt, and was praised for his reliability. He was a pedantic child. He knew he mustn't dawdle, but he mustn't go too fast, either, so as not to fall off. *Slow and steady wins the race,* as his aunt would say: *no Jewish haste* was not an idiom she used. In any case, he enjoyed it all: the freedom, the responsibility, the air whipping past him as he cycled through the vines, especially on the windy crest of the hill, where you looked down on Darkenbloom on one side and Stossimhimmel on the other. He cycled across it as if along the scaly back of a peaceful, sleeping dragon, undulating gently up and down, a competent little courier. The dragon's flanks, saturated with grapes, fell away to left and right. But it was up there, on that splendid ridge, that something terrible had happened. He definitely remembered his mother, in the days that followed, murmuring in disbelief: 'Our lad was right there, just minutes before!' He saw his grandmother crossing herself at the thought; he heard his father scold: 'That's enough of that, just be glad it's all gone quiet now!' For a long time, he felt as if something were expected of him; he thought he saw his neighbours giving him questioning looks, as if he might have seen something important that could help solve the crime. Those memories, he realised, were already fantasies, childishly grandiose falsifications in subsequent years when he may have wished something deep inside him would speak out, as if in tongues, and make him look like a hero.

At any rate, the incident marked the abrupt end of his cross-border messenger service. He never saw the woman from the dilapidated apartment block again, who, if he was honest, he had found unpleasant, almost sinister. She smelled of mothballs, and would often hesitate before handing over the letters, as if it were in his power to reward her with a little extra. He was a child; he only had what his aunt had packed for her. Weren't the two of them friends? Soon after that, the road and the border traffic came to an end, anyway: up went the barbed wire. Everything was sealed off and closed down. Stossimhimmel sank into the past, became a phantom one might simply have imagined, while Darkenbloom fell into the corner of the deep sack. But, as the grown-ups said, at least things had finally gone quiet.

Since Rehberg had started chronicling the history of the town in his spare time, he had occasionally thought about the incident on the crest of the hill, but had never made any enquiries about it. As the Darkenbloomers liked to scoff, he was still stuck in much earlier periods, between pre- and early history and the first documented reference to the town, looking for ways to play up Darkenbloom's role in Roman times. The specialist literature on the subject gave the impression that only Stossimhimmel had been of any significance back then, as a stronghold and centre of trade, whereas Darkenbloom was just a primitive village where messengers got drunk and changed their horses.

One day he mentioned to Eszter Lowetz, more or less in passing, a crime of some sort that had taken place on the road to the border. To his surprise she immediately knew what he was referring to. But he could not accept what she told him; they each insisted on their own version of the events, and it was the only time they parted on uneasy terms. He didn't see her for a few days, long enough for him already to be wondering what pretext he could use to drop by and make peace. But she beat him to it, breezing into his shop unannounced, waving copies of newspapers from the library in Kirschenstein. The reports said that a dental technician from Over There had been robbed and shot dead on the crest of the hill; it was unclear in which order. He had taken the same route every day at the same time, to Darkenbloom in the morning, back to Stossimhimmel in the evening, and had usually had dental gold on him. It could have been anyone; anyone could have done it, everyone had known. Lajos, with the gold in his bag, travels back and forth, Monday to Friday.

A risky thing to do in these lean and hungry times, the article said, quoting the head of the local Darkenbloom police, a certain G. Horka. In any case, the story of the dental technician robbed and murdered on the track through the vineyards fitted precisely; it could have been drawn directly from Rehberg's memory. *Our lad, just before ...* his grandmother's hasty crossing of herself, his father's scolding — whenever he didn't like a subject of conversation, he would shout. There was just one problem, the detail over which he had almost fallen out with Eszter: the dental technician with the bag full of gold had been killed in the second summer after the war, August 1946. But Rehberg wasn't even six years old then. No bicycle, no carrying messages; it was too early. Eszter, on the other hand, knew nothing of any incident on the hilltop around three years later, and it now seemed unlikely to Rehberg as well that there could have been another. Since then, Rehberg had not even trusted his own memories.

A lot of things would have been easier if Aunt Elly had still been alive. He couldn't think why he hadn't started working on the town chronicle years earlier. Then again, his interest had only been piqued when he was no longer able to ask her. Aunt Elly, his father's unmarried eldest sister, born soon after the turn of the century, was, as Rehberg saw it, a moral authority in Darkenbloom; everyone respected her. Rehberg had said something of the kind to her, many years ago, but she had laughed and said, 'If only; I fear it's more the opposite.'

She didn't want to explain what she meant by this; when he asked her again later, she murmured that it had just been a joke. In any case, he had her to thank for his higher education; she had persuaded his father to let him go to the academic secondary school in Kirschenstein. However, she had not supported his going to the seminary afterwards; she never said anything about it, just fell silent and changed the subject when, for example, his devout grandmother got rather too enthusiastic about the prospect of receiving the Last Rites from her own flesh and blood. The young Rehberg was more struck by this silence than by any contradiction, because it was the only time his aunt was not on his side. He suspected he knew now what the reason might have been, although they had never talked about it. So right from the start she had known him better than he knew himself. The thought of it still made him blush.

Without Aunt Elly, he would not have become the person he was. As the only son, he would have had to follow in the footsteps of his father, the master glazier. You didn't just give up a business when the master craftsman was too old; you forced a son to take it over. One of Rehberg's sisters was interested in learning the trade, but that was deemed an *absolutely daft idea*, and she was married off sharpish. Not even Aunt Elly was able to help, which may have been a consequence of her efforts on young Rehberg's behalf. With the daughters, at least, everything had to be done according to convention; old Max Rehberg couldn't lose face completely. Consequently, years later, he couldn't find anyone at all to succeed him, and died soon afterwards, probably from the shame of it. Rehberg's mother also died young, and if Rehberg were honest, it was after this that the best days of his life began. He went on short trips to Venice, Trieste, or Nice with his Aunt Elly, who for many years remained in excellent health, both physical and mental, and was tactful enough to retire early on certain evenings, so her nephew would have a chance to meet people his own age.

A while ago, when the historical research project first began to take shape, and he was at least able to persuade three or four Darkenbloomers to collaborate with him on the chronicle and the planning of the museum, Rehberg had the idea of taking a few lives as examples and portraying them in greater detail. It was modern; visitors would like it; this was how they did things these days in professional exhibitions, using photographs and personal effects; larger museums even showed films. How better to depict history than through the lives of individuals, including so-called ordinary people? Árpád the First of Darkenbloom was on his provisional list, of course, as an important figure, but so was Hans Balaskó, a retired teacher who had been a communist and was in the resistance; then there were some deceased local dignitaries, former mayors, and the legendary leader of the Pinzker Group who composed the 'Darkenbloom March'.

'Why not Ferbenz?' Flocke Malnitz had asked at one of these improvised editorial meetings. 'After all, he's so fond of talking about the past.'

But everyone else thought this was too problematic, at least while he was still alive, and, well, generally.

'You can only talk to him while he's still alive,' said Flocke.

'So you want to take a tape recorder and go and see Dr Alois and let him tell you about the Führer's beautiful blue eyes?' asked young Farkas, polemically.

'Why not?' Flocke retorted. 'It'd be more interesting than these nineteenth-century mayors, anyway.'

'And, of course, a great advert for Darkenbloom,' cried Feri Farkas. 'Hey, look, everyone, we even have a real live Deputy Gauleiter!'

Rehberg was forced to attempt some friendly mediation. 'We need some women, as well — Flocke, I'm sure you could write a nice profile of the Countess? We could get the Countess's office to authorise it ...'

But Flocke sat in stony silence for the rest of the evening, and Rehberg preferred not to know what was going on in her head, or what plans she was hatching.

The question of suitable women eventually led them to Aunt Elly, about whom they all — apart from Flocke, who was still sulking — were quickly in agreement: Elly was an important Darkenbloom personage, although she had never held an official position. Cultivated, a model of social-mindedness, all her life she had passed on to the community all that she knew and was able to do. She had worked for many years in a voluntary capacity, caring for the elderly, the sick, and, in particular, women who had just given birth. Above all, though, she had set up and led the children's art class, which they now came to from as far afield as Kirschenstein. Aunt Elly had succeeded in establishing the art group, which she called the 'Darkenbloom School of Seeing', and making it a permanent fixture. It was still going strong: young women took the children out into the fresh air and taught them how to draw according to nature. It was astonishing to see what the little ones learned in a very short time, about perspective, proportion, and the various techniques. Clearly it made sense to let children draw trees, rocks, fences, and houses first; portraying people came later. The 'School of Seeing' soon became part of the art curriculum, and for some years now there had also been week-long courses in the summer, which busy young mothers were keen to take advantage of for their children. In some of the shops, particularly good drawings by the children of the house had been framed and hung on the wall, but no one had ever gone to the expense of turning the best works into postcards. At any rate, people in Darkenbloom were proud of the young artists, especially since the architect Zierbusch, who grew up here, had said in a newspaper interview that he would probably have pursued a different career if it hadn't been for Elly Rehberg's drawing classes. And this Zierbusch was considered important, partly because of this newspaper interview, although so far he had mostly built car dealerships and supermarkets, in addition to redesigning the train station. The station, though, was no longer in use.

So Rehberg handed over all Elly's documents, photos, and letters in his possession to Eszter Lowetz, so she could write the short profile. As a close relative, he didn't want to do it himself, but Eszter would write it, with her customary warmth and the dry humour that had started to reveal itself so pleasingly in recent years. Shortly afterwards, though, she began asking questions that sounded completely bonkers, at least if you had lived in Darkenbloom for as long and knew people there as well as they did. She seemed well aware of the effect they might have on him, because she asked the questions carefully, and only after a long, rambling introduction that Rehberg had since forgotten. Nonetheless, she asked them, against all reason, and the most upsetting moment still pained him, given all they had worked on together.

Had he ever heard anything about Aunt Elly having been married, earlier? Eszter asked. Rehberg stared at her in bewilderment. Much earlier, she added, long before the war.

'Of course not,' Rehberg answered. 'I would know!'

Eszter placed a wedding photo in front of him, the kind everyone has seen: black and white, extra-stiff card, with a decorative white serrated border, showing a young, nervously smiling couple. The bride did perhaps bear a certain resemblance. He admitted it! It was possible that she might have looked like that at twenty, but that was long before Rehberg had known her. When Elly was twenty, Rehberg's father was five.

'I have no idea who that might be,' said Rehberg, 'but what reason would Elly have had to keep a marriage secret, from me? That's ridiculous!'

'I could think of some possible reasons,' Eszter answered vaguely, but Rehberg immediately interrupted: 'With anyone else, but not Aunt Elly!' She had talked about everything, not like most people who were around back then; she was very critical, especially about the Nazi period. Incidentally, he had heard a lot about that from her; there were quite a few stories he could tell. If there were any dark family secrets, they were other people's — he could name names! — but definitely not hers. This was a person who cut cartoons out of newspapers and stuck them on the fridge, like one of a reporter holding out a microphone to a fat woman with a shopping bag, with a line of dialogue underneath: *Sex? No, no, young man, there was none of that in the old days!*

That was his Aunt Elly, an open-minded woman with a sense of humour. Not at all usual in Darkenbloom. That was what made her special. There were no secrets between them; they trusted each other implicitly. She had even left written instructions for him about the sequence of hymns for the funeral mass and exactly what plants she wanted on her grave. *So you won't have as much to think about,* she had written, with an exclamation mark that he had read as a wink.

And so, a few days after this conversation, when he heard, much to his distress, that Eszter Lowetz had been found dead in her bed, there was a brief moment when he wondered whether perhaps it could have been a sign: that Eszter wasn't right in the head any more. Although apparently it was her heart, which had just stopped beating. He could still hear the last words Eszter had said to him, in her calm, friendly way: *Have another look at the photo, later. I'll leave it here for you. Look at it in your own time. Look closely.*

5.

THE FIRST THE ASSISTANT primary-school teacher Jenő Goldman saw of his future wife was her legs. He was taking his class outside for the first time, to a wildflower meadow just behind the last house on Reitschulgasse. Today, you would have to go at least a kilometre further, beyond Zierbusch the architect's hideous, renovated-to-death train station, before you found an undeveloped space that might possibly even be green; instead of waist-high flowers and grasses, a car dealership now stands in place of the former meadow that proved so fateful for Jenő Goldman. Back then, though, this spot was dominated by a huge, harmoniously proportioned lime, like the tree made by God as the crowning glory of the third day of Creation. And this magnificent lime was to be the subject of the open-air drawing class. As Jenő and the children approached, something stirred beneath the crown of the tree; only for a moment, but Jenő saw it. Two legs being drawn up. He got the children to sit a short distance away, instead of leading them right up under the tree so they could admire the towering, branching cupola from below. He walked up to it alone, to fetch a handful of lime leaves for the smaller children to draw. When he peered up the trunk, a girl was looking down at him from above, forefinger pressed to her lips. Jenő smiled and nodded, but it was clear that the girl couldn't now leave her hiding place any time soon. He went back to the children, carrying the lime leaves. When he walked past later, after school, as if he often had things to do in the vicinity of this tree, she was still sitting on the branch above him, reading.

In a small town in an agricultural region where, at harvest time, some parents still ignored the requirement for their children to attend school, art and literature were a powerful source of attraction between those who were interested in them. This was the case with Jenő and the young woman who would retreat up a tree to read. She was just eighteen; he was five years older. Her father would have liked to marry his eldest daughter to one of the wine growers' sons, at least some of whom had returned from the Great War. Her fresh face encouraged such hopes; her forthrightness dampened them somewhat. However, her father allowed himself to be persuaded to settle for a teacher, even though it was a man from Over There. Elisabeth may well have kept her family in the dark about her fiancé's precise lineage. It is also conceivable that she didn't know. Perhaps Jenő, who, apart from his Eliza, never wanted anything other than to be self-reliant and get through life unscathed, had long possessed an Evangelical certificate of baptism; this was not unusual in the region, unlike in the rest of the country. And, after all, the world had gone completely mad after the death of the old Kaiser, the end of the Great War, and the disastrous collapse of the monarchy. The border that has affected everything ever since was being drawn here at the time, just as Jenő fell in love; a border right through the middle of the wide, yellow-green landscapes that had fed the capital from the east for centuries, not only its people but the countless horses of the monarchy as well. All those hay and poultry farmers — suddenly, from the capital's point of view, they were all foreigners, and subject to customs restrictions. And although the famines that gripped the capital visited Darkenbloom only in the form of dubious traders and desperate hoarders, people had other things to worry about besides a future son-in-law's baptism certificate. Down here in the south the farmers had enough to eat, but the demarcation of the border was disputed, particularly here. For two and a half years there were negotiations, votes, intimidation, threats, shootings. Neighbours attacked each other with pitchforks; young men armed themselves with truncheons and ripped out newly installed boundary stones because individual meadows, fields, and vineyards were suddenly on the wrong side. The people of Here and the people of Over There did not hold back, even if in many instances it wasn't at all clear who belonged to which side, or wanted to, or why. Both sides tricked and cheated as much as they possibly could, as always happens whenever governmental authority is suspended. The law of the jungle immediately takes over, however much we believe, in peacetime, that we have morally refined ourselves.

Then, too, one Darkenbloomer in particular stood out: Benno B., the head of the border police, put together a band of volunteers and comported himself like a marauding robber baron. He was acting *in Austria's interests*, he declared, but this official-sounding claim did not alter the illegality of his actions. Darkenbloom itself had unequivocally been allocated to Austria, Stossimhimmel to Over There. But everything further south than these two towns was contested. And there, in the south, between fields and farmyards, Benno B. and his volunteers fought for every little strip of land.

Compared to all this, a wedding was a thoroughly good piece of news. People here didn't have much, but they knew how to celebrate. And so Jenő, who seemed, curiously, to have no family at all, assigned himself to Austria, even though it meant he couldn't go on teaching: lessons were finally being taught in German again, which was frenziedly welcomed by the majority, whose mother tongue it had always been. It was then, as children, that some of the young pupils in Jenő's drawing class, like the cobbler's son, Alois Ferbenz, who gleamed every morning like a freshly polished doorknob, became German-Austrian nationalists, fighting a defensive war against dirty, foreign, destructive elements all their lives.

For Jenő and Eliza, the years that followed were simple but peaceful. Jenő was the kind of person who made the best of things; he knew how to get by financially, one way or another, and whenever money was tight he would spend a few weeks working in the Rosmarin factory. One year after their marriage they had a son, known as Sascha or Schani.

The birth could not have gone worse. After days of contractions, Dr Bernstein thought the mother-to-be was in a hopeless situation. The black hair on the crown of the boy's head was visible, but they simply couldn't extract him from his mother; he had twisted awkwardly on entering the birth canal and was now stuck fast. Paradoxically, it was Dr Bernstein's fatalism that ultimately brought about the happy ending: after preparing the unfortunate husband for the worst, he returned to Eliza's bedside, reached for the scalpel, and handed the midwife the forceps again. 'Grab firmly and pull,' he murmured under his breath, 'we can't even bury them like this.'

Sascha escaped with nothing more than an egg-shaped head and a few bruises, both of which faded much faster than his mother recovered. He grew up in Darkenbloom like all the other children; the only difference was that he remained an only child. As soon as he could walk, he would run after his mother's youngest brother, only five years older, like a little dog after its master. Eliza's brother Max — Sascha's uncle, strictly speaking — wanted nothing to do with him. He ran away from him, but would sometimes stop as if he had changed his mind before pushing the hopeful little boy over.

At ten, Sascha worshipped Vroni, a blonde girl who was two years above him and had a very refined way of speaking. At thirteen he kissed Agnes, whom he sat next to on the school bench at the time, and who wiped her mouth afterwards with the back of her hand. What was striking was that, unlike his parents, he absolutely could not and did not want to draw. At fourteen he started an apprenticeship as a waiter in the Hotel Tüffer, but broke it off, to his grandparents' horror, to learn bookkeeping from the factory owner Thea Rosmarin instead.

At eighteen he was a confident young man, testing his charm on the older women in the firm. Then his name appeared with his father's on the list that went up outside the town hall. At first, Sascha thought it was a bad joke, and even after seeing it with his own eyes he kept saying that there had been a mistake, until at last his mother explained to him what probably lay behind it. Early one morning, the two Goldmans made their way, with their two suitcases, through Kirschenstein and Stossimhimmel along the complicated route to Budapest, where Jenő had relatives and acquaintances, or hoped to find them again. Sascha clung to his mother's words: *for the time being, just to be on the safe side.* She gave him a little drawing to take with him, a family portrait she had drawn of the three of them. He lost it in the first few weeks. He didn't understand what was happening to him. He had never even been inside the Darkenbloom temple, he didn't know what went on in there, he imagined sorcerers in black pointy hats.

There was never any question of his mother coming with them. Written contact was lost almost immediately; their address kept changing. Jenő searched for ways to save his son, enquired about false papers, smugglers crossing the border to Romania, possible hiding places in the countryside, but Sascha refused to go. He was afraid of being left to fend for himself, and hid this fear behind concern for his father, whom he saw as a defenceless old man, though at the time he was only in his mid-forties. *Stay together at all costs* — when Sascha ran out of arguments, he would declare that this had been his mother's stated wish.

They stuck it out, the two of them, in places they forgot as soon as they left them: attics, storerooms, shared apartments, once even, in summer, a cemetery, until they ended up in a ghetto, which severely curtailed their freedom of movement. They weren't shot into the icy Danube in winter, like a few thousand others. But nor did they have the little piece of luck to come across one of the international helpers at just the right time: Swedes, Swiss, Spaniards, or the Apostolic Nuncio, people in the diplomatic service who were issuing safety passes hand over hand like brothers of Sisyphus. There were never enough. With the Soviet Army approaching Budapest, the Goldmans, along with tens of thousands of others, were driven westwards, back to where they had come from, with their two suitcases, more than six years earlier. The suitcases were long gone, and they were not the same any more, either.

They marched, and they were transported in trains, and from some of the station signs they could tell that they were getting closer to home. They didn't talk about it. All around them people were falling sick with typhoid and typhus, and dying overnight; they froze, they starved. Those who didn't die spent all day digging. They buried the dead, and they built the South-East Wall, proud monument of the final great defence; they built it with pickaxes and shovels, four metres deep and four metres wide, and they lined the walls with wood. In many places, concrete had run out, and so had the labourers' rations. Toilets and washing facilities had not run out; they had never been requested: a few rusty buckets were put out for them in the windowless wine cellars, the unheated barns, the cowsheds and pigpens, in all the miserable, hastily requisitioned rooms where they were billeted and locked in every night; hundreds, thousands of people the length of the border, who defied death for as long as they were able to dig. The buckets in the sheds were also intended to reduce resistance to death; simple techniques like this are excellent for spreading intestinal diseases, and lice, which transmit typhus. It really is a most effective method: lock them up in close proximity and mix them with their own excrement.

And when those who were left — the old, the war-wounded, and the farmers' wives — and still had a home and somewhere to wash and could still present themselves, outwardly at least, as civilised, in spite of the approaching front; when, in the mornings, these neatly combed locals saw the procession of the damned dragging themselves to their trenchwork with pickaxes and shovels, they were able to see, understand, and testify that these were not humans but vermin in human form: filthy, riddled with lice, stinking, wretched, so ghastly that you just wished they would quickly move on out of sight and disappear, perhaps straight into the trenches they were digging. The mere sight of them seemed to bring bad luck. No one wanted to see this, not so clearly. But the train kept bringing more of the ragged figures.

Let us set aside the big questions of human dignity and maximum human evil. Let us try to distinguish a strategy, or less than that: an intention. What did they actually want, the Ferbenzes and Neulags, the Horkas and Stipsitses, the Podezins, Nickas, and Muralters who were responsible for these conditions? What did their superiors want? Did they really want to build a wall that would keep the Red Army at bay? Or did they want to kill a large number of people as fast as possible while also saving ammunition? *Extermination through labour* — while their ideological leaders had a specific term for it, someone like Horka probably at least had a clear sense of what was required. At any rate, they don't really seem ever to have decided between these two objectives. The objectives contradicted each other. Half-starved typhoid patients build neither quickly nor well. Disposing of their inconvenient, infectious corpses also wastes time and manpower. Oh yes, they did indeed kill many thousands of forced labourers this way, and many thousands they intentionally let die. And yes, they did build a long, long wall, but in most places it was overrun soon afterwards, like a barricade of toothpicks.

One person did notice the discrepancy between the two objectives. That was Josef Graun of Darkenbloom, stationed at the time in Steinherz, around one hundred and fifty kilometres south-west of Löwingen, which also meant that he was no longer able to visit his fiancée, Resi, later Reschen, every weekend; it was simply too far. He was in command of the Steinherz section of the Wall's construction, and he was proud of how well he had organised it. As usual, he got Hitler Youth and people from the *Volkssturm* territorial army to guard the labourers, but he set them to work on carefully, topographically selected sections of the construction. Each of these smaller, and thus more manageable, groups started digging at a certain point, from which they slowly moved out in two directions, southwards and northwards, so that each group divided once more. Ideally, after a few days, the northern half of group B would meet up with the southern half of group A, and each would start cladding in the opposite direction. This made it much easier to oversee the progress of construction, and sections that were lagging behind could swiftly be identified and supported by bringing in fresh labourers or stricter guards, depending on the reason. Graun was determined to avoid mass construction sites like those to the south of Darkenbloom, where Horka was sowing his usual chaos. He regarded them with a pedant's secret contempt. When you got there, the labourers were swarming around like ants in confusion, no order, no overview, and they were probably only digging if a guard kept a close eye on them. Which was difficult, with all that running around. His section was nothing like that; there, all was order, overview, control.

He had sketched out his system on a beer mat for Horka one Saturday evening, when they were sitting in the bar of the Tüffer: the separate sections, the digging towards each other. But Horka had just stared at him with his drinker's eyes and said, yeah, Josef, right you are; you do it your way, I'll do it mine.

Afterwards, Resi had whispered to him that he ought to be careful around Horka, that he was more or less in bed with Ferbenz, at least by phone. Josef made fun of the telephonic bed-sharing, and whispered in Resi's rosy ear that Horka, the gypsy bastard, wouldn't always be the most Aryan of Aryans, you wait and see; we'll be having a chat about his parentage when the war's over! But Resi had just opened her eyes very wide and begged him not to say so out loud; please, Josef, do it for me, at least.

Not long after this, one after another, Graun's construction sites fell behind; everything got slower and slower, as if somewhere a brake were gently being applied. He patrolled the individual sections and took a look at what was going on. It was clear to Graun that you had to keep the labourers in at least basic physical condition if their man-power was important to you. It doesn't mean you have to like them, he told his subordinates, but if they're meant to work, they have to eat. Now he learned from one of the guards that they had had no food for days. Which was what they looked like. These people simply couldn't go on, not just the ones who had been digging nicely a week earlier, but the ones who had only arrived a few days ago, as well. They'd not had much before, but now they literally got nothing at all. In Section C a man collapsed before Graun's eyes; his knees simply gave way, and he fell forward into the mud, and was immediately taken away. I'll send some new ones, he promised his deputies at the site, got in his car, and drove back.

What Josef Graun found out over the next few days was both shocking and dangerous. However, after checking the lists of supplies and comparing them with previous ones, after making phone calls and speaking directly to some of his men in the labourers' various billets, he had collected sufficient evidence. It appeared that the district administration was misappropriating provisions earmarked as trench workers' rations — hundreds of kilograms of them. But this was sabotage! Perhaps it was only at this point that Josef Graun realised how many of the highest offices in the region were occupied by Darkenbloomers, and that they were almost all his age: Neulag and Horka in that district administration, and Ferbenz, Dr Alois, of whom everyone was so proud, the local boy with the PhD, up there in Graz. Graun had to report his discovery to one of his superiors. His immediate superior was Neulag, the very man who was presumably misappropriating the supplies. There was nothing for it but to skip several ranks and speak directly to Ferbenz.

Ferbenz received him almost affectionately, the Blood Order pinned to his right breast pocket. Since meeting the Führer in person, he mentioned it in every conversation; Graun had heard people talk about it. And so he listened reverently, picked up the word *Führer* and tossed it back at him like flattering confetti; he described the son of the Darkenbloom cobbler, now a Deputy Gauleiter, as a born leader himself, since his very first day at school! 'The only one who didn't get it straight away was Horka. Remember how we all jumped him, after he attacked you? We practically killed him. That taught him a thing or two.'

Ferbenz laughed conceitedly. However, when Josef Graun got around to the reason for his visit, the laughter died. After the first few sentences, Ferbenz stood and walked over to the window. Graun had to relate all the information he had gathered, all his clues, suppositions, and half-proofs, to Ferbenz's uniformed back. As he was getting no reaction, he got particularly carried away on the delay to the construction of the Wall. He had told himself he would avoid the word *sabotage*, but it must have slipped out. 'All I mean is: the front is getting closer, and we're in danger of failing — failing at the sacred task the Führer ...'

Ferbenz turned and looked at him, with his pale blue, slightly watery eyes. There was a moment's silence. Then the Deputy Gauleiter, his voice expressionless, recommended that he report it to the police. 'With the best will in the world, Josef, I can't advise you to do anything else. But be so good as to leave me out of it. I'm sure you've got enough to go on.'

6.

THE TRAIN CARRYING THE Goldmans took them as far as Kirschenstein; they had to march the rest of the way. Just outside Darkenbloom, Sascha deliberately fell and buried his hands deep in the earth. Jumping up again, quick as a flash, he rubbed his hands across his face to blacken it. His father was beside him, but for several days he had barely spoken. Sascha suspected he was giving up. Like most things now, the thought seemed to arrive from some distant place of no emotion. They were taken to the castle, to the stables where the Countess's racehorses used to stand. The following day, they were led to the nearby section of the Wall, where they dug and shovelled again, as on their previous stops. For the first time in a long while, Sascha's thoughts were less of food than of escape. Where, if not here? But it was hopeless. Anyone who started running was shot. It had happened again and again. Just three, four streets from the castle, and he would be home. But his mother would want to save his father, too, which would be dangerous, fatal even, for them both. And so he had to stay. It was impossible for both of them to flee. And as soon as his disappearance was noticed, his father would be shot. There was no way out. He had to stay.

I have to stay, he was telling himself, in time with his footsteps, as they walked back to the castle in the evening, *I have to stay*. As they were going in through the gate, the rows in front came to a standstill; someone had stumbled, and others were falling over him. His father gave Sascha a sudden, hard, sideways push, grabbing his shovel as he did so. Without moving fast, without a last look at him, Sascha stepped aside, veered off and casually strolled away, like a passer-by. He straightened up slightly and walked on, keeping the rhythm. He waited for the shot. A bead of sweat formed between his shoulder blades and ran down his spine, as if tracing the invisible line to aim for. In front of him was the main square, the plague column; ten more paces and he would be behind the war memorial, out of sight. Twenty paces to Karnergasse. Hide in a corner, in a shed, under a car. Wait till everything's quiet, maybe sleep a bit. Around two or three in the morning, go home. Let them come and fetch him from there.

In the dead of night he found the door locked. He reached up and knocked quietly on the windows. Nothing happened. He knocked louder. Where were they, where were his grandparents? He waited, and knocked again. The door opened a crack; it was dark inside. 'Mother,' whispered Sascha, stepping closer. Behind the door stood his Uncle Max in pyjamas, pointing a gun at him.

'It's me — Schani,' whispered Sascha. 'Let me in, I've run away.'

'Piss off,' said Max, so loudly that Sascha flinched. 'Piss off. Elisabeth is dead, you hear, dead, no one here wants you any more, go away, you're putting us all in danger.'

As he closed the door, a child began to cry inside the house.

At half past two in the morning, that pitch-black hour when, all through the ages, the old and sick die especially quietly and easily, Sascha ran through the oldest part of Darkenbloom, zigzagging across the cobblestones, along the house walls, wherever there was least light. He just wanted to get out of town, into the forest; he wasn't paying enough attention to where he was going, seven years had gone by since he had last been there. And so he blundered into a dead end.

And as he was spinning around, looking for a way out between the walls and fences, someone spotted him, in the middle of the night, a horror-struck but compassionate soul. A young woman called out to him quietly in Hungarian; he answered. Moments later a gate opened and he slipped inside. They only exchanged a few sentences; she asked if he had come from the castle, if he was one of the labourers, he said yes, and that was enough for her. She led him through to the courtyard at the back, into a brick-walled shed. She lit a candle, and together they pushed aside the firewood as fast as they could, so he could squeeze in behind it. She brought him a blanket, two hard-boiled eggs and an apple, and left him alone in his hiding place.

It was two women who brought him supplies, one of whom he never saw. He spoke Hungarian with the one who had let him in, but only the bare minimum. The other gave a short whistle when she left his food in the shed, and he didn't come out from behind the woodpile until she had gone. The food — eggs, boiled potatoes, a crust of bread — was simply wrapped in paper; nothing could indicate that the women had helped him. A tiny jack-knife with a horn handle had been left the first time. He had kept it; presumably he was meant to. At night, he used the Hungarian woman's privy. It can't last much longer, she had told him. She was about his age. The first few days, both women brought hay and straw so he wouldn't freeze to death behind the wood. Sometimes he heard a child crying or babbling; luckily they didn't have a dog. He made a notch in a log for each day that passed. It grew a little warmer. For two days there was no food, because no one came. The noise of battle was so loud that Sascha decided to stay behind his woodpile. Suddenly his saviour was back. She was weeping. The Russians had been in the town, but the Germans had driven them out again, she stammered; she had no idea what would happen next, they were shooting everything to pieces. She was going to flee to the forest with the other women. She gave him a little package of food, probably the last that she could spare, and wished him luck. He asked about the labourers in the castle. She bit her lip. 'They've been gone a while now,' she said, 'and the castle's on fire.'

'Thank you for everything,' he said, as she turned away. He suspected she was still weeping as she left.

Soon after her husband and son had fled, Eliza Goldman had surrendered her two rooms in her parents' house to her brother, and moved out. Max cheered on all that Neulag and his people promoted as the great new era: the white flags, the new racial purity, the so-called economic reawakening that, as she saw it, had first created shortages in healthcare provision, and was based on robbery and theft. But she said nothing; her position was precarious enough already. After even old Dr Bernstein was driven out, she managed to rent Room 22 in the hotel on a long-term basis. She worked in the kitchen, washed up and peeled potatoes, and she was so grateful to the indefatigable Resi for this arrangement that she wordlessly accepted being called by her maiden name and addressed as Fräulein.

Towards the end of the war, when everything was falling apart, she fled in good time to Kirschenstein with her mother, where relatives took them in. They returned in the late summer of 1945, when the worst was over. Max had been arrested and was being held in an American camp. As her parents' house was still standing, the easiest and most obvious thing seemed to be for her to move back into her childhood room and look after her little nephew and her sister-in-law, who was pregnant again.

One year later — Max was still in detention, his daughter had been born — Resi whispered to Eliza one day that Jenő was alive. He was in Stossimhimmel, waiting to be brought to Darkenbloom to give a witness statement. Eliza wanted to find out more from the Russians who were headquartered in the Hotel Tüffer, but Resi forbade it. She would pass on everything Eliza needed to know, she said, but right now she should keep quiet, go home, and say nothing to anyone for the time being.

'Witness to what?' Eliza asked, and Resi said, 'Oh, all these Nazi crimes, who can tell one from another?'

And no, she hadn't heard anything about Sascha, Resi insisted, only about Jenő and a second witness. Perhaps the second witness was Sascha? 'Let's wait and see,' said Resi, ending the conversation. 'There's nothing we can do right now.' With that, she hurriedly took her leave, and went back to the bar to serve the Russians her one-armed husband was playing cards with so skilfully.

A few days later, a grubby boy knocked on Eliza's door. He asked her name; she told him; he shook his head, fist clenched behind his back. 'Who are you looking for?' Eliza asked. He shook his head again, and made to turn and leave. She gripped his shoulder and switched to the other language. 'Goldman,' she said, 'my name is Erzsébet Goldman.' The boy gave her a note and ran away. The note asked her to come to the border at midday with her passport: *just to be on the safe side*, it said. Signed with a *J*.

So she set off immediately and by half past eleven she was standing at the border, waiting patiently, for a long time. It was September, no longer hot, hardly anyone around. Russian soldiers, Austrian border guards, mostly military traffic. No one paid her any attention. She waited. Later, she didn't know when exactly she first became aware of what was referred to afterwards, curiously, as *the shootout on the border*, as if someone had shot back.

She had been staring fixedly down the road that led from Over There to the border installation. But because there was nothing to be seen for so long, her attention flagged. Green military transport vehicles arrived from time to time. Then, finally, a white truck came lurching towards the border. It was kicking up dust and seemed in permanent danger of coming off the road, first to the left, then the right. Everyone looked up, then the border guards started shouting and holding up their red signalling discs. The truck kept weaving towards them. A few soldiers started running. Someone fired a warning shot into the air. It looked as if the truck was going to drive straight into the border guards' hut. They had started to close the barrier; there was a shrill blast of the horn and the guards leapt back. Miraculously, the truck made it through the remaining gap. Later, Eliza often wondered if she had really seen it or had just imagined it: a shadowy figure that could have been her husband, trying to reach the steering wheel, which seemed to have no one behind it. Struggling to get the vehicle under control; not really succeeding. It was a few split seconds. She could have imagined it. The horn blaring: the whole time, or only as the truck came hurtling across the border? Three border guards ran in her direction. Someone grabbed her from behind and pulled her to the ground. The truck was peppered with bullets; everyone knew that, later; it sat around for a long time afterwards like a forgotten prop. Many Darkenbloomers saw it sitting there in the weeks that followed; they saw that someone had been deadly serious about stopping it. Afterwards, two men, one dead and one seriously wounded, lay in the dust on the Austrian side, and the Russians decided to send the wounded man back to Hungary. The dead man was swiftly covered with a grey cloth; Eliza didn't know where it had come from. Nor did she know where Agnes Kalmar had come from, who was suddenly standing beside her, hugging her, holding her tight and murmuring crazy things in her ear. She had suffered bouts of madness since being raped, but in the years that followed Eliza was almost certain that this one, on the border, had been feigned.

Jenő lay in the dust, shot and wounded, but he seemed to still be alive. She wasn't allowed to go to him; someone was holding her in an iron grip. It felt like forever before people arrived to help. Dr Sterkowitz was driven up in a Jeep; he leapt out and proceeded to bandage the injured man. Jenő's head turned; she didn't know whether he had turned it himself, or whether it was the doctor who had moved it. His face was covered in blood; she couldn't tell if he was actually looking at her. It looked as if he was just staring at her legs. Then he was lifted up and put on the bed of a truck. It turned round and drove back to the other side. The dead man was still lying there. More soldiers came; a lot of policemen came. Eliza sat with Agnes by the side of the road. Agnes held her tight. Finally, the officials noticed the two women.

'She can identify him,' cried Agnes, holding her tight. 'She can identify the man! The dead man is her husband! Listen — she knows him!'

They uncovered the body for her, briefly. She had never seen him before; it was just some man, a bit older, but because it wasn't Sascha, and because it seemed so important to Agnes, she eventually nodded and confirmed that this was Jenő Goldman, born 16 January 1895. And the man was buried under that name in the Jewish cemetery in Darkenbloom; a rabbi had to be fetched specially from Graz to conduct the short, unfamiliar ceremony.

Elisabeth Rehberg, who, as Darkenbloom seemed to expect of her, never used her married name again, corresponded for another ten years with Jenő, her former husband. For safety reasons, the letters were exchanged via a third party. The go-between was a greedy woman in Stossimhimmel who took money for her services. The letters were primarily about what the two of them were doing in their respective countries to try to discover what had happened to their son. In the refugee winter of 1956, when chaos and confusion reigned in Darkenbloom, Eliza worried for several days that Jenő would simply turn up on her doorstep. But when she heard from him again, it was by letter. He was already in Vienna; he wrote that he planned to go to Israel and keep looking there. He promised to write as soon as he found anything out. After that, she never heard from him again. But she knew he would not have broken his promise. She knew that, if she heard nothing, it meant there was nothing to tell.

7.

THAT NIGHT IN THE summer of 1989 when the storm drove the people of Darkenbloom out of their beds, old Frau Graun was so drunk that she was the only one who heard nothing at all. As has been mentioned, her alcohol consumption would increase steadily throughout the week, usually reaching its peak on Saturday evening. For years now it had fallen to her daughter-in-law to make excuses for her absence at church on Sunday, on account of illness, though no one even bothered to ask any more, except perhaps some joker making fun.

'Vroni not manage to get out of bed again today, then?' one of them would say, and Karin would answer stonily that unfortunately her mother-in-law had not been feeling well that morning.

'She didn't get out of bed, she fell out,' the joker's wife may have whispered, 'and couldn't get up again!' Suppressed grins all round. Frau Karin, however, pretended not to hear. She dragged the children away and made a great deal of pushing them into the pew. She was proud that her children crossed themselves with conspicuous precision.

That Sunday, old Frau Graun had appeared in the early evening, in surprisingly good spirits, had poured herself a large glass of diluted apple juice, gulped it down, and asked her daughter-in-law what had been going on in town that afternoon. She seldom asked, but when she did, Karin had got used to telling her the truth. It was a sort of contract between the two of them. Karin would seek the old woman's advice whenever she feared her husband was about to make his next tactical or financial error. She would ask her for arguments or reassurance, depending on the situation. She never presented any of these arguments as having come from his mother; that would have been counterproductive. But Karin hoped that, with vigilance and the old woman's advice, she would be able to prevent the worst. Basically, she couldn't stand her mother-in-law, but she respected her more than she did her husband. They're two different things. Karin was vaguely aware that the old woman provided some sort of protection; she conferred upon them a certain standing in Darkenbloom that, without her, they might lose. And so she definitely did not wish her dead. Although often enough she did mutter something along these lines, through gritted teeth, when cleaning the old woman, and her bed, and her room, after a bad night.

Old Frau Graun wanted nothing more from life; she had no desire to influence anyone, either, neither her son nor her daughter-in-law, she just wanted her peace and quiet. That, at least, was what she had believed for a long time, ever since her son had taken over the business, in fact. Recently, though, she had wanted to know things from time to time, because there seemed to be something stirring in the town. And so, occasionally, she asked. In her opinion, her daughter-in-law was definitely not the sharpest knife in the drawer, and in this respect well suited to her permanently resentful son, the wimp. But Karin was at least smart enough not to pick a fight with her. She had never even tried. As far as Frau Graun was concerned, this clearly indicated a bare minimum of intelligence.

And so that Sunday, which could have ended as a quiet evening in front of the TV with her son and daughter-in-law, she learned that human remains had been found up in the Rotenstein meadow.

That a fairly large official delegation had arrived from Kirschenstein, consisting of the public prosecutor, crime scene photographer, and forensics team, even though it was the weekend, and that they had already examined and cordoned off the area. That this find had caused quite a sensation in Darkenbloom, and that as it was Sunday a lot of people had driven up there and stood around speculating wildly. That — strange coincidence — Heuraffl had, just then, caught a fugitive from East Germany in his forest cabin and had given him a terrible beating. One of them, either Heuraffl or the fugitive, had almost been arrested, but then Malnitz had intervened and it had all calmed down again.

So many strange events: something really was going on for once. Karin laughed when, at the end of her tale, she recalled the misunderstanding: someone had asked the local reporter how many there were, and he had answered *maybe fifteen*. The person asking had meant corpses, while the reporter was talking about the commission of inquiry ...

'Yes, yes,' said old Frau Graun dismissively, who, as always, grasped what was being said faster than Karin could say it. 'That's actually not nearly as funny as you think. But tell me: whose land was it on? Ours or Malnitz's?'

'Ours,' said Karin, beginning to realise that it might have been better if she had been a little less forthcoming. With two more curt, pointed questions, the old woman found out that her own son, Karin's husband, had been digging there because he had joined the water rebels and had heard from Toni Malnitz ...

At this point the old woman interrupted with a wave of her hand. She heaved herself up from the table, muttering, and left the room. 'But Vroni,' Karin called after her, 'supper'll be ready in a minute ...?'

Old Frau Graun, shuffling back to her room, responded with her rusty witch's laugh. 'I have a son who goes and digs up the Rotenstein meadow of his own accord because a Malnitz tells him to,' she called over her shoulder. 'I certainly don't need food after that, I feel sick already!'

The door slammed. Karin shook her head. Ten minutes later, her husband came home.

When she told him what had happened, Young Graun groaned. 'All the old stories,' he said, 'one way or another they're all obsessed with the old stories. Mama, Ferbenz, old Malnitz, the whole lot of them are screwed up by the war.'

Nonetheless, because his wife entreated him, he went to his mother's door, knocked, and urged her to come and eat. There was silence on the other side, but when he knocked again, *bam* — heavy objects flew against the door, probably books; *bam, bam.* Young Graun knew what this meant. He retreated to the kitchen and wondered, yet again, how much longer she could survive it. She had been like this for decades. As a child, he sometimes used to stand beside her bed — it must have been in the daytime, because the image in his mind was so bright and clear, of her lying on her back with her mouth wide open, saliva trickling out. Back then, he had never worried that she might die, because he hadn't known it was a possibility. His childish yearning for her to wake up and be normal again was agonising enough. But perhaps she belonged to a special, alien species that schnapps, instead of killing, preserved from the inside out. Perhaps the schnapps was deliberately not doing what she hoped it would do. Perhaps it was all just a ghastly conspiracy, thought Young Graun. It wasn't the first time his thoughts had taken this turn, and when they did, he realised that, in this respect, there was not much to choose any more between him and his relatives and acquaintances.

Somewhere deep inside the mean, drunken old Frau Graun there was still a little bit of the blonde Veronika who spoke so nicely and once caught the eye of the debauched young Tüffer son. At fourteen, under the hotel owner's cold gaze, she had understood that being pretty, on its own, was not enough, and nor was any amount of *how do you do* and *at your service*.

Everything she had wanted back then had been snatched from under her nose by Resi, her former best friend with the fat, lopsided peasant face who acted as if she couldn't count to three and wouldn't have a clue how to differentiate between the male and female of the species. Resi, with her gormless expression, whom Vroni had so unforgivably underestimated, had even duped the boss of the Tüffer. And so one thing had led to another: Resi got the apprenticeship, because while old Frau Tüffer knew an awful lot, she clearly didn't know that for what her son was always after, it wasn't the face that mattered. And later, when the Tüffers left, it was Resi who was given the keys to the whole hotel. As the Tüffers never came back, the apprentice became the boss. And with that, of course, she immediately became a great deal better-looking, at least in the eyes of all the young men who were regulars in the hotel bar and at the Sunday morning drinks. In the white boss's smock, ordering her employees around in an authoritative voice, and just as good at arithmetic as her schoolfriend Veronika, Resi automatically looked a great deal better, and her backside and bosom really weren't bad at all.

In the last winter of the war, shortly before everything fell apart, Vroni unexpectedly encountered Josef Graun. She hadn't seen him in Darkenbloom for ages. Resi had supposedly been engaged to him for a while, but engagements were quickly made and broken off again in wartime. Most of the men were gone; brothers and fathers were at the front and Vroni, as the eldest, had to accompany her grandfather, doing the rounds of the few markets that were still taking place.

And there, right down in the south, halfway to Graz, Josef Graun, who had always been so good-looking, was suddenly standing in front of her. He pointed to the sack of potatoes and asked the price.

'How many d'you want?' asked Vroni, not understanding.

'The whole thing, lass,' Graun replied. He really did buy the whole sack, then and there. Vroni could hardly believe her luck. Her grandfather wanted to carry it over for the gentleman, but Vroni said, 'No, stay there, I'll do it.'

And so she carried the sack over to Graun's car herself, and as he took it from her and was setting it down in the back she quickly adjusted her hair, pinched her cheeks, and moistened her lips. When he looked up again, he finally recognised her. She smiled.

'Give my best to Resi, won't you,' said Graun, as he handed her the money. And Vroni plucked up courage and looked him dead in the eye.

'Resi ...' she said, slowly, 'she's been with someone else for a while now.'

'Is that true?' he asked.

'Oh yes,' asserted Vroni, who knew it wasn't the whole truth, and added, 'He's living with her already, helping her run the hotel.'

Graun leaned against his car and felt for his cigarettes. When he found them, he offered her one.

'Not Neulag, though,' he asked, 'or Horka?'

'God forbid,' she said, 'no, no one from round here, an invalid, he's only got one arm. Reschen, he's called.'

He lit her cigarette; his fingers were trembling. She touched his hand briefly. They stood there, smoking. Vroni fought back the urge to retch and cough, but she held the cigarette very elegantly. Finally, Graun gave a deep sigh and said, 'I'd forgotten how fetching you are.'

'How can you forget a thing like that?' she answered. And then he asked if she felt like coming with him for a bit, and she did feel like it, and while her grandfather waited for her at the market, she was being driven around in the car, and relishing the fact that this man still had both his arms, and that they were handsome and strong, that this suited her and her famous face much better, and that everything was finally working out as it was supposed to.

A few weeks later, the day before Palm Sunday, Vroni was also on duty at the party in the castle. Resi had sent for her and some other women to come and help out; Resi herself was downstairs in the kitchen, overseeing it all. Vroni was upstairs, serving in the dining room along with Agnes Kalmar, and Theresia Wallnöfer, who was shot dead by the Russians not eleven days later. The pretty ones served the food, the less pretty ones ran between dining room and kitchen, and the unpretty ones cooked: the Tüffer boss decided who did what.

Although they had known Neulag forever, they were all afraid of him. For some time now, he had been coming and going at the castle as if it belonged to him. The Countess laughed when she saw him, and the Count took him hunting, as he had done for years. To the gossips of Darkenbloom, these two things seemed irreconcilable, because they didn't want to believe that the Count was capable of such stupidity and blindness. They also didn't want to imagine that the Countess could be properly, or rather improperly, involved with Neulag — with one of them, one of the common people. Their unshakable belief in the divinely ordained distinctions of class prohibited them from even thinking such a thing. They revered the Countess because she was the Countess. They had always had a countess here. That the counts, or the counts' sons, might occasionally sample the tender fruits of the peasantry was not so unimaginable: it happened. That was just nature; it was practically an honour for the girls concerned. But the countesses? They were what you might call representatives of the saints on earth. The women of Darkenbloom almost curtseyed whenever they heard the title. If there had been a few more subjects this reverential in Austria as a whole, the restoration of the monarchy might have had a real chance, even then.

Neulag is trying his luck, shamelessly, as if the Countess were a bar-girl, and because she quite likes him, too, she finds it amusing, otherwise she'd have to punish him severely. This was more or less what the gossiping young women imagined, in their naivety; this was the full extent of what they believed possible — well, not just possible, it was exactly what they saw, with their own eyes.

The idea that the Count might simply not care if the Countess was kept distracted and in good humour, or that he might even have reasons of his own, was equally far from their minds. They curtseyed and blushed and lowered their eyes, and congratulated themselves on being allowed to work in these magnificent rooms instead of in the stables, in the fields, or in a shop, on being able to tell everyone at home about the chandeliers and the gilded chair backs, and when they served the guests they tried to look only discreetly out of the corners of their eyes, or up through their eyelashes, never at anyone directly, in the face.

At Neulag's party, the serving girls had their work cut out for them; there was eating, drinking, and dancing, and they didn't get to stop for a moment. Later, some of them testified that Neulag was called to the telephone at some point, but Vroni didn't see this. And she stuck to her story, although the official from Vienna who interrogated her about it was keen to squeeze this small admission out of her as well.

'If everyone's saying he went out to take a telephone call,' said the official, 'then you can admit it as well! What good will it do you not to?'

'What good will it do me if I admit to something I never knew?' countered Vroni, who by then was already the truculent, despairing Widow Graun. 'I don't know anything about any telephone!'

She had, however, happened to be standing right by Neulag's table, with the bottles of wine, white and red, when Josef Graun appeared — *her Josef*, as she already thought of him, with a leap of the heart. There was no mistaking the fact that he was uninvited, unwelcome, a nasty surprise, because Neulag's table fell silent, and even the

Countess, sitting at Neulag's side and leaning in towards him, paused briefly in her laughter. But at the other tables the drinking continued uninterrupted, which was why the little localised silence was probably scarcely noticeable, except to those who were there. The officials were far less interested in all this than in Neulag's phone call, about which Vroni really did know nothing.

Neulag saw Josef and jumped up, the chair toppling over behind him. 'You dare to come here,' he said.

'A misunderstanding,' said Josef, pale as a trout's belly. 'Give me five minutes, I beg of you, I can explain.'

And then they stood outside, the two of them, in front of the dining room, having a heated discussion; Vroni knew this for certain because after a while she made a point of going down to the kitchen laden with dirty plates and bowls, even though this wasn't her job. Other girls cleared the tables. She was a server, one of the elite. She even got told off by Resi because she appeared in the kitchen, which meant that she was missing upstairs, but she talked herself out of it by saying that she needed to go; she wasn't a man, after all, able to hold it in for hours on end. And as she had walked past the two of them, very slowly, because she was carrying so many heavy things, she had heard Neulag say to Graun, 'Well, you can prove it right now, your loyalty and trustworthiness! We need every man. Go downstairs to the gun room and check everything's ready.'

And Josef Graun, her future husband, had clicked his heels and saluted, as she walked past, hidden behind a pile of plates. 'At your orders and at your service, Herr Sturmscharführer,' he had answered.

And only the last part was a lie. Vroni had not actually heard the sentence about proving himself; it was Josef Graun who told her about it, not long afterwards, when the war was over. But she had no reason to doubt him. Quite the reverse. This was the sentence on which her truth and at least a modicum of peace of mind depended. By claiming to have witnessed a sentence that, strictly speaking, she had not heard, but which had absolutely, categorically been said, she supported Josef's version; it could be argued that anything he might have done, he was forced to do. Join in or be court-martialled, that was what Neulag's sentence meant; the threat wasn't even all that veiled. Soon she was convinced that she had indeed heard the sentence herself; her memory played it back to her on request, word for word, pin-sharp, as if engraved in vinyl. Josef, her husband and the father of her son, had been a decent Nazi. When he had noticed that someone was misappropriating the rations for the labourers working on the Wall, he had turned to the Deputy Gauleiter and followed his advice to file a complaint. We're talking hundreds of kilos of food! Unfortunately, in those last few months of the war, everything was already so chaotic that the law was no longer functioning properly. Because, yes, even the Nazis had had a form of law, though that was now disputed. The front was getting closer, the Wall was being built; even we women and the old people, those who were left, had to dig; everywhere was full of foreign workers, most of the men were at war, and there were Jews all over, those starving, louse-ridden figures. Just as *her Josef* discovered the theft of the provisions and filed the complaint, they introduced the *flying courts martial.* Josef had told her this, and it was true. Neulag had threatened, several times, that Josef would be court-martialled, and someone had tipped Josef off. To stop it coming to that, he had immediately driven to Darkenbloom to speak to Neulag face to face. He explained that he had only filed a complaint against persons unknown, that he had never thought Neulag himself was guilty. Rather, he was hoping for an investigation in which he and Neulag could work together closely to apprehend the embezzlers! That had not been entirely true, the despairing Widow Graun, whose scrawny child wasn't even walking yet, admitted to the Viennese official, but that's what he said back then, to gain time and avoid a court martial.

And then Neulag, who was coming under pressure from all sides, had ordered Josef to prove his loyalty and trustworthiness then and there, and had sent him to the gun room. 'I heard it myself,' the Widow Graun concluded, 'that's exactly how it was.'

'But how was he being asked to prove his loyalty?' the official asked. 'What did they do with all those guns?'

'How should I know?' moaned the Widow Graun. 'Josef cleaned and checked the guns and oiled them if necessary; he was very good at that.'

'Where did they go afterwards,' the official persisted, 'your husband, Neulag and all the others?'

'Josef was in the gun room all night,' Vroni Graun declared stubbornly, 'seeing to the guns and ammunition. Like I said, he was always very good at that, he knew what he was doing.'

'Frau Graun,' said the official, 'what happened in Darkenbloom that night? What have you heard from others? What did your husband tell you about it?'

'He was in the gun room,' repeated Vroni Graun, 'he was in the gun room all night, handing out guns and ammunition to the others, and later, at dawn, I had to wash and iron his uniform because it was so covered in oil. It took me ages to get all the stains out, it was a nightmare, I rubbed and rubbed, I thought it would never end, and everything was soaking wet and I had to iron it for hours. Listen — that was why Neulag shot him in the forest, and set fire to him as well, to cover his tracks, all because of that complaint during the war; why won't you finally do something about it? I'm stuck here all on my own with the farm and the boy! I don't know anything about a telephone, and I don't know who was in the ballroom, or outside for a moment, or when, I only know that Neulag, that criminal, had reason to kill my husband!'

Tears sprang to her eyes and she bit her fist.

'But Frau Graun,' said the official, 'as I'm sure you know,

Sturmscharführer Neulag is very unlikely to have survived the end of the war.'

She slammed her palm down on the table. The official flinched. 'Do you have a corpse?' she screamed. 'Show me Neulag's corpse!'

The official shook his head in resignation. 'You're a right bunch down there, in Darkenbloom,' he said.

'Young man,' said Vroni Graun, wiping away the tears and trying to smile, 'I don't suppose you have a little schnapps, do you? I feel so dizzy, I really could do with one.'

8.

SHE HAD SUSPECTED EVEN then that it couldn't have been Neulag. She knew, almost for certain, that it was Horka. But she couldn't say so, because, unlike her husband and Neulag, Horka was still there. And how: more terrible, more brutal than ever, completely out of control without his friends and superiors to rein him in. Years, decades later, she sometimes wondered whether it had been the wrong thing to do: leaving Horka out of it, instead of ensuring that he was at least detained for questioning. If he had been taken into custody, perhaps a few others would have spoken up as well. Back then, she hadn't dared. She didn't want to be the only one. She understood the balance of power; everybody did. Later, she sometimes thought she should have risked it, that even if she had failed, it would have been worth trying. She herself would have been no great loss; neither, with hindsight, would her drip of a son. But back then she was young and desperate, she still had her life ahead of her, so she clung to what little she had left: the child and the farm, which at first she didn't have the faintest idea how to run. It was all she had left of Josef, who, after his sensational death, was transformed for Vroni into a tremendous romantic hero, the great happiness of her life, in a time between bombs and shells, between Nazis and Russians. Alas, the happiness was over too damn soon.

She hadn't been seeking justice or atonement; those weren't terms she used. She wanted to protect her Josef, even though he was dead. Or for precisely that reason. The newspaper had used the word *execution*, after a projectile was found in the burnt corpse, and she couldn't get it out of her head. Her Josef had been one of the good ones, the decent ones, and he had been killed: after the war, after the victory over the Nazis, in so-called peacetime, in a country occupied by the Allies where, so the politicians kept claiming, a new era had dawned. As if! The evil Nazis went on killing the good Nazis with impunity, and all sorts of others as well. There were at least three murders just in that first year: the cyclist in the vineyards, and a shoot-out at the border, in which an unwanted witness was apparently killed. And her Josef. The Russians just looked on, or looked the local girls up and down, and you could count yourself lucky if looking was all they did.

As to whether she should do battle with the all-powerful Horka or devote herself to the memory of her husband, Josef with the strong arms, Veronika Graun chose the easier path. But what does that mean, chose? She simply took it, just as water flows whichever way it can. If it encounters an obstacle, it will flow around it, without any effort, without hesitation or comment.

Sometimes, very rarely, a tiny, individual decision is enough to steer history in a different direction. But only in the rarest of cases does someone have enough of an overview to still be able, later on, to identify other potential versions, and to see *logical consequences* beyond the ones that became fact.

What would have happened if the young but articulate widow Veronika Graun had told the external official interrogating her all that she knew? If she had divulged the shocking statement *her Josef* had planned to make? To save his own skin, mind you, not for any other reason.

The first to speak becomes a witness for the prosecution. And everyone else gets hung out to dry. If, however, as in this case, the first who wants to speak is successfully sidelined — *executed*, as the newspaper kindly made known to all and sundry — it has a lasting impact. And the wait for a second person who wants to speak will be a very long one. Perhaps that second person will never come.

The whole of Darkenbloom had an idea of what Josef Graun was planning to do. Clearly he had started to panic when the investigations began; he had made telling remarks.

Perhaps Veronika Graun might not even have had to tell them everything. Perhaps it would have been enough if she had told them that her husband had been planning to make a statement. That she didn't know what about, only that he had been afraid. And that she suspected Horka of having something to do with his death. That Horka had showed up at her house and ordered her to spend the day in Kirschenstein.

'Take the kid and go to Kirschenstein, now, this minute,' he said. 'There's something we've got to see to today, your husband and me; women'll just be in the way.'

'Is your wife going, too?' asked Vroni, who detested Horka; but he grabbed her by the arm, hurting her.

'D'you understand me,' he growled, twisting, 'or do I have to make it plain?'

And so she did as she was told. Josef had already gone out, so it was too late for her to ask him. It was too late for her to ask him anything ever again, because she never saw him again. They kept her away from his charred body.

If Veronika Graun had made a start, would a few others have been nudged into action? Might they perhaps have made witness statements, too — for example, about how Georg 'Schorsch' Horka had absolutely not been persecuted by the Nazi regime, as he had told the Allies, but had, on the contrary, been one of its most fervent and brutal defenders?

Sometimes, one tiny, individual decision is enough. What would have happened if, in 1938, the weak, faint-hearted Chancellor Schuschnigg had actually given the order for the military on Austria's borders to resist? Wouldn't one skirmish, however small — a dozen shots fired — have completely altered the image of Austria later on? Or would there have had to have been at least a dozen dead to prove there had been a willingness to resist? Who can say? These dozen dead: would they have been twelve young Austrians, whose posthumous medals *for Austria's freedom* could only be awarded seven years later? These young men — who, thanks to Schuschnigg's hesitation, did *not* die back then — are sure to have fathered a number of children, and their countless children's children are still making the world better, or worse, each according to their lights.

And Austria's image did remain intact for a while, despite Schuschnigg's hesitation. It wasn't until forty years after the war had ended that anyone challenged its honorary title of *Nazi Germany's first victim*, but they did so so forcefully that it shattered forever into tiny pieces, like the hand mirror of the evil queen. Since then, it would seem that the opposite alone is true. Everyone immediately points to the pictures of the cheering, waving crowds lining the streets to welcome the Führer. But that isn't wholly true, either. And that is precisely the problem with the truth. The whole truth, as the name implies, is the collective knowledge of all those involved. Which is why you can never really piece it together again afterwards. Because some of those who possessed a part of it will already be dead. Or they're lying, or their memories are bad.

That was how it was in Darkenbloom. And there was also another reason why no one said anything, about anything at all, after Josef Graun was found dead in the forest at the age of thirty-six; a very good reason why, for Darkenbloom, after the war, unlike for Austria in the year of the *Anschluss*, there were no other conceivable versions of events. Horka, the one to whom everything pointed, concerning the murder of Josef Graun and so much else as well; Horka, who was never an ideologue, planner, commander, or organiser, only an assiduous implementer and bloodthirsty executor of every shameful order, a sadist, a thug, a lusty murderer — this Horka was now very far from being just a simple labourer from Zwick. Nor was he Ferbenz's or Neulag's underling any more. At that time, Horka, incredible as it sounds, was, by order and with the approval of the Soviet occupiers, the head of the Darkenbloom police. And this was the man the Widow Graun and others should have accused, to the investigating officers from Vienna? The investigating officers would eventually leave; all the others would stay.

And so, just as water flows whichever way it can, Vroni Graun devoted herself to the memory of her Josef. According to her, he had been a good Nazi, because he had wanted to see his workers fed. She didn't know that his true ambition had been for progress on his section of the Wall to outstrip everyone else's, making him an even better Nazi, and it wouldn't have changed anything for her if she had. By filing the complaint against those who were stealing the provisions, he had put himself in terrible danger. And it wasn't just Vroni saying this — it had been verified. Neulag had written a letter in which he stated his intention to bring Graun before a court martial, and when the war was over, the letter was found, which resulted in Josef being released from custody after just a few weeks. Whereas a man like Ferbenz, the pride of Darkenbloom, was sentenced, and served two and a half years in prison.

Veronika Graun did the obvious thing. In order to preserve the memory of Josef Graun — who was found in the forest burnt beyond all recognition and identifiable only by his boots, his rifle, and the remains of his dog — as a good man driven by concern for the trench workers, practically a resistance fighter, there were many things about which she stayed silent. She added her voice to the deafening silence in Darkenbloom.

This aside, she was fighting for her survival. And that fight required everything of her. In a remarkably short time, she learned about wine growing, she taught herself to drive, she bribed an official to give her a driving licence, she found out where to hire the best seasonal workers; she made mistakes, too, oh yes, of course she made some bad mistakes, but she usually identified her mistakes pretty quickly. She borrowed money, everywhere; she learned how to talk to the rich farmers, half coquettish, half heart-rending. The farmers' wives hated her, not least because she, a woman, had the audacity to go on running the business on her own. They were all dead now, those farmers and their wives. She stole, too, from time to time, in those first few years. Only when she had absolutely no alternative. She would dress up smartly and drive to Graz or further afield, meet a man and, when the right moment came, relieve him of his wallet. The men were always very drunk by then.

As the economy slowly began to pick up, she became an expert on obtaining credit. She calculated and compared. She got very little sleep in those early years. She kept herself awake with wine and schnapps. This works for quite a while, if carefully controlled and deployed at the right moment. When her child fell over, she shouted *Get up*. When he cried, she shouted *Pull yourself together.* When the boy confessed that he was getting beaten up at school, she ordered him to stop his constant complaining right now. He should always be the first to throw a punch, then it simply wouldn't happen to him any more.

One day, when the child was at primary school, his music teacher called on her to extract permission for him to have violin lessons. She didn't really object. In those days, you did what teachers said. She didn't have to pay, either; the son of the husband she missed so sorely was awarded a scholarship for talented pupils.

It came as a surprise to her when he wanted to play the violin all the time. She made clear to him that the business came first. If he could find time to fiddle as well, that was up to him. Still, she let him carry on with his hobby after he finished school. He worked on the farm, he didn't talk much, his hair was too long, but other than that he made sure she had nothing to reproach him for. He went off somewhere else to practise; she seldom heard him play. She realised that this battle was becoming harder than she had anticipated. And that she would have to win it by cunning, not force. On a few occasions, he disappeared for a whole day; when asked, he mumbled something about trying to find a new teacher. Already he was spending far too much money on this nonsense; he seemed to be handing over everything he had to his teachers in Kirschenstein.

She found out that he was sometimes seen with a girl from Kalsching. One Saturday evening, she staged a total power cut on the farm. She went to Café Posauner, where the young people hung out in those days, fetched her son, and sent him home. Then she sat down at the table for a moment, with the girl. The girl looked uncomfortable. As soon as the door had closed behind her son, Vroni asked her if she intended to go to Vienna, or abroad, even, as the wife of a penniless musician. The girl, scarcely more than a child, shook her head shyly. 'Let me know when he has his big audition,' said old Frau Graun, 'and I promise you he'll never find out.'

And on that day, of all days, the tractor broke down first thing in the morning and had to be repaired. And then firewood was delivered, and stupidly it was dumped right in the entrance so you couldn't get past it. He could have got past on his moped, of course, but there was no question of the wood just being left there. Old Frau Graun, the inevitable fag in the corner of her mouth, calmly surveyed the mess. 'The idiots are out in force today,' she told her dumbfounded son, 'but since you're clearing these logs now anyway, you might as well chop them, too.'

He put off the wedding with the completely unmusical girl for so long that it was almost as if he sensed the betrayal. For a few years, he seemed to be numb. Then, suddenly, he stopped sitting with the youngsters, and sat at the regulars' table instead, with Ferbenz, which old Frau Graun was not at all happy about. Ferbenz, Neulag, or Horka, it was pretty much one and the same: she loathed them all. But her son had stayed: he hadn't simply vanished from Darkenbloom one day, like some of the other boys, and he did finally marry Karin from Kalsching, who wasn't the sharpest knife in the drawer, but who was at least reliable.

The tension of fighting for survival eased at last for Frau Graun, and she began to drink even more, much, much more, as systematically as she calculated different finance models. Her once-beautiful face had been ruined long ago. Little Lowetz, the son of Eszter from Over There, was not the first or last Darkenbloom child to get the idea that old Frau Graun could have been the model for the ghastly beggar on the plague column. From a young age, Darkenbloom children learned to look closely. They learned it better than they learned to speak. And so children often observed the likeness: the haggard face, the frozen despair. But it was only children who noticed it. Once they were grown up, they didn't seem to see it any more.

9.

THE OLD PEOPLE WHO remembered the end of the war in Darkenbloom couldn't have said exactly when it was, because it wasn't important. You could look up the fact that on Maundy Thursday, 29 March 1945, the Red Army, under the leadership of Marshal Fyodor Tolbukhin, crossed the border between Hungary and the German Reich in Burgenland. The South-East Wall, built on rivers of blood, the final, grandiose Führer-bunker fantasy, barely hindered them. They took Darkenbloom the same day, were unexpectedly ejected again two days later (Graun and Horka, drunk on victory, shouting after the retreating tanks), and fought their way back in over the first dismal days of April, with many victims on both sides, and on the third side as well, to be precise, because more than twenty civilians died, including the grandmother of little Fritz Kalmar, who also caught a piece of shrapnel in his head, in the same attack. No white flags were raised this time, either; the fighting continued until it was over. At that point, the rest of the regular defence troops, most of them very young Dutch and older SS men, retreated and fled westwards. The so-called *Volkssturm* territorial army, consisting of local youths and old men or invalids, surrendered. The Russians established their headquarters in the Hotel Tüffer, waited on by Resi and her one-armed husband.

They came uninvited. The people arriving now, the ones who were compulsorily billeted in every house, who commandeered all the schools, the presbytery, the Rosmarin villa, and the counts' two manor farms — these were the same people who, for seven years, had only ever been spoken of as vermin, subhuman, the Bolshevik-Jewish scum of the earth. Unlike the occupiers in the west of the country, they didn't hand out chewing gum and Cadbury bars; they tore the watches off people's arms. No one was glad to see them. No one waved and no one welcomed them. The Darkenbloomers kept their heads down and carried on; they tried to get used to the sight of them, to the sound of the language and the new rules. Everything was in flux, the rules included. A Russian Guards major in Kirschenstein who wanted to celebrate his birthday sent his men out into the town. They were to *collect* one litre of wine, two kilos of flour, and two eggs per household. The operation was called off after the mayor of Kirschenstein, taking his life in his hands, went to the commandant and complained. The collectors and the giver of the order were punished, but the story was told for years throughout the region as an example of what could happen *just because it's a Russian's birthday*.

The world had been turned on its head, but it still had to keep on going. The occupiers confiscated wood constantly, everywhere, and used it to build their barracks at lightning speed. Sometimes the number of soldiers stationed in the area was considerably greater than the population of Darkenbloom. They needed accommodation. Not a single plank was safe; Darkenbloom's sheds and hay barns all disappeared, and from the ruins of the castle they dragged every beam and every scrap of wooden flooring that hadn't been burned to a cinder. And so these first weeks were reduced to a grey monotony of hardship, fear, and the struggle for survival: difficult, in retrospect, to get an overview of or decipher them.

There was, however, a particular day from this period that the old Darkenbloomers did remember, a day sunk into their memories like a gatepost, as deeply as that other one, the night before Palm Sunday when the wild party was held in the castle, just before the downfall. Really, they might as well have set fire to the castle that very night after the last guest had gone.

The second unforgettable day was the summer's day Horka returned. He had vanished off the face of the earth in the interim, just like Neulag, Ferbenz, and all the other dashing commanders. The day he came back, the post-war period, which in previous weeks had been in a confused state of flux, began to solidify. And Darkenbloomers would have had some justification for thinking that there was not much difference between the before and after. Life was hard — it was made hard for them, as if the difficulties of living on the border weren't already enough. *You don't want to get involved in anything, not after all we've lived through ...*

Horka reappeared, not humiliated, emaciated, and in chains, like the defeated in Roman triumphal processions, but in a neat new uniform, smoking and laughing with the foreign occupiers, clapping each other on the back. It was as if he had always been their best friend, better even than one-armed Reschen, whom one might also ask what he saw in these boorish fellows from the East.

But how had this come about? No one really knew. Horka had fled westwards with the last of the SS men. They had intended to join up as quickly as possible with any units that were still fighting. But Horka had disappeared at the first opportunity, ducking off to the side when no one was looking, into the bushes, into the woods. Later, much later, people said he dug up a half-buried forced labourer along the way and swapped clothes with the corpse. The truth of this story can no longer be established. It may have originated in a boast of his own, but it's more likely that it endured for so long because it is a perfect description of Horka's ghastliness. Horka was capable of anything, and would do it with his bare hands. *Just you wait: if you don't behave, Horka will come and get you.*

What is certain is that he fled far into the west, where no one knew him any more, to Salzburg or Tyrol, and got himself papers that identified him as a victim of persecution under the Nazi regime. He returned with said papers and was given his neat new uniform and appointed chief of police. As a person with knowledge of the local area, he helped catch people the Soviets regarded as criminals, such as those suspected of war crimes committed against Soviet soldiers, prisoners of war, or forced labourers; also the so-called Werewolves, secret, unrepentant Nazis who carried out acts of sabotage and planned terrorist attacks on the Allies. In most cases, the charges were of spying or unlawful possession of a gun, this last an offence of which almost anyone could be accused, especially here in the countryside. In any event: those who had shot Hungarian Jews, had beaten or tortured them to death during the war, did not fall under the definition. Horka soon found this out. The fate of some Jews on German or Austrian soil was not something the Soviets were interested in, not unless they had been Soviet citizens. From this point of view, a person like Horka was better off in the Soviet sector than in those of the more ethical Western powers.

The occupiers punished most harshly when their instructions were not followed. They were only interested in themselves and in their own. An unfortunate young man in Löwingen slapped the Soviet commandant's son three times and disappeared to Kolyma for six years. Two years for each slap. At least Horka had nothing to do with that.

What he got up to in Darkenbloom was more than enough. He named names to his Russian friends, and those people were picked up. In the beginning he also named the names of people who simply irritated him, or had made pointed remarks to him after his return, along the lines of *You've got a nerve*. In the first weeks and months, when the occupiers were acutely on edge, fearing resistance, sabotage, and attacks, this was child's play. They were dependent on their intermediaries, and Horka was the local. Several Darkenbloomers were picked up. None were sent to the gulag, as happened elsewhere; it was enough that, for a few weeks, no one knew where they were or what they had been accused of. Horka was setting an example, as a warning, consolidating his reign of terror. After this, he only had to threaten, eventually just raise an eyebrow, and the turkeys, the bacon rinds, the potatoes, eggs, flour, and jam all came to him of their own accord, as if they had legs.

And so it went on for several years. Gradually, the situation eased; most of the foreign soldiers withdrew and went home. Little by little, the new Austrian institutions and departments took up their work, more and more areas of authority were handed over to them, and one day Horka, still only in his early forties, was pensioned off. It came as a surprise, and so abruptly that it is reasonable to assume his previous life must have had something to do with it. Somewhere, something had filtered through. No one ever knew who gave the order, who it was who kicked him out. It must have come from high up, and far away.

Still: pensioned off, meaning benefits. He had lost his job, but the state looked after him. Whoever had had him replaced clearly did not want a scandal. Horka and his family got by, after a fashion.

There were incidents, because he found it hard to adapt to being deprived of power. Once, a man was pushing a handcart laden with leather and furs down Tempelgasse. Horka stepped out of his house and asked him if he wasn't afraid someone would take his nice leather. 'Who would steal it from me?' asked the man. 'There are no gypsies any more, no outsiders at all, in fact.' Horka slapped him on the back and laughed.

'How right you are,' he cried, laughing, 'to have such faith in your own people!'

Not long afterwards, though, at nightfall, this man was attacked from behind, beaten to the ground, and robbed of his leather. He had thought he recognised Horka's stocky silhouette just before he was hit, but he refused to report the crime, nor did he do anything else about it. He let his wife scold him for his stupidity, gritted his teeth, and worked long and hard to recoup the considerable financial loss. And he never pushed his goods openly down Tempelgasse again.

Horka was also said to send out one of his scrawny, frightened daughters on occasion with a note declaring that he, Horka, had to borrow a certain sum of money urgently, tonight, without delay. The people to whom these notes were delivered complied with the written order without a fuss, although they knew they would never see the money again. Some reportedly sighed and said: *Lucky it isn't more.* But no one stood up to him about this, either. No one wanted to see what would happen if the child went home to Tempelgasse 4 without the required sum. Everybody knew what those children, and the wife, endured. The people of Darkenbloom wouldn't have cared, except that, after venting his fury on his family, Horka would emerge like a wild animal from its cave, which he otherwise seldom left. He just sat in there smoking and getting drunk. Sometimes he would grab his rifle and head off into the forest to go poaching. He'd had a gun licence back when he was chief of police — even though the Russians were so restrictive and hysterical about giving them to anyone else — and he never lost it. He went to the forest and shot game that wasn't his; he relieved people of their money, and sometimes even full bags of shopping; at home, he abused his wife and children such that the whole street could hear. But what was anyone meant to do? That was just how it was. *If you don't behave, Horka will come and get you.* The Darkenbloomers kept their heads down and hoped he wouldn't target them, or, if he did, that they wouldn't be hit too hard.

Five years later, the Russians withdrew and Austria was a free country again. It didn't change anything. Horka was still Horka — he became violent without warning, and had ways of getting an entire town to stay silent and submit to his reign of terror. Were they just threats, or were they based on actual information? Did he fashion one from the other?

It wasn't until twenty years after the war, fifteen years after he was pensioned off, that what some later referred to euphemistically as the *Horka nightmare* came to an end. Several factors were involved. First, Horka was getting older; already there were occasions when groups of youths no longer got out of his way in the street, but, on the contrary, forced him to step aside. Furthermore, Horka's brain was severely addled by decades of boozing. Perhaps he had even drunk himself into a form of dementia, because he grew forgetful on the one hand, and talkative on the other, about subjects that were far from advisable. His aggressive episodes became even more sudden and unpredictable, if such a thing were possible. When the young louts refused to make way for him on the street, he shouted after them something about cans of petrol he would empty for them in the forest, as he had for others. And his youngest daughter, who was ugly as sin and a halfwit since birth, announced at the butcher's, while it was packed with customers, that her father was a good hunter: he shot deer and stag, pigs and Jews. It was obvious she didn't know what she was saying. The butcher's wife's hand froze briefly in mid-air. She handed the unfortunate girl the packet of cheap, fatty leg meat and said, in a friendly, over-emphatic voice: '*Birds*, love, you mean he shoots *wild pigs and birds*.'

And so finally Horka overstepped the mark. First he was irritated by the music from a wedding at the Tüffer, grabbed his gun and burst through the door, in among the wedding guests, stamped about like Rumpelstiltskin and fired a few shots at the ceiling. 'Fuck off, you shitheads, you filthy arseholes,' he bellowed, and the wedding guests fled, along with Resi Reschen's serving staff.

Then he gave his wife a beating, worse even than those she had been accustomed to for years; she crawled across the street, bleeding, knocked on someone's door, and now there was no way around it: the police had to be called. There was an investigation, there were interrogations and witness statements, even though the wife, who initially, surrounded by shocked neighbours and the soothing murmurs of Dr Sterkowitz, bravely gave the nod to making an official complaint, retracted it again the next day.

But this time word got around, presumably even as far as Graz, where Alois Ferbenz had been running a successful menswear business since getting out of prison, and was now a well-respected citizen. He had seldom visited Darkenbloom in the intervening years, only for family celebrations. This time, it seemed, he arrived with no particular engagements, and strolled through town like a rich uncle from America who has finally found the time to come home from across the pond. He honoured the mayor (at the time it was one Bastl Csarer, whom we no longer know much about) with a visit, and quite by chance a reporter from the local paper happened to be there, and took pictures. Ferbenz was also photographed, looking troubled, outside the train station, which was in dire need of renovation. He remarked that, with the right connections, it would surely be possible to bring in investment, at both the district and national level. He had lunch at the Hotel Tüffer (the bullet holes in the ceiling had already been filled in and painted over), kissed the hand of the blushing Resi Reschen, and took his afternoon snack at Café Posauner, which had opened fairly recently. He praised the walnut strudel and the Somlauer dumplings, one of Gitta's local specialities, although she was actually from Styria. Everywhere he went, Darkenbloomers came to his table; everywhere he shook hands, everywhere he encountered radiant faces. To people here, Dr Alois, so friendly, elegant, and well dressed, seemed like a man of the world. And at the end of this long and triumphant day he also remarked, here and there, in a low voice, that he had another visit to make before returning home that evening, not easy, but it really did now have to be done.

IO.

BY THE FOLLOWING WEEK, Horka had disappeared. People wouldn't have noticed straight away, but his wife and daughters were clearing out the house. For the first time, the windows and doors stood wide open; the yellowed curtains, thick with smoke, were taken down, and — this was most surprising for younger Darkenbloomers — the grocer Antal Grün was seen going in and out again, with a yardstick. Afterwards, he stood outside for a long time in his blue overall, looking thoughtful. The Horka women, eyes lowered, carried their unspeakable chattels out in baskets and plastic bags and loaded them onto a trailer. Antal Grün and his mother packed up their one-room shop in the Kalmars' house, and the lively little son of their neighbours, the Lowetzes, helped them move. As they were painting the rooms the Horkas had vacated — *whitewashing* them, one might say — the boy suddenly asked why nasty Horka was so nasty that he'd had to go away. Antal Grün put down his paintbrush and considered.

'There isn't really a reason,' he said at last, 'he always was as mean as a spider whitewashed into a corner.' The Lowetz boy hadn't heard this delightful expression before and made a careful note of it, but he didn't understand what Uncle Grün was trying to tell him. He was too young, and it would have been too disturbing.

Soon afterwards, extensive building work began on the old Ferbenz house. It had not been occupied for a long time, and Zierbusch, the architect, was glowing with pride. Here at last he could once again give his skills free rein. Dr Alois was sparing no expense on his homecoming. Scaffolding was erected, the stucco façade renovated, the windows removed and carefully sanded down. At ground level, however, where Ferbenz's father used to nail and sole shoes, they ripped the doors and windows out completely. A lorry with a crane mounted on the back brought and unloaded a rectangular steel girder. And so the first shop window was created in the centre of Darkenbloom, and a sloping, wine-red script, cut en bloc from a convex sheet of metal, proclaimed *Boutique Rosalie*. This was the name of Ferbenz's wife; later, strangers were sometimes puzzled that Boutique Rosalie sold only menswear: socks, shirts, trousers, jackets. For Darkenbloomers, though, this, like many other things, was normal; it was what they knew, what they were accustomed to.

A crypt was a building, too, Zierbusch the architect pontificated at Sunday morning drinks at the regulars' table; unfortunately, back in the olden days, the builders who had constructed the counts' family crypt had not understood this. They had thought that a crypt was just a better, nicer grave, and so had not applied standards anything like as rigorous as they would to building a wine cellar, for example.

The Heuraffl twins bellowed, uncomprehending, 'Why would you construct a crypt better than you would a wine cellar?'

'You're such idiots,' said Zierbusch good-naturedly, signalling to Resi to bring everyone another round. 'Not better, but just as good! If they'd built the crypt back then as well as your grandfathers did the wine cellars, there'd be no problem, none at all. The wine growers cared about what they put in the cellars,' he went on, 'they loved it, looked after and treasured it. Whereas people just wanted to forget the dead; it was no different then and now.'

And he got sidetracked by protracted descriptions of porous mortar, of groundwater, rainwater, mould, of damp-proof courses and drainage that were complicated to install but necessary if the crypt housing the Darkenbloom counts were not to collapse one day like a house of cards. Then the rows of ancient, ornately decorated stone, and metal coffins, lined up from old to new with their explanatory plaques, would all be buried underneath.

People had already stopped listening. Everyone talked over everyone else at the regulars' table, except when Dr Alois's soft but compelling voice chimed in. Then they fell silent. Zierbusch the architect was the only one who felt he had as much right to speak as Dr Alois; because, like him, he had a university degree, and he was converting his house, and for both these reasons he believed he was important. Usually, Dr Alois just sat and listened. Occasionally he would ask questions, but mostly he let the men talk. In this way he unobtrusively gathered information about the years in which he had been absent; he soaked up all he could glean about friendships and enmities, old quarrels and new antipathies. There were some things he still had to piece together: whose daughter had married whom, who had inherited or sold which field or wood, who had gone bankrupt, and who had moved away. It had been clear to him for some time that, with all his talk of damp in the crypt, the architect was fishing for a follow-up commission as cushy as the one he was currently fulfilling for Dr Alois, with all that expensively renovated exterior stucco and the modern, structurally demanding shop window. The house of his ancestors — Ferbenz really did refer to his forebears, those diminutive, bullet-headed tanners, saddlers, and cobblers, as *ancestors* — must shine *in new splendour*. Ferbenz had also joined the shooting club, the savings bank association, and the tourist board as soon as he moved back. He was still hesitating over the *fellowship association*, but the *fellows*, naturally, expected it of him. He would certainly become a member, but he would prefer to do it a little later, once all the attention had subsided. There had already been a disagreeable newspaper article in some commie rag, which Resi Reschen had stopped ordering afterwards. He very much appreciated this, and complimented Resi a great deal. Not about that — he pretended he hadn't even noticed the tabloid — but about everything else. She had the business well in hand. No one would have thought she had it in her, back then, when the poor thing had to take over the hotel from one day to the next. Quite an achievement: she really was stuck here day and night, she'd barely left the hotel in almost thirty years. And through all the trials and tribulations of war and occupation ... *trials and tribulations* were the exact words he used to Resi, who nodded reverently. Dr Alois always talks so nicely, she liked to tell people.

If the ancestors were seeping, the Count certainly wasn't going to spare any expense, Zierbusch the architect told them, slapping the table with delight; that was what the Count had said, those very words. And so he, Zierbusch, had seen no point in explaining things to His Serene Highness in detail. 'I mean, come on, what a phrase: *the ancestors are seeping!*'

Zierbusch's gaze fell upon Ferbenz, and the laughter died in his throat. 'Loiserl, d'you think that was wrong? I just thought, if he's more likely to shell out for the dead than for the walls around them, I'll let him go on believing it. Either way, it's got to be done!'

Ferbenz smiled, though not with his eyes, and raised his hand placatingly to indicate that everything was fine. However, a few days later it so happened that they, Zierbusch and Ferbenz, bumped into one another and had a little tête-à-tête. It was early afternoon, and the bar of the Tüffer was empty. Zierbusch was just leaving when Ferbenz walked in. Resi darted out of the kitchen; no matter where she was, she always sensed when someone important had arrived. Ferbenz winked at her. With the merest hint of a curtsey, she vanished back through the swing door so fast it was as if she had never been there.

With his quiet voice and beautiful intonation, Ferbenz gave the architect to understand that he would like to know in future when major construction projects were being planned. Just as he must be informed about everything that ultimately affected the whole town. 'You see, my friend,' said Ferbenz, smiling like a shark, 'there are a great many things here that have to be taken into account, at both district and state level, and for this you need connections and expertise. I am in the fortunate position of having both.'

At first, Zierbusch seemed not to understand. 'But Loiserl,' he asked in astonishment, 'do you mean I should ask your permission before I accept a commission?'

Ferbenz acted offended. 'Stuff and nonsense,' he cried. 'What do you mean, permission? It's about knowledge that we share among ourselves equally, matters that concern us all, because they benefit our lovely town.'

He took Zierbusch by the shoulder and steered him towards the door. 'We stick together, we close ranks, we march in step to the new glory of our homeland,' warbled Ferbenz, on the way out; he continued on the main square until they had almost reached the plague column, and Zierbusch nodded along, in a daze. 'But most importantly, we have no secrets from one another! Tell me: how old are you exactly?'

This seemed like an abrupt change of subject, but of course it was no such thing. Before Zierbusch could reply, Ferbenz had already continued: 'Zierbusch, my friend, you look so much younger; enviable, truly, you really are very well preserved, I tip my hat to you, yet you're actually even a little bit older than the Heuraffls, and the same age as Berneck and Stitched-Up Schurl, aren't you? But you're the only one who wasn't banged up back then, just afterwards? You were clearly very lucky there, yes, indeed. There are those Fate raises up, and those it casts into Hell ...'

He let go of Zierbusch, as if to dismiss him. But as he held out his hand for a last, friendly handshake, something else occurred to him. As they stood there shaking hands, in the summer sunshine in the middle of the square, clearly visible from all sides but much too far away for anyone else to hear, Ferbenz said in a low voice, and in dialect, which he never normally used: 'And you'll stop calling me Loiserl from now on, d'you hear? I don't like that one bit.'

As he said it, though, he smiled with such sardonic enthusiasm that, if anyone had been observing the scene from a distance, they would have been convinced that these two local dignitaries, Darkenbloom's best of friends, could hardly bear to part.

From then on, Zierbusch the architect seemed withdrawn, and the necessary phone calls with his client, the Count, who lived in Switzerland, were much less enthusiastic than before. Apart from him, everyone in Darkenbloom was infected with cheerful excitement. Construction work began on the comital crypt. Zierbusch employed additional workers — temporarily, he stressed, just temporarily, for as long as the order book allows. At last, though, there was a sense of growth and real progress in the air at this easternmost end of the Western world, at the closed-off border with Over There. Finally the town would blossom, as its name had always promised, because a splendid cultural monument was being renovated. Darkenbloom's crypt was second only to the world-famous Imperial Crypt in Vienna, in both size and number of residents. However, the people of Darkenbloom were much less clear as to what exactly they expected from the renovation. Tourists streaming into the crypt? They didn't actually like outsiders, but these, if they came, would be clean, paying holiday guests, which was all right. In any case, when the crypt was finally sealed, the Count would come and consecrate it; there was sure to be a festival for which the children could make garlands and the old women iron their traditional costumes. That really was something to look forward to, and the future that lay beyond this new beginning seemed brighter. When the women went to buy things at the grocer's new shop, they looked a little less strained. They no longer stepped up onto a platform, as onto a little stage, but a friendly little bell would ring the moment they opened the door. Gisella Grün, the mother, served them with exquisite politeness, smiling, never looking above the collarbone. She knew what constituted good manners. Some of the women who shopped here had once worked in the castle, and this was the first thing they taught you there. You do not look the ladies and gentlemen in the eyes. You certainly do not stare at them. You lower your gaze, and you forget everything you might hear. This is the behaviour of a good underling. Here in the grocery, though, they themselves were the ladies and gentlemen, charmingly complimented by Antal, with whom they could even flirt a little because he was, of course, utterly taboo.

In his new-old premises, Antal Grün had extended his range. He now stocked Italian soaps, the kind that smelled of rose, vanilla, or lemon; his customers no longer had to wash their hands with Nivea, which had replaced the brown curd soap. Some of the older ones shook their heads over such frivolities, but the first to buy rose soap was Leonore Malnitz. She was the queen of Darkenbloom, beautiful, confident, with a tongue like a rapier. True, she had a hot-tempered husband, three small daughters, a large business, and in-laws who still persisted with the old, conservative wine-making methods. But she didn't seem to let all her obligations and stresses get her down. Time will tell, said the envious local women, knowing that the ravages of time would take their toll on Leo Malnitz's beauty, too. What they didn't know was whether they would live to see it. However, there were also younger women who took the proud Frau Leonore as their role model, and resolved not to neglect their hair and clothes simply because the day was long and the work never-ending.

II.

A STRANGE LITTLE THING happened in the summer after Ferbenz's return and Horka's disappearance, in those bright months during which Darkenbloom, purring with anticipation, lived for the September day when the Count's family would return and the crypt would be blessed. In those airy, sunny weeks, it really did seem to people that everything was being mucked out, freshly painted, and made new, inside and out. The ancient Frau Stipsits, who would soon celebrate her hundredth birthday, sat in front of her house in the sun and announced to everyone who stopped and chatted with her that Zierbusch was even going to renovate the castle now, imagine that. And the people smiled at her charming mistake, instead of grimacing as they usually would when confronted with claptrap, codswallop, babbling, twaddle, and bluster. 'You're right,' agreed Eszter Lowetz, as good-natured and friendly as ever, 'that's all we need, for him to do the castle as well.'

And who could blame the old lady? Frau Stipsits had been born just as the American Civil War was ending, Karl May was being sent to the workhouse for the first time, and *Max and Moritz* was published. No one in Darkenbloom made such associations, though, not even Rehberg, because he was still at the seminary at the time; all anyone knew was that Frau Stipsits was as old as the hills, and so was permitted certain liberties.

One Friday that summer, a stranger appeared in Darkenbloom, a person whose visit, as Antal Grün later discovered, was observed by nobody at all. And that was very unusual here, where the walls had ears and every flower had little eyes it could turn this way and that as required. But it seemed that absolutely no one had noticed this man.

Antal's shop was empty; it was a little after twelve. He was about to close for lunch, as shops still did in those days, when suddenly this person was standing outside his door, wanting to ask a question. He spoke no differently to any of the locals — he didn't even have a Styrian or city accent, he sounded like a Darkenbloomer — but he looked different. Perhaps it was the cut of his suit, the fabric, its fashionably pale colour, or his hairstyle; Antal's overall impression was that he was dealing with someone from far away. He didn't know why this immediately struck him, but he thought about it sometimes, later on. There he stood, the stranger; he gave a name that Antal didn't initially take in, and explained that he was looking for two women who had hidden him during the war. He wanted to thank them; they had undoubtedly saved his life. Unfortunately, he could no longer remember exactly where the house had been, only that it was at the end of a cul-de-sac.

Antal Grün stood there with the keys in his hand, trying to compose himself.

'And why have you come to me about this, particularly?' he asked in the end.

They looked at each other for a long time.

Antal thought: I've seen him before. But where?

The stranger replied that the town grocer usually knew everything — the grocer, the hairdresser, and the innkeeper. He hadn't been able to find the hairdresser; he wasn't where he used to be any more, apparently. He hadn't wanted to go to the Hotel Tüffer, as it had passed out of the hands of the original owners a long time ago, who would probably have understood what this was about. And so finally he had come to him, also because of his name — *bistu beyz oyf mir?*

Antal closed his eyes for a moment and ran his hands down the front of his overall as if they were damp, but they were just cold. 'Nonono,' he said finally, 'of course I'm not cross with you; if you don't mind waiting a minute, I have to lock up first.'

Then he walked with the stranger — who he guessed was about his own age, early forties at the time — through the midday town, which appeared to be deserted. Everywhere people were eating lunch, or were out in the fields and vineyards; not a soul was standing at a window looking out. The only thing twitching the curtains was the gentle breeze drifting down from the peak of the Hazug, which made it easier to breathe. The Darkenbloomers' sixth sense had deserted them at the critical moment; or, on the contrary, it was this that kept them glued to their dinner tables: they were eating dumplings and brains with eggs and thinking, as they chewed, of nothing at all.

Antal and the stranger didn't walk far, just a little further down Tempelgasse, round one corner and then another; you needed to know your way around the maze of the old town. The sun was directly overhead; the two men cast very short shadows. Geraniums, chives, and parsley spilled out of earthenware pots in front of the old houses. The façade of the Lowetz house was covered in wild vines, and the little apple tree the couple had planted for their wedding was already a good size; it had been fruiting for several years now, and was spreading towards the fence. Eszter's flowerpots, standing against the wall, were decorated with blue glaze. Antal knocked, and called out over the garden fence. Eventually, as was customary here, he even opened the front door and called inside. But no one was home. The stranger stood a few steps behind him, as if poised to run away, squinting at the house with narrowed eyes. Antal suggested they could try next door as well, at Agnes's; the two houses shared a back yard. And hadn't he said that two women had hidden him? Probably in the brick-walled shed where they stored the wood ...

'Agnes?' the stranger rejoined. 'Agnes Kalmar?'

'Yes,' said Antal Grün, 'that's her name.'

'Thank you,' the man replied, 'but I think I'd rather not. I've seen the house now, and I'm very grateful to you.'

'You know,' said Antal, 'until recently I had my shop right here, next door, in that one room facing the street — see?' He went and stood underneath the windows, and indicated with sweeping gestures the dimensions of the platform, which had since been converted back into firewood. 'Isn't it incredible,' he said, 'the circumstances we live and work in sometimes? You don't even realise till it's over.'

'You started up here after the war?' the stranger asked.

'Yes, of course,' said Antal. 'My mother and I came back a few years after the war ended.'

As they walked back to Tempelgasse, the stranger asked Antal to give his regards to the two women when he saw them, and to thank them on his behalf. 'You'll do that for me, will you,' he asked, 'you'll find the right moment?'

'Of course,' Antal Grün assured him, still trying to work out whether he had met this man before. 'I'll do that — but, I wonder, might I ask you something as well?'

'By all means,' said the man, and stopped.

'Let's go back to my shop first,' suggested Antal, who didn't want to ask his question in public. It was only in the days that followed, when he thought back on this visit without being able fully to make sense of it, that he realised with surprise not a single face had appeared at a window, not one person outside a house, not on the way there, and not on the way back. Everyone must have been sitting down to lunch. It had also been very hot. The sun was burning down, which was another reason why he wanted to get back inside where it was cooler. When they reached the shop, he first asked the man to write down his name and address on a slip of paper. 'In case Eszter wants to get in touch,' said Antal, immediately mentally excluding this possibility for Agnes, in her fragile state. He would only speak to Eszter for the time being; with Agnes, you never knew what would set her off again. You had to be careful, especially with the old stuff. But details like these were of no interest to the stranger.

Dr Alexander Gellért was written on the piece of paper, and an address in Boston. Antal Grün never forgot the name, though he gave the piece of paper to Eszter Lowetz soon afterwards; an expression of alarm flitted across her face, and she squirrelled it away in her apron pocket. Antal didn't know anyone named Dr Gellért, but what was a name, after all, in the times of which he was thinking.

He might not even have asked his question if this man Gellért hadn't reminded him as they were saying goodbye.

'Ye–es,' said Antal, not knowing where to begin. His gaze fell on the till, and, as he considered, he absent-mindedly loosened the roll of paper from its clamp, because it seemed to him that it had run right down again. But he pulled himself together, put down the almost-empty roll, looked up, and said, 'It's really just a quick, simple question. Were you on the breakwater, too, by any chance?'

The fan rotated overhead; a fly buzzed about the room. The roller blinds were still down, so the light was pleasantly diffuse; a cool room in summer, as if underwater, at the bottom of a clear ocean full of brightly coloured fish.

The man's expression didn't change. 'I'm afraid not,' he said, and it sounded like a question, because his intonation rose slightly at the end of the sentence and hovered there, on high.

'Never mind — forget I asked,' said Antal. He cleared his throat and held out his hand. 'Goodbye, then, and mazel tov.'

'Bye, Tolli,' said the man, and they shook hands.

Antal smiled. 'That's what they used to call me at school, when I was a lad.'

'Exactly,' said the man. And he left the grocer's and walked all the way to the station. And once again it seemed that no one saw or noticed him; it was as if this visit had never taken place. Antal had the slip of paper, though: a provisional piece of physical evidence, even if ultimately it was of no use to anyone.

12.

IN EARLY SEPTEMBER 1965, preparations for the counts' first visit in two decades were coming to a head. The choir of the Catholic church was practising '*Nun danket alle Gott*' and '*Tauet, Himmel, den Gerechten*', which was thought to be the Countess's favourite hymn, the mother of the new paterfamilias. No one knew whether she would come, but if she did, they would have the right music. In the Tüffer they were kneading and baking mountains of *grammelpogatscherl*, little savoury pastries to complement the wine, which would be served in the main square after Mass and the consecration ceremony. No one had seen the current count since he was spirited out of Darkenbloom with his mother and some of the riding horses, barely twelve hours before the Russians marched in. However, he clearly shared his ancestors' delicacy of feeling: through his master of ceremonies, who had been sent on ahead, he arranged for the wine order to be placed just as it used to be — fairly divided among the local heroes, Heuraffl, Malnitz, and Graun. Toni Malnitz invited the purchaser to try the sparkling rosé he had been experimenting with for a while, which had already produced excellent results. But the Count would never permit any inferences to be made from the distribution of his favour, which would have been the case if he had taken only Blaufränkisch and Welschriesling from one, and pink champagne from another. The envoy breathed not a word of such deliberations. He declined the champagne with consummate politeness, saying he had only been instructed to buy wine. His Serene Highness would, however, be delighted to hear that his beloved Darkenbloom was making further encouraging developments in this field, and would surely take the Malnitz champagne into consideration at a later date. Toni Malnitz shrugged and wrote down the wine order.

Elly Rehberg and the children from the Darkenbloom School of Seeing had been working for weeks on a large-format picture to present to the Count as a welcoming gift. For a long time they were unable to agree on a motif, as the exterior of the crypt wasn't particularly interesting and the entrance was currently covered in scaffolding. Elly rejected the idea of drawing the castle from old photographs, as some had suggested. Her pupils drew from life, that was the whole point of the project. Let others produce copies; she taught the children to depict what they could touch or, if need be, walk around. However, by resolutely insisting on the rule about touching and walking around, Elly had also inadvertently ruled out her own personal favourite. For a while, she had thought — not least because all her pupils were to contribute to the big drawing — that a panorama of Darkenbloom viewed from above, from the Rotenstein meadow, for example, halfway up the Hazug, might be the best idea. The more talented artists could do the middle of the picture, where the houses appeared tectonically compressed together, sitting almost on top of each other like the bottom layer of a densely packed chest. The smaller children and the less gifted ones could scribble and cross-hatch around the edges, sketch the meadows, woods, fields, and vineyards in lots of pretty shades of green, brown, and yellow, all that rugged, delightful scenery that only rose up here, on the border — that had, as it were, heaved itself up off its belly and onto its knees way back in the mists of time. However, what Elly had thought an elegant solution, an agreeably detached bird's-eye view and ambitious motif, was dismissed by the landlady Resi Reschen with the deadening verdict *impersonal*. From above, it could be anywhere, she grumbled; Kirschenstein and Tellian look pretty much the same, from above. What a daft idea!

In fact, although Resi herself was unaware of it, it was a diffuse class consciousness that made her object to the suggestion. Not only the Count, but the cultivated Elly Rehberg, and even the Malnitzes, who were no better than they should be, with all their posh champagne and fancy ideas — they were already quite *from above* enough as far as Resi was concerned. There was no need for the children to be drawing things from above as well.

The church was also dismissed as a potential subject, although the Count, who was said to be very religious, would doubtless have been delighted with that. But some of the children in the drawing class were Evangelical, and they already found themselves playing a rather awkward role in the festivities. They would join the others on the main square only after the Catholic Mass. It was particularly important to Elly Rehberg that they should be there, so they could all hand over the drawing together.

What is it with her and the Protestants? the younger Catholic women asked each other after choir practice, when the conversation turned to the picture, the children, and the ceremony. The older women exchanged glances. 'What are you winking for?' one woman asked her mother.

'Oh, Elly Rehberg's always had a soft spot for the different ones,' the mother replied, with an ingenuous expression, and the two sixty-year-olds who caught her eye laughed as if they were coughing.

And so, eventually, the older and marginally more attractive of the two comital manor houses was chosen as the subject, a dull building, plainly agricultural in function. Elly herself sketched the dimensions of the picture on a big piece of card, which was then affixed to a thin wooden board and required several children to carry it up to the meadow each time; the outline of the building was a long rectangle in the middle, but it was small enough for there to be plenty of space for nature all around. The building stood alone in the landscape, and although Russians had been billeted there for ten years, it had retained most of the scant ornamentation above its windows. Elly presented the children with their assignment: the white block in the middle, nestled amid the green. The young ones should do little strokes and cross-hatching around the edges, occasional flowers allowed. The older ones would take on the house. The Lowetz and Zierbusch boys were the most talented artists, and they were also friends; they tended to lead the group. Their behaviour was very different, though: the Lowetz boy usually did as he was told, while the Zierbusch boy almost always started arguing. Elly shouldn't have put the house in the middle, she should have positioned it off-centre; like this, the picture was just boring. From a distance it would look like a white rectangle inside a green one, and then with a frame around it, probably brown — I mean, really.

'Do you have a suggestion?' asked Elly, who knew her pupils well and could tell that here was a little boss in the making.

'There's something missing,' the Zierbusch boy insisted, 'it's much too symmetrical. We should put a big tree in there on the left — preferably the old lime tree, the one we've all drawn so often.'

'But the lime tree's somewhere else,' objected Toni Malnitz's eldest daughter, who looked so like her father it was almost comical, a little Toni caricature in plaits. This objection was typical of her, too; she was a no-nonsense child who couldn't tolerate deviation.

'The Count doesn't know that, though,' said one of the many Farkas children. 'He doesn't know Darkenbloom at all.'

'Right,' said Joschi, Ferbenz's nephew. 'The old God-botherer's only coming here to swagger about and act important, then he'll clear off again.'

This led to a discussion among the older children about whether it was permissible to lie to the Count, or rather: to delight him with an especially beautiful picture, of artistic worth. *Artistic worth* came from young Zierbusch, who must have got it from his father. But because some of the younger children seemed relieved to be allowed to draw something they had already practised for this important picture, Elly conceded. Perhaps another reason for her concession was that she saw it as a small act of rebellion to present a retouched image of Darkenbloom to the Count — him and his noble family who, despite taking their name from the town, had always seemed pretty indifferent to all that happened here.

The reception on the main square was long and the Count's speech somewhat tedious. But no one minded, because all those present were keen to savour the historic moment. The Count had returned! He had brought his wife, his brothers and sisters, and various other family members with him! There was also a fresh swarm of progeny, in sweet little dresses and suits, whose well-bred confidence set them wholly apart from the children of Darkenbloom in ways only children can appreciate.

The school choir was waiting beside the plague column, lined up in three rows in their Sunday best; the other children formed a guard of honour in front of them. The older residents, some with tears in their eyes, were laced into their traditional costumes; Resi Reschen's serving staff stood bolt upright in their white aprons behind tables laden with wine and *grammelpogatscherl*; they looked as if they were about to fold their hands in prayer. Two dozen chairs had been set out for local dignitaries and the numerous members of the Count's family, who, it was noted, chatted among themselves the entire time, even when the mayor was talking or the choir singing. Only when their leader, the young paterfamilias, began to speak did they fall silent and listen, with amused expressions. *Look at him, our Epsi,* the faces of the Count's innumerable uncles and great-aunts, nieces, cousins, and brothers-in-law seemed to say, *see how grown-up he is now! And you can hardly hear his lisp any more ...*

The speech given by Count Paul Edmund von Darkenbloom, known to his friends by his childhood nickname, Epsi, essentially consisted of a biographical listing of the dead who awaited Judgement Day and the return of the Messiah safe and dry in the renovated crypt. Paul Edmund did not say *safe and dry*, only implied it, having heard it from Zierbusch the architect; the rest, though, about Judgement Day and the Messiah, he said word for word.

He talked about Árpád the Strong, regarded as the founding father of the noble line, who had established this crypt of such great art-historical significance way back in the seventeenth century. He praised his piety, fortune in war, and loyalty to the Emperor. He even made brief mention of Árpád's father, Franz, commonly known as Ferenc, who had returned to the Catholic faith after the family temporarily went astray down the path of the Reformation. Epsi didn't say *went astray*; he didn't even say *Reformation*; he only mentioned the other, more welcome part: *a true conversion.* The family understood his meaning. The people's mouths were already agape.

And so the current count ambled through his centuries-old family history, dropping an anecdote here or a colourful detail there about one of the personages now lying in the crypt. He spoke, of course, of the famous Géza of Darkenbloom, martyred by the Habsburgs, but also of his grandmother Alix and her talking grey parrot that could mimic the then mayor of Darkenbloom so convincingly. He had to admit, said the Count — and his family began to smile, because they already knew what was coming — he had to admit that the parrot had also, from time to time, come out with comments so appallingly rude that they could not be repeated here, but it had been a remarkable creature. He concluded with a casual mention of the important races won by the horses of his beloved Mamma, the Countess Margarethe, who so deeply regretted that, for health reasons, she had not been able to travel to her homeland of Darkenbloom. But she was with them all here today in spirit.

'The history of Darkenbloom,' he concluded, as the noses of the first children were turning pale at the tip from having to stand for so long, 'is the history of my family. For all of us, dear people of Darkenbloom, history remains at all times the root from which we have grown, and which we remember with gratitude, because it supports and anchors us securely in our present. Only those who know whence they come also know whither they go. Our ancestors are at all times our role models and our comfort. Their example illuminates and guides us. They live on in our memory. The burial of the dead and the maintenance of their resting places is what distinguishes man from beast. That is why we, like every other family, preserve the honoured memory of our dear departed who have gone before us into the eternity of the Lord.'

The very old Darkenbloomers cried *Vivat*, as they knew to do from their childhood; some of the younger ones mistakenly murmured *Amen*, but so quietly that it didn't matter.

It was a wonderful day that was talked about for many years to come. The *grammelpogatscherl* went beautifully with both the Grauns' Blaufränkisch wine and the Heuraffls' Welschriesling, and especially with the so-called *Heanzen* wine from the Malnitz vineyard, which, in contrast to its folksy name, was actually a sophisticated cuvée, the first in a long line of *chefs-d'œuvre* from Toni Malnitz. The noble family mingled and chatted with the people after the school choir had sung the Burgenland anthem: *The flag is blazing red and gold — red and gold are your colours! Red was the motto of the ardent hearts that died for their homeland.* No one would have been able to say who the red-hearted dead actually were.

Count Epsi spotted the radiant Frau Leonore, kissed her hand, and, *pogatscherl* between thumb and forefinger, devoured her with his eyes as he drew her into a conversation about viniculture, hunting, and her three delightful little daughters, who — a harmless compliment readily presented itself here — would surely also grow up to be great beauties and garland Frau Leonore as the planets do the sun. Just then, Young Graun popped up in front of them out of nowhere and asked in a strained voice whether they would like more wine. The Count stared at him in astonishment. Frau Leonore smiled and said, 'Yes, thank you, but some of yours, please, I don't like Heuraffl's and ours I know already.' Young Graun, who had recently been close enough to Frau Leonore to know what the scarf around her neck concealed, was reassured, and retreated, bowing.

Only Zierbusch the architect was tense. He was waiting for an appropriate moment to take his leave. When he finally worked his way forward to the Count, he excused himself, without thinking, by saying he had work to attend to, whereupon the Count sternly exhorted him to respect the Lord's day. Zierbusch's face fell, but Leonore Malnitz came to his aid. 'On Sunday,' she explained to the Count, 'work here just consists of putting in an appearance at the right regular's table.' She smiled knowingly at Zierbusch as she said it, who vowed to himself that he would never forget the favour she had done him — and then, soon afterwards, forgot.

13.

ZIERBUSCH HURRIED TO CAFÉ Posauner, where Ferbenz was en-
sconced with his trusty followers and things had already got pretty
raucous. They wouldn't even let him sit with them at first.

'You wanna have your cake and eat it,' shouted Berneck, and
Stitched-Up Schurl cried, 'Can't have it both ways!'

'Get back to yer toffs and yer Holy Joes,' shouted the Heuraffl
twins, noses red with drink; one even held a fist to Zierbusch's chin.
But after he had waited a few minutes like a supplicant at the big table,
where the company was almost exactly the same as the membership of
the *fellowship association*, Ferbenz gestured to Gitta the landlady and
she brought over a stool.

And here Zierbusch the architect learned things he had previously known nothing about, or at least had never fully realised.
While the gang roared, cursed, and shouted, and sang the first
verse of the 'Horst-Wessel-Lied' over and over again because they
couldn't remember any of the others, Alois Ferbenz kept talking to
Zierbusch in his quiet, fervent voice. He said some things that left a
deep impression on the architect. For example: that in Germany, after
the First World War, they had taken away the nobles' property and
left them only their titles, but in Austria it had been the other way

round. Wasn't that just typical? And they had always set themselves up very nicely, hadn't they, those barons and counts and princes, for centuries? Which was why he, Ferbenz, found it outrageous, the way the whole town was paying homage to this boy who had showed up here in his buckhorn buttons. Who was he, if you please? A clueless God-botherer, still wet behind the ears and as green as his loden hunting jacket. He probably had no idea how keen his beloved Mamma had been on playing stud farm with Neulag in the comital bedroom — the only unknown was whether or not whips had been involved. Ferbenz insistently reminded Zierbusch that the Count's family had of course allowed Neulag to send them forced labourers, whom they had put to work in the castle and the paddocks. And the ball, the night before Palm Sunday? Why another ball, with the end so near? That was a splendid distraction, wasn't it? And such a coincidence, too, that on that particular night, rather than any other ... Ferbenz stared at Zierbusch with his watery blue eyes that sometimes seemed to be lit from behind.

Zierbusch began to sweat. He knew what that look signified. He, Zierbusch, had been there, with the two Heuraffls, Berneck, and Stitched-Up Schurl, Hitler Youth, all of them, sixteen, seventeen years old. That night, Horka had got them out of bed, and they had done what they were told to do. Dawn was breaking by the time they came home to their anxious mothers, who had had to wash their clothes. But he, Zierbusch, was the only one who had not been sentenced, or even charged, or even interrogated; to this day, he had no idea why. His name had not appeared anywhere at all; either the others had not betrayed him, or someone had wiped his name from the records. He couldn't understand it, because everyone had known, back then, that he was involved. Even now, if the doorbell rang late at night or early in the morning, he was afraid that, all these years later, they had come to get him. The lack of any official interest in him remained a source of unease; he would rather have gone to prison back then, for twelve or seventeen months, along with the Heuraffls, Berneck, and Stitched-Up Schurl. He had already been working in the family business at home when the others, his buddies, were up in court in Vienna — only the Hitler Youth, no one else, no other perpetrators were ever found or named. Zierbusch raised his head. Ferbenz stared at him with a fierce expression, his hair standing on end. Things had to be decided between them. Zierbusch took a deep breath. 'You're right, Alois,' he said, 'it can't all be a coincidence. Thank you: you've really opened my eyes.'

That sunny September, while her son and most of their relatives were demonstrating their affinity with the ancestral seat with such ceremony, and offering a Mass for the renovation of the family crypt, the Countess Darkenbloom passed an unpleasant few days at home in Switzerland. She had not wanted to accompany them to that wretched border town, anyway; the only thing of beauty there had been her castle, and that had been gone these twenty years. As it turned out, though, she couldn't have travelled even if she had wanted to. She had more important and much more disagreeable things to do.

A man had checked in at the Grand Hotel Splendide, and had had the audacity to leave a card requesting that she present herself for tea at a particular hour. The Countess ignored the card — she was not to be summoned by anyone, certainly not by some unknown. The sender's name on the envelope meant nothing to her. The following day, another envelope was brought to her from the Splendide at the same time. It contained nothing but a lock of hair, which she was reluctantly forced to admit that she recognised. She sent her lawyer to the hotel. 'So what does he want, the crook?' she said afterwards to Dr Lendvai, the third of a succession of Lendvais to have worked for her family. Lendvai named the sum. When she said nothing, the lawyer asked if he should report it to the police. 'Certainly not, my dear sir,' said the Countess, rather shocked, and went out for a ride.

And so now she had this to deal with, while her son was probably eating Somlauer dumplings with chocolate sauce and playing the count, with all those grovelling peasants and half-gypsies doubtless delighted to play along. People there still curtseyed of their own accord, not because they were on the payroll!

The other lawyer had to be called, the one in charge of the money. There was a great deal of property, there were investments, and the foundation, but hardly any gold or shares; it was not at all easy quickly to realise such a sum. 'You'll manage, dear sir,' coaxed the Countess, but the money lawyer, whose name she could never remember because he was so new and disagreeable, had the nerve to declare it impossible.

'If you need money quickly, if I were you, I would sell a couple of racehorses,' the upstart advised her, whereupon she wordlessly extended her hand in farewell. And so she had to get the art historian to come as well, and send Lendvai back again to the hotel to ask for an extension. She was much less attached to the paintings than to the racehorses; nonetheless, it was difficult to decide. The art historian seemed to be in physical pain when she ordered him to give approximate valuations as they strolled past the paintings together. She decided on a small, very old Dutch one she had never liked, that, with a bit of luck, would bring in three-quarters of the sum demanded. She would get the money lawyer to scrape the rest together. The art historian was sent to the art dealer. The business was in hand, but she needed more time. This was precisely what the scoundrel who had, regrettably, been in possession of the lock of her hair, and had certainly not handed over all of it, seemed to be short of right now. Perhaps he also lacked patience. To go there herself and ask for a reduction was unthinkable. She might possibly have considered it if she had calculated that it would have even the slightest chance of success. But it didn't; she knew the man. In her youth, his uncompromising nature was what she had particularly liked about him. Back then, she had thought he was the only person who could match her in hardness, and perhaps this was closer to the truth than she was willing to admit.

She sent Lendvai to the hotel with an offer to advance the man's travel expenses and costs for the first weeks of his stay. She also instructed the lawyer to pay the hotel bill so far, and not to mention it. 'Not mention it?' the lawyer repeated, uncomprehending.

'Yes, precisely as I say,' said the Countess, and smiled to herself, lost in thought.

As she waited for him to return, she read the newspaper more closely than usual. She discovered a short item that said the Federal Republic of Germany was hunting several Nazi war criminals via Interpol. The names were not currently being made public, so as not to jeopardise the investigations. When Lendvai returned and informed her that the new offer had reluctantly been accepted, with accompanying warnings about statutory declarations, also concerning the Countess, that could be deposited with Swiss lawyers and leaked to the press at any time, she merely nodded. 'Yes, yes,' she said to Lendvai, who once again was wearing his neutral expression as naturally as his stripy tie: the crook sticks to his agreements, and he knows that I do, too.

But later, out riding, she had a good idea. It took Lendvai quite a while to locate the right public prosecutor's office in Germany. It was astonishing how badly organised the German justice system was at that time, and how reluctant to give out information. Lendvai was surprised. When at last he found the right authority, he called to propose that the Countess give evidence as a witness. An appointment was made. A few weeks later, the appointment was cancelled. It was the public prosecutor's office that cancelled, not the Countess. And that was just fine with her.

14.

FARMER FALUDI GOT BUSY early on Monday morning, right after the big storm. It was still drizzling, but the previous night's fury had abated. The sun could be assumed to have risen behind the thick, grey rainclouds, as it was lighter, if not actually light. A runny yolk, well hidden behind thick, frosted glass: that was the atmosphere of this melancholy day. But it was up there, the sun, as surely as a powerful network of springs and little streams flowed all around and beneath the municipal territory of Darkenbloom. Farmer Faludi grabbed his staff and sought out his supporters, one after another, all those who already shared his opinion: that Darkenbloom must cancel the disgraceful, overpriced contract with the water authority immediately and access its own reserves instead. On a day like this, the water would be easier to see than the sun. The sun had stepped back, deferring to the water. 'Now we can finally get an overview,' he said to each of his allies in turn, thumping his six-foot staff on the ground. 'That heavy rain, after all those weeks of drought, is the best thing that could have happened to us.'

And the other farmers followed his lead. They inspected their fields and meadows, noted where the water was pooling and in which direction it was flowing. Much of what Farmer Faludi had already suspected was confirmed, for example: that many little subterranean streams converged to form a single, larger one beneath the Rotenstein meadow. That was why Young Graun had been drilling an exploratory hole there, at his behest. Unfortunately he had immediately come across the pile of human bones. But it didn't matter too much that they couldn't keep digging in that particular spot, now that the police had sealed it off, because you could clearly see further down how saturated the ground was. And with a bit of thought and some careful observation they could find out where this stream surfaced. It was all connected: underground, but that certainly didn't mean they couldn't figure out the system, couldn't map out the flow of water almost exactly, and use it for themselves.

Toni Malnitz was the only one who didn't respond to his request that rainy morning. His youngest daughter had gone missing the night before and he couldn't talk about anything else. 'Now the bloody rain has washed away any traces, as well,' he cursed. 'And you can only file a missing person notice after twenty-four hours!'

Farmer Faludi observed that Toni's aura, usually warm and reddish-orange, was glowing like fire, and had become unstable and blotchy around the edges, like the sun when it spits its flares out into space.

'May I sit down for a moment?' he asked, from behind his long beard, and Toni was compelled to let him in. They sat around the kitchen table, the three of them; the face of the beautiful Frau Leonore, who also appeared not to have slept, was as white as snow, but her aura was a delicate, frosty lilac, thin and practically motion-less. This was just as unusual as Toni's solar eruptions.

Inside, the house smelled of fear and jam. Toni jumped up again and paced back and forth, stamping like a horse about to bolt. Farmer Faludi drank the glass of water he had asked for, then reached forward and gripped Leonore's hands decisively, making a warm, safe cave for them on the table top between his paws. He looked into Leonore's eyes, held her gaze as firmly as her hands, and said: 'Your daughter, Flocke, is a strong and clever girl; she doesn't just go along with things, like so many here. Flocke's someone who thinks for herself. There are those who don't like that, of course. But if she's on to something, she'll never give up. And the old powers here in Darkenbloom — their strength is waning. Not fast, slowly — but it is.' He squeezed both Leonore's hands again and stood. 'Have faith,' he said. 'Not everything comes to light, but most things do. Here, in this house, I don't see death, I see life.'

And with that he continued on his way, to the Heuraffls and Young Graun, to the cattle farmers and the Darkenbloom forest managers. All of them, the ones who worked outdoors all year round, had some understanding of water, unlike the business people and office workers. They knew that water didn't come just because you turned a tap. They worked together, cataloguing the area. That day, the big hydrological map he carried around, rolled up, beneath his coat acquired many new entries, little crosses and lines, sketched or dotted in pencil. Farmer Faludi began to see more clearly. The hapless ersatz-mayor Koreny, that marmot with the supplicating hands, would have to admit defeat, and he'd have to do it very soon.

Farmer Faludi's speech had not reassured the Malnitzes; quite the opposite. His mysterious words now drew Toni — who until then had been thinking more of car accidents, a hit-and-run in some remote part of the forest, or, worse, of drunk and sexually importunate young men — into the ambiguous world of Leonore's fantasies. As she had sat waiting for hours in Toni's leather armchair, staring at the overflowing gutters practically gushing upwards, she had convinced herself that Flocke's dogged investigation of Darkenbloom's history must be the reason for her disappearance. It wouldn't just be any old thing that happened to her daughter. That was impossible. A deer didn't simply run out in front of her daughter's car radiator grille, she didn't swerve clumsily to avoid it, and so did not fall into a ravine. That was far too banal. It didn't fit Leonore's image of herself and her daughters. So there had to be a reason, a guilty party, and thus the possibility that she and Toni could work out what had happened, put two and two together, and track Flocke down. Just as — an old rule of Leonore's — you didn't find something you'd lost by frantically looking for it, but by stopping and thinking. And didn't it all fit together? Since the last council meeting, people in town had been gossiping about how Flocke had rattled Mayor Koreny with her interjection. They spread it around because they all thought Koreny was a pillock, and smacked their lips with glee whenever anyone did anything to him, it didn't really matter what. However, they all also knew, of course, what it had been about, namely: Flocke's idea of a border museum. Her frequently expressed desire to reconcile with the people Over There, and for them jointly to commemorate the horrors of the two World Wars. Flocke, the young schoolteacher, was proposing Hungarian lessons from the start of primary school! She believed — and Frau Leonore could only agree with her daughter on this — that they should at least be able to say *hello* and *please* and *thank you*, in case it were ever possible to drive across again. But the Nazis and yokels here didn't like this at all, and nor did those who persecuted Koreny with something akin to hatred, over the water business, for example. These provincials didn't want to drive across; at most, they wanted to get back some vineyards and potato fields that were taken from their families seventy years ago when the border was drawn. The yokels didn't speak a word of English, either, or anything else; even their German was essentially incomprehensible to anyone who wasn't from the region. But they were able, at a moment's notice, to reel off in their barked dialect the ancient grievances of their parents and grandparents, the memory of those inconceivable times when everyone here was forced to learn Hungarian.

And hadn't the barn burned down soon after that town council meeting? The fire brigade had partied in Kalsching while Leonore's

Ehrenfeld barn went up in flames. Since Flocke's disappearance, she saw the two as connected. It was incomprehensible to her now that she and Toni hadn't realised it straight away. She thought it suspicious the way Berneck had grinned when she told him she suspected arson, as there had been nothing flammable in the barn or anywhere nearby. Yes, fine, the heat of the previous weeks. But just like that, with no lightning or campfire anywhere near it? She had told Berneck to get his surveyors to make a point of looking for evidence of this when they examined the ruins.

'If it's arson you're suggesting, ma'am,' the sleazeball replied, ''s the police you should go to first.'

He licked the corners of his mouth with the tip of his tongue. She had smacked his face once, when she was a young woman — either him or his brother, she wasn't sure any more. And she should have done exactly the same again now. Instead, she turned on her heel and went to the police station to file charges against person or persons unknown.

The longer Leonore thought about it, the more obvious it seemed to her that someone who was involved in something unspeakable back then, during the war, must be panicked by Flocke's research. She didn't know who it might be, but there had been rumours. That the real perpetrators had never been punished. That the higher-ranking officers had got away with it, as they had done everywhere else.

Just recently, Flocke had told her that several witnesses were killed just after the war, including the husband of that old soak Frau Graun. She, Leonore, hadn't known this, or had forgotten it, but then she had grown up in Kirschenstein. Just thirty kilometres away, but a different world — she couldn't have known all this. If only I'd stayed there, she moaned from time to time, as she'd been moaning for years. This time, though, Toni didn't react. He barely heard. He was ashen-faced with worry; he couldn't even think. He wanted to get back in the car and go on searching.

But Leonore wouldn't let him. She had been going on at him, quietly, agitatedly, non-stop, ever since he had found her at dawn, sitting in his armchair. Why this was now in the bedroom was not something Toni could explain to himself. But when he found her there, Leonore's eyes were as wide as a terrified child's, and for a moment he saw Flocke's expression in them, although she didn't usually resemble either of them very much.

He had to remember, Leo was demanding now: 'Remember — you must already have been about twelve or thirteen, back then? You must know something, about that time, or at least what people were talking about? Darkenbloomers are talkers; they've never kept a secret in their lives. What did you lot get up to back then, in your vile Nazi backwater? And didn't Sterkowitz do post-mortems on corpses after the war, a whole load of them shot in the back of the neck, even I've heard that — Toni, please, remember!'

Toni stamped up and down, trying to clear his head. He remembered the rumours like a red label on a box, the contents of which he no longer knew anything about. The word *rumours* stood for something that was always there in the background, but he simply couldn't remember what it was.

All he remembered was this: back then, he had been friends with the son of a gendarme who was the police chief's right-hand man. And his friend's father had once said to the two of them that the Darkenbloomers were all just telling stories, there wasn't a scrap of truth in them, it had all been thoroughly investigated, several times. By the Russians, and by the officials from Vienna as well. *Not a scrap of truth, all ruled out, and now, boys, forget the whole thing, once and for all!*

Toni was resisting Leonore's line of reasoning. She had probably gone mad with worry.

'But Flocke wasn't the only one who was interested in all that,' he protested. 'Rehberg started it, with his town chronicle, him and

Eszter Lowetz; there's a whole group of them now, who ...'

Then it occurred to him. He sat down again.

'What is it?' asked Leonore.

Toni poured himself some water from the jug, into Farmer Faludi's glass. Then he told her about the postcard Flocke had taken from the Lowetzes' fridge. When he went looking for Flocke there yesterday afternoon, to tell her ... 'You know, about the Rotenstein meadow. I guessed she'd be interested. And on the postcard there, in Eszter's kitchen — it had the castle on the front; you know, the postcard everyone's got now — it said: *Stop lying.* Flocke even read it out loud to the son, young Lowetz, but none of us knew what it was supposed to mean. And besides, there was the business with the Rotenstein meadow, which seemed more important.'

Leonore stared at him. 'Eszter died very suddenly, didn't she?' she asked, slowly. 'She wasn't even ill.'

Toni could see from her face that she herself didn't want to believe what she was saying.

They both sat there for a few more minutes, until — as often happens with people who, even if their feelings for one another have soured, have lived together for decades — they both had the same idea. Like it or not, they would have to go and see Old Malnitz, whom they hadn't spoken to for years. Old Malnitz, who for a long time now had behaved as if he had only one son left, namely the one who ran the filling station in Zwick.

15.

LOWETZ SLEPT UNTIL LATE into the grey Monday morning. There was nowhere he needed to be. No morning sun woke him through the east-facing window of his mother's bedroom, unlike all the days before. No early-morning sneeze, no flakes of gold dancing in the air, which he had gazed upon every morning until now, unexpectedly close to happiness. Lowetz, too, had been kept awake late that night, before lightning and thunder despatched him into uneasy dreams.

Around eight o'clock in the evening, long before the storm began, Flocke's father had brought him the blond-bearded refugee. The first thing the man asked to do was take a shower, and he disappeared into the bathroom so fast that Lowetz only just managed to dig out a towel and throw it through the door after him. He offered Toni Malnitz a beer, which he accepted, standing, as people did around here.

They stood shoulder to shoulder, gazing out into the courtyard.

'What do you plan to do with the house?' the older man asked, and Lowetz answered that he didn't know yet.

'It'd be a shame,' said Toni, and Lowetz nodded and said, 'Mmm.'

Fritz walked across the back garden, carrying a long plank of wood to the shed. When he re-emerged, he spotted the two of them and waved. Lowetz waved back, and Toni raised his bottle in greeting.

'Does anyone still see Agnes at all?' asked Malnitz.

Lowetz asked, 'She's still alive? Is she here?'

'Sure,' said Malnitz, turning to face him. 'Are you telling me you didn't know?'

'Not a clue,' said Lowetz. 'I thought she died years ago.'

'Ah, come now,' said Malnitz, shaking his head. 'Where's Flocke gone, anyway? I could've sworn she'd still be here.'

Lowetz grew chatty, perhaps because he wanted to gloss over his cluelessness, or because, faced with the indeterminate prospect of an evening with the fugitive stranger, he wanted to keep Flocke's father with him a little longer. Until now, Lowetz had had a different image of Toni, one from years ago, that was already dissipating in the light of his own impressions. Malnitz had had the reputation of being grouchy, someone you were better off avoiding. Lowetz didn't find him like that at all — quite the opposite. Compared with drunks like the knuckle-dragging Heuraffls, or Schurl, whom everyone called Stitched-Up, with his terrible scars, or the hostile characters who had challenged him that afternoon up on the Rotenstein meadow, Toni Malnitz was practically a revelation. And his daughter definitely was — no *practically* about it. And so Lowetz told him quite openly that Flocke was at the Tüffer, with that elderly man, Dr something-or-other, who'd been staying there for a while. 'He's some sort of historian,' Lowetz declared, 'he knows all about our region. He's involved with the Jewish cemetery, too; they're going to rebury some bodies there soon, or something. And he knows Uncle Grün, I mean Antal; he knows him from before.'

'When, before?' asked Toni. 'Before the war?'

'I don't know,' Lowetz had to admit. 'I just had the impression it was a pretty long time. He wasn't too pleased, though, Antal, recently, when this doctor tried to ask him some questions.'

Toni finished his beer and set the bottle on the table. 'It's understandable,' he said, 'that Antal doesn't like to talk about it. Whereas some others around here ... well, never mind.'

And with that he said goodbye, to Lowetz's disappointment.

The East German refugee called from the bathroom through a little crack in the door. Lowetz couldn't understand him; he had to go over and ask him to repeat it, twice. It wasn't just his accent; it was also that this man was obviously embarrassed at having to ask for anything at all. Now, though, as Lowetz eventually understood, he didn't want to put his dirty garments back on, and was asking, in a roundabout way, whether Lowetz could *borrow* him anything. '*Lend* — he wants to me to lend him something,' murmured Lowetz, and sorted through his own things before finally bringing the man some underwear, a T-shirt, and some tracksuit bottoms.

And then he was standing in Lowetz's kitchen, arms dangling, a lost traveller with no luggage. Lowetz's pity was suddenly aroused; he needed a bag of his own, at least, he thought.

'Everyone needs something to put their things in, even if they don't have any things right now,' he told his guest, encouragingly. 'Tomorrow morning we'll buy you the basics, and you can put them in here.' At this, he pressed upon him a cheap cloth bag he had noticed in his mother's wardrobe. It was nothing special, just a marketing freebie with the slogan of a light-bulb company; it had a zip, and there had just been a few notepads and envelopes in it, scraps of paper and pens. Lowetz had simply emptied it into the wardrobe — that was quickest. A small notepad caught in a corner; Lowetz shook harder, until finally this too slipped out. 'Just take it,' he said, pressing the ridiculous bag into the refugee's hand, dimly aware that with all this gruff, unnecessary activity he was really just asking him to please not burst into tears.

After this, he chattered away while making the man some sandwiches.

With wet hair and beard, Reinhold looked older, and Lowetz began to believe him when he said he had a sixteen-year-old daughter. He insisted that none of his cuts needed attention, and didn't even seem angry with the mad Heuraffls; where he came from, too, he said, thieves and robbers would get a punch in the *gob* if ever they were caught. Other than this, he said little, and his dialect was hard to understand. He was despondent with worry about his wife and daughter, and the days alone in the forest had frayed his nerves. While Lowetz had been enjoying his holiday and reigning supreme in his mother's house, this man had crossed the border, broken through the Iron Curtain, something for which people used to get shot. It had almost never happened around here, as far as Lowetz could recall, but what did he know. He had been living in the capital for years and had done his best to iron out his regional accent. Since coming back, he had let it slip, and this felt surprisingly good. He had stopped trying to pull himself together as far as this was concerned; that is to say, *t'gether.*

'We all forgot, somehow,' said Lowetz, almost guiltily. 'About how things were for all of you, over there.'

Reinhold shrugged, turning his palms upwards, and said it was their own fault as well. Then he apologised and asked if it was all right if he went to bed early; the following day he wanted to try to find out what had happened to his family.

He had already gone out when Lowetz got up the next morning. On the kitchen table was a note saying he had taken one hundred schillings from Lowetz's wallet: *to make phone calls, you'll get it back as soon as possible,* three exclamation marks. Lowetz suspected Reinhold's fear of overdrawing some imaginary account and being driven out of town after all, with Heuraffls raining down blows on him, had gone into those exclamation marks. At least written communication with him was easier. Lowetz made himself coffee; the biscuit tin of sugar was still on the table from yesterday. He ought to go over to the joinery and ask Fritz about his mother. He must pay Agnes a visit. Was she really in there, hidden inside the house, never coming out? All you ever heard was the circular saw. She used to scream from time to time, he remembered that; it had almost been one of the familiar sounds. How was she? What in heaven's name was Fritz coping with, without letting on? Eszter had probably helped out there on a regular basis, had cooked, washed Agnes, and changed her clothes, or whatever needed doing, but his mother had been dead for several weeks now, and he, Lowetz, hadn't even realised that Fritz's mother was still alive.

He needed to go for a walk and have a think. What was he doing here? Why couldn't he leave? Was he really planning to stay? He took the old book of traditional Darkenbloom tales and went out to the car. It was raining. Luckily, his jacket was on the back seat. He hadn't driven for days, and noticed that he needed petrol. The nearest filling station was in Zwick; there was one in Darkenbloom too, now, but it was inconveniently located, at the opposite end of town. So first to Zwick, then Rehberg, and after that he would see.

The petrol station was full; people were standing around inside discussing the previous night, the storm and the damage it had caused. Lowetz considered getting crisps, bars of chocolate, and beer for Reinhold, but that would have been a betrayal of Uncle Grün. Eszter had always bought all of his products that she could possibly use; it was a question of friendship. So Lowetz took a magazine from the stand by the counter instead, and leafed through; he was in no hurry. The subject had changed now, and people were talking about the water authority; they were saying it was a scandal, and were clearly all of the same opinion. Of course Balf took a bribe, one asserted shrilly, and another countered: well, if he did, he didn't get to enjoy it.

'Dear God, he's still alive, though, isn't he?' a woman asked.

'Yes, yes, we're sure to have heard if there was any news,' came the reply, from several people at once.

These were typical provincial topics: the water authority, which people in bigger towns didn't even know existed, with the casual addition of malicious gossip, who was already dead and who was on their way out. Lowetz tried to picture the office and his colleagues. How it would be if he told them he was moving back to Darkenbloom. For the time being, he skipped over the question of what he would live on — some brilliant idea that he just hadn't had yet. Maybe he could work for Toni? Maybe he needed new labels, brochures, marketing material? That wouldn't be enough to survive. Maybe he could start an advertising agency in his own house. Lowetz Advertising? With an antiquated sign, like the one for Boutique Rosalie. Lowetz grinned. He needed to find out whether the town had anything like that already.

He became aware of a familiar smell, one he hadn't smelled in a long time. What was it? Not lavender. Mothballs? Could it be patchouli? What was the difference? He looked up. Beside him, a woman who looked like a ghost took a puzzle magazine from the stand, unobtrusively rolling it back a little as she did so. Lowetz studied her. She was almost bald; sparse tufts of feathery grey hair stuck out from her head, and her huge eyes were emphasised still further by the big bags underneath them. In her hand she held a straw bag, large and light and almost empty, with only a piece of cloth, a scarf or jumper, nestling at the bottom. The woman probably had some sort of wasting disease, she was so scrawny. Her eyes darted around the room. Lowetz took a couple of steps back to stand by the window, and half turned away, as if needing more light to read by. From this position he saw that the woman, still holding on to the newspaper stand, was slowly pulling it towards the shelves on the wall behind the counter. The filling station attendant hadn't noticed; he was working the till and chatting. The other customers were still discussing water pipes and water meters. Just as Lowetz was beginning to wonder whether he was witnessing shoplifting preparations, the scrawny woman made a grab for the shelf behind the attendant, and from amid the wall calendar of naked women, the family photos, trophies, and medals she extracted something round and not exactly small. At almost precisely the same moment, she gave the newspaper stand a powerful shove, pushing it away from her and out into the room. There was a crash, the magazines flew everywhere, and then the woman was lying on the floor beside her shopping bag. She wept and wailed. Someone bent down and set the newspaper stand back on its feet while others tended to the woman. Lowetz stood, clutching the magazine he had been leafing through to his chest, in shock. With others supporting her, the woman managed to kneel, apologising non-stop: slipped, always so clumsy these days, so terribly sorry.

'There now, Inge, no need to cry,' said the filling station attendant, 'there's no harm done.' Lowetz put his magazine back on the stand, as if he were helping to tidy up. Then he paid as fast as he could. The creepy woman had just stolen, before his very eyes, the steel helmet that had sat on the shelf in the filling station for years. It occurred to him now that the filling station attendant was presumably Flocke's uncle. But should he announce the theft of the helmet when everyone else was comforting the woman, who must be terminally ill? He didn't feel he could do it, and he wasn't really all that bothered.

When he pushed open the door of the travel agency, the book of traditional tales concealed beneath his jacket, Rehberg was standing behind his window display, staring out at the rain, past the pile of sand, the steamboat, and the leather camel. 'If I may, Herr Rehberg,' said Lowetz, as people used to years ago, when he was a child. 'If I may, Herr Rehberg, it's me, Eszter's son, and I'd like to …'

'If I maaaay,' Rehberg interrupted him, 'you're just what I haaaad in miiiiiiind.' And he burst out laughing.

Lowetz stared at him, perplexed. For a moment the experiences of the last few hours merged into a sequence of crazy incidents: a drenched and frightened Saxon who had crossed the Hungarian border without being shot there, but was beaten up over here; a scrawny woman smelling of patchouli who successfully stole a Second World War helmet; and now Rehberg, who was reputed to be gay, greeting him with incomprehensible sentences in front of a huge inflatable steamboat.

'Sorry,' said Rehberg, still grinning. 'No need to stand on ceremony; I know who you are.'

And then he explained that the old-fashioned *if I may* reminded him of an anecdote, the only Hollywood anecdote that could be said to take place in Darkenbloom. When the soon-to-be-world-renowned director Michael Curtiz was still called Mihály Kertész and often passed through this region, travelling back and forth between Vienna and Budapest, he saw a good-looking young man sitting in the bar of the newly opened Hotel Tüffer. Apparently, the man was just the type he had been seeking, in vain, to play the lead in his new film. At first, he pointed to him excitedly and whispered to his wife; finally, he got up and introduced himself to the man with those very words: *If I may, you're just what I had in mind!*

Lowetz was surprised. Eventually he said that what *he* had had in mind was that this valuable object here — presenting his dog-eared collection of tales — would be a perfect exhibit for the proposed folk museum. He was only too happy to donate it, but he felt he should point out that it contained certain anti-Semitic tropes that unfortunately were common at the time it was written.

Rehberg did not take the book. It hovered in the air at the end of Lowetz's outstretched arm until he withdrew both arm and book again.

'Couldn't you write about it?' Rehberg asked. 'Now your mother's gone, I don't have any help at all any more; a couple of others, but you can forget about them ... And I've finally got the Countess's approval, for the museum — well, sort of, anyway.'

He offered Lowetz a coffee. He looked so dejected that Lowetz sat down on one of the customer chairs, as if wanting to book a trip on the beach bus to Lignano. But soon the two of them were chatting like old friends. Lowetz talked as if he had already decided to keep his parental home and perhaps move back to Darkenbloom, though Rehberg's delight at the prospect made him uncomfortable. 'Too late for Mama,' he qualified, and Rehberg cried: 'She would have said, better late than never — I know it! That's exactly what Eszter would have said!'

He urged Lowetz to search for the papers and documents connected to their work on the town chronicle. There were some irreplaceable items of his Aunt Elly's among them, photographs and letters. Lowetz said he had heard this from Flocke already, but he hadn't found anything. Strangely, the whole house had been virtually paper-free; Eszter had apparently given away all her books, as well.

He smiled uneasily. 'The longer I'm here, the more I feel I didn't know my own mother,' he confessed to Rehberg at last. 'Almost every day I find out something about her that I didn't know. I'm even hearing things I would never have thought possible.'

'You're not the only one,' said Rehberg, wringing his hands. 'Since I started working on the town chronicle, it happens to me all the time.'

16.

ON MONDAY MORNING, STERKOWITZ'S surgery was as empty as if
the rain had washed away all illnesses as well. Of course, this wasn't
the case. The storm and its aftermath had sapped the strength of those
who weren't especially sick, who would only have needed a prescription or a vaccination. And as it was still raining, the rest preferred
to stay at home and wait for the doctor to visit. Frau Sterkowitz,
who was also the doctor's assistant, had time to flick through the
magazines again. She was a particular fan of the Monegasque royal
family, and couldn't get enough of the beautiful Caroline, her young
Italian husband, and their three delightful children. They were quite
different from the not-very-chic Darkenblooms, who only showed
their faces once in a blue moon. Frau Sterkowitz regretted that she
didn't speak French — how could she? If she had learned it, she could
have dreamed herself far away, atop the densely populated Grimaldi
cliffs beside the azure sea.

Sterkowitz, her husband, had been preoccupied since the previous evening. He was muttering and huffing less than usual, but
there weren't any children or especially anxious patients who needed
reassuring, so it wasn't that noticeable. Once the last patient of the
morning had been attended to, he got into the orange Honda and

drove up to the Rotenstein meadow.

The rain was starting to abate as he clambered down from road level, across two planks and into the white tent. Here you had a roof over your head, but it was humid. His Kirschenstein colleague had with him a portable radio that kept announcing traffic obstructions: mudslides on the Hazug road, trees brought down by lightning and the storm. The main street in Tellian was closed for a fire brigade operation, please to give it a wide berth. Further west, in Löwingen, two people had been injured by a falling branch and were in intensive care. 'Our patient here is the only one not bothered by the weather,' said the Kirschenstein colleague. 'He's been dead for forty-five years.'

'Is it a soldier, then?' asked Sterkowitz, picking up the left thigh-bone and scrutinising it. His colleague had laid out the individual bones more or less in human shape, but some were still missing.

'Actually, it looks like a woman to me,' his colleague replied, holding up a piece of ilium. 'This is all we have of the pelvis so far, but the rest must still be in there.' He pointed to the pit, where two assistants were kneeling and scraping very gently at the earth.

'And apart from that,' asked Sterkowitz, 'you haven't found anything? No buttons or weapons or belt buckles?'

'As I said,' his colleague repeated, 'it could be a woman. Unless a helmet turns up after all!' He laughed. 'But that means we've got a problem.'

Sterkowitz observed the two assistants in the pit. They were wearing white plastic overalls, goggles, and face masks; they looked like little Michelin men. Sterkowitz thought it was a bit over the top, going to such lengths because of some old bones in the Rotenstein meadow. They weren't TV detectives, after all.

Then one of them pointed something out to the other, not at the bottom of the pit but in the side wall, quite low down. He lay on his side with his knees bent and started drilling with his tools. 'More light,' he said, his voice muffled by the face mask; he had to repeat it, and both of them laughed. The second man lay down behind the first, spooning, as it were. He shone a torch over his colleague's shoulder, and Sterkowitz noticed that his arm didn't tremble and didn't wobble, it stuck straight up in the air like a lamppost, as still as the dead themselves.

The sight of the sharp angle of their knees as they lay there, pressed together, one behind the other, suddenly cast Sterkowitz back, way back, to a different time in his life. People lying on their side in the spoon position are tidied away into the smallest possible space; it's also the best way of offsetting differences in height. Not that that had been the case in the scene that rushed back to him now. But the two had been lying like this, one behind the other, as if snuggling up. The pits they lay in were not rectangles or squares, as one might have expected; they were narrow and ran in short zigzags, so that they too made sharp angles like interlocking knees. Considering the circumstances that had put them there, the position these two found themselves in was utterly improbable. Had they fallen like that, or had they been placed that way? Was that what had upset him so? The way they were lying was so ... peaceful and tender. He hadn't seen much yet, back then: corpses of almost every age, of course, but they were usually on a table with a tag on their toe. And he never encountered anything like it again, thank God, thank God ... There were maybe ten or twelve in each grave, but he wasn't required to count; the Russians did that. He and his assistant, Lajos from Over There, only examined two or three, maybe four of them closely: the soldiers took these ones right out for them. In all of them they immediately found the entry wounds, in the cervical vertebrae or in the head. After that, they just did random checks, with a torch. That was how he had come across the two lying close together. Brothers, perhaps, or a father and son. Or just coincidence? He didn't examine them; they would have had to pull them apart first. He picked others who were easier to reach, whose heads and necks were easier to reach. He did no more than this; no more was demanded of him. He established cause of death, recorded the death as unnatural. Once, when he didn't find a hole in the same place as in the others, the soldier beside him said something. He didn't understand, but Lajos pointed at what the young lad clearly meant. They had been quicker to see the smashed-in forehead. No need to look for a hole after that. Sterkowitz stumbled and put his hand over his mouth. Lajos had tied strips of cloth over their mouths and noses, but they were no use. The stench was appalling. The extent was appalling and utterly indescribable. The Russian commandant kept talking down at them, non-stop; he sounded furious. Someone else kept a written record. He and Lajos didn't have a tent, they didn't have anything, just a few black-eyed, starving soldiers with spades, who thrust them in wherever they were told and often had to dig with their hands, too, between the bodies. At some point Sterkowitz raised his head and looked up at the commandant. He was barking at him in his own language, although he knew that Sterkowitz didn't understand. The gestures were clear, though: he could stop. He climbed out and they handed him the report. The soldiers stood above the pit again, at the edge, and filled it in. Open it up, then close it again. They showed him and Lajos where to sign. He had no idea what he was signing, but he assumed that everything was in accordance with the law. And if it wasn't, there was nothing he could do about it. He was a young doctor; he had heard about these things, but it surprised him that there were so many. Many of them had been driven out, hundreds, thousands probably, on those marches, away from here. That was why he hadn't thought there would be so many in the graves; just a few, the sick, the ones who had died anyway. The pits he was recording told a different story. He couldn't say how many there were. They didn't open up anywhere near all of them, they only scratched the surface. The zigzag trenches seemed to go on forever, as far as the horizon. He couldn't bear the stench any longer. The stench was abominable. He pressed his hand against mouth and nose, he staggered.

'Everything all right, Doctor?' asked his colleague from Kirschenstein. The assistants in the space suits were standing next to Sterkowitz, one on either side, as if conjured out of the pit. One of the spacemen, who, when he removed the goggles and face mask, turned out to be a woman, was even steadying him by the elbow. For a moment Sterkowitz thought he had spoken his thoughts aloud and his three colleagues were staring at him, aghast, because of what he had said. Then his brain kicked back into gear. He had been oddly silent, holding his hand in front of his mouth; they must think he was feeling sick. They weren't horrified, they were concerned. Sterkowitz huffed and mumbled, 'I'm fine, I'm fine, at my age you sometimes drift off a bit when you remember something from years ago.'

'What was it?' the woman asked. 'Something important?' She was small and blonde and wearing that suit. Sterkowitz wasn't sure it was desirable for women to be doing work that until now had been the preserve of men. Who wanted to marry a woman who dug around for bones in the dirt?

'Many years ago, not long after the war, I had to perform an autopsy on an employee of mine,' said Sterkowitz, and this sentence, which he had reached for as if for a lifebelt, had the desired effect. His three colleagues forgot what had just happened, and he almost forgot himself.

'It came to mind when I saw your lovely bones here, laid out so neatly,' Sterkowitz lied, huffing. 'Mine was fresh, of course, not skeletonised, but he was lying just like that on my table in the surgery. My dental technician, robbed and murdered, imagine that! He was an excellent specialist, too, Lajos, from Over There.'

And then he told them. That, over forty years ago, the general practitioner did teeth as well, as best he could. Although he himself couldn't, at all, when he first started here; he would freely admit it now, if they promised not to betray him. They all laughed. What was there to betray? Sterkowitz was a respected, experienced doctor. His good reputation certainly extended as far as Kirschenstein. The idea that at some time in the past he had, for years, relied on the dental technician and the midwife until he had learned everything from them was no more than an amusing anecdote, a particularly candid joke.

'And then they just went and killed my dental technician, right there on the border, when he was cycling home, as he did every evening,' Sterkowitz continued, shaking his head. 'They never found the dental gold, and the murder was never solved.'

'How did he die?' asked the colleague from Kirschenstein, pre-sumably out of professional interest.

'Shot in the head at close range,' said Sterkowitz, and sighed. 'Such a nice guy, Lajos.'

When Sterkowitz got home, his lunch was on the table. He told his wife that they were still none the wiser, but his colleagues would doubtless soon have recovered all of the find. He didn't say that they currently believed the skeleton to be female. It seemed somehow indecent to him that his wife should picture someone of her own sex lying up there in the mud. Besides, he had always taken the view that you only imparted facts, not speculation.

When she brought him his coffee, Sterkowitz mentioned that he had found himself thinking about Lajos again today, for the first time in ages; about how he had analysed his corpse just as his colleague up there was analysing this new skeleton.

'Disgraceful that they never found the murderer,' he said. 'I'd have thought that at least some of the gold would have turned up again someday.'

Frau Sterkowitz bit her lip, stood up, and cleared the table.

'Come on,' she said, addressing the top of his head. 'Back then, with Horka and the Russians? They were busy looking out for themselves.'

'You're right, of course,' Sterkowitz agreed. 'The medical care is often a lot better than the policing.' He laughed.

'That'll depend on your successor, too,' said Frau Sterkowitz, sounding strained. 'But if he don't come soon, you'll be the oldest doctor in the country.'

Sterkowitz suddenly thought of his predecessor, how he must have waited for his replacement to come at last. A friendly gentleman with gold-rimmed spectacles, who had seemed ancient to him then. Today, he could almost have been his son: Dr Bernstein, who had had to leave Darkenbloom on foot, travelling light.

'Make sure you always wash your hands thoroughly,' he had advised him, and Sterkowitz had taken this to be typical Jewish irony. He had long since admitted to himself what a pathetic spectacle he must have been, snapped up fresh out of university, essentially clueless. And that you really did have to wash your hands thoroughly, always.

Frau Sterkowitz was energetically stacking plates, but inwardly she was listening, shocked, to the echo of her own words. *Horka* — she had said it out loud, for the first time in decades. Because it had been from him that she had heard that Lajos was dead. She had had to pretend to her husband, later, that she didn't know. Horka had snuck into their house through the cellar, grabbed her in the kitchen, by the neck, and forced himself on her. Standing up. She hadn't made a sound; she had just tried to get enough air through the hand he was pressing into her face, until it was over. Afterwards, he had told her that Lajos was dead. Because he talked too much; and that she had to take care the same thing didn't happen to her husband. 'Not a word, you hear me?' he had hissed, and she had flinched and nodded vehemently.

When he reappeared in her kitchen a few weeks later, she almost collapsed with fear. The cellar had been kept locked ever since, but perhaps locks were something Horka could simply open. This time he didn't do anything to her; he even caught her before she fell to the floor and sat her down roughly on her kitchen bench. He placed some banknotes on the table.

'So far, you've done what I told you,' he said. 'Just make sure it stays that way.' She nodded again, gasping for breath. Then he was gone. The money went into her emergency reserve, stuck with drawing pins to the back of the wardrobe, behind the moth papers. They had had great need of it back then, in that first, dreadful period after the war.

'You're just too good for this world,' she told her husband, and, arms laden with plates, closed the kitchen door behind her with her foot.

17.

WHEN RESI RESCHEN GOT out of bed at dawn and saw the heavy rain, her dreams mingled unpleasantly with the events of the previous night. She had a sudden surge of anger, and began to feel like the proverbial spider whitewashed into a corner. No matter where the spider runs, a deadly white paintbrush comes sweeping towards it. It wasn't clear to Resi why she felt such rage, but she sensed the formless grey outside creeping in through the windows and into her body, moving right through her and sloshing everywhere, like the streams and gutters in the night. Grey versus this insolent white. Various people — she wasn't thinking names just yet, it was just initial, blind fury; she pictured a sort of faceless, hostile crowd slowly advancing towards her — were about to destroy all that had been built up over so many years. They were ripping open windows, wounds, trenches, for no reason, even though none of it was conducive to fruitful coexistence. Dr Alois often spoke of *fruitful coexistence*, and since he had come back, and Horka had gone away, everything really had changed for the better. Didn't these smart alecs realise they would provoke a backlash with all their poking around? Everyone knew how it went. In the end, someone else would be found lying dead somewhere. The inquisitive girl, maybe? Those who talked about coming to terms with the past, museums, reconciliation with the people Over There — none of them could imagine what it was really like back then, during and after the war. They didn't know the risk they were taking if they didn't stop their self-important nonsense. Some of them were just children — that Flocke Malnitz, for example, they only cut her plaits off a few years ago! And Rehberg, the glazier's only son, he was scarcely born when things were at their worst. Resi remembered how, not long after the war began, they'd spent a whole day looking for the midwife. It hadn't actually made much difference, because the labour went on for several days. But mothers are often hysterical when giving birth for the first time. And the young glazier's wife, still practically a girl, had been particularly hysterical, as if people didn't have other things to worry about. But the fact that Rehberg had only just been born in the war years meant that he didn't know anything.

If Resi Reschen had been honest with herself — something her internal apparatus was absolutely not configured to do — she would have realised that it wasn't the chronicle, the museum, and all the other modest attempts at artificially imposing a few tourist attractions on Darkenbloom that bothered her. It was that she was afraid: afraid of what she didn't understand and couldn't categorise. This seldom happened to her. But why did the guest in Room 7 think he could address her as if they'd known each other for years?

Resi whirled through the establishment like an iron broom. She made Zenzi lay out the sausage slices on the breakfast platter all over again because she decided they weren't even enough. When the Croatian chambermaid vacuumed under the tables, she kicked her bottom and pretended it was an accident. Things went on like this until after midday. It was only late in the afternoon, when she had had enough of chasing her employees around and really couldn't find anything else to complain about, that she retreated, glowering, to her office in the corner. She always kept all her papers, even the oldest ones, in the same place; half of life is organisation, so they say, and if anyone had asked her she would probably have replied that the other half was hard work. Equipped with one-armed Reschen's reading glasses, God rest his soul, she picked up an old leather briefcase and took out documents she had hoped she would never have to look at again. She studied them carefully, though she already knew them well. She tried to compile a Tüffer family tree on a piece of paper she set out for the purpose, but failed. Young Herr Tüffer, who had been so taken with Vroni, had had young children, but she could no longer remember their names. Frau Tüffer had had other sons and daughters who emigrated earlier; Resi didn't even know how many of them there were. Suppose, somewhere in the world, one of young Tüffer's sisters had married a Gellért? She had no way of checking. This was why she was even looking at the signatures on the documents, right back to the time of the monarchy, surveys and certificates of land acquisition. An official, or notary, or witness? Did anything point towards someone by the name of Gellért?

She had never let on to a soul how much she feared the Tüffers' return. Though that wasn't entirely true. If old Frau Tüffer herself had come back — right after the war, for example — Resi would probably have curtseyed and gone to fetch the big bunch of keys. But you sometimes heard about letters that resulted in legal disputes, lawyers, expenses. You heard about a lot of impersonal, faceless trouble. There had been a handful of similar cases in Tellian and Kirschenstein, where someone had taken over a business and had had to give it back later on, or else pay a great deal of money so it finally really did belong to him. At least one family had been bankrupted by it, not long ago. According to Resi's personal interpretation of the law, it must all have passed the statute of limitations by now, especially after last year's anniversary. Fifty years! How long would she have to live in fear? Would her heirs have to live in fear, as well?

When he was drunk, her one-armed husband had sometimes vilified Resi as a *Jew-whore*. Because whenever people talked about the Tüffers, she insisted that old Frau Tüffer had always treated her decently. *In the land of the Jews, the decent Frau Tüffer is king*, Reschen would roar, lashing out at her with his arm. In later years, though, he wasn't so fast any more, her husband, with his great belly. Greater even than his belly was his hatred of the Jews. On one occasion it even led to a dangerous argument with a Russian, because Reschen simply hadn't thought it possible that the Russians would allow Jews to become officers. Over the years, his hatred slowly ebbed away. It ebbed away the more time passed since the war, and the longer the Tüffers did not return; the longer, in fact, they didn't hear so much as a whisper from them ever again. As if they had never existed. Perhaps, strictly speaking, Reschen had only hated the Tüffers, although he never even knew them.

There was never any question of them changing the name of the hotel to Reschen. They didn't have money to spend on appearances, and the name, as Resi explained to Reschen often enough, was an established one, since the days of the Empire. *Established*, Reschen bellowed, *kiss my arse*. But the name remained, as did the Art Nouveau elegance, though the Reschens camouflaged it as much as possible with a great deal of rustic pottery and plaited straw.

A shadow fell across Resi's documents and her pitiable attempt to make sense of the various branches of the Tüffer family tree. She glanced up. Zenzi stood before her, looking fearful. 'Old Graun,' she whispered, 'sorry, Frau Veronika Graun, she'd like to speak to you.'

Resi slowly rose to her feet and grabbed Zenzi, who was trying to step aside, by the hips. Holding her in front of her like a human shield, she peered over Zenzi's fleshy shoulder at reception. There indeed stood Vroni, all done up in hat, coat, and handbag; she could hardly believe her eyes. Astonishing that she still possessed any respectable clothes, the old alky! Resi instructed Zenzi in a whisper to seat her at the corner table in the bar, and once the coast was clear she went to change. Equality of arms had to be established.

The salmon-pink blazer Resi selected was stretched as tightly across her chest as the stand-up collar on Vroni's flower-patterned blouse was frayed. They sat opposite each other, well aware of the sartorial inadequacies, including their own. If one of the usual guests had entered the bar of the Tüffer early that rainy evening, he would have been surprised to see the two women sitting facing each other, tense, as if in the presence of a lawyer or notary. But no one was there yet; business was always slow on a Monday and, after the previous night's storm, the first drinkers probably wouldn't show up until later. Vroni Graun ordered a coffee with milk, and Zenzi, unasked, brought a large glass of tap water for her boss. Then she was waved out of the room.

'Long time no see,' Vroni Graun began, with a tiny hint of irony.

'Indeed, madam,' said Resi, with exactly the same degree of irony. 'How can I help you?'

Frau Graun stirred her coffee thoroughly, after scooping in two large spoonfuls of sugar. Typical alky, Frau Reschen observed; she also noticed the sweetish body odour, like a rancid chocolate liqueur. Nonetheless, Vroni was in better condition than the rumours would have led her to expect.

Finally, Frau Graun looked up. 'Tell me, did you actually have a thing with young Herr Tüffer, back then?' she asked, and winked.

Resi froze. What the hell did she want? That couldn't be why she'd come! But with just a few words Vroni had managed to acutely embarrass her, as if they were still fourteen years old. Resi considered her answer carefully, stuck her nose in the air, and said, 'As you well know, one didn't *have* anything with the bosses. They gave, and they took.'

'I'm just saying,' said Frau Graun, 'that a bastard was left outside the church in Ehrenfeld, back then. And just supposing it was yours, you'd sort of have a legitimate heir.'

299

Outside, the clock on the tower struck twice for the half-hour. A delivery truck rattled past. Because Resi was trying hard to breathe without a sound, there was a moment's silence, until old Frau Graun gave a rattling laugh. 'Shame no one knows what happened to him, that bastard child!'

Resi stared at the table top, and clenched her fist beneath it. 'What do you want?' she asked eventually. 'I have other things to do besides sit around here.'

'Of course, apologies,' replied old Frau Graun. 'Our industrious Resi, who never gets to leave the hotel, not ever, day or night. But I have another question.' She changed her tone, becoming more urgent. 'Tell me, Resi, do you by any chance know what Dr Alois has on my boy? He leaps to attention whenever the old Nazi snaps his fingers, has done for years.'

She looked up again, friendly, beseeching, and for a moment Resi saw her best friend, as she once was, so beautiful and blonde and smart; back then, on the way to the Tüffer for the interview, neither of them had known what misery and misfortune they both would have to endure. Yet they had made it this far: had not been shot by the Russians like Theresia Wallnöfer, had not disappeared like Inge Stipsits, had not gone mad like Agnes Kalmar, but were now seventy years old, with children and grandchildren and a secure, established status in the town.

'Even if I did, why should I tell you?' Resi retorted, because she did owe herself that. She looked at Frau Graun again, the childish blouse with the stand-up collar, the amber brooch, and the old-maidish felt hat, with which she was obviously trying to look grand. She did seem sober, though, and somewhat on edge.

'You scratch my back and I'll scratch yours,' Frau Graun suggested. 'I think I know who your guest is — the one who keeps bone boxes in his room.'

'Bone boxes,' Resi echoed mechanically, without allowing the words and their meaning anywhere near her. For a moment she thought she smelled freshly sawn wood.

'Tell me what Ferbenz has got on my boy,' Frau Graun insisted.

'Nothing that matters any more, if you ask me,' Resi answered finally. 'He arranged for charges against him to be dropped, more than twenty years ago, for shoplifting.'

'Shoplifting?' Frau Graun repeated. She looked surprised. She doesn't know everything, then, thought Resi smugly, before nodding.

'But that can't be it,' Frau Graun complained, not satisfied. 'It must be something else for my boy to jump whenever Ferbenz lifts a finger.'

'He was probably looking for a father figure,' said Resi coldly. 'Or just *someone* who was nice to him.'

Old Frau Graun stared at her. Resi went on: 'And who was interested in music, and something other than just debts and your farm. Ever take a look at Malnitz's youngest, by the way? She doesn't exactly look like Toni.'

There was a long pause.

'What did he steal?' asked Frau Graun finally, her voice hoarse.

'Precious stones of some kind, as lovely as the lady Leonore,' said Resi, grinning. So much for bastards, she thought.

She had stripped Frau Graun of her superior manner, that much was clear. With every minute that passed, Vroni seemed to dwindle from an almost-lady to a wizened wreck.

'Tell me, Resi,' she began again, and now she sounded almost tearful, 'Josef, back then, that night, you know what I mean ... was he in the gun room all night, or did he go as well, with the others? You were in the kitchen till the end, you saw!'

'Oh, come now, Vroni, don't act stupid,' said Resi impatiently. 'They were all there, all our men — no one was left behind!'

'Yours was left behind,' said Frau Graun. 'He only had one arm.'

Resi Reschen nodded and hunched her shoulders, feeling a

sudden chill. 'Now tell me what you know about my guest!'

And Veronika Graun told her what had suddenly been clear to her when she woke up that morning. She hadn't even set eyes on this man who, her daughter-in-law said, had been wandering around the town for days engaging Darkenbloomers in very specific conversations. But she didn't need to. Someone like her, someone her age, only needed to put two and two together; and she'd always been good at that. If Resi hadn't already worked it out herself, it could only be because the mysterious guest was right there under her nose, every day, morning and evening, at hotel meals. That distracted from what ought to be obvious.

'But he says he's been everywhere else already, all over the region,' Resi protested feebly. Now she was the one acting stupid. 'In Löwingen and Mandl, in Kirschenstein and Tellian! And they've already found them everywhere else!'

'If I'd wanted revenge, I'd have done exactly the same,' said Frau Graun, and tapped her temple knowingly. 'Deal with everything round about, and home in right at the end. And now I think you could actually offer me a schnapps.'

Resi immediately got up and fetched the bottle, glad to have a reason to move about again. She treated herself to a double as well, something that only happened once in a blue moon. The two women, who had known each other all their lives and had not spoken for most of them, raised and clinked their schnapps glasses, but without a hint of a smile. It was clear that this conversation had never taken place; neither of them needed to say it. There was a long tradition of that here, and it had always served them well.

PART III

Historical is that which one would not do oneself.

ROBERT MUSIL

I.

CURLY-HAIRED MARTHA WASN'T QUITE like the other young people who were dedicating three weeks of their summer holiday to the Jewish cemetery in Darkenbloom. The others were all students of contemporary history who regarded themselves as left-wing, fighters against Austria's historical amnesia, and she had only known one of them before this: Andreas Bart, whom everyone called Bartl. Bartl was tall, blond, and articulate, very full of himself, and, although his surname meant *beard*, devoid of facial hair. He seemed to purchase his T-shirts on the basis of colour (predominantly red), and he was the one who usually handled communications with the local population. It irritated her somewhat that he barely concealed his irony and condescension when doing so.

Martha didn't know why, at that noisy, smoky party, Bartl had asked her of all people, a film student, if she wanted to come with them on the cemetery project. Even by the standards of what the capital considered provincial, there was, nonetheless, a hierarchy. There were the rich federal states, and those renowned for their beauty; there were the ones that were famous throughout the world for their mountains or lakes or festivals. Out of every imaginable provincial possibility, the narrow eastern border region where Darkenbloom lay was by far the least attractive. German and Swiss people had never even heard its name, but they already had difficulty distinguishing Upper from Lower Austria. Even Austrians who tried to list the nine federal states sometimes forgot this most recent, small addition, especially if they were from the west of the country — perhaps because *Burgenland* sounded almost like the word for *federal state*. Hardly anyone knew an actual Burgenlander; they seemed to appear in large numbers only as the protagonists of jokes. Every country has its Irishmen, and in Austria they're the Burgenlanders. The shortest joke Martha had ever heard went like this: *Two Burgenlanders meet at university.*

Martha knew all this because she was from here. She had spent most of her childhood and youth just a little further north, in a village not far from Kirschenstein. When she was sixteen, both her grandparents died in quick succession, and she went to live with her irresponsible mother in the capital. She lasted only a few months with this woman, who was a stranger to her, and whom she detested. Instead, she took refuge with false friends, quit her apprenticeship, earned money waitressing, then as a cleaner, took a lot of drugs, was beaten up multiple times, and raped — she was almost surprised to note — only once. She could no longer recall what got her back on her feet. Just that she woke up one day under a stinking blanket with the taste of blood in her mouth and vowed to herself that she would at least give it one more try. She could always jump off a building later on. The years since that moment, Day One after her absolute nadir, had been hard. She had totally abandoned herself to the freefall, and was now equally relentless in forcing herself to climb back up again. She earned just enough to get by. She studied at night school for her school-leaving certificate, passed on her first attempt, and was accepted by the film academy on her second. She would rather it had been the other way around, but if it had, perhaps she would have given up earlier.

She was twenty-three years old, and in possession of a video camera of her own for the very first time. She had dragged herself up by her curls and put herself back on track, but sometimes she felt as if she were standing on top of a huge mountain of scree that at any moment could start, imperceptibly, to slide. And so spending a few weeks exterminating weeds and cutting down trees in familiar surroundings had seemed a sensible idea, more sensible than staying in the city with all its unhealthy temptations.

On Monday morning, once it had stopped drizzling, she told the others that she wanted to film outside, just because — you never knew what it might be good for. The others understood perfectly what she meant by outside, because they were all inside most of the time, within the high walls, as if in a secret garden. The others didn't care that she was going off on her own for once; after all, she had special status, in that she was documenting the project.

It seemed to her that until now she had stuck too close to it all. She had filmed almost exclusively in close-up: nature without people, or only hands and arms, but mostly snapped-off flowers, falling branches, thick, prickly carpets of thorns, and creepers that fiercely resisted their forcible removal. She liked these sequences; it looked like the battle it was. Never showing whole people, only hands or feet ripping at or treading on them, made the plants seem almost like equal opponents. They were passively resisting, like demonstrators who make themselves heavy when police try to carry them away. And this was how she had filmed the other side, too; in the close up, a sort of personification: stones laboriously righted, or at least uncovered, seeing sunlight for the first time in decades; fingers running along their chiselled letters and wiping away the dirt.

After that crazy storm, though, Martha felt the need for other pictures. Her instinct told her that she needed camera movement, sur-roundings that would put the close-ups into context. The gaze needed to move now, the objects staying still and as silent as the people who lived here. She wanted to film along the length of undamaged walls, to show distances and expanses as a counterpart to the toppled and shattered stones. Darkenbloom stood erect, albeit crumbling in places, but the forgotten, moss-covered stones lay flat on their backs and fronts.

Martha hadn't seen much of the little town so far. She and her colleagues always took the same routes. At midday, some of them would go to a little shop in the old town and buy provisions: ham rolls, biscuits, crisps, and drinks. The man who served them there made Martha uncomfortable. He seemed to have more muscles in his face than normal, especially around the eyes and forehead. And he was so nervous, constantly wiping his hands on his overall and clearing his throat. She didn't like him; she found him almost creepy, although he smiled a lot. But she did want to ask if she could film his postcard stand. She pictured his hand in its blue sleeve setting the stand in motion and making it spin. All those views of the town, the main square, the aerial view, the plague column, as well as a castle that clearly no longer existed, would rotate before the eye of her camera, blur, then come into focus again. This should provide a useful summary. She didn't intend actually to film the so-called sights of the town.

But the shop was shut, the door locked, and a sign stuck to the window: *Closed due to illness.*

And so she walked on, observing the town more closely. She strolled past the houses, and after looking at a street she would go back to the beginning and film it, slowly, all along its façades, front doors, and little walls.

She wasn't looking for people, but she noticed that they were watching her. This amused her. Open staring — that, here, was practically an invitation to chat. She was familiar with this from her village: living in such close proximity, bumping into each other all the time and knowing almost everything about each other, you pretended that the opposite was the case. You nodded sullenly and lowered your eyes; you acted as if you only noticed a fraction of what went on around you. It was less a question of tact than of self-protection.

Whereas stopping, looking, noisily opening a window, or even stepping outside the door meant almost the same as someone in the city holding out their hand and introducing themselves. And Martha could guess why: it was the camera. The people drawing aside their curtains and sticking their noses out of their windows did not immediately see this as an unwelcome event. They were hoping that this unfamiliar girl would film them. It might be an honour, being filmed. Until now, cameras had seldom come here, to Darkenbloom, so a student filming was interesting enough.

Martha nodded to them, but she didn't speak to anyone. In doing so, without realising it, she was putting out bait. She acted as though she wanted nothing from them. To begin with, she really didn't want much. Just to film the crooked streets in peace, the window ledges where geraniums bloomed with touching abandon, peeling fences, archways with heavily laden hay carts driving through them, and, occasionally, a bent-backed woman in a traditional blue-patterned skirt shuffling back inside her house and closing the door behind her.

She was standing in front of a clothes shop window, zooming in from various angles on the claret-coloured metal script above it, when an old man came out of the front door and walked into her shot. She lowered the camera to give him time to move away, but he kept walking towards her.

'Now then, young lady,' he said, 'what're you filming here? Got a permit?'

Martha frowned. 'Do I need one?' she asked.

'Only joking,' said the man. 'I'm just interested to know what you're doing.'

Martha murmured a few non-committal sentences about being here with friends and having a little look around town. 'Most visitors have ordinary cameras,' she said. 'I make moving images, that's really the only difference.'

The man seemed satisfied, but he still didn't go away. He launched into a little speech about how Darkenbloom was an insider tip, though the town hadn't always had it easy, on account of its location. But anyone who takes an interest will find undiscovered treasures and hidden delights, believe you me. Around here, our country is still exactly the same as it's been for hundreds of years, he said. We can be proud of that.

'Have you already looked at the painting in the church with the feathered devils?' he asked. 'And the plague column with the beggar woman in the town square? As plague columns go, it's in a class of its own; you won't find many to compare with it anywhere in the country, I'm telling you! The same with the crypt ... Alas, our plague column is sorely in need of renovation. It really is heartbreaking: the figures barely have noses any more — wind and weather, you can imagine. But no tourism means no money, and no money means no renovation.'

He twinkled at her. 'Our wine, on the other hand, is particularly good,' he added, 'but I expect you've already tried it?'

Martha nodded. The way older people had around here of quickly shifting to the informal *Du* when addressing younger people was also familiar to her. It was by no means an invitation for the younger person to do the same.

'Might I perhaps film you from behind?' she asked. 'Just walking away? You won't be recognisable, but it would be nice if the street wasn't empty ...'

The man, whose watery eyes were a striking pale blue, nodded. 'Gladly, young lady, happy if I can contribute in some way ... Everyone knows me around here, anyway. Where would you like me to walk?'

'Wherever you were going is fine,' suggested Martha. 'And I'll just follow you with the camera?'

And so, on Monday morning after the big storm, the day after Flocke Malnitz disappeared, Martha the curly-haired student and her camera followed Dr Alois Ferbenz as he made one of his charitable visits. Dr Alois was the good uncle of Darkenbloom, by no means only in his own immodest perception — or perhaps now, given his advanced age, the good grandfather. He knew everyone, and for many — for most, in fact — he had a friendly word. There were a few absolute exceptions. But since stepping down from all public offices, and having also persuaded his wife finally to hand on the business to the next generation, charity and helping his neighbours were what gave pleasure and purpose to his life, even more than before. Ferbenz supported people in need, he mediated quarrels, he helped people navigate the planning permission process and other bureaucratic mazes. And just recently, having successfully sued over a foreign holiday ruined by serious defects, he had publicly donated the few hundred schillings compensation to a mother-of-three whose husband was in a wheelchair following a tragic accident at work. He had also ensured that the municipality found a long-term solution for the family. Not that Mayor Koreny had been much help. But he did at least do what Ferbenz suggested and freed up a ground-floor apartment in one of Darkenbloom's municipal housing blocks. *Koreny always has to be goaded into action!* A phrase that was taken up by the people of Darkenbloom and often repeated, with glee.

And so, in his eightieth year, Alois Ferbenz strolled at a leisurely pace through Darkenbloom's narrow alleyways, and everyone who saw him greeted him or tipped their hat. He waved back. Little girls who curtseyed received particular praise. He walked along Tempelgasse, past number four, which, in his mental address book, was still the Horka house; he didn't so much as look at it. The old house stood there; let it stand. It was of no interest to him what was in there, whether a shop was open or closed. His wife did the Ferbenz family shopping, and she certainly didn't do it here. He walked on, turning right, then left, until he came to a blind alley, at the end of which the simpleton Fritz was sitting on a stool outside his house, smoking.

When Ferbenz stopped, Martha was still behind him. She slowly walked past, panned round to the very last house, paused for a few seconds on the dense foliage of an apple tree, allowed it gradually to blur to a veil of green, and switched the camera off.

Fritz had stood up and trodden out his cigarette. He held out his hand to the old man and waved to Martha, gesturing her over. The man she had been filming glanced briefly in her direction. He probably thought it was on his account that she too was invited in.

Behind the front door it was dark and cramped, but Martha soon got her bearings. It was like her grandparents' house. At the front, facing the street, were the two so-called good rooms; behind them, at the back, facing the courtyard, was the kitchen. After that, the house narrowed to a long, thin tunnel, a succession of small and even smaller rooms. This was where later generations had added sanitary facilities whenever they could afford it.

'Just wanted to see how the two of you were doing,' the old man she had followed said to Fritz, the carpenter who carved so well. He mumbled and babbled something, and Martha noticed that, this time, she could hardly understand him.

'Are you managing to get by without Eszter, more or less?' the man asked. 'And is it possible to see your mama?'

Fritz babbled and mumbled and went on ahead, into the second of the two good, large rooms. A small woman was sitting at a table, drawing. Martha stopped in the doorway and narrowed her eyes. It was like a picture from a book of fairy tales. The decor looked as if it had never been changed; the air was stale, the heavy curtains drawn, and the only light came from the lamp on her table. Pale and fragile, the woman was wholly absorbed in her work. Her long white plait hung down to the seat of the chair, where it lay coiled like a friendly snake.

'Mama,' said Fritz — and now he was easy to understand — 'Mama, visitor, Dr Ferbenz.'

The woman dipped her pen in her inkpot and went on drawing. Martha thought perhaps she was deaf and they might be about to startle her.

'Dr Ferbenz,' Fritz repeated, and his mother nodded and leaned back slightly, away from her picture, to examine it.

'What's this pretty drawing, then, Agnes?' asked Ferbenz, stepping closer. Fritz took his elbow, pulling him back and to the side. He led him round in the widest possible semicircle to approach his mother from the front.

So she is hard of hearing, thought Martha; best not to come up behind her. She raised the camera.

Fritz pulled up a chair for Ferbenz.

'Hello, Agnes,' said Ferbenz. 'I thought I'd come and see how the two of you were doing. Do you need anything?'

Agnes drew. Martha zoomed in. It was the portrait of a girl, composed of a multitude of fine lines. Martha thought it was pretty good, but what she liked best was that Dr Ferbenz clearly didn't know what to say.

'Do you always draw the same thing?' asked Ferbenz, pointing to a pile of papers lying on the table. Agnes drew. Fritz shook his head and reeled off a list of names Martha didn't recognise or understand. It seemed his mother was drawing the women of the town from memory.

Ferbenz laughed. 'Frau Stipsits hasn't looked like that for a very long time,' he said. 'If these women knew, they'd pay you good money for portraits of their youthful selves.'

There was silence for a moment.

'Now then, Agnes, come on, talk to me,' said Ferbenz, and put his hand on her left forearm. Agnes sat bolt upright and froze; even her plait seemed to stiffen with fear. Fritz babbled urgently.

'I don't think you should touch her,' said Martha.

'Who asked your opinion?' said Ferbenz, and there were shards of ice in his voice.

Fritz intervened. He pushed Ferbenz's hand aside, placed his own over Agnes's left hand, stroked it, and said: 'Dr Ferbenz, Mama, Ferbenz.'

Agnes Kalmar put down her inkpen. 'Ferbenz — Szinnyei,' she said, seeming gradually to relax again. 'Fiedler — Fenyö, Fischer — Halász, Follath — Faludi, Freud — Barát, Fuchs — Földes.'

'My name is Fürst,' said Martha, from the doorway. She peered out from behind her camera, which was still running.

Agnes turned to her, beaming from ear to ear, and said, 'Fürst — Karakay!'

Ferbenz stood, patted his thighs, and said that Fritz could turn to him any time if he needed anything. He shouldn't be proud; everyone was always too proud. But in a town like theirs, people liked to help; really, it would be a pleasure, any time. Eszter had always been so stubborn; she wouldn't hear of it, always maintained she didn't need anything; one day she was saying this, and then the next she was dead. 'It can happen that fast,' said Ferbenz, shaking his head, 'you really have to watch out.'

As he passed Martha, he nodded to her and said: 'Went through an awful lot in the war, Agnes Kalmar; never recovered, sadly. Those really were terrible times — the things the Russkies did here, literally went on the rampage, they did, the Russkies.'

Martha threw a look at Fritz and gave him the camera to hold. She ran out into the street after Ferbenz and asked, 'May I come and visit you as well sometime, Doctor? And would you tell me a bit about Darkenbloom?'

'Certainly,' said Ferbenz, who seemed tired all of a sudden. 'Come by whenever you like, my girl.'

2.

AT EIGHT O'CLOCK ON Tuesday morning, Herbert Koreny was already in his office in the town hall, with the files on the water issue piled up in front of him.

The texts of the contracts between the municipality and the water authority were long and tedious; Koreny had great difficulty concentrating on the German legalese, and secretly knew that reading them was pointless. However, he wanted to have studied everything else before he picked up the file labelled *Surveyor's Report*; he considered it his duty. He wanted to be able to say that he had inspected everything, absolutely everything, once more, closely, from start to finish.

Eventually he opened the last file, and found a letter from Farmer Faludi right on top. It listed the names of three surveyors who, he claimed, were closely connected to the water authority and had already filed reports for other municipalities in the authority's favour. Above this, a note in Balf's handwriting read: *Strategy of conspiracy!*

Koreny leafed through the file from beginning to end. The reports had indeed been compiled by the three surveyors mentioned, but how was he supposed to check whether they were in cahoots with the water authority? He didn't even know why they, of all people, had been entrusted with these surveys. How many surveyors might there be who specialised in this field? In the state? In the country? He started reading from the top. The first surveyor took a clear position: he recommended joining up with the water authority immediately *to avoid serious shortages, especially, but not only, in the dry summer months.* The second strove for neutrality; he wrote that with a detailed survey of underground water sources, the construction of static water tanks, and the installation of water meters it might be possible to guarantee additional supplies even without joining the water authority. The current situation, though, was entirely insufficient. He did, however, state that he was not qualified to assess the quantities of water that could potentially be exploited, and recommended an expert by the name of Kolonovits. He was sure to be able to provide an answer that would facilitate the decision. Balf had underlined the name Kolonovits several times.

The third report was the one Koreny remembered best; not the details, but the main thrust of it. Balf had quoted from it numerous times in that meeting of the town council, when Koreny was still a deferential, wholly unimportant deputy mayor, and the actual mayor still opinionated and healthy. This surveyor said it was imperative that the question of whether Darkenbloom had enough water to supply its own needs also be considered in terms of the costs and obstacles on this path to self-sufficiency. Excavations, new water pipes, permits, and obtaining consent from the affected parties would all be expensive, would take a huge amount of time, and success, ultimately, was not guaranteed. *Pig in a poke*, murmured Koreny, recalling the phrase from that heated meeting, *expensive, unpredictable pig in a poke, and no guarantee it'll work.* Whereas with the water authority you knew what you were getting: you paid, and they connected the Darkenbloom network to their crisis-proof pipeline. The water came from far away, from the mountains, the Schneeberg, the Semmering, or somewhere else, it didn't matter where. End of story. Koreny sighed.

On Friday, after work, he had dropped in at Heinz Balf's; his house, that is, where Balf's wife was bracing herself for bad news. She didn't open the door when he rang the bell, so he went round the back of the bungalow into the garden. She was standing there with her back to him, watering the flowerbeds. He watched her for a few moments. A tranquil picture: a woman with a garden hose, the mist from the spray glittering in the evening sun. Balf's wife was known for her magnificent garden. Would she feel constrained in her watering if the water were metered?

Eventually she turned and greeted him. 'There's no news,' she added, before he could ask.

Koreny murmured words of regret. They stood there. Koreny pointed to the pallets of paving slabs lined up along the house, next to a small excavator with its arm at half-mast, as if it had been switched off mid-movement. The excavator had already devoured part of the lawn and spat it out in a heap.

'New terrace?' asked Koreny, trying to sound upbeat.

'Bloody thing,' said Balf's wife. 'Heinz arranged it, and now it turns out it's not even paid for. I don't know where we'd get the money. He must have been off his head already on the medication. How could he order something we don't have money for? He never used to do things like this. And I can't even tell him off about it.'

She laughed, too loudly, and her eyes filled with tears. Even recalling the shrillness in her voice made Koreny uncomfortable. He had quickly made his excuses and left.

The rumour was that Balf had taken a bribe for the contract with the water authority. Koreny knew this, though no one had said it to him directly. Over the past few weeks he had often got embroiled in a war of words with opponents of the water authority, when everyone talked at him at once, until eventually someone was bound to shout or hiss the words *bribed, bribery.* Koreny never asked what they were talking about. If he had asked who was alleging this, and on what basis, he would have been the first to say the words openly. *You said it, not me,* they would claim, and afterwards they would repeat it and pass it on, smirking, forever in conjunction with his name.

On the last page of the third survey someone had written an address in Graz, and the initials *E.K. Emmerich Kolonovits,* said a voice in Koreny's head; it sounded almost like Farmer Faludi. Koreny was surprised. Was that actually his name?

He got up and fetched the file of correspondence, H–K. Under Kolonovits there was indeed a letter in which Mayor Balf asked him to quote for a survey of *Darkenbloom's natural water reserves and their possible exploitation.* But nothing else. No reply. Shouldn't the reply be in the file with the surveys? Koreny leafed back and forth in the correspondence file, thinking. Would he, personally, commit a crime in order to get a new terrace? Back when Dr Sterkowitz found the lumps in his armpits, had Heinz for some reason wanted to placate his wife? Or impress her? And why did it absolutely have to be Italian terrazzo?

Leafing through, Koreny came across his own name, but not in reference to him. The municipal authorities had sent his second cousin a letter ordering him to cut back his thuja hedge *by at least one metre in width,* because the dung cart was having great difficulty turning round outside his property. *We would like to draw your attention to the fact that cuttings from the thuja plant are poisonous and, as hazardous waste, must be disposed of professionally. Confirmation of its disposal must be retained for presentation. Yours sincerely.*

Kolonovits. Koreny. His cousin didn't have a terrazzo terrace, and neither did he. His cousin had thuja, he had box, and they both had washed-concrete paving. Herbert Koreny felt strange, light-headed, and it seemed as if there were voices whispering nearby. As if someone were standing behind the curtain, almost touching his collar, gentle, nudging. It was absurd. He should relinquish the office of mayor, step down; these conflicts were not good for him. His wife and children had advised him against it right from the start, though they did enjoy taking on more responsibility for the family firm. They probably didn't even need him there any more now; Electro Koreny did well with him or without. What was he actually good for? He had difficulty kneeling down to test a power socket. He had even more difficulty getting up again. It was the same with being mayor. For Heinz, his old friend, the only one who deserved it, he had bent the knee. Now he couldn't get up again.

Koreny, commanded the voice in his head that sounded like Farmer Faludi: *in a different file!*

Herbert Koreny obediently went to look. Where did Frau Balaskó keep old correspondence? He finally found it in a box in the outer office. H–K. He leafed through to the copies of letters he himself had received: new assessment rate for property tax, permission for a garage enlargement. After that, more letters to his second cousin. Ha, at one point he hadn't paid any wastewater treatment fees for a whole year; interesting! Payment demand, another payment demand. And then suddenly Koreny was holding a page that didn't belong there. It was the last page of something, clipped to the back of his cousin's payment demand, signed *Emmerich Kolonovits*. Koreny leafed back and forth. Behind every second or third letter in section K was a hidden page, cunningly slipped between the copies. There were only seven of them. Koreny tried to prise open the staples, but after stabbing himself and leaving a bloody fingerprint he simply tore them off. He wasn't the one who had hidden them, he hadn't had any secrets before now, so there was no need for him to cover any tracks. Seven pages. He took them all out and replaced the file.

Then he sat at his desk and thought hard. Kolonovits's surveyor's report with the torn corners lay in front of him on the desk. Frau Balaskó appeared at nine o'clock and called good morning to him through the door. She brought him a cup of the bitter coffee she made every day; it ought to be banned, that concoction burned holes in the stomach. He didn't say so, just thanked her.

Koreny sat there and asked her to close the door. At a quarter to ten she came back and announced that the farmer Faludi was here to see him. Koreny felt an immediate rush of anger, burning temples and itchy palms. So now the man had appeared in the flesh! He slid the folder with the documents awaiting his signature on top of the surveyor's report, and got to his feet.

Farmer Faludi entered with his six-foot staff like a hiker in the high mountains, and thumped it on the parquet floor as if beating time for a brass band. Koreny's gaze travelled to the bottom of the staff.

'I wipe it on the doormat, like my shoes,' said Farmer Faludi. He often knew what you were thinking; Mayor Koreny had noticed this before.

He didn't want to sit down, he would only stay a few minutes, he said. So the two stood facing each other, the edge of the office chair digging uncomfortably into the back of Koreny's knees. Before him, invisible, lay the suppressed report, which Farmer Faludi would probably have given his staff to lay his hands on.

'There's enough water there, Herbert,' he said calmly. 'I can prove it now. If you don't look into it, and insist on joining the water authority, it'd be cheating the taxpayers.'

'Even if you were right about the amount of water,' Koreny answered, rubbing his itchy palms together, 'no one knows what it would cost! How long it would take! Whether the water would be sufficient!'

He fell back onto the chair and stretched his belly. He felt almost nauseous; his bowels were rumbling, and he thought of his friend Balf lying there, so helpless, tubes hanging out of him left, right, and centre, while this man dared to come in here thumping his staff.

'I just don't understand,' said Farmer Faludi, who was standing in front of the desk like a chief, so erect and proud, with his absurdly long beard. 'I just don't understand why you're taking it so personally. Anyone can make a mistake.'

'We have contracts,' Koreny whispered. 'We're committed; they've got us over a barrel.'

'Who's got us over a barrel?' asked Farmer Faludi, looking genuinely astonished.

'Everyone,' cried Koreny. 'You have no idea what this is really about!' He slammed his fist down on the desk, causing the document folder to shift a few centimetres. The torn ears of the report peeked out from underneath.

Farmer Faludi said, 'I wanted to settle it with you amicably. But if you're digging in your heels, we'll hold a referendum. Come over to the Tüffer at twelve; there's going to be a public meeting.'

Koreny sat there, saying nothing.

Farmer Faludi waited a moment, shook his head, tapped his felt hat, and left.

Koreny went on sitting there for another ten minutes, during which the only practical strategy unfurled, slowly and clearly, in his mind's eye. Put simply, this strategy was a combination of ashes, and gaining time. As soon as you'd got Faludi out of the room and out of your head, you could think for yourself again. It wasn't actually all that hard.

Eventually he got up, shoved Emmerich Kolonivits's seven pages into his inside jacket pocket, walked past Frau Balaskó to the lavatory, locked himself in, and burned the paper in the toilet bowl. Afterwards, he relieved his agitated bowels, blissfully excreting a massive turd, almost half the Hazug, on top of the ashes. He opened the window, lit a cigarette before leaving the cubicle, and as he walked back to his office, smoking, past Frau Balaskó, he said, 'I've eaten something that didn't agree with me. Probably the Posauner egg salad; not a good idea in summer.'

Frau Balaskó shook her head sympathetically and confirmed that no, eggs of unknown provenance really weren't a good idea in summer.

It had burned brightly and swiftly, the surveyor's report. The double page with the construction drawing was the last one he lit; he was still staring at it as the rest disintegrated, as if committing it to memory. As well as the necessary pipelines and pumping systems, this Kolonovits had projected the construction of several high-altitude water towers and elevated tanks. He had marked everything in. The biggest and most important was situated on the Rotenstein meadow. Now the flames were consuming it, this drawing of an elevated tank whose foundations must surely extend several metres into the ground; already it had vanished, was gone, forgotten, burned and obliterated, along with the monstrous and unreasonable suggestion that any extensive digging and excavating should take place in the Rotenstein meadow. Herbert Koreny wondered why his friend Heinz hadn't simply destroyed the report. Balf, the great strategist.

3.

IT WILL NEVER BE possible to reconstruct in its entirety all that occurred in the Hotel Tüffer from midday onwards that Tuesday in August 1989. This is a banal statement, because it applies to all events that involve a lot of people with different wishes, intentions, and feelings. The memories of individuals can only be trusted so far; most people only remember what suits them, what casts them in a better light, or spares their feelings.

The plain facts have been more or less established, although even on these there are dissenters. The Heuraffl twins, for example, apparently still lay claim to a different and completely illogical sequence of events. But everyone knows what the Heuraffls are like. In a word, one that Darkenbloomers might agree on to describe many others as well: alcohol-addled.

If anyone had asked him, Alexander Gellért would probably have taken a rather different view. He had no memories of the current Heuraffls, Berneck, or Stitched-Up Schurl from his youth in Darkenbloom; they had still been children when he had had to pack his suitcase and leave town. However, since taking lodgings as an observant guest in the Hotel Tüffer, Room 7, and conducting all manner of enquiries, he had, of course, come across them. Gellért's explanation would have focused not on the lifelong consumption of wine, which almost everyone here indulged in, but on a certain lack of intelligence, exacerbated — as in, further diminished — by the fear and aggressiveness of beaten dogs. Gellért knew something about this: he had had plenty of opportunities in his life to study this particular combination.

That Tuesday, he had breakfasted late and read the newspapers in detail. There were already more than a hundred East German citizens in the West German embassy in Prague, and others were scaling the fence every day. Gellért wondered where they were putting them up. After all, an embassy was not a hotel where Frau Resi Reschen was at your service day and night, although since Sunday evening she had been eyeing him with suspicion. The situation at the Hungarian border, just round the corner, within spitting distance, was also starting to get out of control, if he understood the insinuations in the local papers correctly. Gellért certainly conceded that the newspaper commentators found themselves in an absurd position. On the one hand, they had always condemned, with the utmost disgust, the communist Eastern Bloc that imprisoned its own population. On the other, they deeply mistrusted the activities of Otto von Habsburg. And suddenly the two seemed to be working together! Of all people, the son of the last emperor — who had also been the king of Hungary — was promoting a pan-European picnic, right here on the border, with the new Hungarian prime minister, a so-called reformer. There were some Austrians who, given their country's less-than-glorious history over the past century, ascribed to it a national talent for making a hash of things, and they already had a sneaking suspicion that some divvying up was going on again behind the scenes. Why else were the goulash communists suddenly so pally with the Habsburgs that they should want to go picnicking together? Gellért found it entertaining, in the paradoxical way in which, since his return, there were many things he found both satisfying and shocking.

Otto's ancient mother, Zita, the last empress, had only died in March, and the country had almost disintegrated again over what to think of the funeral ceremonies, which had gone on for several days. One side complained, saying they couldn't believe that Austria was playing at being a monarchy again, with such anachronistic kitsch and pomp, as if the Emperor Franz Joseph and his Sisi with her floor-length hair had departed a second time, simultaneously. On the other side were those who made the spectacle possible. Subjects with their inquisitive noses held aloft, right hands permanently poised to cross themselves, waiting to present their condolences in a queue that circled three times around the cathedral; they lined the streets for kilometres to see the 1876 royal hearse, and dabbed the corners of their eyes with their handkerchiefs when the coffin containing the embalmed corpse was carried into the Imperial Crypt, the only crypt in the country that was bigger than Darkenbloom's — much bigger, and world famous, but still: Darkenbloom was right behind it, in the hierarchy of crypts.

Zenzi cleared the table. 'Would sir please be so kind as to move to a side table,' she requested. 'We've got a meeting here shortly.' Gellért nodded and ordered another coffee with milk.

The young man he had asked to come appeared. He looked as if he hadn't slept; or, on the contrary, as if he had just got out of bed and come straight to the Tüffer restaurant without making a detour via the bathroom. He stuck out his hand, mumbled his name, which Gellért already knew, and said, 'You wanted to speak to me?'

Gellért invited him to sit. 'I knew your mother slightly,' he began, carefully. 'That is, we corresponded recently. She invited me to come and visit her, but I'm afraid I arrived too late.'

The young man nodded absently.

Gellért waited a while, then said, 'May I ask how your mother died?'

The man, who must have been in his thirties, raised his head and looked at Gellért with red-rimmed eyes, like a distraught child. He said, 'I don't know. I don't actually know anything, I mean, nothing that I can really be sure of, that I could swear to in court, or to anyone else, but I'm probably just too, too ...'

Gellért waited.

Slowly, young Lowetz composed himself. 'Please excuse me ... So: my mother died in her sleep, she didn't wake up one morning, our neighbour found her ... The doctor said sometimes the heart just can't keep going any longer; you can't foresee it, unfortunately, sometimes it just stops.'

Gellért said, 'My condolences.'

Lowetz nodded, and there was silence again, until Zenzi started demonstratively clattering plates on the other side of the room.

Gellért held up a palm in her direction, asking her to be patient. 'I don't want to shock you with what I'm about to say,' he said quietly.

Lowetz looked at him.

Gellért said, 'Your mother saved my life during the war. I don't know whether you know that. She hid me for two weeks.'

Lowetz stared at him and said nothing.

Gellért said, 'I don't know whether anyone else knows about it, either. Apart from the second woman who helped your mother.'

'The second woman?' Lowetz repeated.

'From the house next door,' said Gellért, 'the family with whom I believe you share the courtyard.'

'Agnes,' said Lowetz quietly, and nodded slowly, as if his head were underwater. 'Agnes Kalmar.'

Resi Reschen approached them noisily. 'Gentlemen, please, a public meeting is about to take place in here; you're very welcome to stay, but you won't be able to continue your quiet conversation. How about moving over to our nice bar?'

'Thanks, Resi,' said Gellért pleasantly, noting how she bridled at the implied familiarity. 'We're almost done; it's not worth the trouble.'

Resi retreated again.

'Is that why you wanted to speak to me?' asked Lowetz, who seemed to be waking up.

'Well, actually,' said Gellért, 'there was something else as well.'

He placed a postcard with the historical view of the castle on the table in front of him.

'They're all over the place now,' said young Lowetz. He suddenly seemed annoyed. 'Everywhere — the town is full of them, I've no idea why. Didn't you buy a whole stack of them recently?'

'Yes, I did,' said Gellért, and thought for a moment. 'I don't know why, though. Perhaps I wanted to take them out of circulation. Anyway: this one is from your mother.'

He turned the card over and pushed it across the table.

Lowetz recognised Eszter's round, childlike handwriting. *Many years ago ... your address with our grocer ... something concerning your family ... perhaps better if you were to visit us in person ... if your health permits you to make the journey. Yours sincerely, E. Lowetz.*

Lowetz said, 'And? I don't understand.'

Gellért sighed. 'I wanted to ask you if your mother had left anything behind, notes, papers, that might give some indication of what she wanted to say to me? The gentleman at the travel agency told me she had collected all sorts of things. It seems the two of them ...'

'I know,' Lowetz interrupted, 'the town chronicle. The museum. The interviews. Her missing notes. I'm afraid I have to tell you that I don't know anything, can't find anything, and I've practically turned the house upside down twice already over this. It's almost as if it's cursed.'

'*Cursed*,' Gellért echoed. He slid his visiting card across the table. 'Just in case anything does turn up ...'

Lowetz put the card in his breast pocket. 'Did you hear the girl's disappeared?' he asked abruptly.

Gellért nodded. 'Yes, of course,' he said. 'Her parents came to see me. But none of the perpetrators from back then are still ...' He glanced up.

Lowetz asked, 'None of them are still what? Alive? That's not true!'

'Look,' said Gellért, 'here comes the armada to do battle with the water authority.'

'Herr Gellért,' Lowetz asked, 'please tell me whether ...'

But they were already coming in, all of them at once, and soon every last seat in the Tüffer's spacious restaurant was taken.

Because there wasn't much going on at the height of summer, and almost everyone was able to take a long lunch break, a great many people had come: the small shopkeepers and the bigger employers, Zierbusch's architectural practice, the staff of Wallnöfer's car dealership and Stipsits's pharmacy, the estate agent employed by Balf, bank and post office workers, Rehberg from the travel agency, his younger sisters and their husbands, Gitta, the owner of Café Posauner, and her husband, the Slovenian hairdresser, pensioners and young people and, of course, the farmers: the wine growers and cattle farmers and cereal farmers, led by Farmer Faludi with his tall staff and long black beard. Dr Ferbenz also snuck in and sat down near the exit. Among those missing were Dr Sterkowitz, who was with his patients, and Antal Grün, who was lying in bed in Tempelgasse 4, still feeling rotten, cold and damp and anxious from his feet right up to his neck. Agnes Kalmar, of course, who hardly anyone knew was still alive, was also missing, but her son Fritz had come, because although he couldn't speak clearly, he was tremendously curious.

Last of all, the mayor's secretary, Frau Balaskó, teetered across the square from the town hall. A short, spherical person, she floated in on the highest of heels, an astonishing display of almost artistic balance.

She felt that these shoes were a requirement of her position, but at the end of the working day she took them off as soon as she got to the car park and swapped them for the slippers she kept under the passenger seat. Today, though, she was here in her official capacity, and so was balanced on the thin, perilous needles. Keeping her gaze firmly fixed in front of her and an eye out for potential obstacles, she squeezed through to a free chair, and only when she was happily seated and the blood had begun to reach her squashed toes again did she look up. She was being stared at from all sides as the provisional focus of this murmuring assembly. Frau Balaskó glanced at her watch and pointed to the door. She was not responsible for her boss, but she assumed that he was coming. Outside, the church clock struck the hour: four times the high bell, the deep one twelve. It was only on the final stroke that he entered, Deputy Mayor Koreny, and unlike his floating secretary he looked as if his feet were too heavy to lift. His expression, though, was determined, almost haughty, and compared to its usual state his face was pale and almost free of sweat.

A lone chair had been kept free for him in the middle of the front row, as if the sole purpose of all this was for the mayor to sit through a remedial lesson with all his citizens watching.

Farmer Faludi unrolled his map with deliberation; he was unrolling his argument. He knew what he was talking about. When it came to some of the outlying sections of Darkenbloom and Zwick, this autodidact, who was also a talented politician, let other farmers step forward and speak, more or less proficiently, about the water resources they had discovered and measured.

When they had finished, Farmer Faludi summarised it all once more. He said there was no longer any doubt that the municipality could source its own water independently, without having to pay the water authority's excessive fees. It was the most sensible, most economical, and, last but not least, the most environmentally friendly method. Koreny grimaced. The environmental thing was a new fad, and, like every fad, it would pass. But Farmer Faludi was greeted with thunderous applause; when Koreny looked around, there wasn't a single person who wasn't clapping.

So he had to get to his feet, and, as many would later concede, he gave the best speech of his life. He didn't even need notes; he spoke extempore, freely, as free as he now felt, having reconciled himself to the idea of doing something for reasons other than the usual ones — out of a different sense of propriety, as it were. First he talked about the constitutional state, about contracts and contractual fidelity, about reliability and liability, about the many levels of politics, which were inextricably interlocked: the communal, district, state levels, right up to the national. He found a broadly comprehensible, memorable image for these interconnections: everyone should think of their television cabinets at home. At first there were just one or two cables; later there was one for the video recorder, one for the lamp, eventually maybe a stereo system with loudspeakers as well. Soon you had several socket extensions and a right old tangle of cables, and sometimes it was hard to figure out which cable you could unplug without switching off all the appliances at once. And that was what it was like with big decisions that had to be weighed up carefully, that were far more complicated than the question of whether there was enough or too little water underground.

For a few sentences he made as if to respond to Farmer Faludi's arguments, recounting in detail what he remembered of Emmerich Kolonovits's report — without ever mentioning his name, and exaggerating everything he had suggested, presenting it all in the worst possible light. He raised the prospect of excavations and drilling that would go on for months, probably years; of fields dug up, gardens destroyed, access roads blocked; he painted worst-case scenarios of floods in the lower part of the old town and the inadvertent draining of subterranean springs, side effects that could hardly be avoided with such a fundamental restructuring of the watercourses. It would be a gamble, he cried, but one that would not pay off. Nature, which Farmer Faludi made such high-minded claims about protecting, was in reality wild and cruel; their forefathers had been right to pay her the respect she was due.

By this point, Koreny had even earned the admiration of an astonished Rehberg, who was wondering whether the mayor had recently taken on a speech writer, and who in the world it might be. Someone from Kirschenstein or Löwingen at the very least, thought Rehberg, because he couldn't think of anyone closer, himself excepted, who fitted the bill.

It was only at the end of his speech that Koreny got around to speaking of Mayor Heinz Balf: one of the best mayors we have ever had.

'How true,' shouted someone at the back, but no one laughed.

Heinz Balf, whose friend he, Koreny, was proud to call himself, had, as everyone here knew, made this matter his top priority; he had commissioned survey after survey and had carefully familiarised himself with all the arguments for and against.

Farmer Faludi shook his head.

Just a few days ago, he, Koreny, had gone to visit Balf in the Vienna General Hospital, up on the seventeenth floor. Koreny paused for a moment and swallowed. The room was silent.

Koreny lowered his voice and said, 'You can't begin to imagine the state Heinz is in. The tubes hanging out of him everywhere. How weak he is. And despite it all, the only thing he wanted to know was how everything was going here, in his beloved Darkenbloom. He squeezed my hand, and he gave me a task. Don't give up on the water, he said; stay strong, hang in there.'

Koreny paused and blew his nose. Farmer Faludi turned down the corners of his mouth in disdain, but no one noticed, and no one would have condoned it, either. The rest of the assembled company was glued to Koreny's lips and eyes.

'And so I say to you: out of respect and appreciation for Heinzi Balf and his lifelong work on our behalf, I will not cancel these contracts,' thundered Koreny, in conclusion, 'because I have not yet heard a good reason to do so! Everything that's being claimed, people have been claiming for years; none of it's new, and no one knows whether it would work. What I do know is this: Heinzi Balf didn't want the Rotenstein meadow dug up — he didn't want everything up there, in the midst of our beautiful countryside, turned over again and again just so a massive elevated tank could be sunk metres into the earth! Heinzi didn't want our landscape blighted with these concrete constructions, and I speak for him, and I'm on his side, even if, sadly, he cannot be here today.'

Koreny's gaze swept across the rows of seats, looking for the older people who would have understood the message. Some stared back with horror in their eyes. They hadn't known anything about reservoirs, elevated tanks, and their planned locations, that much was clear. He gave them an imperceptible nod, these ones who understood him better than the others.

Then he sat down; and although it had been the best speech of his life, and no one could recall anyone ever speaking in such a statesmanlike, responsible, yet humane and moving way, no Balf, no priest, and certainly no count or anyone else in the whole of Darkenbloom's long and painful history, no one clapped. The room was silent. For a moment, the people of Darkenbloom seemed wholly at a loss as to what to think or do.

4.

THERE WAS MOVEMENT NEAR the door, where those who had arrived too late to get a seat were crowded together. Toni and Leonore Malnitz entered and walked straight to the front, and many of those present thought it embarrassing, ostentatious, and melodramatic that they were holding hands, like children or young lovers.

'Good speech, Herbert,' said Malnitz loudly, 'but not good enough.'

Koreny's temples grew hot and his palms itched. He was no friend of Malnitz, not this one, nor the other who ran the filling station in Zwick, but they, along with their father, who had been *political*, and the beautiful, outspoken Frau Leonore were an undeniable force in Darkenbloom, economic and social. No one liked them much; people thought they considered themselves a cut above, but for precisely that reason they listened to what they had to say. Besides, their artistic and cultural ties reached all the way to the capital. The fact that Balf was lying in a private room up there on the seventeenth floor, operated on by the senior consultant himself, was attributed to Frau Leonore's connections. The Malnitzes were all Social Democrats. It did not bode well that Toni, one of his own town councillors, was the first to stab him in the back.

Malnitz adopted a power stance and, holding his wife's hand, announced that he was fifty-five years old and couldn't stand this typical Darkenbloom dishonesty a day longer. The water saga had played out exactly like everything else, exactly as it always did: a few bigshot con-artists divvied things up behind the scenes, then the whole of Darkenbloom had to live with the consequences for decades. If you yourself were not a con-artist, you were treated with contempt, exactly as Koreny had just sneakily implied — you were the kind of person who didn't understand anything, who was too stupid to sort out their own television cables! And, as if that wasn't enough, you were calling for a breach of contract — disgraceful!

'If you lot hadn't already signed contracts that no one asked you to draw up, we wouldn't be in this position,' cried Toni Malnitz. 'Instead, we now have to open everything up again and take it all apart, and search for evidence that you lot have carefully erased.'

Some of the people listening cheered, others banged on the table, but the noise quickly died down as they wanted to hear what else he had to say.

'Because you've always had something against it,' cried Toni Malnitz, 'against clarity, openness, humanity, honesty — none of which have any tradition here at all, unfortunately.'

'You voted for it, too, Toni,' bellowed Koreny.

'Based on lies and deception!' Toni bellowed back. 'Scratch the surface with your fingernail anywhere in Darkenbloom and you uncover some new abomination!'

'Don't exaggerate,' bellowed Koreny. 'This is slander!'

'Listen to him, threatening again,' said Toni. He spoke more quietly now, but this sounded more menacing than his bellows. 'We really should take a very close look at the conduct of our so-called people's representatives in this affair.'

The audience muttered and growled.

Farmer Faludi stood and rapped on the ground twice with

his staff. 'Ladies and gentlemen,' he said, 'we are here to discuss a difference of opinion about the Darkenbloom water supply; let us return to the matter in hand. I would like to make a suggestion. From what I can see, all the members of the Darkenbloom town council are here present. I would like to ask the councillors to take part in a quick indicative vote. That way we can all get an idea of what might be possible, in terms of reversing the decision that's already been taken, which so many of us believe was wrong. A relative majority of the town council would be enough to approve a referendum for the municipal district of Darkenbloom. So, town councillors, if you would: please stand if you want to give your fellow citizens the chance to vote on this important issue.'

Farmer Faludi rapped on the ground with his staff once more and looked around expectantly. Toni Malnitz finally let go of his wife, raised his hand, as he was already standing, and went over to join Faludi. All around the room sweaty men were struggling to their feet. Others stayed in their seats, looking flushed. Three elderly Christian Democrat councillors, all of them over seventy, who had long been advocates of a self-sufficient water supply, remained seated. Joschi, Dr Alois's nephew, also remained seated; he had caught a look from his uncle and decided to do as he was told. And because Joschi remained seated, the other Freedom Party councillor also kept very still and hoped that no one would pay him any attention. On the other hand, several young Social Democrats who had previously voted for the water authority, in line with party policy, rose to their feet, warmed by the sense that, in doing so, they were helping the will of the people to prevail, even if that might not suit Koreny, their leader. They wouldn't have dared to voice an opinion on what was right or wrong in this business, but they could sense the hostility of the people. And so they were more comfortable with this decision, which really did affect everyone in Darkenbloom, being taken by everyone collectively. It was the most democratic solution imaginable.

And then there was a tiny movement from Dr Alois. Once the young Social Democrats had stood, he turned his palms up and gave the merest hint of a gesture, as if lifting a tray. At this, Joschi too leapt to his feet, as did the second Freedom Party councillor, baring his teeth in a smile intended to convey the same message as on the election posters: *We're here for the people, we understand you, we're fighting with you against all the bigwigs, even if there aren't actually that many of them.*

So the vote, although it was only indicative, went quite differently to the first time around — almost the reverse, in fact. No obligation to vote according to the party line, but a vote of conscience. They know not what they do, thought Koreny, watching his young, misguided councillors glowing with democratic pride. They're acting in the name of conscience without knowing what that will actually have to encompass. An image popped into his mind's eye of a white linen sheet that was too short. It only covered the sleeper to just below the knee, halfway down his calves at best. Or was he not sleeping at all, this scrawny, brown, wraithlike individual — was he already dead? Are there shrouds that are too short? Are there consciences that are too short?

Koreny suddenly felt dizzy, and turned to where he guessed the hotel manager would be to gesture for a glass of water. She was already bringing over a half-litre of lemon soda. Resi Reschen's attentiveness was worth its weight in gold.

'Sixteen votes for a referendum,' announced Farmer Faludi, 'with all twenty-three town councillors present.' The whole room erupted in yelling and cheering. Koreny gulped down his drink, but the soda bubbles travelled in the opposite direction, like a knife up into his sinuses. If I choke now and start coughing and spitting, he thought, I might as well pack up and move to the other end of the country.

As he gasped for air, the room went quiet again. He looked up. Toni Malnitz, arms raised, was asking for silence, and the beauty of

Frau Leonore beside him was almost unearthly.

'On Sunday evening,' she said, once she was able to make herself heard, 'our daughter Flocke didn't come home. She's been missing for three days. We don't know what's happened ...'

Leonore stared into space for a few seconds, as if she had lost her train of thought. Toni Malnitz moved a step towards her; she came to, and continued, 'We don't know what's happened. First our barn in Ehrenfeld was set on fire, the very same evening the volunteer fire brigade were busy partying in Kalsching, just up the road. That was already a sign. Flocke's interested in history, including the crimes committed here among us during the Second World War, which we all keep nice and quiet about. Eszter Lowetz, who was helping Flocke with her research — she received threatening letters; they're still stuck on her fridge. I've started to wonder whether she really did just die in her sleep ...'

At this, the room began to grow restless.

Leonore Malnitz raised her voice, although she found it difficult. 'Herr Gellért has been among us here in Darkenbloom for the past two weeks. I'm sure a lot of you have already seen him. He's looked for victims of the Second World War all over this region — you know what I mean ...' She cleared her throat, held her hand in front of her mouth, and stared at the ground. 'Labourers from the East, who died here at the end of the war; that is ... were murdered. They've already found graves in Tellian and Kirschenstein, in Löwingen and Mandl. Herr Dr Gellért sees to it that the ... the mortal remains can be laid to rest according to the proper ... rites. But here, in Darkenbloom, not a single person has been able to help him! People are acting as if that sort of thing didn't happen here, with us. But Herr Gellért knows more or less how many are missing. And they must be somewhere!'

There was a long pause. It was so quiet that all they could hear were the flies hurling themselves kamikaze-fashion against the windowpanes, again and again, in the unshakeable hope of one day breaking through to the sun and the light.

Leonore continued, 'And Flocke must be somewhere, too. Please, tell us if you know anything, even if you think it's just a rumour. Any little tip might help. You can do it anonymously — you could just put a note through our letterbox, or hand something in here, at the Tüffer, or get someone else to hand it in. Please ... I'm begging you. Even if you all know nothing about anything and you can't do anything, you've always had so much to do, you couldn't pay attention, not to anything at all ...' She started to weep.

Toni went to her at last, put his arm around her shoulders, led her to the side of the room, and made her sit down on a bench.

The room erupted in shouting that, with the best will in the world, could no longer be brought to order, not even by Farmer Faludi and his staff. Some people were demanding to know what Flocke's disappearance had to do with the other matter, if you please? Had Leonore completely lost her mind? Couldn't her husband have left her at home if she was this crazy? Others were shouting that people needed to calm down, for heaven's sake, and not take everything so personally — a young girl was missing, after all, it was understandable if her parents were clutching at straws. And a third, strikingly large, group of younger people was trying to find out what all this was about, what these allusions were to crimes and the end of the war, to graves and labourers and unfamiliar rites. Faces flushed with horror, they badgered the older residents, who squirmed, protested, refused to answer; some hobbled hastily away. The longer people like Gellért and Lowetz, who were essentially uninvolved, sat picking up scraps of the sentences flying about the room, the clearer it became that the town was splitting into two groups: those who were saying nothing, and those who, in all seriousness, *I swear by God and my children*, insisted they had never, never, never heard anything about it. That there was supposedly something no one ever talked about? A secret, a crime, an atrocity, a skeleton in the cupboard? 'Just the one?' someone shouted, voice cracking with excitement: there's always that person, the one who simply has to make a joke.

Who, when, why, how many? the young people demanded of their relatives, their parents, grandparents, neighbours, and acquaintances. They felt like shaking them, but the old people were already shaking their heads and talking about hearsay, dodging the question, or naming names no one had ever heard that sounded like excuses, myths, and fairy tales: the bogeyman, and that other one, the devil on horseback, the Countess's lover, and so on. Finally, the crowd turned it back onto the Malnitzes, saying that they had gone mad, madder than they were already, the eco-farmer champagne-manufacturer and his fancy lady from Kirschenstein who'd had the bathtub put next to her bed. Folded toilet paper and whatnot, all of that. Screw loose, the lot of them, always making a fuss, always sticking their necks out to make sure they grabbed all the attention.

Dr Gellért sat silently at his table with young Lowetz beside him. Eventually Rehberg was swept past; he scrambled onto the empty chair next to Lowetz as if onto a lifesaving raft of tranquillity and reason.

Gellért was paying close attention to the forces that had been unleashed. He had planned to talk about his work himself, as there would be so many Darkenbloomers gathered in one place. But there was no question of that now, amid all the tumult.

The Malnitzes had visited him in his room at the Tüffer the previous evening. They had wanted to speak to him again about their daughter, about what she had wanted from him, and Gellért had told them everything, just as he had Flocke. He explained about his difficult work, which he nonetheless found so gratifying, and which he had been doing ever since he had retired and come back to Europe. But had not told them, or Flocke, that he was born in Darkenbloom.

That, he felt, would be going too far. He feared it would compromise his position, make it look as if he had come to take revenge. He knew what people were like: men like him had been accused of this elsewhere. When they had said goodbye, Toni Malnitz had declared that he would use the water meeting the following day to inform as many Darkenbloomers as possible about Flocke's disappearance. 'There's nothing else for it,' Toni had said, 'we have to ask the whole town for help. Even my father says so.' And that was when Frau Leonore had blurted out her request that Gellért say something, too, about his search — the other search, which was important in a different way, and which Flocke supported so enthusiastically.

Now, though, in her despair and confusion, she had effectively stolen his contribution. She had mixed up the stories in a nonsensical way, and it had made people angry. This had not been Gellért's intention — absolutely not. He was sure it hadn't been Leonore's, either. He had wanted to do it gently, affably, as in all the other places. Everywhere he went, his aim was to secure cooperation; he tried to draw people in by appealing to their ambition, their powers of deduction and regional knowledge. *Where might it be, here, in your town? You're the ones who best know the local landscape. Because the possibilities aren't unlimited with a thing like this. It's a big area we're talking about.*

These were the phrases he used wherever he went. He knew he would find them harder to say here, but nobody needed to know that. He had, however, brought one of the bone boxes down from his room, like a talisman, something he never usually did. Darkenbloom. He was here, in Darkenbloom. That was the difference. Had he really believed that this small, innocuous, neatly constructed box would overcome their resistance to the unwelcome subject matter? That the citizens of Darkenbloom would vie with one another to provide all the hastily buried dead with such attractive boxes?

5.

THAT SAME AFTERNOON, ORF television journalists arrived from the capital. The minivan with the broadcaster's familiar symbol, a stylised red eye, parked up right in the middle of the town square, a spot where no vehicle had stood for as long as anyone could remember — not since the Red Army's first advance at the end of the war, to be precise. It was here that the first Soviet tank had caught that rocket-propelled grenade, and from here that the second tank, coming up behind the first, took out the *Volkssturm* man who had shot it down — him and the war memorial and the corner of the house overlooking Karnergasse, in one fell swoop, as the saying goes.

After two hours, one of the journalists moved this peaceable peacetime van to one side, but the vehicle was still parked there like an exclamation mark: *Hey, everyone, the television's here!*

The passengers took rooms at the Tüffer, and Resi Reschen was immediately dancing attendance, though unsure how to address them. One of them wore a suit and tie, and after some deliberation she plumped for *Herr Editor*. Nobody corrected her, so she seemed to have got it right. With the others, she initially took refuge in the third person. They were more casually dressed, in what people called sports shirts; they probably operated various pieces of equipment, Resi didn't understand any of that. There was also a skinny little dogsbody with them who was sent running hither and thither with the baggage. They had coffee and cake in the bar, and presumably felt that by engaging the landlady in conversation they had already embarked on their work. Resi, however, was famously not born yesterday. To those who didn't know her, the scarlet blotches on her cheeks made her look a bit slow-witted; she smiled stiffly, and launched into a detailed account of the genesis of the so-called water dispute, beginning, as the editor later commented to the cameraman, somewhere shortly after the birth of Christ. The editor soon interrupted her and asked her straight out about Darkenbloom's Nazi crimes.

Resi deflected. The discussion that afternoon had been about the water supply.

'But a young girl is missing, isn't she?' queried the editor, fumbling for his notebook in his inside pocket. 'The girl who uncovered these crimes? And her foster mother died in unexplained circumstances?'

Resi Reschen put her hands on her hips. 'What a load of nonsense,' she said. 'The Malnitz girl's mother is very much alive — you shouldn't believe every silly story you hear, Herr Editor! As I was saying, there was a meeting this afternoon about the water supply; we were run off our feet. I served well over a hundred drinks, in and out all afternoon, scarcely a moment to catch my breath.'

'But the girl has disappeared, hasn't she?' the editor insisted.

'Heavens,' said Resi, 'there's usually a perfectly ordinary reason for a thing like that.'

'For example?' asked one of the casual dressers.

'A young man, for example,' she said, raising a bristly, blonde, barely visible eyebrow. 'Or how did sir come into the world?'

The editor laughed at this, and the second casual dresser laughed as well, and then at last they got up and went on their way. Resi watched them suspiciously as they left. She could tell that this wouldn't be the end of it.

Even as the ORF was confidently and visibly invading Darkenbloom, teams of reporters from the two big national newspapers were also infiltrating the town. One was the penny press tabloid that, in terms of readership as percentage of national population, was the most successful daily paper in the world; the other was its sworn rival, a rag that looked even cheaper, although it was printed in colour throughout. Full colour was intended to symbolise a new era, but the cheap production meant that the cyan, yellow, and magenta printing blocks didn't precisely align, creating pictures that shimmered psychedelically around the edges. The thrifty Darkenbloom housewives didn't even like to wrap kitchen scraps in this paper, because of the colour; perhaps this was given insufficient consideration as a reason why it always placed second.

These teams were much more inconspicuous than those of the state broadcaster. The reporters mostly went about on their own, rarely together, partly to conceal from the competition who and how many they were, and to whom they had already spoken. They also had female interns, which bordered on a disgrace. In those days, young women were still not taken seriously; a questioning look was all that was needed, and elderly men would gladly explain the world to them in exhaustive detail. This trick apparently enabled some female reporters to obtain information incognito: if someone tells you something you haven't actually asked them about, you're not absolutely obliged to say you're from the papers. In fact, you're not obliged to say anything at all — just make sure you remember everything. Even later on, it was never clear how many reporters there had actually been, or who had spoken to them, and about what. The only ones who could be identified were the photographers, but they too worked quickly and inconspicuously. Later on, some Darkenbloomers claimed not to remember being photographed, even though they had indisputably been pictured posing outside their house or garden gate.

Young Lowetz had been in a strange state of mind for several days. His vague, pleasurable sense of being on holiday had well and truly gone. He didn't like the way these mysteries kept materialising one after another, like evening drinkers at the Tüffer, or how, like the drinkers, they would stick together after hours. He always tried to keep things meticulously separate; he thought it a bad idea to conflate them, to surrender to the superstitious belief that everything was connected beneath the surface. If anything, he believed in coincidence, that some things just happen to occur simultaneously. At the moment, though, it was becoming very difficult for him to maintain this point of view.

The heated exchanges after the water meeting, and the shocking new information, which was not in fact new at all, but had been hushed up for years, did not surprise him. Rather, he felt that he had known it all already, even though just one day earlier he would have been unable to answer a single question — from Dr Gellért, for example — about the matter. It had all been there, though, beneath the surface, and he was almost relieved that it wasn't just him — that there was actually an identifiable reason for the suspicion and unease he had sensed in Darkenbloom all these years. It made him suddenly like the Darkenbloomers more. There was an explanation for their obdurate behaviour, and it was not only, as they usually asserted, the border, their border location, the fact that history had shoved their backs against the wall, that this was the last stop before Asia. It turned out that, unsurprisingly, they were no better than anyone else. Lowetz had more or less known what had happened in the region towards the end of the war, albeit not in detail. Forced labour, war crimes, the usual — terrible times. And so it had occurred here, too, which was hardly unexpected; the lack of ambiguity was almost liberating. It was a long time ago, after all, and in other places, in Mandl and Kirschenstein, they were coming to terms with it. So Darkenbloomers could finally start doing the same, for God's sake. He understood Flocke now. He understood her perfectly. If you lived here, you probably wouldn't have any patience with the fact that people were still obstructing and lying and keeping schtum. How he would have liked to say this to her, to admit his ignorance. She would have puffed at her fringe, taken a drag of her cigarette, and grinned, with that tiny wrinkle in her nose. Not even a wrinkle — her nose just scrunched up a bit when she grinned, as delicately as her wrists ... But this brought him to the first of the two painful issues. Flocke was gone; she was registered as missing now, and the police were looking for her. Her disappearance could no longer be traced to some unfortunate series of mishaps, as he had continued to hope. He couldn't get her mother's face out of his mind. The mixture of fear, hope, and love, as well as disbelief: perhaps there was a simple explanation? Why couldn't she figure out where her daughter was? Surely she should know — she had given birth to her, after all. That face and its torments tormented him, too. Anyone who saw Leonore Malnitz was compelled to turn away, or else they suffered with her; there was no alternative. Amid the tumult at the end of the meeting, Lowetz had pushed his way forward to Flocke's parents and offered his assistance: 'Please, tell me what I can do, I'd really like to help.'

'Eszter's son,' Toni Malnitz had said, by way of explanation, and Frau Leonore had turned her head and stared at him with that shattered expression.

'What happened to your mother?' she asked. 'Can't you find out?' Toni pulled her away.

And now he was hooked. Someone had died, and someone had disappeared. Both could have the most banal of explanations, or the most serious. It could be coincidence, or they could be connected. Although death was more common than disappearance. In the latter instance — Lowetz still wanted to believe it was highly unlikely — the implications were enough to make your head spin.

At the end of their relationship, Simone, his ex-girlfriend, had accused him of being *indolent*. As she said it, her mouth had for the first time seemed ugly to him, almost repulsive. Only for a moment, but he couldn't forget it. What she called indolent he preferred to call circumspect, and it was with circumspection that he wished to proceed. There was no point in allowing himself to be driven mad by possibilities and speculation, which always had a tendency to pro-liferate uncontrollably. But there *were* routes that he could take. He wasn't going to find Flocke by getting in the car and driving around aimlessly, as her father had been doing for days. But he could talk to Dr Sterkowitz, who had been his mother's general practitioner and must know what medications had given her such a craving for sugar. Sterkowitz had probably issued the death certificate; he would know what needed to be done if there were any justifiable reason to doubt that she had died of sudden cardiac arrest. She had only been sixty-five; no age at all, really. Yet these things did happen. Process of elimination, systematic, step by step. However, Lowetz was not entirely comfortable with this route. His mother was dead and buried. Whatever had happened to her, it could wait. Whereas Flocke was probably urgently in need of help.

Lowetz got up, took his jacket off the back of the chair, opened the front door, and recoiled. Right behind it stood a young woman with a notepad, scribbling with inexplicable zeal.

As of Thursday morning, Darkenbloom was famous throughout the country, from Lake Neusiedl to Lake Constance, albeit not in a good way. And so it would remain for a while. The two competing newspapers sold out before noon, and anyone who was too late to buy them went and read them at their neighbours'. The ones in the Tüffer and Café Posauner were stolen, and scarcely had Gitta clipped her own copy of the tabloid into the bamboo holder before the relevant pages were missing again. At midday the rumour went around that Antal Grün, who was more or less back on his feet, still had copies, but it wasn't true: that morning, his bell shrilled so often and so piercingly that he wished it were still clogged by the lump of dried chewing gum with the little stone inside.

Town of Terror was the headline, announcing a forthcoming series of reports, starting with a big interview given to the paper by the architect Zierbusch, son of Zierbusch the master builder. After much soul-searching, this respected citizen of Darkenbloom had decided to speak, for the very first time, about the events of almost forty-five years ago, because, as a contemporary witness, he felt it was his duty to contradict false rumours, partly in order to restore peace to his community.

'So this is what it's come to,' Rehberg complained to Dr Gellért. 'Those who've never opened their mouths before get to masquerade as peacemakers.'

Rehberg accosted everyone who didn't turn away fast enough, declaring that the level of this tabloid was immediately apparent from its use of formulations such as *false rumours*. He only stopped after the Tüffer landlady took him to task: 'I don't know what you're trying to say, Herr Rehberg, but they really are false, the rumours.'

In any event: Zierbusch had given the tabloid a detailed insight into his activities as a Hitler Youth. As a boy, he said, you had no choice but to join, regardless of your political views. The interviewer didn't ask Zierbusch about his views, either then or now. Instead, he asked about the night of the ball, just before the end of the war. Zierbusch prefaced his answer with the portentous declaration that he had never spoken about that night to anyone, not even his wife or children. The interviewer asked why he was breaking that rule now. 'Young people cannot begin to understand what it was like back then. The coercion and threats we faced. It's easy,' Zierbusch said, 'to point the finger when you haven't experienced it yourself, the violence and repression. We saw such accusations when our president, Herr Waldheim, was elected. Here in Darkenbloom, the Jewish cemetery is currently being renovated — with foreign money, incidentally, which can only mean Israel and the East Coast. And there are those among us who are forever talking about setting up a museum and remembering, commemorating, and what-have-you. I've nothing against it in principle. But it's only those who were there who can actually remember!'

And then he described the night when he and the other Hitler Youth were dragged out of their beds by a certain Horka, whom the communists even made chief of police, later on. 'The Russians,' said Zierbusch, 'you could do a whole story on them, as well, but let's not go there.'

'You can speak freely,' the reporter assured him. 'What would there be to say about the Soviet occupation?'

'Looted and raped, they did,' said Zierbusch, 'rampaged all over the region like swine. And no one held them accountable. We were as powerless then as we were under the Nazis.'

This was the only thing he said about that specific night: that they, the Hitler Youth, had led the forced labourers the last bit of the way into the forest, from where the trucks had dropped them off. All they had done was lead them there. After that, the SS men had taken over again. And yes, they had heard the shots, but they hadn't been standing close by; he couldn't remember exactly now, but no, he didn't think so. Filling in the graves — they, the Youth, had had to do that as well, all night long. He hadn't looked, he'd just shovelled. By the time he got home it was already light; his mother had clapped her hands over her head because he was so covered in earth and blood.

'Were the people responsible for this deed held accountable?' was the penultimate question.

'Not one,' said Zierbusch. 'All those fine gentlemen got away. It was only the boys who were accused and sent to prison, us sixteen-year-olds, because they couldn't lay hands on anyone else. But tell me, what could we have done? We couldn't have run away, right at the end of the war! We were minors. The way I see it, we were victims of those criminals, too.'

'But you yourself didn't go to prison?'

'No,' was Zierbusch's answer to the final question, 'and to this day I still don't know why. Back then, of course, I was glad. But now, believe me, in all my life it's the thing I regret most.' The interview ended with one word, italicised and in brackets: *(weeps)*.

6.

ON SUNDAY, AROUND MIDDAY, Gellért and young Lowetz happened to bump into each other outside Rehberg's Travel, and, after a bit of polite back-and-forth, they both decided to go in. Rehberg was sitting at his desk with a stack of papers in front of him. He gazed at them, hollow-eyed, then got up and fetched two mugs of coffee.

'Well, haven't we made a good impression,' he said.

'There's going to be something on TV tonight as well,' said Lowetz.

Rehberg nodded, and said that he had also spoken to the TV crew; he hadn't been able to see any way round it.

'And why not?' said Lowetz. 'You're exactly the right person!'

'Because blind loyalty will be required of us again, just you wait and see,' cried Rehberg. 'Silent as the grave!'

'Required by whom?' asked Lowetz. But the only answer he got was a vague wave of the hand that presumably meant *everyone*, or *someone or other*.

Dr Gellért, whom until recently Lowetz had thought of as 'the mysterious visitor', before starting to feel a certain affection towards him, as if for a distant relative — Dr Gellért was suddenly holding *Traditional Tales of Darkenbloom*.

Lowetz flinched. Reaching for it, he said, 'That's my old book of fairy tales; I wanted to donate it to the museum. Please could you give it to me for a minute, though? There was something I wanted to look up.'

Gellért handed it to him. Lowetz leafed nervously back and forth, wondering how he could take it back. As a boy, he had loved this book; it wasn't easy to let go of it, or of his nostalgia for the past. He hadn't been poisoned by it; his mother had made sure of that by censoring it as she read it aloud. Now he wanted it back; he wanted to see what else she had changed. That was sure to be interesting: he would read it from cover to cover and hope that, as he did, he would hear her voice in his head. It had been over-hasty of him to give it away, to want to get rid of it. And on no account should Dr Gellért get hold of it; he mustn't stumble across the fascist elements, the buried, hunchbacked Jew and the other arch-Catholic crap, the Christmas roses on Christmas Day. This Gellért had a good opinion of Lowetz's mother, probably far better than of the rest of Darkenbloom, and he'd been through more than enough already. Lowetz wanted at least to spare him this.

'It's got the Devil and a count and a knacker man in it,' he said, and pretended to find this amusing. 'Do you know what a knacker man is?'

Gellért turned to him and opened his mouth. He closed it again, sighed, sat down, and sipped his coffee.

Lowetz seized the opportunity to change the subject. 'Hey, Rehberg,' he said, 'what I don't understand is why you're so, so ... pissed off. I mean, it's what all of you wanted, Flocke, Mama, and you — it's all coming out now at last.'

Rehberg shook his head. 'You've been away far too long,' he said. 'You have no idea. It shouldn't have happened like this, not like this. It's all going to backfire.'

'I don't think it will,' said Lowetz. He noticed that he was starting to get angry, even though Rehberg was clearly not the right target for it. 'You can't sweep this sort of thing back under the carpet. No one has the power to do that! Look at Kurt Waldheim! What do you reckon, Dr Gellért?'

Gellért sighed again. He put his hand in his trouser pocket and took out a piece of folded paper. He placed it in front of him on the table and said, 'I found this in my hotel pigeonhole today.'

Lowetz lurched towards the table: he wanted to pre-empt Rehberg, but the travel agent didn't even move, just sat there looking grey and tired. 'At least it's not a postcard of the castle, for once,' Lowetz murmured, as he reached for the note and unfolded it.

He flung it down again almost immediately, turned to Gellért, and said that the hotel manager had some questions to answer about who had accessed his pigeonhole. Who even knew his room number? 'I mean, she's got more than one room, for God's sake, that sneaky Frau Reschen! At the very least, the hotel employees must have had something to do with it, for crying out loud!' If he were Gellért, he would threaten to report it to the police. This had to be cleared up — what a preposterous note, they won't get away with it! Not these days; not any more!

Rehberg gave a cough that could have been a laugh. He leaned forward and picked up the note. He placed it on the stack of papers in front of him and stroked it flat, back and forth, as if trying to iron it with his hands. Lowetz was reminded of Uncle Grün, the way he ran his hands up and down his overall. He hadn't visited Antal for days; someone had said that he was ill. Or was he just imagining it? He felt as if he had dreamed certain things. Or everything. That spectral woman who had gone to such lengths to nick the steel helmet off the shelf in the filling station? Had he really seen that helmet? Or had he just imagined it, because there used to be a helmet there? Hadn't the woman simply fallen over, tripped awkwardly on the rotating newspaper stand, wasted as she was by her illness? And just happened to have a big, empty bag with her? If he'd asked the filling station attendant afterwards whether he was missing a steel helmet, he'd probably have called the men in white coats. The same men in white coats who came when Agnes started screaming, and who, as far as he could recall, he had never seen, but only ever imagined. What does a man in a white coat look like? Is he accompanied by assistants bearing the neatly ironed straitjacket? *Agnes is back in the loony bin*, people would say, each time. Agnes, who wasn't dead at all, like most of the others, though unlike his mother she had probably wished often enough that she was. Agnes, whom he was gradually starting to fear as he would a ghost, though he knew this was ridiculous. She was probably just a confused old person, like so many others, who needed nothing more than a comfortable chair, sunshine, and cocoa. But she could just as easily be the one who knew everything. Instead of speaking it, she had screamed it, like the drunken, drugged-up oracles of classical antiquity, Delphi, Olympia, Cumae; like Cassandra. For those who know, their knowledge is often too much to bear; it makes them lose their minds. As I will, if I stay here much longer, thought Lowetz. Or have I gone mad already? He was immediately disgusted that he should think of himself like that, dramatic and self-pitying, and so, in an attempt to distract himself, he forced a grin and asked: 'If I maaaaay, my dear Rehberg, might I have another coffee?'

But just as Rehberg was getting to his feet, Gellért began to speak; the words spilled out of him like a quiet, silvery thread, and the coffee failed to materialise, because Rehberg stopped and stood still.

'Two years ago,' said Gellért, 'I met a French priest, a man who was already doing then what I do now. I accompanied him on a trip to understand how to go about it, this work. In a little village in the Balkans we questioned almost every single inhabitant, because it was clear that it must have been there somewhere. But no one knew anything, or no one wanted to say anything. Probably a bit of both, as everywhere. Also, we tend not to realise how much landscapes change in a very short space of time.'

Lowetz laughed and said, 'Some people — me, for example — get lost in their home town after just seven years away!'

'Well, yes,' Rehberg interrupted. 'If it's in the forest, I can believe that, but from everything we know, they didn't go to that much trouble; it had to be done quickly. Everything indicates that it wasn't very far away, on the edge of town, just outside, only slightly, it really can't be that ... I simply can't understand ... There must still be someone who ... not just one ...'

Lowetz gesticulated furiously with both hands; Rehberg fell silent.

Gellért said, 'There are fast-growing plants — lupins, pines, dog roses — local people are familiar with them. In many spots where things like this took place, they afforested them afterwards. That's what they called it: afforestation. These people, the perpetrators, became landscape gardeners, so to speak.'

He went on talking, slowly, almost as if he were just relating it all to himself. Back then, on their first trip, they were just about to give up when an old man came cycling towards them. They stopped him and asked him as well, whether he knew, whether he had seen or heard anything, back then. And this old man on a bicycle was very friendly. Answering questions and giving information was as natural for him as it was for everyone else to know nothing and be angry just about being asked. 'It's possible he wasn't quite right in the head, this man,' said Gellért, 'a bit like your Fritz.'

Rehberg raised a hand in protest, but said nothing.

'He led us to a deep hole in the ground,' said Gellért. 'When we got there, he told us that, when he was still a child, the last knacker man had died. They hadn't been able to find anyone to replace him, which was why this hole had been created. Perhaps the hole had always been there; that seems more likely to me now,' said Gellért, 'a geological peculiarity, a deep fissure in the rock. In any case, it had once been used as a bait trap; this used to be fairly common. People would throw in animal carcasses that no one wanted to or was able to process. And then, during the war, it was the logical place: a deep hole, and that was that. Near the village, easily reached from everywhere. In their midst, so to speak. Later, when it was all over, animals ended up in there again, ones that had died of old age or sickness: first animals, then people, then animals. I often find myself thinking about it,' said Gellért. 'That was the beginning for me, of dealing with all of this. If there'd still been a knacker man there at the time, they would've had to do things differently. Perhaps then they would never have found this hole. Perhaps there would have been something left to salvage. But it's understandable; it's an unpopular, disreputable profession.'

'Please forgive me,' squeaked Rehberg, from behind his desk.

'Forgive you what, for heaven's sake?' asked Gellért.

'For talking about the silence of the grave, earlier,' whispered Rehberg.

'You're very kind, and sensitive,' said Gellért. 'There's really nothing to forgive.'

'But the knacker men,' said Lowetz, looking desperate, his face crumpled, with red-rimmed eyes, like a child about to cry, 'the knacker men usually doubled as the hangmen, the executioners or whatever, as well.'

'True,' said Gellért, 'but that was much earlier. In the period we're talking about, that aspect of the job was long forgotten. It really has nothing to do with it any more, my dear Herr Lowetz.' He reached out and touched Lowetz's arm, whereupon the latter sprang up and said, 'I'm going home now to look for my mother's papers. They must be somewhere.' And he stormed off, and when he grabbed his tatty book of fairy tales on the way out, it came across as absent-minded. But neither Rehberg nor Gellért was paying any attention.

On the way home, Lowetz was already going through his parents' house again in his mind, from top to bottom. It was a small house;

there weren't many places where papers would have been kept, but if Eszter had hidden them, perhaps he should think about it differently. She had been an imaginative woman, his mother, even if she hadn't had much chance to express it: in this place, in her marriage, or in her life. Lowetz pictured himself finding a way of reaching her mentally, almost psychically, telepathically, or whatever it was called; he had known her well enough, after all. If he just made an effort, he would be able to feel his way into her mind. *If I hide something only my son should find, where do I put it?* Would he have to dismantle the tumbledown shed in the courtyard as well, the place where a young, an inconceivably young Gellért had huddled for two weeks behind the firewood? No, that would definitely be going too far. He would go and sit in the parlour, Lowetz decided, where the finger of sunlight crept across the wooden floor in the afternoons as if trying to show him something. He would wait, picturing her as she used to be, hair down to her apron strings, slicing apples, and turning to him: *Kisfiam, bring me the big casserole dish.* And then she would laugh. Whenever she sent him to fetch something, she would ask for the *big* something, even if the thing itself was not particularly big, or there was only one of it. That was the way it was; it had amused her, and he hadn't thought about it for so long. *Kisfiam, the big scissors, the big ball of string, the big dustpan, over there, open your eyes.* This was why he didn't need a first name, or rather felt no connection to the name that appeared on his official documents. The one on the documents was not familiar to him. Lowetz had never wanted or needed a first name; certainly not at school, and afterwards he had only ever introduced himself as Lowetz. If anyone insisted, he would fob them off, saying that this was what everyone called him; just Lowetz, that was enough. His relationship with Simone had probably come to grief because she refused to call him by the same name as everyone else, forcing him, with her, to be a stranger.

As he was crossing Spiegelgasse, he stopped. Uncle Grün's shop was on the next corner. Apparently Antal had been ill and had missed all the drama. Lowetz needed to look in on him, he needed to tell him everything, and perhaps it also made sense for him to start his search there. They had been so close, his mother and Uncle Grün, former neighbours ... and, when he thought about it, Uncle Grün's position in Darkenbloom was a pretty unusual one. What had actually happened to him, *in those terrible times*? Hadn't Dr Gellért said, before Lowetz had known who he was, that Antal had *got the house back*? From Horka? Horka, the Darkenbloom bogeyman, who people were now saying had ...

Yes. He and Uncle Grün had sat on the step outside the shop, smoking.

'They used to threaten us with Horka back then, when we were young.'

'I can imagine.'

I can imagine. That had only been about a week ago; to Lowetz, it felt like years. Still standing at the small, curved crossroads, he decided to go and visit Antal then and there.

The grocer's was open, but the bell on the door was not working again. Antal was sitting rather than standing behind his counter, on a stool or stepladder, visible only from the chest up, and regarding him as inscrutably as an old owl. 'Uncle Grün,' said Lowetz, 'for heaven's sake, what's the matter? I only just heard ...' He blushed, hoping the older man wouldn't spot the lie.

'Just a little dizzy spell,' said Antal, giving him an ironic look. 'That's what Sterko says, anyway. And that I should take it easy, and always open the windows. Unfortunately, not even I am getting any younger, though I deserve it more than anyone.'

'Have you heard what's been going on?' asked Lowetz. 'Flocke Malnitz has disappeared, and Koreny was outvoted, and now there are reporters swarming everywhere ...'

Antal Grün pointed to his newspaper stand. At the top were

the postcards; the lower section, where the papers usually were, was half empty. He chuckled. 'People are even buying the *Presse* and the *Arbeiter-Zeitung*, though there's nothing in either of them yet. Frau Reschen will soon be so full she'll have to make up Room 22, just you wait and see!'

Lowetz fetched beers for them both, although Antal hardly ever drank. But Uncle Grün was in a strange mood, like an old man in high spirits, with nothing left to regret.

'The body suddenly becomes unreliable, from one day to the next,' he told Lowetz, 'and you have to learn to live with that realisation.'

They sat together again on the step, and Lowetz asked, 'Did you know about it, Uncle Grün, this business with the forced labourers?'

'One did hear things,' said Antal.

'Yes, but,' said Lowetz.

'I wasn't here at the time,' said Antal emphatically. 'I can't tell you anything about it. When you look at it like that, you know as much about it as I do.'

'Yes, but,' Lowetz repeated, 'what about you? After all, you ... you were ...'

'I was sixteen years old, and I was kicked out, just like all the others,' said Antal, raising his voice slightly. 'Mama and I simply came back again afterwards. That's the only difference.'

'Why ...' asked Lowetz. 'How could you ... I mean, sorry — did you do that on ... on purpose? Come back?'

Antal burst out laughing, and didn't stop for some time. Lowetz was mortified. He simply couldn't find the right words; everything he knew, as well as all the things he didn't know, surrounded him like a hostile force that messed up everything he asked. When Antal had finished laughing, and had wiped his palms thoroughly on his overall, he said, 'Ah, come now, lad, you really are a one! But seriously: no, it wasn't on purpose, it was just that we couldn't think of anything better. At least here we knew the region and the language. And you can never see inside people's heads, not here, and not anywhere else, either.'

Lowetz shook his head. 'Where were you, actually, in between, you and your mama?' he asked, finally.

But Antal said, 'Ah, come now, please, let's drop it.'

7·

MEANWHILE, REHBERG WAS TELLING Dr Gellért that the trouble
with the past was that it was a slippery business. Ever since he had
started compiling the town chronicle, things had only got less and
less certain; facts practically dissolved in your hands, which was the
opposite of what you wanted to achieve with a work like this. These
days he was even suspicious of professional historians, people he had
essentially plagiarised — he would happily admit it — when writing
about prehistory or Roman times. 'These academics,' he said, laughing
mirthlessly, 'at least they've got the advantage that they don't have
contemporary witnesses coming along complaining, saying things
like *it's only those who were there who can remember.* Talking about
false rumours. So what they write is true in a different way, even if it
wasn't true at the time. You, Herr Gellért, on the other hand, you've
specialised in such a small, precisely defined detail that everything
you discover is true. Either you find the dead, or you don't find them.
A or B. If you find some, it's evidence that a crime took place, and
that's that. I hope I'm not saying anything wrong?'

Gellért sighed. 'No, no,' he said, 'I understand what you mean.
But it's not about truths for me; it's about giving the dead a decent
burial. Also, in my experience, once I've finished my work, that's

when the furore really starts, among the local population.'

They had both got to their feet and were standing side by side, gazing out of the shop window, past the leather camel, the palm tree, and the beautiful, tempting steamboat, objects the two of them had arranged so recently, just a few days ago, in a different time. Outside, Darkenbloom lay in the summer sunshine. Soon, people would be able to travel again not only to Jesolo and Lignano, but to Prague, Budapest, and Lake Balaton, to Chernivtsi, Lviv, and Ternopil. Closest of all, though, was Stossimhimmel, very close, and you wouldn't need a travel agent to get there, just a bicycle. But at that moment they didn't know any of this, although it's possible that Gellért may have guessed.

'Right from the beginning,' said Rehberg after a while, 'I've felt I could speak openly with you. After all, we both belong to persecuted minorities, don't we?'

Gellért turned and looked at him in astonishment.

'Well,' said Rehberg, blushing slightly, 'I ... am not married, and never wanted to be, if you get my meaning. I'm ...'

Gellért nodded. 'I understand. That wouldn't have occurred to me.'

'Thank you,' said Rehberg, relieved, 'that's very kind of you. But people figure it out more quickly nowadays than they used to; I don't know why.'

And then he told Dr Gellért about his most vivid childhood memory, the day something happened on the path through the vineyards. He described his childhood courier rides, how he had regularly taken letters and packages to Stossimhimmel for his aunt and delivered them to an unpleasant, almost sinister woman there. Once, out of nowhere, she had yelled at him in Hungarian; he hadn't understood a word, but had guessed that it was something about Nazis and Jews;

he didn't know what to say, and just stood there, head bowed, until it was over. He hadn't said anything about this scene to his aunt; the letters he brought back for her on his bicycle had meant a lot to her. To this day he still didn't understand what his aunt had liked about this woman; she hadn't seemed friendly, or even particularly intelligent, just bitter, nasty, not at all his aunt's sort of person.

'Those letters were probably in there as well, with the papers I gave to Eszter Lowetz,' said Rehberg despondently. 'I'm pretty sure they were in there. Eszter would have been able to read them. Do you speak Hungarian, Dr Gellért?'

'Yes,' said Gellért, smiling vaguely, 'from my father's side.'

'Excuse me for asking,' said Rehberg, 'it's just that people here often have names from Over There, but don't speak a word.' Gellért waved his hand to indicate that there was nothing to excuse.

'But I digress,' said Rehberg.

He told him how these excursions had come to an abrupt end one day, how as a child he had always believed it was because a crime had taken place, something really terrible, and that a murder *had* been committed there, but much earlier, too early, 1946, when he was still too young for cycle rides across the border. Eszter had proved it all to him beyond a doubt.

'She was a really talented researcher,' said Rehberg, looking very sad. 'In any case,' he went on, 'this is what I've thought since then. This murder, of Dr Sterkowitz's dental technician, was a topic of conversation in the town for years, and as a child I probably associated myself with it. So that I'd have a reason for why I wasn't allowed to ride across any more. Typical delusions of grandeur.'

'That seems plausible,' Gellért agreed. 'We like to connect things, and soon we start to believe that they're the truth.'

'Yes,' cried Rehberg indignantly, his voice rising in pitch again, 'but that's not what happened, either! And that's what I mean when I say the truth is a slippery business. It's driving me crazy! Nothing, absolutely nothing, is the way we thought it was! The skeleton in the Rotenstein meadow will turn out to be an Indian in the end, or — what did Lowetz say recently — *Homo darkenbloomiensis*!'

Gellért laughed.

'Yes,' cried Rehberg, 'you laugh, but it isn't funny at all. It's complete madness! And Flocke Malnitz has probably driven over the border and won't come back, because they'll think she's East German, which wouldn't be surprising in that clapped-out old Opel! I'm telling you, Dr Gellért, everything here is so messed up, absolutely everything; you only need to glance at the newspaper for evidence.'

Rehberg jumped to his feet and paced up and down. Eventually, he opened the shop door and hooked it back. A hot wind gusted briefly in, as if curious, and decided to blow on outside instead. Leonore Malnitz was walking past on the other side of the street, a pug under one arm, pulling the other along behind her on a lead. Rehberg waved, but she was staring straight ahead and was clearly in a hurry. Other than that, the place was dead — typical for August. Very occasionally, a tractor rattled past; there were hardly any cars about. The office workers who could afford it were all sunning themselves on the Adriatic — Rehberg could have told you exactly who and where — but the farmers were in the fields and all the others were at their posts, behind the tills and counters and the hotel reception desk, at the filling station, in the businesses, Electro Koreny, Zierbusch Housing and Construction, Boutique Rosalie, Berneck Insurance. The only people in evidence were children, roaming around in small groups; teenagers too, here and there. Some were sitting just a few metres away, on a low wall at the next corner, smoking. Rehberg stepped outside his shop and shouted, 'Don't throw the butts on the ground again, if you please!'

The teenagers made obscene gestures and laughed. One of them dropped his cigarette in the road and spread his arms wide, as if he couldn't think how it had happened. Then he got off the wall and gyrated in a circle, waggling his backside.

Rehberg went back into his travel agency, sat down again, and groaned.

'There was something else I'd like to ask you,' Gellért began. He proceeded to enquire about Rehberg's family history, about the family name and how common it was. Had Rehberg ever compiled anything along the lines of a genealogical chart?

Rehberg was immediately in his element. He hurried upstairs to his apartment and fetched the family tree he had drawn up years ago. 'This was where it all began, actually,' he explained, unrolling the chart. 'It was back then that I had the idea of compiling the town chronicle — when I realised that you really do come across Rehbergs everywhere you look.' He looked up at Gellért. 'And I thought: it's not just about the individual, you know? Each of us is the product of our environment, not just our family.'

He held forth for a while about the first Rehberg, and his pride in his discoveries was unmistakable. He had been able to prove that this first one, a master saddler from Stuhlweissenburg, had settled in Darkenbloom at the end of the seventeenth century, after the Turkish wars, perhaps because he had married someone here, perhaps because he was able to purchase a piece of land at a good price — the available evidence from so long ago is, of course, thin on the ground. And this master saddler had established the family in the region; he had had seven children, and they in turn had each had ten, or even more; Rehberg had compiled the record as best he could.

Gellért ran his index finger around the bottom of the chart, where all the many different branches stood almost illegibly close together. 'Aloys Rehberg,' he read aloud, 'died and was buried in Löwingen in 1863, in the neighbourhood of Deutsch-Gollubits?'

'Yes,' said Rehberg. 'Are you interested in him for a particular reason? I should have a bit more information about him somewhere ...'

'No, not him especially,' said Gellért. 'I just wanted to know what comes after this? Does the family tree carry over onto the back, or where does it continue?'

'It just got to be too many,' said Rehberg. 'We're spread out all over the region; all the cemeteries are full of Rehbergs, right the way down to Steinherz and Löwingen. I wanted to document the family's advent in this part of the country, as it were, which begins with our excellent master saddler here. We can be absolutely sure he was the first.'

Gellért took a deep breath. 'I'm interested in an Elisabeth Rehberg who married a Jenő Goldman,' he managed finally. 'The wedding was somewhere round about 1918.'

'Right,' said Rehberg. 'That's one of the names that crops up most often, though; it was my dear Aunt Elly's name, as well. You could search for her specifically in the registers of christenings and deaths; I'd be happy to help. I'm at your disposal!'

Gellért said nothing; he still seemed to be contemplating the family tree.

After a long pause, Rehberg asked, 'May I finish telling you my story?'

Gellért looked up.

'Are you not feeling well?' Rehberg asked in alarm. 'Would you like a glass of water?'

'Yes, please,' said Gellért, 'and perhaps a glass of the schnapps you offered me last time. But what story did you want to finish telling me? I'm not sure I understand what you mean.'

'You know, the incident on the path through the vineyards,' cried Rehberg, 'when I was a child and used to cycle over on my bike!'

'Is there more?' asked Gellért. 'That wasn't the end?' He looked as if this were too much for him to deal with.

'No, it wasn't,' said Rehberg unhappily, 'and I need a schnapps for this, as well.'

Here they were again, sitting just as they had one week earlier, the catalogues behind them on the shelves replete with the blues of sea and sky, two men in the empty travel agent's with an inflatable steamer, an indoor palm tree, and a disgruntled-looking leather camel for company. Since last time, the sun had travelled another eighteen million kilometres along its annual path, and the evenings were gradually getting darker, but the heat of summer, the heavy scents and the sweetness of the fruit, particularly grapes, seemed to want to linger at their height, bracing themselves against the inevitable descent into autumn, prolonging time. Rehberg took a photocopied page from an envelope and put it on the table, a section of the penny paper from June 1954. The article bore the headline *Naked Man Apprehended*. It reported that a police patrol had come across a man wearing nothing but a shirt on the old track from Darkenbloom to Stossimhimmel, and had picked him up; a man against whom, the gendarmes discovered when they brought him in to the station, an anonymous complaint had already been filed concerning *homosexual fornication*. The man had refused to give a statement of any kind as to how he had ended up in this humiliating situation, and had not spoken at all except to give his name. If there were any witnesses, they were requested to pass on whatever information they might have to the local police station.

Gellért asked Rehberg where it had come from.

'It came with the post today,' answered Rehberg. 'No stamp, no sender's address, just like the note at your hotel. And I think it means something similar.'

He leaned forward. 'I have to confess that the exact same thing happened to me, though again it was around four years after this incident. The Heuraffls and their friends caught me with someone who fortunately managed to escape. They beat me up, and stripped me of everything but my vest. I had to run home like that, which I managed to do without being seen. But now, of course, I'm wondering whether

I had something to do with this earlier incident as well — do you see? Whether perhaps I saw it? Or was even involved? But I don't remember anything, nothing at all; no matter how hard I try, there's just a blank wall in my head.'

Gellért said it was because the incidents were too similar; Rehberg probably couldn't differentiate the memories clearly, especially if he was still very young the first time. 'I suppose it's out of the question to ask the Heuraffls about it — about that first time?'

'You've seen what they're like,' groaned Rehberg. 'You can be sure they'd shout it from the rooftops; and now, with the reporters in town, it'd ruin me. Perhaps they've told everyone already. They're probably the ones who put this in my letterbox in the first place!'

Gellért rose to his feet, with an effort. 'If you'll excuse me,' he said, 'I have to go and lie down for a bit.'

'Of course,' said Rehberg. 'You go and lie down; you look as if you need it.'

And so Gellért left the travel agency and walked slowly through the narrow streets, crisscrossing the uneven cobblestones, past luxuriant tubs of flowers, towards the Hotel Tüffer, Room 7. Plenty of people saw him on his halting path; here and there a curtain billowed slightly, back and forth, as if fanned by quiet breathing. The Darkenbloomers who saw Gellért walk by as if his feet were weighted with lead didn't just stare after him, they also projected onto him their worries and fears, their curses and anger.

Rehberg lost sight of him once he turned the first corner. He picked up the small, crumpled note again, addressed to Dr Gellért; it even had the accent in the right place. Rehberg stroked it flat, but only at the edges; he didn't want to touch the script. *If you don't stop, you'll soon be lying with the others.*

8.

ON THIS SCORCHING LATE-SUMMER evening, Stitched-Up Schurl was irresistibly drawn to the south-western border of his plot of land, where he paced up and down, smoking. The best fruit trees in Darkenbloom stood here, majestic ancients that had borne fruit for many decades, providing his family of handymen and labourers with sorely needed additional income. Their lives had revolved around this orchard ever since his father had seized it; he and his brothers and sisters had seen to the maintenance, harvest, storage, and sales. He clearly remembered the days of the construction of the wall that had structurally annexed the impressive rows of trees — you could almost have called them a plantation — to his family's property. Schurl's father and grandfather had acted boldly and swiftly. While others were assisting Horka by kicking in doors and bringing in trucks for those who didn't leave straight away, while they were writing lists and ransacking the temple, Schurl's forefathers were feverishly organising as much bricks and mortar as they could lay their hands on, and, with considerable difficulty, the transport of same. When little Schurl, sweaty from carting bricks around, asked if they were finally extending the house because yet another kid was on the way, his father just laughed. 'You'll see, lad,' he said, shooting Schurl's grandfather a look.

The first brick of the wall was laid at practically the same moment the last member of the Rosmarin household passed across the threshold of the villa: as the Rosmarins were closing the front door, they started constructing the wall at the back, at the bottom of the small but tasteful formal garden. News had got around town of what had happened prior to this, namely: Frau Thea Rosmarin, the factory owner, had gone to see Ferbenz. *Unreasonable behaviour* was how Frau Ferbenz described it later, and the Darkenbloomers passed this on. Schurl's mother translated it to her son as follows: insolent, she was, complaining, banging on about her connections, threatening with the police, but her kind don't get to complain no more, them days is gone. Schurl's father had already started sourcing bricks, which wasn't easy, as he couldn't actually pay for them. He placed his biggest order with a brick manufacturer in Kirschenstein, so big that it caused a row between Schurl's parents. Things only calmed down when the grandfather came home. "S fine,' he told his daughter-in-law, 'you just hold your tongue.'

And then, early one morning, as young Schurl was coming out of the chicken shed, the brick manufacturer himself was at the front door. The gentleman was as well dressed as you'd imagine someone from Kirschenstein would be, and he politely requested the outstanding payment for the bricks he had supplied. Schurl's mother didn't know what to do. However, when his father appeared, he just slammed the door and shouted that the man should come again next month, then he'd get what he was owed. And laughed.

Maybe, Stitched-Up Schurl thought now, three months before his sixty-first birthday, maybe it wasn't actually okay just to kick them all out. That was simply how it was back then; it wasn't forbidden, it was positively encouraged, in fact. But the Rosmarins were grateful to them for bringing the trees over to their side; Schurl's mother had often stressed this, later on. Who was going to look after them? If it hadn't of been us, it would've been someone else! You could hardly argue with that. Schurl's parents knew how to take care of them, because they had done it for years under the supervision of the Rosmarins' gardener. What a disaster it would have been if someone inexperienced had cocked it up, the formative pruning of younger trees, the renewal pruning of older ones, the propagation of the vineyard peaches. If this inexperienced person had mowed the meadow more than twice a year. A few years later, the roses came scrambling over the new, whitewashed wall from the garden on the other side, as if pining for their fruit trees.

And that was how Schurl's family's little farmer's cottage, extended bit by bit over the years like a child's sandcastle thanks in part to the income from the fruit, acquired the enormous walled orchard behind it, unequalled anywhere in the region. It used to be the other way round. The radiant front of the Villa Rosmarin had shone down on Reitschulgasse; at the back lay the park-like garden where the poor children of the town were remembered with clothes and shoes at Christmastime, and behind that, further still, right at the bottom, like an enchanted grove, the orchard Frau Thea had planted in her youth. There had been a long line of sight from the windows, an axis from the villa over the box bushes and roses to the apples and pears, plums, damsons, and mirabelles at the far edge of the picture. This visual depth no longer existed, because now there was the wall, and the little formal garden was ruined, recently paved over with washed concrete slabs as a break area for the assistants of the tax advisors who worked in the *historic Villa Rosmarin*, unthinkingly proud of their *outstanding Art Nouveau treasure*. The axis had rotated a hundred and eighty degrees back then, along with everything else.

Naturally, Stitched-Up Schurl didn't see it this way. He only saw his trees, which he had tended all his life as best he could, and which he loved more than his children or his wife. For a while now he had been plagued by a feeling of inner unrest, what with all this talk of commemoration and mourning and reconciliation, which they'd never heard before and which could not bode anything good. There was an irreparable loss to be mourned: that was what the politicians had said in the anniversary year. But he hadn't lost anything, back then; he had only gained. The idea that something had to move, to loosen and change, as that cocky Malnitz girl was always saying, felt threatening to him. What did she know? Whenever anything moved, all that happened was what always happened: the poor got poorer and the rich stayed rich. He liked the world the way it had been since he was ten years old, apart from the few years of the war. At last they'd had a livelihood; at last it usually stretched to cover even the smallest brat, though sometimes only just, depending on whether or not it rained enough, and whether they were spared the damaging late frosts. Stitched-Up Schurl was opposed to movement, physical included; his back and knees had troubled him for years. Now, though, even the border was moving; he had seen it on TV, people picnicking on it, then running across like rabbits.

Once, just once, unlike the others, he had made a move, and what had he got from it? A cut-up face. The jagged red scars that had crisscrossed it like a net ever since had brought him the nickname Stitched-Up, and the name had transferred itself to his whole family. *One of the Stitched-Ups* — that was how they were spoken of in town, him, his brothers and sisters, his children and his children's children, and perhaps it was also an indirect comment on the matter of the wall and the orchard. He himself seldom thought about that any more, just as he rarely thought about the day they cut his face to pieces. All these were thoughts he usually brushed away, like the creepy-crawlies that fell on him in the trees.

Frau Thea, though, was a pleasant memory, like an image from a dream. She had been beautiful and kind, and when she gave him the padded boots she took a handkerchief from her pocket and wiped the snot off his nose. He was embarrassed; the handkerchief smelled good, and it was soft. He was not even six years old; all his brothers and sisters wore the boots after him, right down to the last, belated arrival, who was a skinnymalink and halfwit. But he had worn them first; he was the one who wore them in. The civil war began just a few weeks later, and he didn't know whether the Rosmarins continued to dispense their Christmas charity over the next four years, in that formal garden shimmering with icicles where the children lined up in shivering rows and curtseyed and bowed as their mothers had drummed into them to do.

Perhaps that was why he snuck into the villa during the construction of the wall, slinking off in a break from work, into the house from the back, through the conservatory. He knew that they were all gone, that he wouldn't see the regal Frau Thea again, and she wouldn't wipe his nose any more, but a niggling curiosity drew him inside. He saw paintings and figurines, and glossy, varnished furniture and embroidered wall hangings; he had no words for any of it and didn't understand what it was all for. A fringed curtain hung around her bed. He pulled it back, and suddenly Horka flew at him like a shrieking devil and carried him out by the scruff of his neck to his father, who gave him his just deserts. 'If anything's missing,' said Horka, 'you lot are for it, because all you're getting is the trees, that should be enough for you,' and Schurl's father thrashed him on the spot, even harder than usual, so Horka would be satisfied.

From then on, the young Schurl had believed that Horka knew and saw everything, that he lurked everywhere you weren't supposed to be, and if you kept anything from him, you would suffer a terrible punishment. As soon as he joined the Hitler Youth, he tried to emulate him, though he was terrified of him at the same time. Sometimes he would think of the moment Horka had caught him in the industrialist's bedroom, and was plagued by a baffling illusion: that, before he grabbed him and dragged him outside, Horka's flies had been open. It was all forgotten now — the decades drew a veil over everything — but whenever he heard someone say the name *Villa Rosmarin,* a sour feeling rose up in him, like acid reflux.

Later, when the war was over, he stood trial along with the Heuraffls and Berneck. As the lawyer who represented them had advised, they admitted everything — that they had met the people off the truck and accompanied them into the forest. They all pleaded *irresistible coercion*, reiterated their remorse, and looked ashamed. The judge just kept shaking his head. Finally, he asked if they would have shot the men with their own hands, too, if they been instructed to do so. The lawyer made the gesture for saying nothing, as previously agreed: both hands flat on the table, fingers spread. They said nothing. Then the judge said something Schurl didn't really understand, but old Balaskó shouted it so often in the Tüffer afterwards that in the end he was beaten up and thrown out: *He cannot plead irresistible coercion who never made the slightest attempt to evade said coercion.*

These were Darkenbloom stories. Old Balaskó had never set foot in the Tüffer again because of a sentence spoken by the judge in the trial of Schurl, Berneck, and Heuraffl, a sentence Schurl had not understood and would not have been able to repeat. When he got home sixteen months later, the first thing he did was visit the orchard.

It was mid-February; the frost had everything in its icy grip, and the winter sun was struggling through the fog. Schurl had studied his trees, grafting knife in hand. In this light their trunks glowed like dark silver. Soon the other three appeared among the trees. The Heuraffls were already out, because their longer time in custody had been taken into account, and Berneck had only got twelve months, as he was younger when the crime was committed. Schurl could guess why they had come. Something was up with the fifth, Zierbusch, who had not been tried alongside them, even though he was in the forest too, back then, the night of the ball. Schurl thought it stank. He could guess the reason. Their fathers were farmers and day labourers, whereas Zierbusch's father was a master builder and had been a high-ranking officer during the war. Zierbusch's father was only a few years older than Ferbenz; they were both doing time now, in a denazification camp somewhere in the West. Maybe they would even get to America that way.

When he was behind bars, Schurl had made no secret of his anger; he kept going on about it, to his cellmates and to others who were there for similar reasons: it was always the small fry that were hauled up in front of the judge, while the big fish got away; it had always been like that, all through the ages, whether it was the Kaiser or the Führer or the People's Court. Schurl's mother had visited him once; his father had never come. Even in the prison visiting room you could tell that she was a day labourer from the back of beyond. She kneaded her apron with her chafed red hands and whispered that people at home were demanding that he stop running his mouth off. His pals would explain it all to him later, but right now he just had to keep his trap shut for a change — and above all, no names. His mother glanced around fearfully. Schurl rose angrily to his feet, shoving the table a few centimetres towards her. The guards looked up. 'Shut the hell up and stop sticking your nose in,' he told her. 'You women are the last thing I need.'

And now they were all standing together again, the Heuraffls and Berneck, just as they had stood beside each other in court. The other three grinned and asked how he was doing, and he, Schurl, wanted to puke at their hypocrisy. 'What's with Zierbusch?' he burst out. 'Why's he out when we were all inside?'

The other three went on grinning and said that there were reasons, but he needed to keep his mouth shut, he'd get something for it if he did, and he had the knife in his hand and could smell the fruit trees again for the first time, even though it was winter. At last he could shout and let rip and no one would hear him but his friends; and so he let it all out, the shame of those sixteen months and the fear of the years before, including when they had stood on the edge of the forest with the spades in their hands and heard the shots. It wasn't just a few shots, it was like a solid mass, a thick black wall of shots that echoed back and forth and wouldn't stop. Enough, Schurl shouted, Austria was supposed to be free now, wasn't it; there had to be an end to it, only the poor, the little people, never the bigwigs and the rich; and Zierbusch, it was only fair, no one was going to stop him from ... He didn't really mean it like that, he just wanted to shout for a bit, and perhaps he wanted an explanation, too, one he couldn't think of, stupid as he was back then, but it makes everyone stupid, being inside. He hadn't understood that it was just a question of money, that they had all let themselves be bought and now he was supposed to get his share as well; nor did he understand how threatening and out of character his fury seemed to them. He had always just kept his mouth shut, little Schurl, had gone along with things, a fellow traveller; at most he had shouted along, and now, just for once, he wanted to act as if he wasn't like that, as if he was grown up and able to stand up for himself. He was twenty years old; next year he would be of age, but what did he have to show for himself? A criminal record as accessory to murder, a few fruit trees, and eight brothers and sisters. That'll never add up, he thought, nothing is ever going to add up. And what really doesn't add up is Zierbusch getting off scot-free and becoming the next master builder. But when he lowered the knife, which he had been waving around, his friends all jumped him, three against one: they flung him to the ground, and he defended himself with all he had, but again it wasn't enough.

The hardest part, Dr Sterkowitz said later, was stitching the cut that ran from the corner of his eye to his temple; there wasn't much skin left for him to work with. Although Schurl had been lucky on two counts — neither the eye nor the crucial nerves at the temple had been damaged. 'You're a very lucky lad,' Dr Sterkowitz admonished him as he stitched him up. 'But you really ought to say who did this to you.'

Schurl gritted his teeth and said nothing.

'It makes no sense,' said Dr Sterkowitz, with an encouraging snort. 'If everyone always holds their tongue, it doesn't make anything better. Someone has to start the ball rolling, eh, Schurl?'

But from that day onwards, Schurl's mouth stayed shut.

This trickiest stitch, which wasn't nearly as obvious as some of the others that crisscrossed his face like red zips, gave him a crooked, shifty look that wasn't like Schurl at all. But it's as true as it is unfair that outward appearances are what make an impression. Little children were scared of Schurl, just as he had been scared of Horka, and soon the whole of his extended clan were dubbed *the Stitched-Ups*.

Frau Thea Rosmarin was not rewarded for all her charity of the preceding decades. She had distributed warm shoes and clothing to children in need at Christmas, and in summer had given baskets of fruit to all her employees, not just the gardening assistants and harvest workers. But the proud Frau Rosmarin was supposed to be both charitable and meek, as if this were a fitting and obvious combination. Darkenbloomers didn't grasp that a meek industrialist would never be successful, and an unsuccessful one would not be bountiful. Perhaps they never even thought about it. What is clear is that Frau Thea went to appeal to Ferbenz about some aspect of the new regulations with which she felt she could not comply, be it the enforced sale of the factory on ruinous terms, the very short notice she had been given to vacate her home, or the minuscule amount of luggage they were permitted to take with them. She went to him and asked for a concession, an easing of conditions; he refused, whereupon she called him a *primitive swine*, a cobbler's boy who was no better than a *primitive swine*. Unreasonable behaviour, as Frau Ferbenz said later, pursing her lips, and, back then, the punishment for this was Horka. So Horka was given the nod, and Horka dealt with it: he would beat anyone up to order, man or woman or child, itinerant labourer or industrialist.

And shortly after this the Rosmarins all left town with what remained of the proud Frau Thea, and as they closed the front door overlooking Reitschulgasse, Schurl's family started to erect the wall, brick by brick, and brought the fruit trees over onto their land.

'What're you doing, Grandad?' asked his grandson, Karli, appearing suddenly next to Schurl as he patrolled the south-western border of his plot of land, smoking and ill at ease, shortly before his sixty-first birthday. Karli would soon be seventeen — his eldest grandson, a wild lad with smooth, handsome features. Schurl didn't reply at first; he kept walking slowly up and down, along the rose-covered wall. Karli stayed at his side. And after a while, as they walked, Stitched-Up Schurl said: 'Y'know, Karli, stirring up all this old stuff, it ain't right. 'S dangerous. We got to stop it; affects us as well. Someone's gonna have to do something, and soon.'

Karli nodded, and his eyes glittered.

9.

LOWETZ SLUNK HOME, MORTIFIED. He felt his visit to Uncle Grün had gone awry, and he was embarrassed. He was out of place here; he had never paid any attention to what was really going on, to all that lay behind Darkenbloom's familiar, apparently provincial façade. He had picked up a few things here and there, but had never understood that they were important. Or how they fitted together. Now, potential theories were interlocking with such force that it was impossible for him to make sense of it all. He urged himself to concentrate on what lay within his grasp. He absolutely must find those papers, his mother's research for the town chronicle that might contain God knows what, about the fate of Dr Gellért's family as well as the background of Darkenbloom's terrible crime. Something about the perpetrators, even? Their names were known, more or less: Horka, Neulag and Co., the majority dead or disappeared, but of course it was possible that a few no one knew about were still living — pretty much next door, in fact. And a great deal else was unknown: the exact sequence of events, the chain of command, and, above all, the scene of the crime.

But there were no files or documents anywhere in the house; he had searched everywhere, he and Flocke, right up to the attic ... And that was when Lowetz had a brainwave. It seemed crazy at first, but with every step he became a little more convinced. If he sat on the so-called sofa, his father's repurposed bed, and watched the beams of sunshine move across the room, they finished exactly in the corner where his mother's low, untidy bookcase had stood. The bookcase to which printed matter had seemed to migrate overnight. Migrating print ... Why had it migrated? Did Eszter read at night because she couldn't sleep? Why couldn't she sleep? Then there was the business with the sugar tin, which he still wanted to get to the bottom of. At any rate: the longest, thinnest fingers of sunlight pointed there, into the corner, to floorboards that were paler than the rest. It sounded a bit far-fetched, but shouldn't he take one of them up and see what was underneath? Why else would she have got rid of the bookcase? It could be a message: *Look, here my books are missing, but some papers are still there — the sun is showing you where.* Lowetz straightened his shoulders and walked faster.

At home he fetched his father's toolbox and located some files, a saw, and a small crowbar. Getting it between the boards wasn't easy, though. They were tightly fitted together and sealed, as if they had formed a unified surface, smooth and impenetrable, since the dawn of time. If she had hidden them here, he would have been able to tell, surely? But if they had been instantly visible, it wouldn't have been a very good hiding place. He assuaged his doubts and carried on. Twice he whacked himself painfully on the thumb and urged himself to concentrate; then the froe slipped and only just missed his thigh. It occurred to him that there was a main artery there; he couldn't remember exactly where. Better not hit that with the froe; they had shown a film on his first-aid course about using a belt to tie off a thigh that was spurting blood. After that, amputation loomed. Like all inexperienced workmen, the more incompetent he felt, the faster he tried to complete the task in hand. Applying force instead of thinking. Nonetheless, after a while it did occur to him to remove the skirting and loosen the floorboard from the short end, easing it away from the wall. The first nailhead slipped seductively into his pincers and came out with a single sharp tug. The beginning had been a success, and for a moment he thought he had made a metaphysical breakthrough. The nails would now slide out like butter, the skirting board would come away, then the floorboard, and underneath, lying flat as if holding its breath, would be a cardboard folder wrapped in tissue and tied with kitchen string that, when at last he found it, would almost sigh: *Well done, kisfiam!*

But the nail proved to be the only thing that did as Lowetz wanted. He couldn't even get a purchase on the heads of the others, they were hammered in so deep. You can't get at the heads in Darkenbloom, thought Lowetz, with an ironic mental nod, they're buried too deep in the ground. He was sweating, and was now switching aimlessly between his two sites of attack: trying to split the floorboards, and trying to remove the skirting.

He heard the door slam, and then Reinhold from Saxony was standing there, greeting him. For a second, Lowetz had considered hastily shoving the tools under his father's bed, but he didn't want to make himself any more ridiculous than he already was. How would he have explained why he was sitting on the floor? 'Can I help?' asked Reinhold, who was sure to be an experienced handyman, and Lowetz, who was definitely losing his equilibrium now, replied, 'Aye.'

Reinhold laughed, and just asked what needed doing. He didn't enquire as to why; his extreme reticence apparently dictated otherwise. Lowetz wondered whether perhaps this was characteristic of East Germans — that they never asked why. Flocke would have given him a slap for that generalisation. Oh, if only she would! Reinhold asked if he could sacrifice the floorboard. Lowetz replied enthusiastically in the affirmative: the floorboard must be sacrificed, absolutely, when all the heads here are buried so deep in the ground! Reinhold didn't know what he meant by this; perhaps he hadn't understood properly, because of the accent. A few minutes passed in silence, during which all that seemed to happen was that Reinhold poked about between wall and skirting board with the flathead screwdriver. With a bit of sensitive jiggling he managed to ease out a second nail. He pulled the skirting away from the wall and carefully sawed out a little section, only just wider than the floorboard. Lowetz began to get bored. Maybe while this was going on he could pop over to Fritz's and pay Agnes a visit? Then, without warning, Reinhold deployed the froe, raised the hammer, and hit it. Once, twice, three times; he pressed it down, levering. Lowetz heard a crashing and splitting that filled him with panic and alarm; he briefly tried to picture the treasure they were about to find, then was overwhelmed by the horror that issued from the blows. It was an act of violence. What this man was doing could never be undone. What in heaven's name was happening? Why was he willingly letting his home be destroyed?

He screamed *stop* and *no*, as if someone had cut his leg right to the bone, or deep into the main artery; Reinhold, shocked, was holding the floorboard he had finally ripped up, as instructed by his host, in front of his chest; and now, as if that weren't enough, Fritz, the carpenter with shrapnel in his head, was standing in the middle of the room. He stared in confusion at the hole in the wooden floor, and began to gurgle. Lowetz was kneeling on the ground as if frozen, awakening from a nightmare in which his mother and the faceless Horka were fighting over a bundle of papers, and old Dr Alois was chasing Uncle Grün — on horseback, weirdly — and hitting him with a riding crop, each blow cracking like a gunshot. He managed to shake off the images when he saw the effort Fritz was making, his mouth, that desperate black hole, laboriously opening and closing as he struggled to form the consonants correctly. Lowetz spoke quietly to him, asked questions, got him to repeat the important points, stood up, brushed down his trousers, and translated to Reinhold that his wife and daughter had arrived. Apparently they were in the town square, or in front of the Hotel Tüffer; Fritz would be happy to take him there, and he, Lowetz, would follow shortly.

Reinhold dropped the floorboard and leapt up, grabbed Fritz by the arm, and shook him; Fritz laughed and hugged him, and a moment later they were gone. The bag Lowetz had given the East German refugee, his guest, had been left behind; a threadbare cloth bag, little better than a plastic one, but at least it had two carrying loops and a zip, and bore the familiar logo: *See better, hear better — Philips lamps and radios.*

Lowetz pulled the bag towards him. In it were cigarettes, a newspaper folded open at the latest Darkenbloom revelations, and a small notepad with a few names and phone numbers. How little a person could have, in such a tatty bag. He had found it in his mother's wardrobe, full of odds and ends, and had immediately felt he should press it upon Reinhold. How humiliating! Lowetz remembered scenes from his early days in the capital, when he too had been fobbed off with cheap, unwanted marketing giveaways, back when he was an intern with a daily newspaper and had still wanted to be a *newspaper hack*, as they were called in Darkenbloom. Perhaps it was because Darkenbloomers felt threatened by *newspaper hacks* that the profession had interested him, but he had soon ended up in sales, and later switched to advertising — similar money with fewer morals. He was still in advertising, but had long since left the newspaper. You could advertise anything, after all — probably even Darkenbloom.

The gesture with the bag must have seemed condescending to Reinhold, or it should have done, if Reinhold had not been such a decent, unassuming person. Lowetz realised that now. He shook his head in disbelief at what he had done, and decided he would give Reinhold and his happily rediscovered family his own suitcase, which was new, good quality, and capacious. It would certainly be useful to them for the journey to West Germany, at least to the first reception camp, if not beyond. He would be generous, would provide the wife and daughter with essentials, cosmetics and toiletries, perhaps, after all those days in the forest. He stared at the ruined floor, the senseless hole. There was nothing underneath but pebbles and flattened clay, not so much as a torn piece of paper for insulation that might send Lowetz off on the wrong track again, even now. He laid the split floorboard back in place, even leaned the piece of sawn-off skirting against the wall, and cleared away the tools.

He sat there, thinking, although he knew he ought to go to the Tüffer. He must invite Reinhold's family to stay with him as well, even though it would be a bit crowded. It was a question of honour. He had stepped forward to take Reinhold in; he would do things properly. They wouldn't be staying much longer. He reached for the Philips bag again and took out the newspaper. He thought he had ... yes, here: a picture of Reinhold, along with a few others, though the photo was small and bad. They couldn't have used it on a wanted poster. Reinhold had also spoken to the reporters, and had had nothing but praise. He was described as an *East German with an unquenchable thirst for freedom*. He couldn't comment on the past, he said, but he had been received with kindness, several Darkenbloomers had looked after him, he had felt welcome and protected. Not a word about the Heuraffl beating — the man had manners. As he wasn't there, Lowetz couldn't ask him whether the quotation the paper had picked out as a subheading in bold type was what he had actually said, those exact words: *Open-hearted people — surely not Nazis*. Perhaps it was just how the newspaper had summarised it, the phrasing deliberately imprecise.

Lowetz put the tabloid, which in his humble opinion was not even fit for wrapping fish, back in the bag and stood up, but he didn't leave by the front door. Instead, he went through the kitchen and out into the courtyard, past the decrepit old shed — his parents used to distil schnapps in it when he was a child; he wondered whether Eszter ever used to think of the young man she had hidden in there — and in through the kitchen door of the Kalmar house. As soon as he entered, he began to call out, mainly to assuage his uneasiness. 'Agnes, are you there? It's Lowetz from next door, you know, Eszter's son; I just wanted to drop in, Agnes, don't be alarmed, Lowetz from next door is here!'

Silence.

'Agnes?' Lowetz called, with a question mark. Suppressing an urge to run away, he opened the doors to the two main rooms. He decided he wouldn't go into the little bedrooms, where she might be in bed. But then there she was, sitting at a desk in the further of the big rooms, half turned towards him and smiling at him. He went over to her and knelt down; she held out her hand, and he kissed it. She placed it briefly on his head.

'Agnes,' said Lowetz, 'I haven't seen you for so long. Please don't be cross that I didn't come before ...'

She said nothing. He pulled up a stool and sat beside her. She was drawing portraits of women in pen and ink. That explained the silver-framed picture in Lowetz's living room. 'Nice,' said Lowetz, talking to hide his discomfiture as he began to realise no words would be spoken in return. 'Do you only ever draw girls?'

She frowned, and pulled a picture out of the pile in front of her. 'No, not just girls,' Lowetz corrected himself, 'that's old Frau Graun. She really does look like the beggar woman on the plague column!'

Agnes smiled. She pulled out another picture and placed it along-side. A young girl, very pretty, a pert expression playing around her mouth. Lowetz didn't recognise her. 'I didn't know you were such an artist,' he said.

Then Agnes said, 'Elly.'

'That's Elly?' asked Lowetz. He couldn't think who this was, though he knew that there was, or had been, an Elly.

Agnes shook her head, frowning.

'Elly taught you?' Lowetz guessed. 'Elly discovered how good you were?'

Agnes smiled.

'We've got one of your pictures on the wall in our house,' said Lowetz, 'a particularly nice one. I think it's my mother as a young girl.'

Agnes reached for the inkpen again.

'I'll bring it over next time, and you can tell me who it is,' Lowetz said helplessly.

Agnes went on drawing. Lowetz realised that there were only a handful of motifs; the pictures resembled one another. He thought perhaps she was drawing herself as a young girl, with the long plait that she still had now. There were lots of versions of this picture, some better, some worse. Half-finished pages, scribbled over wildly and discarded, were strewn across the floor.

'Agnes, I'm going to go now,' said Lowetz. He reached out to her again and touched her forearm. She froze in horror, as if he were someone else, and he withdrew his hand. 'I'm sure Fritz will be back soon; he said he's just gone to the Tüffer. A Dr Gellért has been staying there recently, who …'

'Gellért — Goldman,' said Agnes, relaxing again. 'Gergely — Grünbaum, Gödrössy — Gruber, György — Gschwandtner.'

Lowetz was shaken. In this dim light, Agnes looked like a crazed angel. And once again he was almost choked with longing for his mother. She was the only one who could perhaps have explained this to him. Before, Agnes used to scream, day and night. Now she used her voice only for senseless lists of names, while her son struggled to make his gurgles understood. 'That's lovely, Agnes,' he said, quietly closing the door. 'See you soon.'

IO.

OLD MALNITZ, THE FATHER of Toni and Mick, had been a communist in his youth, and wore the insult *commie* like an honorary title. In the intervening years, his politics had shifted more towards the centre, to the socialists, but he could have provided information about *that time*, if he had wanted to; he had been in the resistance and in a prison camp. The Nazis, he used to say, were *political* opponents; they wanted something similar to us in the beginning, they just went about it differently. We demonstrated together against the Austrofascists' social legislation in the thirties; the Nazis were with us in the Austrofascist detention camps, and ultimately it was just bad luck that they got into power rather than our lot. Went the other way in the Soviet Union, didn't it? Old Malnitz, back when he was still a young Malnitz, had risked his life to oppose the war in Europe — to oppose what the Nazis had unleashed. Because the revolution should have come from below; they could have celebrated friendship among nations with their communist-liberated neighbours in perpetuity. Instead, the Nazis pursued wars of aggression in all directions and failed. *Bit off more than they could chew,* he used to say, *they just bit off more than they could chew.*

Independent of this, he was a lifelong anti-Semite. He considered the Jews to be a *natural* enemy, the ultimate enemy, since the world began, so to speak. Old Malnitz's father was cheated out of almost everything he owned by a Jewish wine and spirits merchant, a man who, it transpired — too late — was a compulsive gambler who juggled funds till they all slipped through his hands. But on his purchasing trips to the winemakers he wore a three-piece suit and silk tie. The merchant would step through the door as gingerly as if he feared for his shoes, and already Old Malnitz's father would feel inferior. And his young son sensed it, and the feeling lodged in his bones and in his memory. How were they supposed to guess that the suit was all this man still had to his name? Then one day the Jew was banged up in jail and they were out of pocket. Nobody knew what had happened to their wine. *Typical*, people said. *Bad luck*, said the other winemakers, who had dealt with other merchants. And this had been the first real disaster in Old Malnitz's life. He had never got over that early feeling of shame and humiliation. It was why, late in the evening, he would complain about the Jews — a few of whom had been killed, yes, but a far greater remainder still sat in the international banks, governments, corporations — and that Thea Rosmarin, too, she bought an old vineyard off them back then, when they were desperate, and cut down all the lovely vines, because of course a plot of land for the factory was more important than the precious grapevines, bloody capitalists. He would keep complaining until his elder son, Toni, said: 'C'mon, Father, enough of the old stories, put down your glass and go to bed.'

But the Jews were certainly not the cause of the rift between them, the discord between father and son that had lasted so many years. They weren't important enough for that. The cause was Toni's wacky ideas, about expensive wine and champagne and bottle fermentation, things his forebears would never have dreamed of. When his son wanted to take out loans to switch to the *top-of-the-range market segment*, before anyone started calling it that, Old Malnitz felt as if history were repeating itself. Loans? Debts? With the banks? With the Jews? Asking for trouble! They'll rip us off again! And for what? Just so we can do everything differently to the way we've always done it?

But Toni had married a woman who reckoned she was a cut above. She had brought a piano with her into the marriage! And she seriously believed that she should have a say. Letting women having a say in the business — madness. Because she had big ambitions, his daughter-in-law, you could see that from the off. One evening, Old Malnitz got so angry that he played the head-of-the-family joker, staked everything on a single card, the one that always came up trumps. He banged the table so hard that the plates jumped, and shouted, 'Either everything stays exactly as it's always been, or you no longer have a father, Toni!'

His wife, old Frau Malnitz, the devoted mother of his sons, dropped the bowl she was clearing away. His daughter-in-law, the much-too-beautiful Leonore, breathed in so sharply it sounded like a whistle. His little granddaughters began to cry. His son, the bastard, was the only one who stayed calm. His hand just shook slightly as he reached for his wine glass, took a sip, and said, 'Father, I was thinking of suggesting the same thing — that we should just go our separate ways. Then each of us can do what he thinks is right.'

And that was how this scandalous state of affairs had come about: that an established winemaker was unable to grow old on his farm, enjoying the fruits of his labours being harvested by the next generations, but instead had to shuffle off to go and live with the other son. No one ever found it worth mentioning that he had been bought out of the house and the business, or that Toni took on a risky amount of debt in order to do it. The young Malnitz had thrown out the old, the sensation-seeking Darkenbloomers whispered among themselves, although everyone knew, more or less, what had really happened.

He himself, Old Malnitz, didn't talk about it. He moved in with his other son, in Zwick, where he was forced to watch the younger one getting nowhere while Toni and Leonore prospered. Then it all came to an abrupt end with the wine scandal, because Mick's wine was adulterated, too: they lost everything, father and son just managing to scrape together enough to acquire the filling station. Mick didn't seem all that bothered; he was lazy, and wine growing had always been too arduous for him. Now he stood around amid the newspapers and cigarettes, crisps, and motor oil, chatted all day, and got fat. Toni, as his father saw it, was the triumphant victor. Toni, in whose bottles no banned substances were found, only award-winning wine — he'd never done anything like that, wouldn't even admit publicly that he had been aware of his competitors' practices, they were so far beneath him. 'I started specialising in the top-of-the-range market segment years ago,' he had told an interviewer, rather smugly, 'and as we know, there's never been any place for artificial additives in that.'

For the past four years, since Mick and Old Malnitz had had to sell their farm, Toni had come by every week and left a case of wine outside their house, without a word. But for three weeks now there had been no case of wine. Something had happened with Mick's wife when the wine was delivered. Old Malnitz didn't ask. He didn't need much wine any more; he was focused on dying. You couldn't tell to look at him, but he could feel it, deep down, in his bones and in his bowels. All he wanted was peace and quiet, a comfortable chair, and some sunbeams on his belly. But on the Monday after the big storm, his eldest, Mr Prize-Winning Top-of-the-Range Winemaker, knocked at the door. He had brought not just a case of wine but the big-headed Frau Leonore as well. 'He wants to talk ...?' said old Frau Malnitz, in a questioning voice, kneading the thin, grey fingers that had dropped the bowl all those years ago, and Old Malnitz sighed and agreed.

He had already heard that something was going on with the youngest girl. He wasn't very attached to her; unlike the other three, he hadn't spent a few years watching her grow up; she was different, wilder, less normal, and occasionally it had even crossed his mind that she might be someone else's child. Lately, too, when this youngest girl paid him one of her rare courtesy calls, she pretended she wanted him to tell her things, when in fact she only wanted to lecture him.

So now they had come to see him as well, the proud owners of the Malnitz organic farm, a posh hotel for druggy artists from the city, where it was said the bathtubs stood right in the middle of the bedrooms. He, Old Malnitz, had declined to view his parental home after the renovations, thank you very much. He didn't need to see it. It was there in his head, the way it used to be: the low ceilings, the little windows, the whitewashed walls, modest but clean, and that was how it should have stayed, and how it was going to stay in his head.

Frau Leonore was crying now, and Toni was scowling the way he used to as a child when he had just been spanked. Suddenly they started to press him, urging him to tell them what had happened back then, in Easter '45; you know, Father, the party in the castle, with the Countess, and the executions in the night. Who was responsible, who gave the order, where did they take them, who was shooting, how is Ferbenz involved, Ferbenz has to be involved, he was the mayor or Gauleiter back then or what was he, what do you know, why was there never an investigation?

They had to explain to him what any of this might have to do with the girl, his rather too impudent granddaughter. They didn't do a very good job of it, constantly interrupting each other. Coming to terms with the past — town chronicle — Rehberg's planning a museum — threatening letters — our barn in Ehrenfeld went up in flames just recently — Eszter Lowetz died, though she was never ill a day in her life — Flocke told us Graun's father was shot dead back then, just after the war, is that true?

Old Malnitz just shook his head and couldn't stop shaking it. What a muddle. 'So my crackpot granddaughter and the poof from the travel agency are writing the history of Darkenbloom. That'll be interesting. And they've found out a few things already. And they're driving everyone crazy with these scraps of information without any order or context. Still, none of that has anything to do with the fact the child hasn't come home, does it?'

'Tell us, Father,' Toni roared, like a wounded animal, and Leonore grabbed her husband by the shoulders and shouted, 'Shut up, Toni, that's not going to get us anywhere.'

A woman appeared in the doorway. Old Frau Malnitz, like a grey shadow. She had heard her eldest roaring. He was quiet now, Leonore still gripping his shoulders and holding him at arm's length, as if to make sure that he really was calming down. Old Malnitz shook his head again. 'She called me an anti-Semite last time, your daughter,' he said finally.

The two of them stared at him, aghast.

'Or is she just *your* daughter?' asked the old man, slyly holding Leonore's gaze.

'What ...' said Toni. But then his mother's grey shadow in the doorway began to speak, quietly, in a monotone, the way the old women in church intoned the Lord's Prayer and the Hail-Mary-full-of-grace, as they had done for hundreds of years and presumably would for a hundred more.

'Out of their heads ...' she intoned, '... they didn't even look to see if they were really dead, the Jews ... they were all so drunk ... I heard the moaning ... sound carries at night, when it's quiet ... I closed the windows, blocked my ears, so I wouldn't have to hear it ... the moaning, those, those ... death screams.'

Leonore let go of Toni, went over to her, and touched her arm. 'Who, Mother,' she asked, 'who did it?'

But the old woman feebly raised her hands and whispered, 'I don't know, and I don't know if anyone knows. And *he* was still in the camp.'

She jerked her chin towards her husband, and a moment later was gone.

'Well, children,' said Old Malnitz, clearing his throat, 'I don't know what good it'll do you, but the man responsible was called Neulag; he was a friend of Ferbenz, Graun, and Stipsits — that was the Nazi gang. Along with that nutcase Horka from the settlement in Zwick; he was their hired thug. The Russians made him chief of police later on — it really was beyond belief. But Ferbenz wasn't here then; he was in Graz or somewhere, so presumably he had nothing to do with it — with that, at least. He was only ever a desk warrior. Anyway, Neulag hasn't been seen since then. First they said he was killed in the last of the fighting, then, later on, that he fled with the Countess's help, supposedly to South Africa.'

Old Malnitz laughed. 'Maybe he's still down there, stuck among the Negroes! Serves him right! But there was an investigation; you've got that wrong. There was even a trial; the Hitler Youth boys were hauled up in court, the Heuraffls and Stitched-Up and I don't know who else. Did time for it, too. You were still too young back then, thank goodness,' said Old Malnitz to his son. He paused, then said, 'You could ask Hans Balaskó, too; he wrote it all down, back in the day. But I don't talk to him any more.'

'Why is that?' asked Leonore.

'He called me an anti-Semite, too,' said Old Malnitz, 'just like your daughter.'

'But you are,' said Toni.

Leonore nudged him.

'That's as may be,' said Old Malnitz. 'All the same, you don't come out and say it.'

II.

ON THURSDAY AFTERNOON, WHEN the daily papers were sold out all over Darkenbloom, Mayor Koreny sat in his office and marvelled. Astonishing how everything could change overnight! Not just a little, but completely. It was like a natural disaster, a snowstorm in high summer. He had asked his colleague, Frau Balaskó, not to admit any visitors for half an hour and not to put through any calls, but it was no good: he could hear the telephone ringing non-stop outside his door. From time to time he caught scraps of sentences, and felt admiration for his secretary. She remained constant. Her voice never altered; she said what she was supposed to say, in a calm and friendly way, because it was not her business and not her responsibility; she was simply carrying out instructions. And if, one day, he were to be driven out of office and a successor installed, she would sit out there just as calmly, occasionally easing a foot out of those instruments of torture that masqueraded as shoes and rubbing it against the other ankle, and perhaps she would say the exact opposite of all that she was saying now. And it was for precisely this reason that people should follow her example, because for her it was not a question of strategy or reputation or saving face; she simply deflected. She effortlessly returned the balls that came flying her way, but with absolutely no intention of scoring points. She just passed them back, softly, without aggression, utilising the energy of the opponent.

On the desk in front of Koreny lay a sheet of paper. He had turned it sideways and divided it into four columns: *Water supply / Hist. find, Rotenstein meadow / F. Malnitz missing / Gen. history questions*, open brackets, *war crimes*, question mark, close brackets. At the edge he had noted lightly, just for himself: *Border security, polit. developments Hungary*. So far the reporters hadn't asked about this, but he needed to deal with it as soon as possible, because his citizens, being so close to the border, were getting nervous.

He had had to speak sternly to each of the journalists in turn and urge them to keep things separate, because these matters had nothing to do with each other. Reporters who didn't even know where Darkenbloom was two days ago were irresponsibly lumping things together, he said; please understand, he wished to speak out very clearly against such nonsense.

After each conversation, he noted down in the different columns what the interviewer had been interested in. Entries in the first column, which in his view was by far the most important, were few and far between. All the newspaper reporters cropped up repeatedly in the other columns, because they kept mixing things up and jumping about all over the place. On one occasion, at the end of an interview when the questions had got too ludicrous for words, Koreny deliberately lied. It was for a Viennese publication called *Wiener*. Koreny had seen it in the newsagent's, a sort of glossy magazine, but he didn't think anyone read it around here. He pretended he had no idea what the caller, who kept giggling shrilly and sounded almost insane, was talking about. No, said Koreny firmly, there hadn't been a murder in Darkenbloom for many years, not even manslaughter; the gentleman must be mistaken. And he didn't know an Erika Lohritz, or Lohrmann, either. When he hung up, his heart was pounding like the clapper of the church bell; he could not have said whether with fear or anger.

When his fellow party members called him, they asked about almost nothing but the *bad press*. A comrade from the regional association, a town councillor in Löwingen, tried to reassure him. Right now, you're being painted as Nazis, he said, but don't worry about it: soon everyone'll be painted that way, and then no one'll stand out.

The marketing manager from the water authority called, as well. He was mainly interested in the find in the Rotenstein meadow; clearly he knew that, if the decision went against the authority, a huge water storage tank would have to be built up there. Not for the first time, Koreny tried to shake the feeling that he was always the last to find out about and understand anything. Once again, he was glad that he didn't have to control his facial expression over the phone. During difficult conversations like this he would pull faces to compensate for the relaxed, friendly tone of voice he was obliged to maintain. Towards the end of the call, the man said, with an unpleasant undertone, that one of the authority's legal advisors would be in touch very soon to go over the clauses that pertained to a withdrawal, if only theoretical. 'Any time you like,' said Koreny, pulling the face of a murderous gorilla, 'have a nice day.'

So there he sat, as the phone went on ringing outside. Frau Balaskó, his saviour, did not put any calls through. He looked at the columns on his piece of paper. He hadn't realised how little was required to connect it all. Just a bit of imagination, and everything fitted together, imagination apparently functioning like mortar or mounting glue. Even the most offbeat ideas slotted in. Into what? Into a decades-long conspiracy of horror. Koreny grimaced. If he looked out of the window, he saw Darkenbloom as it had always been: nice and old-fashioned in parts, ugly in others, but all of it quiet, with a high quality of life, provincial only to those who had something against the provinces. He didn't. He couldn't imagine living anywhere else; larger towns, not to mention cities, made him nervous. Hospitals twenty storeys high! But if he looked down at his notes instead of out of the window, and recalled the questions and accusations, claims and insinuations of the past few hours and days, he felt as if he were living in a film, with mafia and explosions and so on.

With a bit of effort you could take the same ingredients, or other ones, and tell a different story. What if it wasn't a question of truth at all, but of how it was put together? Perhaps the defendant actually needed less imagination than the accuser. Something had already been presented to him: the story of Darkenbloom, incorrigible den of Nazis and murderers. He had to counter it. After all the crazy stuff they were writing in the newspapers! I have every right, he thought, without finishing the sentence, we Darkenbloomers have every right ...

He took a second piece of paper. *Farmer Faludi*, he wrote, and sighed. Faludi could testify that democracy here was alive and well; surely one could expect that much local patriotism from him, in the current situation? *The mayor has always been happy to discuss things.* He could have his official water referendum in exchange, for heaven's sake; Koreny could resign later on, and someone else would have to grapple with the water authority's legal advisor. Why not Farmer Faludi himself, as the new mayor?

Next, with greater confidence, he wrote: *Rehberg*. He had received generous sponsorship for his historical research. He could confirm this publicly, and as far as Koreny was concerned he could go on to talk about the Ancient Romans or Celts. Fortunately, that was as far as he'd got. We've been actively coming to terms with our past for years already! Koreny nodded, then wrote: *Lowetz*. The young man had seemed a bit lost after his mother's death, but he had clearly begun to like it here in Darkenbloom. Koreny's wife had told him that young Lowetz wanted to come back, to keep the house and renovate it. Darkenbloom, a great place to live! A return to nature! And hadn't his mother, Eszter, been received with open arms back then, when she married Lowetz senior, of blessed memory — a good example of the historical ties between here and Over There, even across the heinous Iron Curtain?

Koreny grew bolder. He wrote: *Malnitz*. True, they were preoccupied with their missing daughter. They were the accusers, so to speak; at least some of this mess had come about thanks to them. But there was no reason why that should prevent anyone from talking about their flourishing business, the countless artists and famous visitors who had been coming for years to recuperate in the delightful countryside, to drink the award-winning wine that Toni, a pioneer of organic agriculture ... Koreny grinned. Embrace the opponent. Praise the Malnitzes any way you can! He was beginning to enjoy this. It's not just strategy, my dear Heinz, he said silently to poor Balf. You've got to have a feel for it, too.

When, for one minute, Frau Balaskó was not on the phone, Koreny threw open the door to the outer office and beckoned to her to come in. She stood up and rubbed her ear. 'You're doing a terrific job,' Koreny told her. 'You have no idea how grateful I am to you!'

Frau Balaskó blushed with surprise and pleasure. Her telephone rang again.

'Let it ring,' said Koreny. 'Come into my office for a moment. They'll call back. Now — tell me how your father's doing. Is he still in good health? Might it be possible to suggest he does a newspaper interview?'

The conversation with the daughter was followed by a cheery phone call with old Herr Balaskó, and before he hung up Koreny had no problem responding in kind to the socialist greeting *Friendship!* Balaskó's daughter was quick on the uptake, and immediately knew how else she could help. She informed him that someone from that left-leaning newspaper had called earlier and had left their name and number. 'The *Wiener*?' Koreny asked, reluctantly, but she laughed and said, 'That's a glossy magazine; no, I mean *Profil*.'

Koreny acquiesced, and allowed her to make the call. The

conversation with the editor went very well. To begin with, she just listened to him calmly, which was already more agreeable, and more inspiring of trust, than some of the over-excited accusers he had spoken to that morning. Koreny told her a few interesting facts about the area, the nearby border; he talked about unwelcome and misleading provocations in the relentless tabloid press, the kind we see so often; he thought he could sense that the editor was of the same view, although she didn't actually say so. 'I'm certainly not going to tell you what to write, madam,' said Koreny, punching the air as if hitting an invisible opponent in the solar plexus. 'But I would like to invite you to meet various different Darkenbloomers, so you can get the fullest possible picture — including of the historical facts. For which I offer you, as a representative of the quality press, my full support.'

When he hung up, he felt liberated. He would not resign, not in this difficult situation. He would not leave his Darkenbloomers in the lurch. Calm leadership was called for: experience in office, a feel for things, and strategic thinking. Sod the water authority. Fine, then, they wouldn't go through with it; there were other legal advisors who could take on the water authority's. He just needed to find them. Frau Balaskó should start making tentative enquiries. He was starting to discover his own abilities as mayor. You had to loosen up, as if you were dancing. Throw everything you had believed and feared until now overboard. Surrender responsibility to a higher authority, just like Frau Balaskó. His higher authority was the welfare of Darkenbloom. He would do his very best to prevent any damage to his hometown. That was what mattered. And how.

Koreny was in a cheerful mood when the Kirschenstein public prosecutor called. The prosecutor even commented on the change: 'It really was too hot for you up in the meadow a few days ago, wasn't it?' Koreny said he didn't know what it was like in Kirschenstein right now, but here it was still the same; these were the dog days, but he'd got used to them now, we don't really have a choice, do we? He laughed contentedly and pictured the unusually long bridge between the prosecutor's nose and upper lip, that haughty feature. Surely today, of all days, a fat bead of sweat was forming there that would soon break loose and trickle down as if on one of those newfangled water chutes? Koreny hoped so, and believed that simply by wishing it he could make it happen. He concentrated on the bridge, focused his telepathic powers, could practically see the sweat collecting ...

Meanwhile, the public prosecutor was reporting the preliminary results of the find in the Rotenstein meadow. As they had suspected, the remains were human, and at least forty years old, so presumably a victim of the Second World War. Apart from the left hand and the majority of the pelvis, the skeleton was complete. The absence of the pelvis made it harder to determine the sex, but as a helmet had been found nearby, it was very likely to have been a soldier. The helmet had been sent to the Museum of Military History in Vienna for more precise identification, and the appropriate War Graves Commission would be informed as soon as the results were in. 'Although I suspect that the Russians, for example, might have other worries at the moment,' said the public prosecutor, laughing. 'In any case, the building work or geological excavations or whatever the landowner was doing up there can restart, as of now.'

'Herr Graun will be pleased to hear that,' said Koreny, pulling a face. He thanked his *dear colleague* for the *good teamwork*, said, almost jovially, 'Until next time,' and hung up. For a moment, he puzzled over the missing left hand; unlike the incomplete pelvis, the public prosecutor hadn't commented on that. What could have happened to it? Maybe it had been carried off by an animal all those years ago, up there on the edge of the forest? It really was all a bit gruesome, the stuff that was starting to come to light from that period. He had been ten years old, he had only just joined the Deutsches Jungvolk, the precursor to the Hitler Youth; his main occupation back then had been scrapping with the Malnitz brothers, and he couldn't help it, he didn't know anything. Anyway: he could mark one of his four columns as dealt with.

Already the phone was ringing again. Would he ever be able to get up and go home? He sighed. 'Leonhard is on the line,' said Frau Balaskó, 'from the police station. He says it's urgent.'

'Didn't he say anything else?' asked Koreny.

'No, he didn't,' said Frau Balaskó. 'Can I put him through?'

'Go on, then,' said Koreny. It was hot, and those monstrous house flies were buzzing around his office as well; you never knew how they actually got in. His office chair had imitation leather upholstery; even your backside sweated in this weather. One of those decent lads from the gendarmerie was talking away in his ear; excellent young men, all of them, who, like him, did not shy away from responsibility. This one was now tasked with reporting to him what had happened. You could hear in the young man's voice that he would rather have been somewhere else — on the bathers' bus heading to the Adriatic, for example.

The fly accelerated and slammed into the window behind Koreny like a battering ram. The young man was still speaking. Suddenly Frau Balaskó yanked the door open and stepped into the room, beaming, her fist raised in triumph. The fly slammed into the glass again as if trying to break through. Frau Balaskó gave a silent cheer. About what? Gerald or Leonhard in his ear was telling him, in a roundabout way, that graffiti had been found in the Jewish cemetery, graffiti and evidence of vandalism; the young people from the city who were renovating there had just filed a complaint. Could the mayor perhaps come by and take a look? Please?

'What do you mean by graffiti, lad?' asked Koreny.

'Swastikas, Mr Mayor,' said the gendarme. 'Among other things.'

'Jesus,' said Koreny. 'I'm coming.' He threw the receiver back into its cradle. 'Frau Balaskó, why are you dancing around like that?'

'The girl's back,' cried Frau Balaskó, and actually clapped her hands. 'Flocke Malnitz, safe and sound!'

Right now, though, this wasn't much comfort to Mayor Koreny. She was probably up at the cemetery already with the other comers-to-terms-with-the-past, making a scene. Why was it that each new problem always seemed worse than the one before?

12.

ALEXANDER GELLÉRT FELL INTO a deep sleep after his visit to the travel agency. He never dreamed, or at least he couldn't remember anything when he woke, which, given what others claimed to experience and suffer in their sleep, must surely be an advantage. Normally he couldn't sleep in the daytime, but the heat and the events of the past few days had exhausted him more than usual. Being here, searching here, was not the same as in any of the other places, even Mandl and Tellian, Kirschenstein and Löwingen. This was where his own, old horror awaited him; sometimes he felt it breathing down his neck. He wanted to counter it with something: another, more harmless search, for his mother, who had presumably died of an ordinary illness and would surely have been given a decent burial, even in wartime. But he couldn't seem to muster the energy; even his effort with Rehberg today had been half-hearted at best. Probably, he admitted to himself, seeking refuge on the starched bedlinen as if on an innocently white, cool island — the hotel had considerately removed the eiderdowns at the start of the heatwave — probably he was afraid of encountering something unexpected. And yet it certainly wouldn't be difficult — registers of births and deaths; he didn't need Rehberg for those. Doubtless he could find them pretty quickly, along with cause of death and place of burial. Since returning to the town, he had wandered around the cemeteries, too, in self-imposed semi-blindness. He didn't so much want to read the gravestones as allow the locations to affect him. And until now he had had the girl with him; he didn't want to explain anything to her. Soon he would have to ask himself whether he actually wanted to know. On the one hand, it was inconceivable for him to leave Darkenbloom without even making the attempt. Yet he couldn't seem to start, because as soon as he began to think about it someone hit him over the head repeatedly with a little wooden hammer, which was very painful and bothered him a lot ... Gellért realised that someone was knocking at the door. He extricated himself from the depths of sleep as if from clinging brambles. It took him a moment to get his bearings; there was a smell of cleanliness and starch, the curtains were half closed, and beyond the windows the heat stood over the town square like a shimmering wall. There was another knock at the door.

'Yes, I'm coming,' he called, his tongue furred with sleep, 'just a minute, please.' When he sat up, his limbs were as heavy as if he had been swimming in the river fully clothed. He had learned that some years ago they had constructed a reservoir between Kalsching and Ehrenfeld, with an open-air swimming pool; perhaps that was the place to go in dog days like these. But how would he get there? The nice girl who had been happy to chauffeur him around in her spinach-green car was still missing.

Outside the door stood Resi Reschen, looking unfamiliar, as she wasn't wearing her white work coat. Even the clumpy waitress's shoes with the crisscrossed laces, squares of flesh bulging out along the top of the foot, had been substituted with something more ordinary. 'Has something happened, Resi?' Gellért asked.

'I've got a little bit of time right now, Schani,' said Resi grimly, 'and so I thought I'd show you your grave!'

Gellért exhaled deeply. Now, he thought, at last — and he was as excited as he had been when the old man with the bicycle had trudged ahead of him and the priest through the field of lupins. So: Resi herself. He had been hoping for something like this. It was often the women who gave the crucial tip; perhaps they were more easily moved, because they had so often, for generations, been turned into mothers of fallen sons. And it mattered to them where the dead were buried. *Dead is dead* — it was men who made brusque remarks like these.

'One moment,' said Gellért. 'I'll just put on my shoes.'

And so they walked together through Darkenbloom, the hardworking boss of the Hotel Tüffer, who would soon have to establish her successor, and the retired Dr Gellért from the United States, whom no one had recognised apart from the old lush Frau Graun, who hadn't even seen him in person. Resi set a brisk pace, the rest of her body led by her chin, and her expression remained grim. She was as angry with herself as she was with Schani: that he hadn't stayed where he was, where he must surely have led a more comfortable life than hers; they even had electric garbage chutes over there. Instead, he simply had to come back and spread unease, stir everything up — why, what for? Getting those disgusting, freshly sawn wooden boxes delivered to her hotel, for him to — never mind. She would show him that there was more, that there were things he didn't know. And besides, she told herself, it was an act of compassion. Perhaps then he would be satisfied and go away? He had been two years below her at school, but she remembered that he had been good-looking and funny. She thought she recalled him kissing Agnes, back then.

'I preferred Goldman,' she said snippily, over her shoulder; he was walking half a pace behind. 'Why did you change it?'

'Too Jewish,' he said simply. After a moment's surprise, she gave a dry laugh and nodded, as if she should have guessed.

When he realised she was heading for the Jewish cemetery, which had only recently been reopened, he stopped. She turned and said, 'Come on, Schani, believe me, I'm going to show you something important for you.' Gellért started moving again, but he fell behind. He could feel the warning breath on the back of his neck. A police car was standing right outside the gate, as if waiting for him, the one who got away.

There was a small crowd of people inside. The students who were spending the summer cutting back the weeds and renovating the first few gravestones were all talking at once to one of the two gendarmes, who had a notebook in his hand but wasn't writing in it, just nodding helplessly. The other gendarme was hiding behind his camera, concentrating hard on diligently photographing gravestones daubed with white paint. The slim girl with the curly hair stubbornly persisted in videoing him until he lowered his camera, looked straight into her lens, and said, unhappily, 'Please let me do my work.'

'Am I not allowed to document your work?' the girl asked.

Still looking unhappy, the gendarme carried on.

Borne along on her own determination, Resi pretended not to notice any of this. Now that she had started, she had to keep going; she couldn't let herself be thrown off her personal trajectory. And so she was too quick for Leonhard and Gerald.

'This way, come on,' she urged Gellért. 'It's back here, I think; we're nearly there.' She trudged round the piles of garden waste and foliage, round the tools, round the gravestones lying flat on the ground. Gellért followed her right down to a spot beside the outer wall, where she pulled aside some creepers, trod down the long grass, and finally pointed to a gravestone. *Jenő Goldman*, it read, *16 January 1895–12 September 1946, deeply mourned by his Eliza.*

'That's impossible,' said Alexander Gellért. 'That can't be right.'

'Because you thought he was with the labourers, up in the forest,' said Resi Reschen. Her expression became crafty. 'But things are never that simple. Your father survived what happened to the labourers, fortunately, but I'm afraid he died in a car crash not long afterwards. I'm really sorry, Schani.'

At this point, one of the two gendarmes finally caught up with her and explained that they had to leave, as this was a crime scene and must not be altered in any way. Resi was still clutching the creeper in her hand.

Stupid boys playing a prank, Mayor Koreny, sweating profusely, told the outraged students from the capital. He told the reporters, the ORF camera team, the gendarmes, and the curious Darkenbloomers who had started trickling in because word had got around that something had happened, yet again. *Youthful silliness, a drunken escapade, they can't have thought about or intended the consequences. Definitely not! That's not what people here are like!* He wiped his face with a large handkerchief. 'But we will find the culprits,' he said emphatically, 'we have a very competent gendarmerie here. And we do not tolerate damage to property.'

'Damage to property?' cried the leader of the cemetery garden volunteers, who had been sent and were being paid by Jewish organisations. A tall, disrespectful young man in a red T-shirt. '*Death to the Jews* is more than just damage to property, Mr Mayor!'

'When did the crime take place?' someone from the tabloid paper interrupted. 'Is there anything you can tell us yet about the timing?'

Koreny looked at the gendarmes. Leonhard leafed through his notes, then glanced up at the student spokesman. 'All between six pm yesterday and two pm today,' Leonhard said at last, 'according to these witness statements.' The red youth nodded. A couple of the girls stared at the ground.

'Two pm?' asked the reporter. 'So it could also have been today?'

'Theoretically, yes,' the young man, the spokesman, said reluctantly. 'We went swimming before work.' He smacked his fist repeatedly into the palm of the other hand. 'For the very first time, damn it!'

'No one's going to hold that against you,' said Koreny. 'You've worked so hard up till now.' He glanced around, wiping his forehead. 'These young people have made it really pleasant again here, haven't they. We can all take a leaf out of their book.'

At this, on *really pleasant*, Martha panned away. She walked slowly past the gravestones, which was possible now, since Fritz the silent carpenter had turned up one day with a finger bar mower. They had used it to cut the waist-high grass in the open spaces, and the former layout had started to appear. Chaos still reigned in the oldest sections, where the gravestones were closest together, overrun with brambles, stinging nettles, ground ivy, and sticky willy, which buried the stones beneath them or choked them with their indifferent, chlorophyll-addicted vigour. No one knew what was under there: which names, how many, how much destruction. In some spots the gravestones stood unscathed, while others just needed to be righted once the weeds had been cleared away. Others still were shattered, the engraved side consumed by mould and other spores. Did it bear any relation to the way the deceased had comported themselves on earth? That was how Martha's deeply Catholic grandmother would have seen it; Catholics were the most superstitious folk of all. But it was all just a question of location. The location, how much sunlight it got, and the composition of the soil determined whether plants flourished better or less well, whether the same plants grew, or different ones — there were even corners without any brambles at all. In some areas the earth was damper than in others. The wonder of nature, no mystery to those in the know: strata of humus and rock, sedimentation, angles of gradient.

It was slow work they were doing here, and yet each day saw considerable change. Martha took daily photos, morning and evening. In every photo the funeral steles of the rich rose up like lighthouses, immutable, two and a half metres high, granite blocks that tapered towards the top and stood like watchmen politely surveying the disorder all around them. Even after death the traces left by the rich were more striking, more imperious, more durable. I was David Rosmarin, I was Leopold Tüffer, remember us — we could afford to give ourselves a huge block of black granite or an entire mausoleum; the others couldn't, the Grüns, Arnsteins, and Spiegels, who only have the little white ones that fall over so easily, shatter, become illegible.

Over the past few weeks, Martha and her friends had managed to create paths and corridors, some leading deep into the overgrown sections. Their combined efforts had at least carved out a few avenues of order and civilisation. The attackers had taken advantage of this. Now they, too, had been able to leave their mark on this territory. As she filmed the white paint, daubed on in such a hurry that in many places the letters dribbled downwards like the lettering for the *Rocky Horror Picture Show*, Martha wondered whether they shouldn't just have left everything as it was. With the gate locked, the stone wall would continue to encircle a forgotten realm, like an exclave, the dead inside resting beneath their gravestones, and the gravestones, too, toppled or not, would be left in peace for all eternity, or until the coming of the Messiah. There was no one left to visit the graves of people buried in 1888 or 1912. They hadn't needed to open up the cemetery. Wasn't that what Flocke had said when they met? But they had ripped away the creepers and burrs from the stones in the conviction that they were doing good. And some good did seem to be coming of it. Nice Herr Gellért, who had been trying for weeks now to find the mass grave near here, seemed at least to have found his father's grave instead, which he had not been expecting. They had sat him down on a plastic chair, someone had pressed a cup of water into his hand, and now he was just staring into space. Presumably he needed some time to take it in. But who decided which took precedence, the good or the bad? The graves were accessible not just for visiting, but also for desecration. Martha and her friends had made it possible. Martha stopped in front of one of the graffitied gravestones. Clearly they had tried to kick this over, as well. They hadn't succeeded; the stone had just leaned slightly backwards, like the back of a chair adjusted for greater comfort. *Heil Haider* was scrawled across it, along with a smudged swastika. Could it be that the culprit had painted it first, then kicked it? It almost looked that way. Which would be stupid, because now he would have paint on his shoes and clothes. At least this swastika's legs were pointing in the right direction; there were others where they hadn't even got that right. Were these clueless swastikas an indication that the perpetrators were young? Was the mayor right? Martha remembered a drinking session as a teenager, in her grandparents' village, north-west of Kirschenstein. Bottles of beer, sausages grilled on sticks, bread toasted over the fire. In the dawn twilight one of the boys had stuck two fingers in the ashes of the campfire, painted a Hitler moustache onto his upper lip, and strutted up and down with his right arm extended, snarling a load of nonsense as if barking orders. Others jumped up and pretended to be soldiers, flung their arms up in the air and saluted. Then they all shouted in chorus: *Heil, Heil, Heil!* It was only a joke; everyone had roared and laughed along with them, including Martha. But would she still have laughed, back then, if they'd set off for the cemetery with tins of paint?

13.

AFTER THE EXHAUSTED DR Gellért had left the travel agency and disappeared into Darkenbloom's maze of alleyways, Rehberg kept turning the note over in his hands. He would hold on to it; after all, this sort of thing was part of Darkenbloom, too. It would be pretty daring, he thought, to include an undeniably threatening letter in an exhibition, but perhaps that was the correct response? What was it that so threatened people that they threatened others in turn! It was worth remembering that it was only certain individuals who behaved like savage dogs, presumably those who were not the sharpest knives in the drawer. Of whom there were quite a few. Sending threatening letters really is stupid, Rehberg told himself, aware that he was trying to talk himself out of a kind of fear; the sender could probably be convicted based on a sample of handwriting, or fingerprints. They had very modern methods these days ...

He gathered up the papers: the Rehberg family tree, the day's newspaper articles, which he had already cut out, pasted, and labelled. And that old report they had put in his letterbox, about the naked man on the track through the vineyard, which unsettled him so because it reminded him of his own, vest-clad ordeal: beatings, bruises, contusions, black eye. And then the beating from his father because he refused to say what had happened. His mother standing behind his father, pleading with him to stop, he's bleeding already. His grandmother saying: 'Won't do no harm, needs toughening up, that one.'

It was quiet. Business was traditionally bad at the height of summer; those who hadn't already booked a trip were not going to want one now. He should put together another brochure for *golden autumn holidays* and send it out to his clientele; that had worked well in previous years. Once, he had even been given the opportunity to present his merchandise at a Tupperware party thrown by Balf's wife, at which he was the only man. The ladies, tipsy on sparkling wine, had plumped then and there for a group trip to Trieste. That had been two years ago. In the autumn he mostly sold city breaks, though his customers showed little interest in trying anything new. Many just wanted to go to the Oktoberfest.

Something started crawling around in his brain like an insect under a piece of silk, moving back and forth, trying to draw attention to itself. But Rehberg couldn't think what it was; it remained hidden beneath the cloth. He groaned. He had forgotten something relevant, something important. When he realised that his thoughts were simply going round in circles — *I can't remember, I can't remember* — he stood up, turned the sign to read *Back soon*, and took the documents up to his apartment. He went over to the chest of drawers, opened one to put the papers inside, and that was when it leapt out at him, as if with a shrill whistle. He staggered, and sat down in shock, overcome with emotion. Gazing up at him from the drawer was the melancholic wedding photo Eszter Lowetz had brought him: sepia brown, with a decorative, serrated white border. *Look closely*. The bridal couple were smiling shyly. With a huge effort, it was possible to imagine that the young woman bore a certain resemblance to Aunt Elly — all young women looked alike in those days — but what absolutely could not be denied was that the unknown young man, his eyebrows, his nose, resembled Dr Gellért. Elisabeth Rehberg! Gellért had asked after someone with that name; it was probably this woman. And because they had had the same name, dear Eszter must have assumed that this was his aunt! For once, the skilful researcher had got it wrong. What a shame he could no longer tell her. They had almost fallen out over it; he still regretted their argument. They needed to stick together, Eszter, Flocke, and him, the hard core, the few progressive thinkers in Darkenbloom with an interest in history and genuinely coming to terms with it. Of the three, only he was left. He mustn't think too hard about that. Perhaps Feri Farkas, at least, would stick it out, and he'd already told young Lowetz how much he needed him. But what if it all started up again with the threatening letters? Rehberg was well aware that he was not the heroic type.

Silencings, Aunt Elly had said, in that memorable conversation a few weeks before she died: *they were silencings.* Immediately after the war, the witnesses had been killed, one after another. And he should never forget this, but he shouldn't speak of it to anyone either, not yet. *Just remember it*, Aunt Elly had instructed him, *remember it well, and if someone comes for whom this information might be useful, tell them. Someone from outside, not anyone from here. You'll know when.*

And that was what he had done, just over a week ago. As they sat together enjoying a nice glass of schnapps, he had informed Dr Gellért, in confidence, that there had been a series of silencings after the war, to intimidate people. His aunt had witnessed at least one of them herself: the famous shoot-out at the border. He said what she had instructed him to say: they had been carried out each time with utter ruthlessness, in broad daylight. Including the one when she had happened to be present. First the driver had been taken out, presumably by a sniper, then the lurching car came under heavy fire from the border guards and Russian soldiers. The conspirators must have known nothing would happen to them. They had protection in high places, including from the then chief of police. The exact names and circumstances could be found in any archive; the newspapers had reported on it at the time. Rehberg admitted to Gellért that he had not yet researched it himself; he had found it too gruesome.

Gellért, however, had attached little importance to Aunt Elly's urgent message. 'Yes, yes,' he replied, almost placatingly, 'people always tell me this; it's a story I've heard in every town I've searched in.'

Perhaps he hadn't been the right person after all. When Rehberg thought about it, it was clear that Gellért, too, was from here, and not an outsider. But he hadn't known that a week ago.

After all the man had been through, he could at least present him with the photograph of his young parents. Eszter Lowetz's other papers may have disappeared, but still, Rehberg could give him this nice photo: that was a piece of luck. And so he slipped the picture into his breast pocket and set off for the Hotel Tüffer.

That afternoon, around the time Mayor Koreny was being summoned to the Jewish cemetery and Resi Reschen was dragging her guest, Dr Gellért, there as well, the two Stipsits women came to Café Posauner for a snack. They hadn't been in for weeks, and Gitta, the owner of the Posauner, had actually been hoping they might never come in again. But here they were, claiming their usual table, one of the two next to the big windows. And she could guarantee that they would share a fruit tea and a glass of tap water with their cake. They didn't usually talk. The Stipsits daughter, poor soul, had been a rather unappetising sight for some time now, and Gitta couldn't understand why they insisted on sitting in the window. The idea that they had no interest in being seen, that they just wanted to watch the goings-on outside instead of chatting, was not something Gitta could get her head around. Usually it was pink-cheeked girls who sat in the window, showing off their lipstick or their décolleté in the hope that the other girls, or boys, would quickly find them. Everyone else, the café regulars, the workers who lunched here, the pensioners who came for a snack, preferred the café's cosier, dark interior, where they could sit and chat with Gitta as she stood behind the espresso machine.

One sick, the other depressive: the two Stipsits women, a sad end to that branch of their extended clan. Mother and daughter, mutually dependent, both unmarried and, bar that one calamitous occasion, untouched. All the older Darkenbloomers knew the daughter was a memento from a Russian soldier; the only one who seemed not to know it was the daughter herself. As soon as the conversation strayed anywhere near the topic of her origins — it was usually enough for it to be about *the Russians* in general, and how they had gone on the rampage after the war — she would say, with a strange, almost trans-figured expression: *My father was passing through back then.*

Once, there was someone present who didn't know any of this and couldn't make sense of her remark. When this stranger asked what she meant, and everyone, including Gitta behind the espresso machine, held their breath, the Stipsits daughter casually replied, 'I just wonder whether he knew about it, back then — that the Red Army was committing these crimes.'

At which her mother, face expressionless, said, 'It was mostly the women who knew about it.'

At some point, the Stipsits mother had displaced the whole ter-rible story onto her sister Inge, who was forced to go with the Russians and did not come back. Agnes Kalmar had come back, the Stipsits mother herself had come back (though she never spoke of this); their nightdresses were ripped to shreds, they were alive, but Inge, her sister, had disappeared. She never got over it. Her daughter, born out of wedlock, was named after Inge, like a revenant, and the Stipsits mother resisted all her family's attempts to marry her off during the pregnancy. For generations, the Stipsitses had been one of the rich farming families, until one of her brothers started the successful pharmacy line in the fifties. They would have had no difficulty in drumming up a servant or handyman — one of the Stitched-Ups, for example — to restore her honour. But she refused. From then on, she lived with her daughter, who bore her sister's name and worked, until she got ill, in one of the pharmacies. Since then, the daughter had also got more peculiar; people ascribed it to her illness, which seemed to be burning her up from inside.

The previous Sunday, when the Darkenbloomers had headed to the Rotenstein meadow to see what there was to see, the Stipsits daughter had not gone along. And perhaps that was the only reason the mother had permitted herself a conversation with the local reporter, which had appeared in the paper before all the other excitement. In it, she again recounted what she knew, but breathed not a word of her own experience. Since that time, she told the local reporter, her greatest wish had been finally to learn her sister's fate. And if these remains were, perhaps, her sister's, it would be terrible, but it would put an end to the uncertainty: 'I could bury her at last alongside our parents, in our lovely family tomb!'

'Is there any other possible explanation for what might have happened to Inge?' asked the well-known local reporter with the camera round his neck and the anti-nuclear suns stuck all over his car.

Mother Stipsits answered, hesitantly, 'She might, of course, have gone with one of them of her own free will, to the East. My daughter's sure of it — that she's alive and doing well.'

And now here they were again, the two of them, and in a moment they would both be prodding at their poppy-seed cake. As always, they ordered one tea, one glass of tap water, and *one cake with two forks*, and Gitta needn't have bothered with the question about the whipped cream, but she asked everyone who ordered cake, out of habit. Not to ask would have required additional mental effort. 'Good heavens, no,' said the Stipsitses, almost in unison, and Gitta nodded, retreated from the window to the back of the café, and rummaged in the drawer for the fruit tea, which only these two ever ordered.

The gendarmes' car drove past outside. 'Look — Gerald and Leonhard,' said the daughter. The mother nodded.

'Maybe they've dug up someone else,' she said.

'No, they definitely haven't,' the daughter contradicted her, with the patient sternness of a nurse. 'A thing like that only happens once in a blue moon.'

When Gitta brought their order, she paused at their table for a moment. 'No news yet about your skeleton?' she asked. Mother Stipsits shook her head.

'It could be Inge,' she said quietly.

'It's not Inge,' the daughter contradicted her, 'it's definitely a soldier. They'll find a helmet or a gun next, you'll see; there are usually other finds as well, with soldiers.'

'But where's Inge?' asked the mother, dully.

'Inge is in the Urals,' said the daughter. 'She's got lots of children and grandchildren over there, and a garden with apples and potatoes.'

'But why did she never write?' asked the mother.

With a tender expression on her eyebrowless, eyelashless face, the daughter said, 'Out of love, Mama; out of love for her husband, she forgot. Maybe she was a bit ashamed, as well, that she just ran away like that.'

'That is a possibility,' said the mother, thoughtfully, and Gitta guessed that the two of them had had this conversation many times, that maybe they had it every day. 'It really could be that she was that ashamed.'

Gitta could see the little veins shimmering under the daughter's pale scalp, between sparse tufts of fuzzy grey hair. 'Inge,' she said sternly, 'I'm going to bring you some whipped cream after all. You really must try and put on a bit of weight; you can't go on like this.'

14.

NEITHER THE ORF TEAM nor the film student Martha got any footage of Flocke Malnitz driving up to the Hotel Tüffer in her spinach-green Corsa, only the skinny little dogsbody who usually ran errands for the editors and technicians. For some reason he had not accompanied them to the cemetery. It's not true, incidentally, that Flocke did a circuit of the town square first, beeping her horn; these things were made up later by people who begrudged her her few days of fame. Flocke instinctively made for the Tüffer because it was in the centre of town and there was a public payphone near the reception desk. Contrary to what was subsequently claimed, the first people she called from it were her parents; she certainly did not give long interviews or allow herself to be filmed before sparing a thought for her grief-stricken mother. That is not what happened, but some Darkenbloomers made these malicious claims because since time immemorial they had harboured a deep-seated mistrust of stories that ended well.

The second person she called was Lowetz, because she was trying to reach Reinhold. No one picked up; the ringing may have been drowned out by the hammer blows breaking up the floor of Eszter's living room. Telephone numbers in Darkenbloom were just three digits in those days, and everyone knew plenty of them off by heart.

So the third person Flocke called was Fritz, to send him across the courtyard with the message for Reinhold.

Meanwhile, the two women, Vera and Silke, were sitting shyly in the restaurant, drinking lemonade because it had been urged upon them. Like any spectacle, this, too, had a gradual build-up. For the first half-hour, almost nothing happened. The spinach-green Corsa was parked outside the Tüffer. Flocke made her phone calls, which can't have taken longer than ten minutes in total, then went and sat with the women and encouraged them to try the *grammelpogatscherl* Zenzi had put on the table. At first it proved impossible to translate what exactly these were. Vera asked if these things were *savoury*; Flocke said they were *a bit greasy*, which didn't really answer the question. Mother and daughter smiled uncertainly. They had never heard of *Grammeln* in Saxony, and Flocke didn't know that Germany used a different word for greaves. *Pogatscherl*, she said, was probably just the shape. Maybe it means something like lumps? I don't really know either, to be honest.

And this was when the humble runner who had stayed behind at the hotel caught his big break. Once he figured out what was going on, he leapt into action. He dashed up to his room to fetch the little camera, sidled up to the two women on the bench, asked a few initial questions, then shyly asked if he could do some filming. This was how they got the idea of reconstructing the scene. The young man made out that he simply couldn't believe both women had fitted in the boot of the car, that they'd really been able to get enough air in there, so in the end they all went outside and showed him. Zenzi came out as well, just as Rehberg arrived, hoping to call on Dr Gellért. He was overjoyed to see Flocke again safe and sound, and wanted to hear all about it. Flocke told him: how she had scoured camping sites and bed-and-breakfasts, asking after the two women who had lost their husband and father in the forest. How she had slept in a tent with other Germans, and was able to give them tips: down here in the south, at the Zwick border crossing, the Hungarian guards changed over at four o'clock in the afternoon, and the cabin was unoccupied for just under a quarter of an hour. She recounted how, after two days, she was just about to give up and turn back, but then someone had known something after all … On her quest she had seen a main road full of abandoned Trabants, all lined up in a row like brightly coloured toys, blue, green, white, yellow, red, a phantom traffic jam with no people and no rumbling of engines. They must belong to the people who had taken advantage of the pan-European picnic a few days earlier to rush across; the border had been closed again since then. And think how long they'll have waited for those cars! Her stowaways confirmed this, as they folded themselves into the car boot again for documentation purposes: sometimes you had to wait ten years or more! 'I really wanted to take one with me,' said Flocke.

'One what?' asked Rehberg, who was starting to get confused by so much information.

'One of those cute little Trabis, of course,' she said, giggling. 'A bright red one, to go with my Corsa. But my boot was already full!'

So at first, apart from the young camera assistant, it was just Rehberg, Flocke, and the two women she had fetched from Over There in such daring circumstances. Then Zenzi, the kitchen workers, the chamber-maids, and even the caretaker came and stood in front of the hotel as well. *When the cat's away, the mice will play*, Resi Reschen would say later; right now, though, she was still in the cemetery, determinedly tugging at creepers. Because the young man asked so nicely, Flocke even closed the boot for a moment, very carefully, and turned to him. 'You see — of course it works. It isn't comfortable, but they weren't in there for long, just the last little stretch across the border.' As she spoke, she turned to open the boot again.

'Stop!' the young man cried, the sweat of a once-in-a-lifetime opportunity on his brow. He asked Flocke to take a step back, then step forward again — 'please don't say anything!' — and only then to open the boot. 'And please don't look into the camera; I'm not here!'

Flocke raised an eyebrow, but did as she was told. She opened the boot, and Silke and Vera, exaggerating slightly, stretched up their arms like sleepy mermaids when their shell opens in the morning; they sat up, Flocke helped them out, Vera, the mother, stumbled and twisted her ankle; the runner kept filming. He asked Flocke to drive up again in the car. Not with the two of them in the boot, but to re-enact her arrival outside the hotel for the camera? Could she do that? And then open the boot? They could edit it into the right order later on. Vera was hopping around on one leg, face screwed up in pain, insisting that it didn't hurt and leaning on her daughter, Silke.

Then, to cap it all, the delegation from the Jewish cemetery turned up outside the Hotel Tüffer; quite a crowd, because they wouldn't leave Mayor Koreny alone, although he had declared his inspection of the scene over. Curious onlookers had been swept along as well, like by-catch in a trawlnet. Koreny kept repeating that he had to get back to the town hall, to his desk, but it was no use. They just kept filming and photographing him, and everyone pricked up their ears to listen to the young man in the red T-shirt berating him while walking at his side: if people refused to recognise that the swamp still persisted wherever it wasn't spoken of openly, the mayor should not be surprised if people were painting swastikas. Teenagers don't usually come up with ideas like that on their own! There has to be an environment, a residuum, for something like this to grow! 'Why is it the Jewish cemetery they're defacing, Mayor Koreny? Why not spray the anti-fascist logo on the bank? Is it really coincidence, or do you just hope it is?'

'Look,' said Koreny defensively, his face bright red again, 'look, you and I certainly aren't going to get to the bottom of that right now.'

'I demand that you take back what you said about damage to

property,' the young man cried.

Koreny stopped. 'What gives you the right to demand anything at all of me, young man?' he asked. Several of the bystanders nodded and moved closer, glowering.

Koreny raised his voice. 'Just who do you think you are? Let me tell you how it works around here. First, this will be investigated, calmly, by our efficient young gendarmes, and after that, we'll see. It's called the rule of law. Heard of it, have you, out there at your university?'

'You can talk, Mr Deputy Mayor,' the young man hissed. He turned to face those he took to be reporters from out of town. 'All the papers are writing now about what a nest of Nazis this is. The last Gauleiter lives here, too, by the way,' he shouted accusingly. 'Alive and well! And we're told that, in this town, he's a highly respected citizen!'

At that very moment, Martha, the curly-haired film student, was paying this same highly respected citizen and, in his own presumptuous opinion, benefactor of Darkenbloom a visit. Frau Ferbenz opened the door, Martha drew on all the resources of good manners at her disposal and claimed, rather audaciously but in a tone of velvety obsequiousness, that she had arranged an interview with Dr Ferbenz. It wasn't about the current controversies, she said, noting Frau Ferbenz's hesitation; not at all, I've got nothing to do with the reporters here in town! I'm making a film about Darkenbloom and its colourful history — I've been working on it for weeks. Martha decorously lowered her gaze, and Frau Ferbenz let her in.

It was thanks to Gellért that Martha acted so quickly. She had sat down with him in the cemetery while Bartl and the other students were still arguing with the mayor, the gendarmes, and various Darkenbloomers. They were saying that they had to secure evidence, for heaven's sake, look for fingerprints in the white paint, which was barely dry, while others said it was like when people walked past swanky cars at night and let their own car keys stick out of their pockets for a second — before you knew it there was a scratch across the door. Petty crimes like these — scratching cars, desecrating cemeteries — were almost impossible to resolve; very annoying, but there was nothing you could do about it. That was when Bartl lost his temper. 'It's a question of *wanting to*,' he shouted, 'and not wanting to begins with you seeing scratched cars and *Heil Hitler* as the same petty offence!'

'There's no *Heil Hitler* anywhere, thank goodness,' said Koreny. 'Now control yourself, young man!'

Martha sat on the ground beside Gellért, who didn't seem to be listening. He was drinking a little water from a plastic cup, carefully, in tiny sips, like a bird at a puddle. 'Are you all right?' asked Martha. Gellért glanced up and, to her surprise, he looked happy.

'Yes, my dear,' he said. 'And I think I've got something for you. You should take it to Ferbenz and interview him, with that camera of yours. No time to lose!'

And he slipped her a piece of paper, a page he had evidently torn from the local paper. She unfolded it and read. 'Best go right away,' Gellért insisted. 'Get him to talk. And if you'll take my advice, start with that!'

When Martha was shown into the living room, Dr Ferbenz was sitting in an armchair in the half-light; she couldn't really see his face. She went and sat opposite him as if she had just come for a little chat. 'I read about you in the paper recently ...' she said, as she had been advised, and he immediately took the bait and started to tell her all about it. He was proud of himself; he interrupted himself several times, jumping even further back in the chronology to ensure *the young lady* got the right impression.

'Dr Ferbenz,' she interjected, 'may I switch on some lights first? I'd like to record you telling this marvellous story!'

And she switched on the lights, and skilfully deployed a few volumes of Meyer's encyclopaedia, 1939 edition, to construct a small camera stand on the side table next to her seat. That way she could unobtrusively adjust the camera without having it in front of her face. She hoped the picture would be in focus, and that he would forget about the equipment. And that was how, over the next few hours, she obtained the interview that would have such far-reaching repercussions. Clips from it were also shown abroad, not only in German-speaking countries: Dr Alois Ferbenz with the pale blue, watery eyes, former Deputy Gauleiter of Styria, even had his central arguments subtitled in English. On Austrian television there was an argument on a prominent discussion programme about whether this interview should ever have been broadcast. Or whether it shouldn't immediately have been shut away in a sort of poison cupboard, with only established experts allowed to access it.

'People are nowhere near as stupid as you think,' a supporter of the broadcast said on the programme. 'You don't have to explain to them what an old Nazi is.'

'You're demonstrating that you're completely incapable of seeing beyond your own educational perspective, even for a moment,' his opponent retorted angrily. 'Maybe *you* know how to evaluate it. But young people, or those with a right-wing worldview, might think the nice old grandpa actually sounds convincing!'

And this was just one of the lesser consequences of Dr Alois's late-life candour.

Darkenbloom's physician, Dr Sterkowitz, was sitting in front of the television set with his wife, watching the Ferbenz interview, when a flash of insight struck him like a lightning bolt. It really felt as if he had understood something that had not been clear to him before, accompanied by a physical sensation akin to a blow or a shove. In the days that followed, he wondered whether he had ever had such a sudden insight before in his life, and concluded that he had not. This, too, gave him pause for thought. But what made him most thoughtful of all was that he couldn't even explain to his wife, as they sat there in front of the television with their ham sandwiches on plates, what it was that had, quite literally, struck him. Sterkowitz wanted to wait until the end of the programme, not talk over it; that wasn't something you did in those days. Back then, television programmes were still seen as something precious, like plays. The moment the interview was over, though, it burst out of him. 'I understand it now, Hertha,' he cried excitedly. 'He's saying the same things he always says, but the television makes it worse! Do you know what I mean? All that old nonsense, everyone's heard it from him before, he's often … But it takes on a different meaning simply by virtue of being broadcast! As if the telly does something to it … Why is that?'

His wife looked at him. 'I don't know what you mean,' she said. 'It's obvious.'

'What's obvious?' he asked.

'That you don't say things like that in public. Ferbenz must have gone completely senile. He should know!'

But this was days later. Right now, Martha was sitting opposite Dr Ferbenz, getting him to talk. Gellért's tip was worth its weight in gold. Ferbenz held forth about Egypt, another great and ancient civilisation that had completely gone to the dogs; just *fellaheen*, peasants, no pharaohs any more; greasy pedlars, diseases, vermin; anyone who didn't get gastroenteritis out there must have Teflon insides. We mustn't let it happen to us, such a decline. But his wife had insisted she wanted to see the Pyramids, and after a lifetime of hard work and sacrifice he'd wanted to grant her this wish. He had complained about them performing the Nazi salute as popular entertainment; had claimed it as a travel defect, yes, yes, that was correct. Why? What do you mean, *why*, young lady?

Martha's palms grew damp. She folded her hands on her lap. This was the decisive moment that would determine whether or not she would be thrown out. She opted for a cheeky smile, and the offensive.

'Well, Herr Doctor,' she said, 'I just thought you didn't actually object all that much to the Nazi salute, on an ideological level, I mean.'

Ferbenz said, 'You're right there, girl; no objection to the salute itself. But from those Mohammedan faggots? And the Yankees and the French sitting there making fun of it? No, no — I availed myself of the prohibition laws; they've got to be good for something. And the judge ruled in my favour!'

And then he told her everything, allowed himself to get carried away by his memories, revelled in his swashbuckling past, responded candidly to every question Martha managed to ask. Her reactions would have been apparent; before long, she was unable to control her expression, and began to interject sharp questions, but Ferbenz didn't notice: why should he care about some obscure young girl's opinion? He was elsewhere, in better days. He would explain to her what things were actually like, back then. A dam that, in the past, had only occasionally been crested by frothy little waves finally broke. He was as free again as he had been back then, when he was finally allowed to use his mother tongue in school and no longer compelled to speak the loathsome Hungarian. *Köszönöm!* Free as he had been back then, when the stupid drawing teacher was driven out, the one who had married the glazier's daughter, because even one of their kind would rather stay here than go back where he came from. Because someone was finally asking him, for two hours Ferbenz was young again. He felt himself clothed in his new uniform with the shiny buttons; he saw his men marching, and the sea of flowers, that spring. Never before had Austria offered up so many flowers, he cried; that's not war, that's homecoming, liberation!

And so they went out into the world, all Ferbenz's remarks that, even many years later, were still regarded as a terrible, deranged, senile gaffe, a singular aberration, as it were, to which the wicked media had attached far too much significance — you can find nutters anywhere, after all — until they began to realise how many hearts were moved by these and other such remarks, people who hadn't even necessarily been there at the time, who simply yearned for a greatness they had never experienced, and were fired up by Dr Alois and his ilk, like the torches of which he still dreamed. Some of Ferbenz's remarks concerned parasites: that nature required they be combated, even if they were people. *They're not people, they're parasites, and because that's what they are, you exterminate them!* It was this remark and others like it that were translated into other languages. Above all, though, his rant dwelt on Adolf Hitler's slender hands: an artist's hands, they were, hands of the very first rate. Ferbenz rhapsodised about Hitler's first-rate hands, and shed a few old man's tears over his blue eyes, the most beautiful he had ever seen: it was like a time warp. As he spoke of those beautiful blue eyes, his own grew moist, his chin trembled, his grief for the Führer trickled from the corners of his eyes and made his nose run, and if you were looking as closely as Martha was, you could see that he was no longer neatly shaven, because those moist eyes couldn't see well any more, certainly not first thing in the morning, when it mattered. A few white hairs projected from his trembling chin, helpless and perplexed, in bristly contrast to the artist's hands of silken delicacy he was conjuring in his imagination. The old, badly shaven Ferbenz blathered on, oblivious to the damage he was doing to his town, for many years to come. Darkenbloom, people would ask from then on, or would if they were from outside the region: wasn't that where that mad old Nazi bastard was from?

Whether or not that would have restrained him is debatable. Afterwards, many Darkenbloomers defended him because, after all, they knew what he was like. They would have given a great deal for this interview never to have happened; perhaps even the remnants of the castle, that pointless, lonely tower with its stumpy little wings. At the same time, though, they were able to put it in perspective, because things were not as people believed. The further away people were, the more they misjudged it. This so-called scandal, which even made the international papers for a few days, was like an illusory giant: the closer you got to Darkenbloom, the smaller it became. From far away it was very big, because the people who made a scandal out of it were so inordinately glad that they were nothing like the people of Darkenbloom. Glad, and certain of it, utterly convinced.

In Darkenbloom, though, it was soon referred to as Dr Alois's *unfortunate choice of words — you know what he's like.*

'We've got a lot to thank him for,' elderly farmers' wives said at first, speaking defiantly into the journalists' microphones. 'I can't say exactly what he did back then,' town councillors, wine growers, business people said at first, pursing their lips, 'because I wasn't even born. But he's always been a benefactor and a real pillar of our town — there's no law against saying that.'

Later, they didn't say anything any more; they swore, turned away, and slammed their shutters. Ferbenz's son-in-law chased a camera team out of Boutique Rosalie. A reporter complained to the police that a dog had been set on him at the Heuraffl farm. As he wasn't bitten, though, the case was closed and the newspaper man advised not to set foot on private land unless expressly invited to do so. People round here are a bit sensitive right now, Gerald and Leonhard explained.

'Well, and no wonder,' Joschi, Ferbenz's nephew, said angrily. 'Half his life things were one way, now they're another — Christ, they could at least leave him his memories! He's not doing any harm! For more than thirty years, ever since he was allowed to again, he goes out and votes in every single democratic election, and puts out the flag on October the twenty-sixth! What more do you want from the old man?'

'You'd better not give any TV interviews, either,' one of the wags in the Posauner or the bar of the Tüffer would advise Joschi, those wags that are found everywhere. Secretly, though, they actually agreed with him, even though they howled with laughter when Joschi yelled that no one in Darkenbloom would ever give an interview to anyone ever again, he'd make sure of that himself! Even though they made fun of Joschi and mocked him in his fury, they secretly agreed with him.

15.

IT BECAME THEIR PARTY piece, the story of how Heuraffl, Berneck and Co. helped the citizens of the German Democratic Republic, whose numbers had been swelling for days, creating a diplomatic problem just across the border, to flee. Or rather, how, with the boldness of genuine locals, confident of the protection of their state, they simply beckoned the East Germans over without arousing the ire of the Hungarian border guards. They went about it with such brazen nonchalance that there was no need for the Hungarians to shoot; not, at least, to preserve their honour. The ageing Darkenbloom gang had only driven to the border at Zwick out of curiosity. They took some of their sons, grandsons, and nephews with them, and their desire to see what was going on was definitely born of schadenfreude: there, you see, the Eastern Bloc is collapsing! The same Eastern Bloc that until then had been a source of constant fear and threat, especially here, where for decades people's backs had, quite literally, been up against the communist wall.

So they stood and stared, and over there, beyond the concrete no-man's-land that lay between the Austrian and Hungarian border guards' huts, people with weird hairstyles stared longingly back. Most of those thronging over there were young; there were lots of families, parents carrying children in their arms or holding them by the hand, and these children were presumably the reason they didn't just start running. The situation appeared to have ground to an unsatisfactory halt, the dash to freedom abruptly blocked, and this aroused the playful instincts of the locals who, after all, had nothing to lose.

The Hungarian border guards walked up and down behind their barrier, looking tense, their holsters as clearly apparent as the fact that they were in the minority. No cars from the border region had been cleared to cross in either direction for days. To get to the other side you would have had to drive from Darkenbloom all the way up north, to a bigger border crossing. The Hungarian barrier remained closed; the Hungarian border guards, silently besieged by their East German brethren, were desperately waiting for instructions to come by phone, and received none.

The Heuraffl twins walked up to the first barrier and chatted to the Austrian officials; naturally, they all knew each other.

'What if we bring a few over?' a Heuraffl asked, offering the guard a cigarette. 'What if we say we know them, we invited them?'

The guard accepted a light. 'Hard to say,' he replied. 'Nothing happened at the picnic, but they shot someone just a few days ago.'

'But that wasn't our lot here,' the Heuraffl said, 'and it was the middle of the night!'

'Well,' said the guard, 'you never know.'

'Is shift change at four,' the Heuraffl asked, 'same as usual?'

The border guard nodded.

And so they drove away again, the Heuraffls and their mates, and went home and fetched the biggest vehicles they could lay hands on with loading beds or trailers, as well as a VW bus. They returned with them just before four. At four pm precisely, the Hungarian border guards would march as one to the barracks, where the changing of the guard took place; the vehicles bringing the guards for the next shift were already approaching in the distance. The changeover had always taken about a quarter of an hour, and even on that particular day no one seemed inclined to speed things up. Perhaps the Hungarians were hoping the ritual would have a preservative effect.

'Right then, here we go,' said the Heuraffls. They threw their half-smoked cigarettes out of the car windows, nodded to each other, got out, and, leaving the Austrian barrier behind them, walked towards the Hungarian side. There they began to wave, with both arms, in big circles, like the traditional windmills in the nearby Hungarian lowlands. 'Come on over,' they shouted, in dialect, 'come on over, this here is Austria.'

And then the others started shouting, too, Berneck, Young Graun, Stitched-Up Schurl, and his grandson, bright young Karli; they waved and beckoned, *come on over, come on over*, and a shudder passed through the densely packed block of people on the other side; they began to move as one, advancing noiselessly towards the barrier, glancing cautiously at the border guards, but the guards just kept on walking towards their shift-change barracks, and suddenly looked like nothing so much as tin soldiers.

The bravest among the crowd stepped onto the stretch of concrete that lay, neutral, in the September sun, advanced into the transitional realm between the two countries, and began to run. The block liquefied.

'Well, will you look at that,' murmured Stitched-Up Schurl with satisfaction. 'There you go.' In the space of one and a half minutes, all the East Germans came over, everyone who had been waiting, just over a hundred people, almost as silently, elegantly, and collision-free as a swarm of fish or a flock of birds spectacularly changing direction. They crossed this stretch of concrete where a dead witness, falsely identified by Eliza Goldman, had lain exactly forty-three years ago, and already they had vanquished their political system, already they had escaped to the West, already, with those few steps, they had left everything behind, even their expensive, long-awaited Trabis. The first to cross the Austrian border cheered, but there were some who burst into tears as the tension was released. They climbed onto the load beds of the agricultural vehicles, clambered onto the trailers. This provisional shuttle service brought them to Darkenbloom in several instalments, just as forty four and a half years ago the forced labourers had been brought from the castle to the forest, anxiously guarded by the same people who now were the rescuers. But no one was thinking of that on this happy day. As friendly, pro-active chauffeurs, they divided the refugees up among themselves, the Heuraffls, Berneck, and Stitched-Up Schurl; they each had a few guest rooms on their farm, after all, or relatives and acquaintances with rooms to offer. Only when all their rooms were fully occupied did they drop the remaining people outside the Hotel Tüffer in the town square and tipped off Resi Reschen with what they had learned: 'Just give them a bill to take with them tomorrow and the German embassy'll transfer the money.'

'Tomorrow?' asked Resi suspiciously. 'What's happening tomorrow?'

'Tomorrow the German buses are coming,' crowed Berneck, 'and as soon as this lot are gone we'll drive to the border and get us some more!'

And so it came to pass, because the West German government's representatives abroad worked more efficiently and unbureaucratically that autumn than ever before.

'You've got to admit,' these zealous first responders told each other contentedly, 'things always run like clockwork with the Krauts.'

They charged extra, of course: ten, twenty, even twenty-five schillings over the usual price for bed and breakfast — well, the poor devils wouldn't have to pay it themselves, nor did they have a clue what the exchange rate was from schillings to deutschmarks. The guesthouse landladies — guest rooms were traditionally the woman's responsibility — did feel rather sneaky when they prepared the bills.

But they did have to keep washing the bedlinen, they told themselves in self-justification, every day! Never having travelled themselves, they were mercifully ignorant of international room rates, and never found out that their surcharge hurt no one, nor was ever even noticed.

And so it was that the combination of Flocke's days-long search-and-rescue mission and the Heuraffls' initiative of simply beckoning the East German refugees across, then moving them on again with unctuous smiles and inflated bills, saw to it that Darkenbloom was once again seen in a better light. It was as if the antagonists had instinctively pulled together, a thought that would certainly have annoyed Flocke, had it ever occurred to her. The scale of events was far grander than just these Darkenbloom border antics, but in the autumn of 1989 everyone was caught up again in the tide of history, and acted accordingly. Each responded in their own particular way, according to their standpoint, individual morality, and opportunity.

Closed the heavy, dusty curtains and stayed at home with pen-and-ink drawings, like Agnes Kalmar, from whom all reports about open borders were withheld, just in case.

Complained to the public health insurance company for the first time, like Dr Sterkowitz, bitterly and by registered post, that he wanted to, he must, take his well-earned retirement at last. And what had happened to his long-promised replacement?

Or investigated the possibility and cost of retirement homes in Israel for Holocaust survivors, like Antal Grün. He was careful to make sure that no one learned of his enquiries, though it did pain him a little to be so secretive, at least where his helpful, naive young friend, Eszter's son, was concerned. All the same, he revealed nothing even to him, not a single word, until one day the congenial grocer's in the heart of the old town was simply closed, locked up and dark, as if it had never existed. Antal removed the shop sign, too, and all traces of his and his mother's name; the only thing he left behind was the impersonal A&O sign that adorned so many small shops all over the country.

But that was months later. Right now, everything was happening very fast. After the Hungarians, unnerved by episodes like the pan-European picnic and the porous border in Zwick, which went on leaking for several days, declared that East Germans wanting to leave would no longer be returned to their homeland, the situation in Czechoslovakia intensified. It was only after a diplomatic solution was reached for this as well, and the hundreds of people who had climbed over the railings of the embassy compound in Prague were sitting in special trains bound for West Germany, that people noticed demonstrators had recently started gathering in Leipzig every Monday, and that their numbers had been swelling as steadily as those of the Hungarian campers and embassy climbers before them.

Mayor Koreny, who now settled down in front of the television news every evening with the newly acquired dignity of office and a corresponding, rather coquettish sigh, thought he detected a subtle, physiognomic similarity between the Czechoslovak and East German nomenklatura. Compared with the Hungarians and the Yugoslavs, or indeed the new Soviet general secretary, they looked as if they still took it seriously.

'I reckon they're more dangerous,' Koreny told his wife. 'I can't say why, but I can feel it in my bones. They'd still like to shoot and send in the tanks, like their comrades in Peking.'

'Well, aren't you the clever one,' said his wife.

Her scepticism, however, prompted Koreny to start taking more of an interest in world politics. On one occasion he saw a late-night interview with an East German writer that got him very riled up, and he would have found this as hard to explain as his compelling vision that the statesmen in Prague and East Berlin shared the same implacability. This supposedly very famous man — Koreny had never heard of him, but then he never read novels — made disparaging remarks about his own countrymen, those happy and grateful people whose hands Koreny had shaken by the dozen as they boarded the West German buses beside the plague column on the town square.

The writer, who Koreny immediately thought came across as condescending, said that his own flight had been a matter of life or death, because the Nazis were hot on his heels. Whereas the good people on the Austrian–Hungarian border really had far less dramatic reasons.

Koreny shook his head; he couldn't quite believe what he was hearing at first. Why did everything always have to begin and end with the Nazis!

Many of the young people one saw on Western television every evening telling the story of their escape were essentially philistines, the man continued. 'They have very crude ideas about democracy!'

'This guy's an absolute shit,' Koreny told his wife, who had come in in her nightgown and ordered him to turn it off. He pointed at the screen. 'Listen to what he's saying!'

'What's he saying that's so terrible?' Koreny's wife asked, and, as if in response, the man on the television said: 'The East German leadership are not barbarians.'

'There you have it,' cried Koreny. 'Not barbarians? People who build a wall and shoot at their own people? No? Who are barbarians, then, if you please? Only our old Ferbenz, because he held some position or other back in the day! Everyone can agree on him!'

'If you don't come to bed right now, I'm filing for divorce,' said Frau Koreny. She, too, was affected by the convulsions of the time, which sometimes led her to make exaggerated remarks along these lines. Reluctantly, her husband got to his feet, muttering to himself. He was so agitated that he didn't hear what the famous writer said at the end, and even if he had, he would only have felt vindicated. The writer was expanding on his assessment of the East German leadership. They had been shaped by their experience of fighting fascism, he said, under which many of them had suffered, in the underground movement, in concentration camps, in exile. 'They believe that if they abandon their defensive stance, their life's work will be destroyed.'

But by then Koreny was already in the bathroom, putting on his pyjamas, groaning — wretched knees — and murmuring that there really was something to it: Jews were always such insufferable smart-arses.

16.

ONCE THEY HAD TOLD each other all there was to tell, Flocke and Lowetz sat on the flying carpet in the courtyard, blowing smoke rings in the air. The afternoon sun had already undergone that infinitesimal shift, impossible to anticipate and, later, impossible to pin down, from the glaring, immediate light of summer that outlines every shape with fierce clarity to one that slowly starts to flow along golden edges, transfiguring them. Had it been different the previous day? Or does the shift take place imperceptibly, over several days, until you are forced to acknowledge, with a sigh, that autumn has arrived?

Lowetz had been trying for days to sort his head out. Too much had happened almost at once, and some of the excitement had yet to ebb away; the good and the bad had been stirred up and incomprehensibly mixed. The bones in the Rotenstein meadow apparently belonged to a Second World War soldier, and were not a gruesome harbinger of the thing Dr Gellért had been searching for for weeks. Was that good or bad? If they found the metal tag nearby as well, somewhere in the world, in Kiel or Kamchatka, surprised grandchildren or great-nieces would be notified that the official status of their almost-forgotten ancestor had changed from *missing* to *dead*. It might also be a local *Volkssturm* man; they'd had helmets, but they weren't all given tags later on.

Some lunatics had vandalised the cemetery, and Lowetz wondered if he really wanted to know who. He imagined himself having to lie in wait for this person, then hitting him until he confessed to writing the threatening letter to Gellért as well, perhaps even the postcard to Lowetz's mother. It had to be someone. Someone out there was walking around greeting everyone with a friendly smile, and underneath they were really a sick bastard. When Lowetz shoved this dark shadow up against a wall in his imagination and pummelled him with inaudible, impalpable blows, it was the message on the postcard that he was shouting: *Stop lying!* The fantasy was completely ridiculous; he wasn't a thug. In this, too, the real locals were way out of his league.

The border was now open, and Fritz was still very worried that his mother would find out. He hadn't been heard singing for days. Lowetz doubted anything got through to Agnes any more; she seemed at last to have cushioned herself adequately against all memories, with her curtains, drawings, and lists of names. Besides, things had already quietened down. Hardly anyone came through here any more, since the East Germans were now able to cross further north, which was more convenient, and drive their plastic cars through Vienna and Linz and on towards the West, in the direction of Passau. Hungarians were occasionally spotted in Darkenbloom, looking around, visiting the two churches, or contemplating the elaborately decorated plague column. They nodded and said hello, and sometimes they scrutinised the menu on the board outside the Tüffer. You never saw them go in; they only entered shops that sold electrical goods. It seemed that the whole of Hungary had an insatiable hunger for washing machines, televisions, and stereos.

'I wonder if they'll stay?' said Flocke.

'What?' asked Lowetz, surfacing from the confusion in his head. 'Who, stay where?'

Flocke meant Reinhold and his family, who had transferred to two guest rooms on the Malnitz farm. Leonore Malnitz had insisted on hosting the women her daughter had brought across. Blond-bearded Reinhold was now helping with the grape harvest and seemed in no hurry to decide what would happen to them next. Several times a day, Leonore would tell them they were welcome to stay as long as they wanted. Silke, the daughter, was mad about Hildegard the pug and spent the whole day trying to train her. Clearly there were no West German relatives eagerly awaiting their arrival.

However, Lowetz had missed the latest development: Mayor Koreny had called on the authorities, on television, to officially invite the East German refugees to stay in Burgenland. After all, he said, for years now the state had suffered from outward migration; it was predicted to lose more than 5 per cent of its population over the coming decades, and in Koreny's view they should have developed a strategy for dealing with this long ago. 'So why,' he asked, 'shouldn't we try to help these people? They're motivated, they want to build lives for themselves; they've already demonstrated that by making the decision to flee! And, what's more, they have command of the German language!'

'I'd never have believed that of Koreny,' said Lowetz, and Flocke said, 'He'd never have believed it of himself two weeks ago.'

'So why now?' Lowetz asked.

Flocke puffed her fringe off her forehead. 'Maybe he's rising to the challenge — just like you?'

Lowetz gave her a look that seemed, to him, almost improper. It didn't seem to bother her. He had come to the conclusion that she had to be one of the rare species of *Homo darkenbloomiensis*, possibly the very last specimen before it became extinct. She was different from other people here, both wittier and more serious. With her slightly slanting eyes, hair that could best be described as caramel-coloured, delicate fingers and limbs, she didn't even particularly resemble her parents. Perhaps that was also what made her special: that on the one hand she seemed almost like a rare insect, and on the other was so stubbornly rooted in this region, with a strong, patriotic desire to make it better.

'And did you see the bag Reinhold's walking around with?' she asked, laughing. '*See better, hear better?* Like a bona fide local!'

Lowetz laughed, too. 'I gave him that,' he said. 'As for command of the German language, we just have to train him out of saying *nu* for yes. People round here take it to mean the exact opposite ...' He broke off.

'Nu,' cried Flocke, who was a gifted mimic, 'nu-nu — yes, you're right!' She would have gone on messing about, but Lowetz raised his hand.

'What?' she asked.

He sat up. 'Shit,' he said, 'shit, shit, shit ... and I ripped up the floorboards — I'm such an idiot!'

His mother's papers were not in a yellowing cardboard folder labelled TOP SECRET; they were not, as in a bad film, elaborately tied up with string, or singed on one corner, as if they had only just escaped a fire. His mother's so-called papers consisted of three or four banal, orange A4 envelopes and two squared-paper notepads with the blocky Libro logo on the front, and they were where Lowetz himself had tossed them, the evening of Flocke's disappearance: scattered on the dark floor of Eszter's wardrobe among the dust bunnies, odd socks, scrunchies, drawing pins, a moth-eaten woollen scarf, a pair of plastic flip-flops, and a clothes hanger minus its hook. In the far corner was a crumpled-up piece of linen that turned out to be the twin of the Philips bag, dusty, empty, but in rather better condition.

Flocke stroked the second bag flat on the floor with both hands, as firmly as if she were ironing it with her palms.

Lowetz asked her to stop. 'Please don't be cross, but it drives me crazy when Uncle Grün does that.'

She complied, although she didn't like being rebuked. She sat cross-legged on the floor and gazed around the room as he knelt beside her and leafed through it all, shaking photocopied pages out of the envelope and racing through the notepads as if they were flip-books that would be forced to reveal their tricks.

When he had finished he started again, more calmly, from the beginning. Flocke sat there watching him. After a while he pushed it all together and stared at her, at a loss. He didn't understand what about this could be important. There were a handful of photocopies of newspaper articles about various events from the post-war period: the trial of some boys from the Darkenbloom Hitler Youth, surnames all abbreviated. A border incident involving a car crash and a shooting. The robbery and murder of a cyclist. And finally, a report about the death of a wine grower named Graun — probably the father of the current one — who had apparently been careless while lighting a fire in the forest and had burned himself to death. Whatever next. Then there was a three-page list of addresses, clipped together, that looked as if it was from an old register of residents, and a Rehberg family tree with lots of dates of birth and death, some of them crossed out and corrected. Eszter had tried repeatedly to draw up this family tree by hand; one notepad was completely filled with countless uninteresting Rehbergs who belonged to or were related to one another. Lowetz kept coming across the name of the travel agent, who apparently, like his father, Max, a glazier, had only sisters, all of whom were married and so now had other names. Lowetz knew most of the families the female Rehbergs had married into; everyone in Darkenbloom was related to everyone else, either directly or by marriage, though this might not have been immediately apparent to an outsider. It looked as if one of Rehberg's aunts had married someone from Over There, if you could draw that conclusion from a name like Jenő. Or had this man come over here, like Lowetz's mother, but a generation earlier?

The most interesting thing, for Lowetz, was a page-long interview, typed up, in which Eszter told her life story. He would read it properly later, but skimming through he didn't see any reference to the night of the ball in March 1945, or to the Gellért family.

Finally, there was an envelope containing several pages in a strange quarto format, thin as airmail paper, on which there was writing in fine pencil, just a few words on each page, the text right in the middle, like little labels. These notes were in Hungarian. They might be shopping lists, or memoranda, or brief letters without salutation or greeting that Eszter might have received from her relatives over there. They didn't look important, but they could of course ask someone who understood the language.

'You're disappointed now,' Flocke observed. 'What were you expecting?'

Lowetz considered. 'You know, Flocke,' he said, 'while you were away there was a weird atmosphere here, as if the whole town were under a spell, or a curse. It was after that thunderstorm; everything was so wet and hot, and it felt as if it was all about to start slipping. The whole of Darkenbloom a mudslide. At your uncle's filling station, for example ... oh, never mind, I probably just imagined it ... Anyway, after that water meeting in the Tüffer, where everything got out of hand, when your mother asked people to help with the search ...'

'The search for me?' asked Flocke, uneasily.

'Well, that's what I was about to say,' said Lowetz. 'She meant the search for you, of course, but somehow the thing with the war crimes suddenly came up as well, I can't even remember why, so the word *search* took on a sort of double meaning ...'

'And then?' asked Flocke, when he faltered.

'It's hard to explain,' Lowetz continued, hesitantly, 'and I'm really not one for that sort of thinking, but I was convinced there was a link, or at least that lots of things are connected beneath the surface, like Faludi's water veins.'

Flocke laughed.

'You laugh,' he said, 'but I was consumed by this feeling for days. My mother's death — so unexpected that I'd already thought it seemed suspicious; then Dr Gellért, whom she'd hidden from the Nazis back then, and never said a word about it to me; your disappearance, right after you'd spoken to him; the skeleton in the Rotenstein meadow that made people so jittery; even the book of fairy tales, even Reinhold coming out of the forest from Over There, and all the drama about the water supply. I know it's crazy, but I was certain: that there was a key to it, a code. And I was determined to find it — maybe I was the only one who could? And then I thought it might be in my mother's notes.'

'You ripped up the floorboards,' Flocke asked, 'because you wanted to find me?'

Lowetz started laughing. 'I didn't mean ... no, but actually, you're right. Exactly — I ripped up the floorboards because I wanted to find you! And it worked, almost to the minute!'

'But that sense of internal connection,' Flocke persisted, 'you don't have that any more? Since when?'

'Since you came back,' said Lowetz, very deliberately. And he opened his eyes wide, because he felt a quiet, ink-blue lake of wonder spreading out inside him, an impenetrable blue, but warm, protective, and not at all unpleasant. 'Yes — since you came back, I know I was just being a bit crazy.'

'Maybe it worked the other way round,' said Flocke. She shot him an amused look, stuck out her lower lip, and puffed her fringe off her forehead. 'First I came back, then you remembered the papers, and as to whether there's a key — well, that we still have to find out.'

'Yes, we really do,' said Lowetz, looking her straight in the eye, those slanted, mocking eyes right in front of him that were not ink blue, but just at that moment he was convinced they should have been. He took a deep breath and tensed his lips ever so slightly, but Flocke, her gazelle-like legs still crossed, rose straight from a sitting position to her feet, walked over to the window, opened it, and lit a cigarette. Lowetz was embarrassed. Something was going wrong again, but he simply couldn't work out what. Aimlessly, he reached for the papers and picked up the list of names and addresses at random. It started with *Arnstein, Malwine, Hauptplatz 13*, followed by *Bernstein, Emma, Herrengasse 3*, continuing with *Eisenstädter, Engel, Glück*; then came *Antal and Gisella Grün, Tempelgasse 4*, followed by *Hirschler, Holzer, Pimper, Rosenberg*, at various addresses in the town centre. There were two big families called *Rosmarin* and *Tüffer*, and the list of names went on for two and a half pages altogether, ending with a *Wohlmut, Karoline, Hauptplatz 7*. Lowetz stared at the list without seeing it. His cheeks were burning as if Flocke had slapped him. What a curious name Uncle Grün's mother had, he thought, his mind faltering like a drunk reciting a poem; and how interesting that there really were people called Tüffer, once upon a time. The rest of the family names, unlike the addresses, were unfamiliar. It must be a very old list.

17.

AROUND DARKENBLOOM, THE NUMBER of secrets has always far
exceeded the number of issues clarified. It's as if the landscape, first
pushed and puckered up like velvet trim embroidered in luxuriant
green, before falling away to flat and endless yellow, fundamentally
rejects a clear perspective. And as if this is also true of its inhabitants,
whose behaviour is similarly contradictory: observing everything,
understanding nothing. Commenting on everything, explaining
nothing. The little flowerheads turn busily this way and that, and the
walls prick up their grey and crumbling ears, but they only take things
in, they give nothing away.

And so it was never really clarified why it was that they forgot
to relieve Dr Sterkowitz. His registered letter caused a scandal in
the corresponding department of the public health insurance company — a typically Burgenlandish scandal: someone shouted; that
someone, shouting, threatened to sack various people on the spot;
a door was slammed, coffee cups and cactuses rattled indignantly in
their saucers, and afterwards everyone, especially the door slammer,
worked collectively and determinedly to iron out the mistake and
ensure that it would never be made known. It transpired that the year
of Sterkowitz's birth had been entered incorrectly on his personnel

record, and so he had been thought to be a decade younger than he was. But how had it gone unnoticed for so long! On the cusp of retirement, the good doctor aged tremendously — in the files, that is, which were hastily corrected. And nobody felt guilty. After all, their hardworking, still sprightly colleague had taken up his post at a time when Austria didn't actually exist — there may well have been the odd copying error, what with all those different systems of government, never mind the war, if you please! But it wasn't actually necessary to justify the mistake, because even at the local paper they didn't notice anything when they wrote the big valedictory article.

As far as outsiders were concerned, the state bureaucracy donned its mask of impenetrability. They wrote to Sterkowitz to inform him that they had succeeded in finding a suitable replacement sooner than planned, as if he really ought to thank them for it. If he wished, Sterkowitz could retire at the end of the quarter, on the thirtieth of September. This curt letter made him fear he had pushed too hard. When he tried to follow up by phone, all the relevant administrative assistants were sick, at lunch, out of the office, or could not be located. His successor himself called, though, and they were able to make all the necessary arrangements. Before hanging up, Sterkowitz asked him to spell his name again. 'I'm afraid my hearing isn't as good as it used to be,' he said, apologetically.

'Bello,' repeated the young doctor at the other end of the line. 'Bello, as it's pronounced.'

'Bello, as in the dog's name?' asked Sterkowitz.

'Bello, as in the beautiful one,' said his successor, laughing.

'Well, as long as it's not *bello*, as in war,' said Sterkowitz. 'See you at the end of the month, Dr Bello!'

'What does he sound like?' asked Sterkowitz's wife.

'Pleasant and friendly,' Sterkowitz replied. 'They really do get top-flight training these days; all the places he's already gained clinical experience ... I think he's tall and very fat, though.'

'Wherever did you get that idea?' asked his wife.

'Because of the way his voice booms and resonates,' said Sterkowitz, 'like a bell in a tower.'

Sterkowitz embarked on a farewell tour in his orange Honda. He worked almost as hard as he had at the beginning of his career; he wanted to see all his patients one last time. Like Dr Bernstein before him, he also wanted to leave the files in perfect order. No subsequent medical error should be attributable to incomplete case histories. What had happened to Bernstein, he wondered, back then? Had he made it?

The illnesses, diseases, and injuries Sterkowitz was dealing with did not oblige him by leaving him plenty of time. On the contrary: after the hot summer, and all the commotion around the opening of the border, problems seemed to have accumulated that had previously been suppressed, or had simply never manifested themselves before. There were a number of cardiovascular issues, in younger people, too. Older patients wanted to talk more than usual, including about the new era that was clearly about to dawn. Will my grandchildren soon travel to Hungary for work, asked an old beet farmer; will everything be turned upside down again? And one of the wizened old ladies who wore traditional costume and must have been about a hundred years old — there were quite a few of them — asked him, with rapture in her eyes, whether now the Countess would return at last. Sterkowitz pumped up the blood pressure cuff and said: 'Who knows? Anything's possible.'

Others, it seemed, were calling on his expertise for the very first time because word had got around that he was retiring. Frau Leonore Malnitz, for example, whom he had never treated because, if ever she was unwell, she drove to Kirschenstein — out of habit, she insisted now, very old habit — appeared in his practice asking for something to treat her dreadful insomnia. Sterkowitz examined her thoroughly, did a full blood count, and found nothing more alarming than the menopause. He prescribed *Agnus castus.* As he was writing the prescription, Frau Malnitz quietly began to speak. Was it also part of the change of life, she asked, to have an urgent desire to rid oneself of old ballast? This was how she felt. Lying awake at night for hours, she had the feeling that she, too, needed to come clean — she couldn't just demand it of everyone else. Sterkowitz stamped the prescription and placed his hands on the desk. True to her reputation, she was still a beautiful woman; the air around her seemed to glow. Now, though, he perceived something else as well: a fraught state of mind, a poison forcing itself to the surface.

'Is it really just ballast,' he asked, 'or sins that have gone undetected?'

Her expression betrayed her.

'My dear Frau Leonore,' he said, 'anything that has caused no trouble for such a long time should continue not to do so. And the longer ago it is, the less it's relevant. The passage of time changes things, you know that.'

'So you don't believe in confession, atonement, and forgiveness, Doctor?' she asked.

'I don't know enough about it,' said Sterkowitz. 'But if a bone has healed crooked and you've been walking about on it for years, you can't make it straight. If you're determined to try, you have to break it again. And then it would have to heal a second time.'

When Sterkowitz stepped into the house of the fruit growers everyone referred to as *the Stitched-Ups,* the first thing he did was throw open a few windows. 'Dearie me,' he cried, 'don't bury yourselves alive like this! As I always say: you'll suffocate before you freeze! And it's still so nice and warm outside!'

No one said a word. The Stitched-Up family had always reminded Sterkowitz of a cluster of euglena, little organisms with a prominent eyespot: like dark searchlights, their eyes absorbed everything around them, yet they remained predominantly mute. Sterkowitz knew that, like everything else, intelligence was not distributed fairly in this world. But because, statistically, nature strives towards the middle ground, even this household sometimes produced children who understood more than their elders, and who did at least learn to read, write, and do their times-tables. Sterkowitz had actually thought that this Karli, a grandson of the original Stitched-Up, was one of the cleverest. A few years ago, as a child, Karli used to prepare small animal skeletons: a dove, a marten, a squirrel. Sometimes he would ask the doctor for advice; a bright boy of ten or twelve, eager for knowledge. And this was what had become of him? Why did it always have to end badly? Karli was by no means stupid. But perhaps, thought Sterkowitz, the responsibility of always having to think for everyone else is even more likely to send you off down the wrong track?

The woman who had opened the door to him led him to the sick room, shooing several silent, gawping children out of the way. Karli was lying in bedlinen of indefinable colour and was much as he had been two days earlier, when they had brought him into the surgery with a deep stab wound in his thigh: pale, gloomy, and unwashed. On the windowsill stood a wire-mounted skeleton model of a human hand; no trace now of the squirrels and doves. Sterkowitz inspected the hand; it looked astonishingly real. 'You didn't bag this yourself, though, did you, like the animals?' he joked.

Karli stared at him and mumbled something about having bought it.

'The last little finger joint is missing,' Sterkowitz observed, touching the wire where it stuck out. 'You know what the missing bit looks like? It's shaped almost like a Ludo playing piece, a cone with a little head.'

Karli cleared his throat several times. 'It was like that when I got it,' he said finally, in a choked voice, 'that's why it was cheaper.'

Sterkowitz felt the boy's forehead. He was sweating. 'I'll leave you some antibiotics,' he said, 'to be on the safe side. One tablet three times a day, all right? And it's stuffy in here, too; move the hand somewhere else, let the air in!'

He treated the wound and changed the dressing. Finally, he sat down on an unmade bed — there were three in the tiny room — and asked Karli if he was sure he didn't want to tell him a bit more about the incident. 'Be sensible,' the doctor said. 'If you tell me what happened, I may be able to help you.'

But Karli just gave him that dark look again.

Euglena, Sterkowitz thought, exasperated. He had nagged the young man the day before yesterday, too, while stitching the wound. He had said, straight out, that the two things were bound to be connected, Karli's arrest and interrogation, and now, a day later, this injury to his thigh. That can't be a coincidence! Because even if Karli had done what he was accused of — although he hadn't confessed, Sterkowitz had heard that all the evidence supported this conclusion — still, no one was allowed to wound him with a knife. 'The one has nothing to do with the other,' Sterkowitz told him sternly. 'We don't have vigilante justice here! And I'm pretty sure you didn't ram that knife into your leg yourself.'

Karli said nothing. He had said nothing two days ago, nothing three days ago during the interrogation, and he said nothing now, either, with an iodine-stained line of six clean stitches in his thigh. Sterkowitz got to his feet, with an effort. 'You're all the same,' he said. 'When will you learn that if you always keep your mouth shut, it doesn't make things any better?'

Outside the house he bumped into Karli's grandfather, whose face he'd had to stitch up all those years ago. Back then, he hadn't had the very fine thread, or the practical adhesive strips you could cut to shape.

A few years later and his handiwork would probably have worked out better. Now, though, it would be worse again: Sterkowitz's fine motor skills were long past their best. But they were still good enough to mend a gash in the leg.

'You lot have really got a thing about knives,' said Sterkowitz, jerking his thumb at the house behind him. 'Can you make any sense of this?'

Stitched-Up Schurl shook his head unhappily. He looked as if he, too, were in pain, a twitching, tugging ache in his scarred face.

'I mean, Schurl, really,' remonstrated Sterkowitz, 'what was he thinking, with the cemetery? Where did he get an idea like that? These youngsters don't even know what a Jew is!'

Schurl whispered, 'I don't understand either, dunno what he was thinking. Will he go to prison? He's still a kid!'

'Well, he's really not a kid any more,' grumbled Sterkowitz, 'but I don't think he'll go to prison. He'll just get community service, or a criminal record. Still, there wasn't any need for all this. How did they catch him so quickly?'

'He brought the rest of the paint back home,' whispered Schurl. 'It was the expensive stuff.'

Dr Sterkowitz's last days of work were taken up with stories like this. It was just as it had been for all those long years: sometimes you felt like crying, sometimes laughing, not infrequently both at once. Alois Ferbenz was beginning to worry him; he had lost a lot of weight since all the fuss about his television interview. Contrary to what Sterkowitz had supposed, Ferbenz was no longer able to enjoy his new-found fame, which was really just the exhibition of an old man exerting his fool's privilege. He seemed confused, and spoke to Sterkowitz unintelligibly but with great urgency, something about plots of land in Ehrenfeld, near the border, where no one could be allowed to build, not ever, or it would all start up again. 'If I'm not around to make sure, Doctor, you must see to it!'

Sterkowitz said, 'But Dr Ferbenz, I'm only a few years younger than you.'

'You have to pass the information on to a suitable person,' Ferbenz insisted. 'One of ours, not one of them! No one can ever be allowed to build there!'

Sterkowitz asked, 'Who do you mean by *them*?'

'The Jews and their henchmen, of course,' said Ferbenz.

Sterkowitz wondered whether his patient's permanently reddened eyes required medical attention. Was this the usual *keratoconjunctivitis sicca*, or did he have an allergy?

'My dear Dr Ferbenz,' he muttered soothingly, 'all that has been over for a very long time.'

'Nothing is over,' said Ferbenz, and wept.

Sterkowitz stopped trying to understand the story; his patient was clearly mixing things up. More to the point, he had an irregular heartbeat. Sterkowitz wrote in his notes that a pacemaker should be considered, *cardio in Kirschenstein*, question mark.

The hotel manager Resi Reschen, on the other hand, was fit as a fiddle, apart from her usual high blood pressure. Sterkowitz asked whether she, too, might want to start thinking about retirement.

'I've been thinking about retirement all my life,' the indefatigable Resi retorted.

She offered him a coffee, and they sat together for a few more minutes. Resi explained that, as so often in life, it was hard to see the bigger picture. If the border stayed open, it might revive the region, in which case it would be stupid to sell the hotel as she had intended. In any case, she said, she couldn't market it as a hotel at the moment, only as real estate. The way things were going, she'd try to hang on for another year or two. Maybe hotels would be needed again around here. Maybe someone would preserve it as it was — you wouldn't want to lose the pretty Art Nouveau decor. Maybe it would go back to being a bit like before the war, when people used to come here for the fresh air, the wine, and the gently rolling scenery. And weren't put off by watchtowers, barbed wire, and border installations.

'I always thought you were an inveterate pessimist,' said Sterkowitz approvingly, as he took his leave, 'but above all you're a businesswoman, through and through.' And this made Resi as proud and happy as a young girl, almost as she had been back then, when Frau Tüffer handed her the big bunch of keys.

As Sterkowitz was walking across the town square to his Honda, Farmer Faludi waved to him, and they got into conversation. Sterkowitz asked if it was true that Faludi wanted to stand for mayor.

'*Want* is the wrong word,' Farmer Faludi replied. 'Although I criticise Koreny, I actually think he's got better and better lately.'

'But?' asked Sterkowitz.

'But now he's committed political suicide,' said Faludi dryly, 'by inviting the refugees to stay in Burgenland.'

'You really think so?' asked Sterkowitz. 'It wasn't such a stupid idea, though, was it?'

'I'd certainly have nothing against it,' said Farmer Faludi, 'but the right are attacking him from all sides. Haven't you read about it? Even the Blues' parliamentary leader has said he's comfortable in the *socio-cultural sphere* we have today and he'd like it to stay that way, thank you very much. Our own Joschi Ferbenz is going around parroting this whenever he gets a chance.'

'Joschi couldn't even pronounce *socio-cultural sphere*!' said Sterkowitz.

'True,' said Faludi, 'but in his version it's even worse. *Ethnic replacement* and so on. And these are East Germans he's talking about!'

There was another reason Faludi was considering standing. If, as expected, the referendum prevented Darkenbloom from joining the water authority, the restructuring and provision of an alternative water supply should be supervised by someone who actually understood something about it.

'The site up on the Rotenstein meadow alone,' he said. 'The water tower will be enormous; there are a whole load of other environmental issues to consider.'

'A water tower on the Rotenstein meadow?' asked Sterkowitz, aghast. 'With foundations and so on?'

'It'll be sunk deep into the ground,' Farmer Faludi confirmed, 'with the capacity to store a huge amount of water.'

Sterkowitz held his hand over his nose and mouth.

'Are you all right?' asked Faludi.

'Yes, yes, I'm fine,' said Sterkowitz, coughing.

'Sure?' Faludi asked, sceptically.

'Quite sure,' said Sterkowitz. 'Something just got up my nose, some disgusting smell.'

And he hastily said goodbye, mentioning that he had an important appointment: his successor, Dr Bello, had announced his arrival, and Sterkowitz wanted to check the surgery equipment beforehand.

Back home, Dr Sterkowitz sank onto a chair and told his wife it was just like when you fall ill as soon as you go on holiday: 'It's only once you've made the decision to retire that you realise you really can't do this any more.'

His wife shot him a look. 'You're not coming down with something, are you?' she asked.

'Well, the new doctor can check me out in a minute,' said Sterkowitz, trying to smile. 'And you and I will check him out.'

It felt as if his blood pressure was dropping. Not a good moment for it, but what could he do? He was about to ask his wife for a strong coffee with plenty of sugar when the doorbell rang. Sterkowitz held his hand over his nose and mouth. 'Please could you answer it,' he said, 'I need to catch my breath.'

His wife gave him a worried glance, but went out. She returned looking thunderstruck. Sterkowitz feared that all the blood must have drained from his face, that the classic cold sweat was on his brow. He couldn't feel it, but perhaps any minute he would slither silently off the chair, like a towel? The new doctor would have to raise his legs and hold them in the air. An excruciatingly embarrassing state of affairs. 'Why are you looking at me like that?' he asked, grimly. His wife usually had good manners. 'Is something the matter?'

'No,' she stammered, 'no, no, I ... I ... here's the gentleman ...'

And the new doctor bounced in behind her, in radiant white shirt, midnight-blue suit, all very elegant, a slender, sinewy figure, not remotely tall and fat. A smile almost like an illustration in a children's book, from ear to ear. 'Delighted to meet you,' the man said, sticking out his hand, his voice resonating like a bell in a tower. 'My name is Alphonse Bello.'

The new doctor was Black.

After his conversation with the good Dr Sterkowitz, Farmer Faludi felt drawn, as if by a thread, to enter the church. He had long been in the habit of heeding summonses like these; he lived in harmony with the forces of nature, and these couldn't all be measured and explained in the same way. When he realised where his feet were taking him, he nodded his assent. It was a long time since he had entered the church on a whim, and whatever force or power was asking him to, it was right. Empty churches were cathedrals of contemplation, comparable only to the forest at sunrise. The spirit was free to roam and vibrate; your own spirit, yes, but you could pick up other vibrations, too, even voices from the past. Render yourself pure and empty, expect nothing, just receive whatever is given to you with openness and kindness: that, in Farmer Faludi's view, was how people should enter churches. Then you were safe in God's house and hand. Those who simply forced themselves to follow the rite on Sundays in the midst of the whispering, murmuring congregation were missing something. Even when everyone else was silent, praying or listening to the sermon, the roar of feelings and thoughts, all that pent-up human fallibility, swirled above their heads and pressed against the temples. Whereas an empty, or almost empty, church offered spiritual recuperation, a bath in light and space.

He walked around the marble slab in the vestibule with a few Darkenbloom counts and a bishop buried beneath it. He had intended to sit in one of the pews in the centre of the church and let the silence take effect, but he was drawn on, right to the front, to the altarpiece with the painting of the Last Supper. The apostles sat there eating, knocking back the red and white wine just like the people of Darkenbloom. Did they realise that the very next day it would all be over? Some did seem to sense it; others were celebrating as if there were no tomorrow, or indeed any Last Judgement. A man stood off to one side; he had just come in. Pale and stricken, he was looking at Jesus, who had already got to his feet. The man, of course, was Judas, but he didn't look wicked; he seemed in the depths of despair. His hoof was just visible beneath his monk's habit, along with a glimpse of bristly leg. And behind him stood the famous feathered devils, smaller than children, but dressed in neat little doublets and with naked, human faces, feathers and horns notwithstanding. The betrayer appeared to be in distress. Perhaps he didn't want to betray at all; maybe he just wanted to warn, but the indistinguishable little devils were driving him mercilessly before them. The group is stronger than the conscience of the individual, but perhaps the reverse is also true: the great, upright, complex human being, the pinnacle of creation, is so appallingly weak in contrast with the group, defenceless, like a leaf that has fallen from the tree.

As Farmer Faludi gazed at the Messiah, trying to fathom his expression, the little devils in his peripheral vision began to move. And he heard them whispering. Farmer Faludi sensed that he mustn't look at them or they would freeze and fall silent. Only when they thought themselves unobserved could you eavesdrop on them. And so he immersed himself in the face of the Messiah. The Messiah was suffering, and his silence roared as loudly as that of the empty church. Always the Messiah would suffer in silence; always he stayed silent and suffered, regardless of what was going on around him. But the little devils were constantly chattering; they whispered and laughed. *Is it not*, Faludi thought he could make out, *history, is not, the*. Farmer Faludi held his breath, closed his eyes, and crossed himself. And now he heard it clearly, spoken in chorus by a multitude of evil voices and punctuated by metallic snickers. Over and over they repeated it; they found it infinitely amusing, the little feathered devils on the three-panelled altarpiece of Darkenbloom church:

This is not the end of the story.

Acknowledgements

FOR ASSISTANCE WITH HISTORICAL, criminological, medical, botanical, architectural, dialectal, technical, and other details, I would like to thank:

Manfred Eder, Christoph Gerstgraser, Barbara Glück, Rudolf Gollia, Karl-Heinz Grundböck, Paul Gulda, Nikolaus Heidelbach, Ursula Hellerich, Günter Kaindlstorfer, Gerald Krieghofer, Walter Manoschek, Agnes Meisinger, Ulrich Moritz, Judith Schalansky, Alexander von Schönburg, Ingo Schulze, Walter Ulreich, Mona Willi, Ute Woltron and Christa Zöchling.

Original sentences from the films *Totschweigen* [Wall of Silence] by Eduard Erne and Margareta Heinrich and *Schuld und Gedächtnis* by Egon Humer, as well as the book *Kontaminierte Landschaften* by Martin Pollack, have been incorporated into this fictional text in a few places in a kind of collage. The rights holders have given their consent for them to be used in this way, and I am very grateful for this.

My thanks to Michael Maar for everything.

Quotations

p. 3 'The Austrians are a people ...': Attributed for years to Alfred Polgar, apparently incorrectly; sometimes also to Karl Kraus. It seems most likely that the quotation originated, in a slightly different form, with Karl Farkas.

See https://falschzitate.blogspot.com/2020/04/der-osterreicher-blickt-voller.html

p. 155 Hans Lebert: *Die Wolfshaut*, Europa Verlag GmbH, 1991.

p. 303 Robert Musil: 'Das hilflose Europa oder Reise vom Hundertsten ins Tausendste', in *Das hilflose Europa: Drei Essays*, Piper, 1961.